KERRY BARRETT is the author of numerous novels, including the *Strictly Come Dancing*-themed *A Step in Time*, and *The Girl in the Picture*, about a crime novelist who solves a 160-year-old mystery.

Born in Edinburgh, Kerry moved to London as a child, where she now lives with her husband and two sons. A massive bookworm growing up, she used to save up her pocket money for weeks to buy the latest *Sweet Valley High* book, then read the whole story on the bus home and have to wait two months for the next one. Eventually she realized it would be easier to write her own stories . . .

Kerry's years as a television journalist, reporting on *EastEnders* and *Corrie*, have inspired her novels where popular culture collides with a historical mystery. But there is no truth in the rumours that she only wrote a novel based on *Strictly Come Dancing* so she would be invited on to *It Takes Two*.

When she's not practising her foxtrot (because you never know . . .), Kerry is watching Netflix, reading Jilly Cooper, and researching her latest historical story.

Also by Kerry Barrett

The Secrets of
Thistle Cottage

KERRY BARRETT

ONE PLACE. MANY STORIES

HQ
An imprint of HarperCollins*Publishers* Ltd
1 London Bridge Street
London SE1 9GF

www.harpercollins.co.uk

HarperCollins*Publishers*
1st Floor, Watermarque Building, Ringsend Road
Dublin 4, Ireland

This paperback edition 2021

1

First published in Great Britain by
HQ, an imprint of HarperCollins*Publishers* Ltd 2021

Copyright © Kerry Barrett 2021

Kerry Barrett asserts the moral right to be
identified as the author of this work.
A catalogue record for this book is
available from the British Library.

ISBN: 9780008389765

MIX
Paper from
responsible sources
FSC
www.fsc.org   FSC™ C007454

This book is produced from independently certified FSC™ paper
to ensure responsible forest management.

For more information visit: www.harpercollins.co.uk/green

Printed and bound in Great Britain by
CPI Group (UK) Ltd, Croydon, CR0 4YY

For Bob

Edinburgh Daily News

Friday, April 3

Breakfast television presenter Alistair Robertson has pleaded guilty to two charges of sexual assault and one of attempted rape.

The star appeared at the High Court in Edinburgh yesterday, April 2, and was warned that he would face a custodial sentence.

Adjourning the case for a week, Judge Lady Morpeth said: 'You were in a position of trust and you used that power to assault women who looked up to you.'

Robertson presented Good Morning Scotland *for ten years and was voted the nation's favourite TV star three years in a row. He was a runner-up on* Celebrity Masterchef *and was tipped to be in the line-up for next year's* Strictly Come Dancing.

He shares his million-pound house in Edinburgh's swanky Marchmont area with his wife, Tess – a top lawyer – and their teenage daughter.

Outspoken Tess (pictured leaving court), has been under fire since she tweeted that 'silly girls should think about their actions before ruining people's lives'. The tweet has since been deleted.

Comments:

Hanny said: Disgusting pig. They should throw away the key.

Scottydog said: I hope his victims get some closure now they know he's locked up.

Alphamale said: Me too has gone too far. Soon you won't be able to compliment a girl without her crying rape.

LittleJohn said: Earn £200 a day from home. Click here for more information.

Royalfan23 said: These women knew what they were doing. Bet they were out for revenge because he turned them down.

Rugbylad09 said: Look at her, the sour-faced bitch. Can't blame him for looking elsewhere.

Muffinman said: Face like a slapped arse.

Survivorandlovingit said: Victim blaming is the lowest of the low. She needs to get in the bin.

Proudmum said: She should be ashamed of herself. What kind of woman looks the other way when her husband is up to all sorts.

Sayit said: Agreed. She's a disgrace. Like a Poundshop Hillary Clinton. Imagine putting their daughter at risk like that. I heard the victims were in their teens.

Stayalert said: Paedo scum.

Mumstaxi said: This comment has been removed for legal reasons.

Prologue

Honor

Summer, 1661

I did not like the new laird and he could tell.

I remembered him as a sour-faced boy and surly young man, who was cruel to his wee brother and bullied the local children, but I'd hoped his time away from North Berwick would have softened him. He'd got married, I'd heard, and I thought losing his father might have made him realize that riches meant nothing – that family was the most important thing.

But it seemed Gregor Kincaid as an adult was just as unpleasant as he'd been as a child.

He stood at the front of the meeting hall, chest puffed out, and I felt a prickling on the back of my neck that warned me not to trust him.

Gregor had only been the laird for a few weeks but he had big plans for the town. Plans he was outlining to the meeting.

'The returns are impressive,' he was saying.

'Aye, for you,' said Mackenzie White, tipping the brim of his hat back so he could look Gregor in the eye. 'No for the town.'

3

'That's not true. Bringing larger ships into the harbour will put North Berwick on the map.' Gregor threw his arms out wide, his enthusiasm obvious. 'Making us a trading port with direct connections to the colonies will increase opportunities for everyone.'

'We'd have to dredge the harbour,' Mackenzie said. 'Make it deeper.'

'That's right.'

'And what about the fishermen?'

I sat up straighter. My husband John had been a fisherman. He'd run a fleet of boats from the harbour and when he'd died he'd bequeathed each boat to the men who'd worked for him. They had a trade and an income for life thanks to my John – as long as our town remained a fishing port.

'Fishing could continue,' Gregor said.

The prickling on my neck got stronger and I spoke. 'You can't run clippers and fishing boats from the same harbour,' I said. 'The fish won't bite. The men would have to go north to Fife or even further.'

Gregor's eyes fell on me, in my usual seat at the back of the room, and he raised an eyebrow in recognition.

'Widow Seton,' he said.

'Yes.'

'I believe the fishing would not be affected.'

'You are wrong. Bringing tall ships into this harbour would change the town forever.'

'She is right,' Mackenzie said. 'It's one or the other. And fishing was here first. It gives us a good living and we would be fools to change it.'

There was a swell of murmuring in the room and Gregor cleared his throat for silence, giving me a small, mocking smile.

'Why are you here at this meeting? It is for burgesses only, not women.'

I lifted my chin. 'I am a burgess.'

Gregor laughed but his brother, Davey, touched his arm and nodded. I didn't know Davey well either. I'd not seen much of either of them since they were boys. Like Gregor, Davey too had grown and left, but he'd returned before his father died, with his small son and tales of a wife who'd died tragically. The town gossips told me he had a fondness for playing card games and, penniless, had been forced to come home to North Berwick with his tail between his legs. I had no idea if it was true, but despite the stories, I thought Davey more worthy of respect than his boorish brother because I remembered him as quite a sweet-natured lad back when we were all young. His brother had always been a bully.

'Widow Seton was left her position as burgess by her late husband,' Davey explained now. 'She has the same voting rights as the men.'

Gregor's face went red. He turned to Mackenzie, who'd lowered his hat again. 'You went along with this?'

Mackenzie just shrugged and I hid my smile. I knew the men would never question John bequeathing me my position in his will – that would mean questioning their own inheritance.

'We should vote,' Davey said. I suddenly had another memory of him as a child, forced to soothe the ill temper of his older brother. Poor Davey, having to make room in his life for this coarse, bad-mannered man. I caught his eye, hoping he knew I was behind him, and he smiled at me, showing me he appreciated my support.

'All those in favour of dredging the harbour to accommodate large clippers and other ships,' Gregor said.

A few hands were raised.

'All those against?'

This time, there were many more hands raised – including my own.

Gregor snorted. 'You will believe the insane ramblings of a woman over my own plans?'

There was silence.

5

'Very well,' Gregor said. His voice was light and casual but I felt a darkness descend over the room like a shadow and I shivered in the sudden chill. 'I trust you all know the teachings of good John Knox about women holding positions of authority?'

The men all stared at him blankly. We all knew of John Knox's beliefs, of course. He may have been dead and gone these last one hundred years, but his teachings lived on in the changes to our churches and our lives. And no more so than in the mistrust of women who rose above their station. I fixed my eyes on Gregor and he looked back.

'Beware,' he said. Was he talking to me personally? It felt that way. But then he looked around the room. 'Be careful who you trust and who you follow. For witches come in many disguises.'

There was a gasp from the other council members and my heart lurched in fear. This didn't sound like a warning. This sounded like a threat.

Chapter 1

Tess

Autumn, Present day

I pulled the final book from the box and put it onto the shelf with a flourish. 'That's it,' I said. 'The last box has been unpacked. We have officially moved in.'

My daughter Jemima threw herself on the sofa. 'It's taken long enough. We've been here well over a month already.'

'Don't get comfy, Jem. These boxes all need to go out for recycling.'

Jem gave a huge, over-exaggerated sigh and dragged herself to her feet. 'Can we order pizza?'

I shook my head. 'But there are two in the freezer that I can put in the oven.'

Jem looked like she was going to argue but then she changed her mind and I was glad. Money was tight and little luxuries like takeaway pizza weren't something I could just buy without thinking – not anymore. But Jem had been through a lot and I hated to remind her how much her life had changed. Fortunately, though, she just grinned. 'Actual pizza or your fancy ones with goat's cheese and spinach?'

'Actual pizza.'

She nodded approvingly and started flattening a box to put it in the recycling. I looked round the tiny cottage which was finally starting to look like our home. Thistle Cottage. I'd fallen in love with the name before I'd even seen the house. It sounded like something from the Enid Blyton books I'd loved as a little girl. It had a thistle carved in the stone above the door, and a huge clump of them growing in the tiny front garden. It was very small but it was the perfect size for Jem and me. The front door opened onto the hall and the stairs up to the bedrooms. To the right was the large-ish living room with its pretty bay window and at the back of the house was the little kitchen. None of the furniture from our old house would have fitted in this quirky home, so I'd sold most of it and bought a second-hand sofa, then Jem and I had done an Ikea run to buy bookcases and a coffee table, and a desk for her bedroom. It wasn't top quality but it was good enough. And the best thing about it was how close we were to the sea. Our house faced the beach, though it was set back enough – separated by the road, a narrow car park, and huts that had once belonged to fishermen and were now craft workshops or fish and chip shops and artisan bakeries – to be protected from the worst of the winds and the waves.

Jem took the cardboard outside and I heard her laughing. I initially assumed she was on her phone, but it was there on the shiny new coffee table. I stiffened, listening for another voice. Was she talking to someone? Who was it? We didn't know anyone here really. Not yet. And I liked it that way. It had been six months since Alistair's trial but it still felt raw and I didn't want to face any questions from well-meaning strangers.

Just as I was about to go and see what she was doing, Jem bounced into the room. 'I met our next-door neighbour,' she said. 'She's really sweet. I asked her to come round and say hello.'

I closed my eyes briefly. This was exactly what I hadn't wanted. I'd been pleased so far that there had been no sign of whoever lived next door. Our neighbour on the other side was a church and its residents – buried under the ancient wonky gravestones in the churchyard – were unlikely to cause us any trouble.

'She's been away,' Jem said as the doorbell rang. 'She's called Eva Greenbaum. You'll like her.'

She skipped off to answer the door and I took a deep breath, readying myself for questions from a stranger. I ran my fingers through my newly short hair, which still took me by surprise sometimes, and pasted a smile onto my face.

'Mum . . .' Jem came into the room, followed by a small woman with steel-grey hair in a sharp bob. 'This is Mrs Greenbaum. This is my mum, Tess.'

'Call me Eva,' said the woman, holding her hand out for me to shake. I took her hand, impressed by her firm grip. 'I brought some biscuits.'

She shoved a cardboard cake box at me and I took it, getting a waft of delicious sugary smells that made my mouth water.

'Gosh, these smell amazing,' I said.

She gave me a beaming smile. 'My son-in-law bakes,' she said, and I noticed for the first time that she had the hint of an accent. German, I thought. 'He used to bake Austrian pastries for me when he first met my son, but now he no longer tries to impress me and he bakes whatever he likes.'

Ah, so not German, Austrian. I thought that she looked rather impressed anyway, no matter what she said, which made me warm to her in spite of my early misgivings about meeting neighbours. 'Thank you. Will you stay for a cup of tea?'

Eva nodded. 'That would be nice. I'd been wondering if you would move in while I was away.'

With a little prod from me, Jem took the box of biscuits, then she went off to the kitchen and I heard her filling the kettle and opening cupboard doors. I hoped we had enough milk. Eva and I sat down on the sofa and she looked round at the room with a little nod.

9

'You've settled in well.'

'We've actually only just this minute finished unpacking.' I gave a little laugh. I felt a bit awkward and uncomfortable; I was out of practice when it came to small talk. 'But we're happy with it.'

'It's just the two of you?' Eva looked straight at me and I resisted the urge to duck my head away from her glance.

'Just us,' I said.

Jem came back into the room, holding a tray with the drinks on it. I noticed she'd put the milk in a little jug, which was sweet. And she'd arranged the – amazing – biscuits on a plate for us to share.

'Are you new to town?' Eva asked.

'I used to come here for holidays when I was little,' I said. It was those happy memories that had made me choose this place when we were finding somewhere new. Far enough from Edinburgh that I wouldn't bump into old 'friends' everywhere I went, but close enough for it not to feel too much of a wrench to leave.

'Mum's still working in Edinburgh,' said Jem, taking a bite from a biscuit. 'Oh my god, this is delicious.'

'What is it you do?'

I shifted on my seat. I knew Eva was just being neighbourly but I didn't like being under all this scrutiny. I'd not only chosen North Berwick because of its happy memories, but also because it was big enough that we could simply blend in among the holiday-makers and residents. We'd had enough of being in the spotlight during Alistair's trial and afterwards. All I wanted was for us to be invisible and for Jem to go back to being a normal teenager. So being asked all these questions was making me worried that Eva had some sort of ulterior motive – but I was being silly, she was just an elderly neighbour taking an interest.

'I'm a solicitor,' I said. 'Terribly dull stuff. Wills and property and that sort of thing for dusty old Edinburgh families.'

I'd had a corporate job before my husband had gone to jail. But when Alistair had been charged, my boss had taken me to one side and gently suggested that I should leave quietly with a not-nearly-generous-enough pay-out, or – he hinted – my working life would become very difficult. I'd be side-lined for big projects because no one would trust a lawyer with a husband in prison. I'd thought about fighting it, but in the end I had taken the money and thank goodness I had because Alistair, not content with breaking my heart, had somehow managed to spirit away the contents of our joint account and all of our savings long before my divorce lawyer – aka my friend Lu – had managed to get near it. That money had let me get a mortgage on this tiny cottage and I'd got a new job at Langdown & Son, a family firm in Edinburgh's New Town, with wood-panelled offices and a sweet receptionist called Judy. It wasn't as exciting as my old job, nor nearly as well paid, but the father and son who ran the firm left me to my own devices most of the time and either they hadn't put two and two together – which was unlikely – or they knew exactly who I was and they didn't care. Young Mr Langdown was only in his early thirties but he was already a tweed-jacket-wearing, whisky-drinking carbon copy of his father. They were both very posh, very polite, very old-fashioned and very kind and I was so grateful that Lu had put me in touch with them when my world had fallen apart. Another favour I owed her if I ever got things back on track.

Eva raised an eyebrow as I described my work, but she didn't comment further. I felt oddly like I'd disappointed her. Jem jumped in again. 'Mum's working here, too. At some women's centre.'

'The Haven?' This time Eva sounded like she approved.

I nodded. 'An old friend put me in touch.' It was only a white lie – that old friend had actually been the family liaison officer the police had assigned to Jem and me when Alistair was first arrested. She had been sternly supportive and I'd liked her no-nonsense attitude. 'They needed a legal adviser. It's just voluntary.'

'The Haven is a good place,' Eva said. 'You're doing a good thing.'

I felt that prickle of discomfort again. I didn't deserve Eva's praise. I wasn't working at the Haven because I was a good person. Instead I was trying to make up for all the mistakes I'd made. I spent two days a week there, advising hollow-eyed women on their rights when it came to divorce, or child custody, or maintenance payments. Or helping them prepare to face their rapists in court. It was hard work. Some of the women were scared. Some of them were angry. The stakes were always high. But it was rewarding and I felt like I was helping. Making a difference. Making amends.

Eva drank her tea and I studied her. She was older than I'd first thought. Well into her eighties, I guessed.

'Do you live alone?'

She nodded. 'My husband died twenty years ago.' She gave me a quick, mischievous grin. 'But I am never lonely.'

'That's good to hear.' I wondered – self-pityingly – if I'd be alone for twenty years, or more. 'You keep busy?'

'I play bridge, and I watch television, and I go for lunches,' Eva said, waving her hands. 'I have many friends.'

'And is your son local?'

'London.' She raised her chin proudly. 'He works in the theatre.'

'Is he an actor? Is he famous?' Jem said. I shot her a glance. Was she thinking about our old life?

Eva screwed her nose up. 'He is a producer. So he gets tickets to all the shows.'

'Fabulous,' I said with relief. I didn't want any unexpected paparazzi turning up on the doorstep. I'd had enough of that to last a lifetime. 'If you ever need anything – shopping or anything – just let me know.'

'Thank you,' Eva said. I got the impression she was genuinely grateful. 'And the same goes for you. If you need me, just call. And now I will leave you to your unpacking.'

She got up from the sofa in a very sprightly fashion and said goodbye. Jem showed her out and I sat back against the squishy cushions that had once belonged to someone else, and closed my eyes, exhausted suddenly. Starting a new life wasn't going to be easy.

Chapter 2

Jem

Mum was so jumpy and nervous that I was trying really hard not to make her skittishness rub off on me. She reminded me of those meerkats – you know the ones on that David Attenborough documentary? Always on the alert, looking round to see where the danger was coming from next.

I couldn't blame her, I supposed. Things had been totally messed up for a while back in Edinburgh, thanks to my shithead perv of a dad.

And because of me.

I was only 13 when he was arrested. Just a little kid, looking back, though I thought I was really grown up of course. All pleased with myself going to high school, with its fancy uniform and its amazing facilities. We had to play lacrosse. Like it was bloody Malory Towers or something. Mum and Dad said it was one of the best schools in Edinburgh, which was probably true, but it had been the absolute worst place to be when the truth about Dad came out.

At first I didn't know what was going on. There were a lot of whispers at home and an atmosphere. And then one evening,

Mum and Dad sat me down and said a woman had told the police something about Dad and it wasn't true – of course not – and she was just a bit sad and lonely and it would all be sorted out and I just had to trust them.

I may have only been 13 but I had Google and it took me about five minutes to find out what Dad had been accused of. And it probably took the girls in my class even less time. They started calling Dad names. Saying he was a perv. Back then I'd believed Dad when he said it was a mistake. You trust your parents, don't you? I'd said that, over and over. Madeleine, the girl in my class with the sharpest tongue and the most devoted band of followers, the girl I'd thought was my friend, had laughed when I said it was a misunderstanding.

'They all say that,' she'd said, flicking her silky hair over her shoulder and gazing, wide-eyed, at the girls gathered round, hanging off her every word. 'Let me tell you about the way he looked at me when I went round to Jem's house once after school.'

It was a lie, of course. Madeleine had never even met my dad, because he was never home when she visited. But she'd dropped the little seeds of poison and they were taking root.

I shook my head, not wanting to think about that now. I liked our new house. I loved living beside the sea. And I liked my new school. It didn't have the swanky theatre and sports hall that my old school had, but I liked how it was enormous and chaotic and no one paid any attention to me. Most of the kids were nice. I'd made some friends and there was a girl called Cassie who I really liked. I was even thinking of auditioning for the school play. It was a relief, to be away from Edinburgh and having to be 'on' all the time. And I liked Mum being around more. We had each other's backs.

So even though I felt bad that I'd invited our next-door neighbour in for tea, I was quite pleased that I had. She was nice. And I thought Mum could do with having a new friend, like I had Cassie.

I cooked the pizzas to make up for it, because when Eva left

14

Mum looked totally exhausted. I always got the feeling she'd really like to live miles away from anyone, just me and her. But obviously there was school and work and all that to deal with so she couldn't shut out the world completely. Instead, she just stopped me going on social media and kept her hair short which she said was because she fancied a change but I knew was really because she thought it made her look different and she didn't want anyone to recognize her. She even changed her name – well, she dropped the Robertson and just went back to being Blyth all the time, which she was before she got married, and had always been at work. I did it too. I was Jemima Blyth at school and I quite liked it. It made us feel like a team.

*

The next morning was a bit hectic because I got up late and then I spent too long in the shower. Mum was cross with me because it was one of her days for working in Edinburgh, and I was secretly pleased that she was cross because it meant she was more like her normal self than when she was being super-nice to me the whole time.

'I don't have time to drive you,' she said, swigging at a cup of coffee. 'I've got to catch my train.'

'It's fine. I'm going early anyway. I'm walking with Cassie.'

Mum looked at me, a little frown on her face. 'The famous Cassie I've heard so much about. Just . . .' She paused. 'Be careful, Jem. I remember when you talked about Madeleine all the time.'

'She's absolutely nothing like Madeleine,' I said with a giggle. 'Cassie's a friend. She's in my class. She's nice.'

I saw Mum's shoulders relax a little bit. She was worried about me making friends and worried that I wouldn't. Basically, she was just worried.

'She lives up the road a bit. I'm meeting her on the corner. She's invited me to hers after school actually.'

'For tea?' Mum looked thrilled. She hated when I had to come home from school to an empty house on her work days. I liked it because I ate crisps and watched Netflix until she got back.

'I guess. We've got a history project to do and Cassie says her mum can help.'

'Should I call her?'

'Cassie?'

Mum tutted. 'No, her mother?'

'It's fine, Mum.'

She paused and I thought she might have more questions but then she just nodded. 'Home by seven. Text me when you're on your way back.'

'I will.'

I grabbed my bag and headed out to meet Cassie. I knew that as soon as I'd gone down the path, Mum would run upstairs to my bedroom at the back of the house because it had a good view of the street, and watch me walk to the corner by the church. I could feel her eyes on me as I went. I didn't mind. It was nice to feel safe.

Cassie had said it made sense for me to go to hers after school because her mum worked in the museum in town so she would be able to help with our totally lame history project.

'Is she a historian?' I'd asked, quite impressed.

Cassie had made a face. 'She works in the shop.'

I had laughed along with Cassie. 'She might have overheard people talking about history,' she'd protested.

'She might have,' I'd said, nodding. 'Let's hope she's overheard a lot, because otherwise we're stuffed.'

We were doing a thing about learning from the past. So we had to do a report on one aspect of local history and find lessons in it we could apply to the present day. Our teacher had given us some ideas, but I'd not really been listening and it turned out Cassie hadn't been either.

'What about the castle?' I said later that afternoon, as we

walked back to Cassie's after school. There was a ruined fortress not far from town. 'We could do something about home security.'

'Boring,' Cassie said.

'You're right, it is really boring. What do you suggest?'

'Everyone's doing the prison. We could do that?'

My stomach lurched. 'Why prison? Why would you say that?'

'Duh, because it's such an obvious one.'

'Is it?'

Cassie rolled her eyes. 'There was a prison on Bass Rock.' She nodded in the direction of the sea, where the lumpen island loomed out of the waves. It was a seabird sanctuary now but I hadn't known it had once been a jail.

'It was like Alcatraz,' Cassie said. 'No one could escape.'

'That's pretty cool,' I said, relaxing now I knew she hadn't mentioned prisons because of my dad. 'But how does that link to the present day? What lessons can we learn from it?'

Cassie shrugged. 'Don't go to prison,' she said with a grin. I screwed my face up, thinking she had the right idea. 'This is us.'

She led me up the path to a red-brick semi-detached house with a neat front garden, and opened the door.

'Mum?' she shouted. There was no response.

'She's getting changed.' A tall teenaged boy with wild curly hair like Cassie's came out of the kitchen eating a sandwich.

'How did you get here so fast?' Cassie eyed him with suspicion. 'School only finished ten minutes ago.'

'Long legs,' he said through a mouthful of bread. 'What kept you?'

'Well, what we did,' Cassie said as though she was sharing a secret, 'was we stayed at school right until the end of the day and didn't bunk off early.' I stifled a giggle as the boy – Cassie's older brother Drew I assumed – aimed a punch at her arm and she ducked out of the way. Sometimes I wished I had siblings. It would be nice to have someone who properly understood what it had been like at home. Back then.

'Pig,' Cassie called after Drew's retreating back.

'Scumbag,' he said cheerfully.

'Let's sit at the kitchen table and see if we can get a proper idea,' Cassie said. 'Or old Miss McGinty will be on our case.'

Miss McGinty was about 25 so she didn't really qualify as old but I definitely didn't want her on our case so I obediently followed Cassie into the kitchen. It was much bigger than our little cottage's whole living area with a large table at one end, and shelves groaning with cookery books. It was warm and cosy and I liked it.

Cassie dumped her bag on the floor and got us both a drink and some biscuits, while I spread our books across the table.

'It's so boring,' I moaned, staring at the printed-out instructions for our project. 'I just don't see how history can be relevant to our lives now.'

'I know.' Cassie sat down next to me with a thump and took the sheet from me. 'Boring and pointless.'

Cassie's mum came into the kitchen wearing sports gear. She looked young and fit and energetic and I felt a tiny twinge of envy. My mum had been like that once. Now she was skinny because she didn't eat properly, not because she worked out, and she had permanent lines between her eyes because she was always worrying.

'Hello,' she said, giving me a wide smile.

'Mum, this is my new friend Jem,' Cassie said.

'Hello, Jem.'

I said hello back, as a younger girl came into the house, trailing a bag and wearing a too-big blazer that told me she'd just started high school.

'Oh, Thea, I was wondering where you'd got to,' Cassie's mum said.

Thea, who looked like a smaller version of Cassie, looked at me. 'Was that you that I saw in the drama studio earlier?'

'That was me.' I'd been finding out about auditions for the

18

school play. They were doing *Macbeth* and I thought it sounded fun.

Thea nodded. 'I've got loads of homework,' she said dramatically, throwing herself into a chair. 'I'm going to be up until midnight finishing it all. It's an absolute nightmare.'

I smiled to myself, thinking she should try out for the play, too.

'Us too. Shit history.' Cassie waved the instruction sheet.

Cassie's mum rolled her eyes at her daughter. 'Did you expect me to help with that?'

'No.' Cassie looked innocent but then she grinned. 'Bit. We've got to do a report on some local historical thing and what lessons it can teach us in the present day.'

'What are you going to do?'

'Dunno. Prison maybe.'

'You could at least try to look enthusiastic about it.' Cassie's mother sighed. 'Let me know if you need me to get any books from work.'

'We'll just google for now.'

'Best get on with it then,' her mum said, dropping a kiss on Thea's head. 'I'm going for a run, but I won't be long. Will you need a lift home, Jem?'

'I can walk, thank you. I don't live far away.'

'Jem lives in the witch's cottage,' Cassie said with glee. I looked at her in surprise. I lived where?

'Erm, I live in Thistle Cottage,' I said. I looked from Cassie to her mum. 'It's just by the sea. It's really not far.'

Cassie's mum made for the door, clearly eager to be off. 'Well, if you're sure you don't mind walking?'

'I don't.'

'I'll give your cottage a wave as I run past.'

She headed outside and Thea looked at us both, interested in our conversation. 'You live in the witch's cottage?'

'I really don't. I live in Thistle Cottage.'

'The little white one with the black window frames?'

19

'Yes. And the thistle over the door.'

'That's the witch's cottage.'

I made a face at Cassie. 'Why do you call it that?'

She looked blank. 'No idea. We've always called it that. Not just us. Everyone calls it the witch's cottage.'

'Maybe a witch lived there,' Thea said with a thrilled grin. 'There were loads of witches in North Berwick. I did an assembly about it at primary school.'

I felt a little shiver of interest run through me and I grinned at Cassie. 'Witches,' I said.

Chapter 3

Tess

I had a slight niggle about Jem all day while I was at work. The downside of my new job was that it really wasn't very busy, nor absorbing. And that meant I had lots of time to fret. I was worried that Cassie could have worked out who Jem was, and befriended her just to get the gossip about Alistair. Did teenagers care about old television presenters? I wasn't sure. The girls at Jem's old school certainly had, but I had a sneaking suspicion that was more about them sensing a weakness than the story itself. I had always hated the 'mean girls' cliché but there were definitely some queen bees at that school who had made it their business to make some of their classmates' lives a misery. And unfortunately, Alistair's arrest and trial put Jem firmly in their sights.

I tried not to think about Alistair's arrest and the court case and the awfulness that followed if I could avoid it but I found that no matter how hard I tried to forget, it just kept popping into my head and forcing me to remember how my charming, handsome husband, the darling of the press, became a villain overnight. Of course I had stood by him at first. Why wouldn't I when he was standing in front of me, ashen-faced, telling me it was all a big

21

mistake? That he barely knew this woman who was saying such awful things – he'd only ever seen her in the corridor or maybe taking notes in a production meeting. *She must be mentally ill,* he told me, his eyes filling with tears. *She needs our sympathy, not our anger.* I'd taken him in my arms, amazed by his generosity and promising I'd be right by his side.

But then another woman came forward, and another. And he was charged, and we were hurtled into the awfulness of courts and custodial sentences. And they were so young, these women. Not teens – not like the rumours said – but interns young enough to be his daughter. Fresh out of university and eager and excited to get started in their television career until my disgusting husband made it dirty and spoiled.

I tapped my keyboard to bring my screen back to life and sighed. The will I was drafting wasn't exactly gripping and I needed a distraction from my thoughts, so I pushed my chair back from my desk and went in search of tea. The firm's receptionist, Judy, was in the kitchen with Marcus – a law student who helped Mr Langdown sometimes. They were watching something on Judy's phone.

'Cat videos?' I said, turning on the tap to fill the kettle.

Judy looked up. 'Ooh if you're making one, yes please.'

I took two mugs out of the cupboard and raised an eyebrow at Marcus who nodded, still gripped by the action on the phone. I added another mug and dropped three teabags in.

'What is it?' I asked, wondering what had them so enthralled.

'Some MP has accidentally shared a saucy message on Twitter,' Marcus said. 'Look. It was clearly meant for his wife, but he made it public. It's filthy and totally hilarious. Though people are being pretty mean about her, which isn't great.'

I glanced at the screen as he showed me the comments people were making about the wife's appearance, and made a face. 'Urgh. What happened to "be kind" eh?'

Judy looked half ashamed, half gleeful. 'We're just watching the . . . what did you call it, Marcus?'

'Pile on,' Marcus said with relish. 'He's deleted the message but everyone's screen grabbed it so he can't deny it. Everyone's talking about it.' He bit his lip. 'Shame they're being so nasty about her, though.'

I concentrated on stirring the tea and pouring on the milk, hoping they couldn't see my hands shaking. It was so easy to make mistakes on social media. To write something in anger or without double-checking that your meaning was clear. Or – apparently – to share something publicly that should have been private. Thinking about my own error made me feel sick. My 'pile on' had been quite early on in that nightmarish time when Alistair had been arrested and the police had been in our house night and day, searching our bedroom, and the study, and Jem's room. They'd taken the computer from the lounge as well as my work laptop and Jem's phone. And all the neighbours saw, of course, even though our house was large and set back from the road. You can't miss a load of police cars and streams of uniformed officers carrying out laptops and monitors. I think that's where the rumours that Alistair had groomed young girls started, which is totally understandable. If I'd seen it happen to a neighbour, I'd have assumed that too.

When news of the arrest hit the papers, it got even worse. Jem's school was supportive enough at first but when it became clear that it wasn't all some big misunderstanding, that soon faded away. They had a reputation to protect, after all. So there was no punishment for the girls who followed her round all day asking questions about her 'pervy dad' and no consequences for the former friend who spread rumours about Alistair eyeing her up when she came to Jem's birthday party.

When Jem came home in floods of tears for what felt like the hundredth time, I snapped. On my newly returned phone I typed a tweet about the silly girls who were making my daughter's life a misery.

'Silly girls should think about their actions before ruining people's lives,' I wrote because I had some sort of conscience and I didn't want to name the girls or the school. But that backfired because everyone thought I meant the women who'd accused Alistair, of course – they didn't know about the school bullies. Within seconds I had hundreds of comments telling me I was victim blaming, calling me a sad, vicious old woman who had been brainwashed by her paedo husband, saying all sorts of awful things. I realized how stupid I'd been putting anything on social media and deleted it straightaway but the damage was done. And then it all got even worse . . .

'Tess?' I jumped, startled out of my memories by Marcus who'd put his phone away and was waiting patiently for the cup of tea I'd promised.

'Sorry,' I said. 'In a world of my own.'

He nodded, eyeing me thoughtfully. I wondered if he knew who I was. He didn't appear to and I was glad.

*

Jem was in really good spirits that evening which made me feel more comfortable. I wanted her to make friends, despite my nerves, and Cassie actually sounded really nice. Jem was full of stories about Cassie, and Cassie's bedroom, and Cassie's brother and sister, and Cassie's mum, and chatting about school and how she was going to audition for the school play. She was even excited about her history project which I was pleased about because I liked history. Jem had never shown much interest before.

'Cassie's mum went for a run while I was there,' she said, as we sat on the sofa with an old episode of *Friends* playing in the background. 'I thought maybe you could go running again. You used to like that.'

She looked at me in a way that made me realize with a start that perhaps she worried about me just as much as I worried

24

about her. Poor girl. She'd had so much to deal with the last year or so since Alistair's arrest. It had all just been one long drawn-out nightmare.

'Maybe I will,' I said. 'That's a good idea.'

Jem grinned and I relaxed a bit. 'Tell me about your project.'

'Ohmygod,' she said, jumping to her feet and getting her school bag. 'It's so cool. Did you know everyone calls this house the witch's cottage?'

'I did not know that,' I said, with a small shudder, thinking of the names I'd been called when the truth about Alistair came out. 'It's not because we live here is it?'

'Duh, no,' Jem said. She pulled her history folder out of her bag. 'Cassie's sister, Thea, said there were loads of witches in North Berwick and she reckons one of them must have lived here.'

'Goodness,' I said. 'I suppose this cottage is very old. It's one of the oldest buildings in the whole town, I think.'

'So Cassie and me are going to find out about the witches that lived here. It's supposed to link the present and the past, so it fits perfectly.'

'Cassie and I,' I said automatically. 'What have you found out so far?'

Jem shrugged. 'Nothing yet,' she admitted. 'We got a bit distracted on Instagram.'

My stomach lurched. 'Jem, you know I don't want you on social media.'

She sighed. 'I'm not on social media. I was looking on Cassie's phone.' She turned away from me and I heard her mutter, 'Everyone else is on it.'

I understood that it was hard for her not to be online like her friends, but I knew all too well how easy it was for people to send horrible, nasty messages on social media. Messages and comments that stuck in your head, no matter how much you tried to dismiss them or laugh them off. Threats against you, or your loved ones. Or once, even against our family pets. Rape threats.

Death threats. All sorts. So I wasn't budging on my social-media ban, no matter how much Jem begged me.

Wanting to distract her, I got my laptop from the bookshelf and opened it up. 'Shall we have a look?'

The lure of finding out about the witches who'd lived in our house was too tempting for Jem to keep sulking. To my relief, she turned back to me and smiled. 'Google it,' she said.

I typed in witches and North Berwick and was rewarded with dozens of hits.

'Oh my,' I said. 'It was quite a thing.'

Together, Jem and I read about the witch trials in our town, the accusations of dark deeds, which sounded ridiculous to our modern ears, and the torture of women, which didn't sound so ridiculous.

'It's horrible,' Jem said, wide-eyed. 'Can we try to find the one who lived in our cottage?'

I thought for a second and then searched for 'witch, Forth Street, North Berwick'. Nothing came up.

'Perhaps the street had a different name back then,' I said.

Jem was looking thoughtful. 'I think I know how to find it,' she said.

'Really?'

'Come on.' She jumped to her feet and disappeared into the hall, then came back wearing her coat – finally – and shoes. 'Come on, Mum.'

'Where are we going?'

'You'll see.'

I pulled on my boots and my own coat, and together we went outside into the dark street, Jem leading the way.

'Here,' she said in triumph as we reached the corner. 'I lean against it when I'm waiting for Cassie.'

It was an information board aimed at tourists, showing some history of North Berwick. Jem got her phone out and shone the light at the pictures.

'There's an old map,' she said. 'I was looking at it this morning.'

I squinted at the board in the dim light. 'I think this map is a bit later than the witches would have been,' I said, trying to read the date.

'Still could help.'

That was true. I looked again, trying to get my bearings. 'So that's the harbour, there,' I said, pointing. 'And that's what's now Forth Street. Shine the torch here, Jem.'

She obliged and I grinned. 'It's called Church Street,' I said.

Jem clapped her hands. 'Church Street. Let's go and look that up, then.'

We hurried back to the house because it was chilly, with a real autumnal feel to the evening, and I made tea while Jem googled Church Street, North Berwick and witches, and gave a yelp of triumph.

'I've found them,' she said. 'At least, I think I've found them.'

I took the mugs of tea through and put them on the coffee table. 'Show me.'

'Look, this is someone's dissertation or something. It's like a massive project on witches in Scotland,' she said. She looked up at me and gave me a cheeky grin. 'Maybe Cassie and I can just copy this whole thing.'

'Jem,' I said. 'Don't even think about it.'

'Joke.' She rolled her eyes. 'Look, Honor Seton is on this list here of accused witches. Her address is given as Church Street, and it says she was 35.'

'Considerably younger than me,' I said wryly.

Jem zoomed in on the list, looking pleased. 'And it says she lived with her daughter Alice, who was 16. Maybe Alice was a witch too?'

I felt a bit uncomfortable. A mum with a teenage daughter, in our house, being accused of all sorts. It was a strange coincidence. 'None of them were actually witches, Jem,' I said, more sharply than I intended. I forced myself to smile and look more interested. 'So what happened to them? Were they burned at the stake?'

'It doesn't say,' Jem said, leaning forward. 'There's a photo of the original document. Hang on.'

She enlarged the picture, which was of a list of accused witches from the seventeenth century. It was written in old-fashioned hand, difficult – if not impossible – to read, without the helpful typed text beneath translating it for our twenty-first-century eyes. But there was nothing about the outcome of the trial – simply that it was said to be happening.

'I'm sure we can find out what happened, now we know their names. Cassie's mum could find us some books. Or she said one of the people who work at the museum with her might know more.' Jem's eyes were gleaming with interest. I drank in her happiness, pleased to see how much she was enjoying this. 'Isn't it funny, that we're a mother and daughter living here, just like they were?'

'Let's hope we're not accused of witchcraft,' I said, stifling a yawn. 'Gosh, I'm beat. I think it's bedtime for me.'

'I'll come up too,' said Jem, who may have been bolshy and independent, but still didn't like being downstairs by herself.

I pulled her to me and kissed her temple. 'You go on up, sweetheart, and get your stuff ready for the morning. I'll be up in a minute. Remember to plug your phone in down here, please.' That was another rule – no phones in the bedroom. I didn't want Jem scrolling and stumbling on anything about her father. Or about me. I liked to know what she was looking at, although I knew I couldn't control that all the time.

Jem threw me her phone to plug in, then she stuffed her books back into her bag and headed up to bed, calling a cheery goodnight to me as she went. I took our mugs into the kitchen. As I rinsed them out, I noticed the bin was overflowing. Jem had a very irritating habit of balancing rubbish on top like a smelly game of Jenga. Tutting, I pulled the bag out of the bin, tied it up, shoved my feet into the sliders I kept by the back door for this very reason, and went out to the wheelie bin.

The wind had really got up and the crashing of the waves was loud in the quiet night. I shivered as I dropped the bag into the bin, and let the lid close. Winter was definitely on its way.

A noise in the dark garden made me start, my heart thudding. Those witch stories had spooked me a little. I stayed still for a second, but there was nothing there – it must have been the wind.

I turned to go back inside and jumped again as a black cat ran in front of me.

'Christ,' I said, clutching my chest in fright. 'Where did you come from?' The little cat sat down and regarded me in the light from the kitchen without interest. I reached out a hand to stroke its head, and it hissed at me, making me recoil. 'Oh,' I gasped. The cat darted off into the darkness, leaving me shaking my head at my jumpiness. No more reading about witches before bed, I thought. It was clearly a bad idea.

Chapter 4

Honor

1661

I don't like to go out when there's a storm brewing. Not just because my gowns are threadbare and the soles of my boots so thin I can feel the gravel through them, though that doesn't make the weather feel more welcoming. It's more that when I'm seen around town as the waves are churning and the clouds are whipping through the dark sky, people remember.

So I was scurrying along, hood up and cloak drawn around me to keep the wind out, in case any whispers reached my ears. It was years now, since my husband had died. Drowned when his fishing boat was dashed against the rocks in a storm. But people still remembered.

I knew why they blamed me, of course. I wasn't stupid. Women weren't supposed to hold power – as Gregor Kincaid had made very clear – and I had known that when John left me his position as burgess on the parish council, people weren't happy. But it was perfectly legal and there for all to see in his official papers. There was nothing anyone could do about it. Except talk and whisper about how the storm that killed my John had come from nowhere. How the weather had been fine, until it wasn't, and had someone made it happen? Had someone caused the sea to swell and the waves to crash and the lightning to fork? Someone like me.

Many years had gone since then. I'd been carrying Alice when John drowned, and now she was grown. But people still talked. It wasn't malicious – not often. Just careless gossip and chitter-chatter that had died away over the years and come back just as strong, since Gregor Kincaid returned.

I had reached the fisherman's cottage on the edge of town, and now I knocked on the door. It opened at once.

'Honor,' said the woman who stood there, her white pinny splashed with blood. 'I am pleased to see you.'

I took off my cloak and gloves. 'Where is she?'

'Upstairs. She's in such pain but nothing is happening.'

'Is the bairn's head down?'

'I think not.' The woman – Mary, a capable farmer's wife who often delivered babies in the town – looked worried. 'I tried to turn it before her pains began but try as I might, nothing happened.'

I picked up my bag. 'Take me to her.'

The mother was leaning over her bed, crying with pain, when I entered. She looked up at me with fear in her eyes.

'My baby is dying, Honor,' she said, reaching out to me. 'And I am dying. You must help.'

'Hush now, Bridie,' I told her. 'No one will die today.' I busied myself taking a small bottle of oil from my bag, and some dried herbs. 'Let me see you.'

I helped her up onto the bed, washed my hands in a basin of water that Mary was holding, and then gently examined Bridie. She was exhausted but the baby wasn't coming yet. Mary was right – the little one was trying to come feet first. I looked at Bridie carefully.

'How long have the pains been coming?'

She shook her head, tears welling in her eyes. 'I don't know,' she whispered. 'It feels like days, but it can't be. Two days, I think and one night?'

In surprise, I glanced at Mary who gave a tiny nod.

'You should have come to get me sooner,' I scolded. 'Bridie, I need to turn your baby inside your belly.'

Bridie lay back against the bed, looking pale and weak. She didn't have the strength to say yes or no.

Quickly, I crumbled the herbs into a bowl and with a taper from the fire, I lit the leaves. They caught straightaway and burned well, filling the room with scent. Then I uncorked the bottle and rubbed the oil into Bridie's bulging belly. More smells filled the air.

'What is that?' Mary said, her brow furrowed in suspicion.

'Lavender,' I told her honestly. There were other things in there too, but I never told anyone what was in the tinctures and oils I cooked up. Only Alice, who was proving to be a capable and creative apprentice.

I put my hands on Bridie's skin, feeling the baby move beneath my fingers. 'Come on, wee one,' I said softly. 'I know there's not much room, but you have to move.'

Bridie groaned and I stroked her head gently. 'It's going to feel odd for a minute, but you'll be right as rain after. Ready?'

I thought Bridie would agree to anything I asked of her, so worn out was she. She nodded and I pushed on the side of her abdomen, not hard but with just enough pressure in the right spots, and then I gently rubbed and coaxed as the baby wiggled round, making her taut skin ripple like the waves on the sea on a calm day.

'Ohhh,' Bridie moaned and then her eyes widened. 'I'm sorry,' she said.

I looked down at the bed, where liquid was trickling. 'It's your waters,' I reassured her. 'Things are moving now.'

I helped her back onto her feet, so she could walk around the room.

'Don't let her lie down,' I warned Mary. 'She's tired but she needs to stay upright. It'll help.'

Mary rolled her eyes but she nodded. 'And keep the herbs burning,' I added. 'They're soothing.'

I packed up my things and pulled on my cloak. Mary pushed some coins into my hand and I tucked them away without looking. Then leaving Mary tending to Bridie, I quietly went downstairs, pausing only to look in at Bridie's husband, Conall, who was asleep in a chair by the fire. He'd never know I'd been here unless Bridie told him. I wondered if she would.

Outside, the weather hadn't worsened as I'd thought it would, but it was still cold and windy. I headed for home through the dark lanes and found my daughter, Alice, standing at the side of our cottage looking at the sky.

'I think we're over the worst of it,' I said.

'It's passed,' she agreed, still staring at the heavens. Then she dropped her head and looked at me. 'Did the bairn live?'

'He's not born yet, but he will.'

'It's a boy?'

I nodded. I always knew if babies would be boys or girls. Just as I knew Bridie's wee one would survive.

'Did you tell Bridie?'

'No,' I said with a chuckle. 'Though I don't think she'd have heard if I had. She was worn out, poor thing.'

'How much did they give you?'

I put my hand in my cloak and pulled out the coins Mary had pushed into my hand. It wasn't much. Alice made a face and I waved away her disapproval. 'Better than a kick in the shins,' I said. 'Come inside and we shall have some warm milk.'

Thistle cottage was small, but it was plenty big enough for Alice and me. We didn't have a lot of room inside, but we had a great deal of it outside. My husband had been a clever man. He went from having one fishing boat to running three boats out of the harbour every night. He made money and he spent it on land. And because he was a landowner, he was entitled to be a burgess with a seat on the parish council. He was older than me, my John, and had always thought he would never marry. But marry we did and John built our cottage with his own hands – and some help from the men in town. I named it for the thistles that grew in the garden, and we made our home together. Our land stretched from the Kincaids' estate to the south, and Old Man Fraser's farm to the east. The churchyard was our border to the west and at the front of the cottage was the sea.

'Did anyone see you go to Bridie's?' Alice looked worried as we went inside.

I shook my head. 'Just Mary.'

'I hate looking over our shoulders all the time,' Alice said with a groan. 'We are doing good work. You have saved that baby's life, and Bridie's too I imagine, and still we need to keep it quiet.'

'It's for the best.' I poured some milk into a pot and set it on the fire to warm. 'We can't be too careful. Not with Gregor Kincaid dripping his poison into the ears of the town.'

Alice pushed her hair back from her face and I thought how much she looked like her father. 'It's not fair,' she said. 'We do nothing wrong.'

'There will always be those like Gregor who think women should not own land, or hold authority over men,' I said, wrapping a cloth around the pot handle and pouring the warm milk into mugs. 'And for that reason, we must give them no cause to suspect us of any wrongdoing.'

With a sulky nod, Alice sipped her milk. 'You are right,' she said. 'But I don't like it.'

'We are doing well enough. Don't we have a good life? We're luckier than some.'

Alice looked as though she was going to argue, but she didn't. I was pleased. My daughter had grown to have a stubborn nature and a mouth that often ran away with her, and while I admired her ferocity, it wasn't always fun to be on the receiving end of it. She was clever, too. John had taught me to read and write and I'd taught Alice, and she'd picked it up in no time. She had persuaded me to keep records of my remedies, writing down the combinations of herbs, flowers, thistles and other ingredients that made up my tinctures. My potions, Alice called them with a wry smile. Now we had bundles of paper, tied up with string, with remedies for every ailment you could think of, from heartburn to unwanted pregnancies. And more besides. People from all over town came to us for help, but they did it quietly, because ten years ago, and twenty years before that, and decades before that, over and over again, women like us had been taken from their beds and punished for being different or having knowledge. So we worked quietly and I saved most of the money we earned. Because I never knew if one day we would have to run.

Chapter 5

Alice

I was born too late, my grandmother used to say. Too late to save my father. I arrived still floating inside the caul; I slipped out of my mother encased in a raindrop. My grandmother, who delivered me, had to burst the sack and let the water run away before my mother could take me in her arms.

I'd heard people say that babies born in the caul were blessed. The cauls were sold to sailors because it was said that if they carried one in their pocket, they would never come to harm at sea. But my father had drowned before I was born and my mother kept the caul I'd been born in, wrapped in a cloth on a shelf. When I was wee, I would sometimes ask to see it. Ma would take it down and gently peel away the cloth and let me touch the soft skin.

'I was inside this?' I would say, astonished. 'Before I was born?'

'You were growing in there,' she always said. 'Floating inside your bubble, kept warm inside me.'

'Then I came out to meet you.'

'You did. And I'm very pleased about it.'

And I would snuggle in beside her, pleased too.

Caul babies were rumoured to have powers. We were said to have second sight, or the ability to raise a storm on a sunny day. But I had lived sixteen summers and never seen any sign of these powers. And I was glad about it, because at times like these it didn't do to stand out. Wasn't I already strange enough with a healer for a mother, and my knowledge of reading and writing?

Not many people knew I could read. It wasn't wise to show too much learning, Ma always said. The only person I told was my best friend, Kyla. I'd tried teaching her letters as well, but she was too fidgety and ready to jump up and run off somewhere, so I gave up on that.

Ma didn't like Kyla. We didn't argue about much, me and Ma, but we argued about that. Ma said Kyla gave her a bad feeling. I ignored that. I didn't ignore all of Ma's feelings – I'd be a fool to do that. But I ignored this one, because Kyla and I had been friends since we were bairns and Ma was wrong.

Kyla was a bit older than me, and she worked at the big house on the estate. The Kincaids' house. She'd worked there since she was a little girl. Her mother had been a maid there, and Kyla grew up running round the enormous garden like it was her own. But when her ma died, she was left with no one to care for her. The other maids at the big house knew her, and they gave her food from the kitchen and let her sleep by the fire and sometimes she came to us and Ma would feed her. And when she was old enough – still no more than a scrap of a thing – she started working for Mrs Kincaid as a maid, like her mother had. But Kyla wasn't satisfied with that. She saw every problem as an opportunity and soon she was in charge of all the other maids and her not even 20 years old. She wanted to be the housekeeper, she told me. Now Gregor Kincaid had returned with his wife, and his brother Davey's son was growing up, the house was full of people again. Another opportunity for Kyla.

Kyla lived at the big house, in a tiny bedroom in the tower on the side of the house. She could see our cottage from her room.

Sometimes I'd leave a candle burning in the window and put my hand in front of the flame, flashing a greeting to her. She would do the same. I liked knowing she was there.

The day after Bridie's baby boy – of course he was a boy, Ma was never wrong about that – was born, I was eager to go and find Kyla. She would be working all morning. The Kincaids got their money's worth from their servants, everyone said. Gregor was throwing his weight around, according to Kyla. She didn't like him much, though she never said that out loud.

So I had to wait, impatient to get away, while Ma made me hang herbs for drying and add Bridie's name to her notes. My mother was a careful and precise record keeper. She kept a list of every person she had helped, and what their ailment was, and what the treatment was, and how they recovered. It was a worthwhile pursuit but I found it achingly boring. Especially today because I wanted to talk to Kyla about women and men – and love.

Eventually, I heard the clock on the church chiming the hour and I looked at Ma. She rolled her eyes but she nodded.

'Why are you so desperate to be away?'

'I'm meeting Kyla.'

She tutted, as I'd known she would. She always did when I mentioned Kyla.

'Be back before dark.'

'I will.'

I pulled my cloak over my shoulders and danced out of the cottage and down the street to where I would meet my friend. She was there already, wrapped up warm against the cold.

'Why couldn't you come to the hall?' she complained. 'Why drag me out here in the freezing cold?'

'Because I want to talk to you about something, but it's easiest if I show you,' I said. I looked up at the sky, which was already darkening. 'Come on. We don't have long.'

Grumbling, Kyla followed me as I darted along the street towards the harbour. 'Alice, where are we going?'

I didn't reply, just pulled her arm to make her hurry. I could hear the shouts of the fishermen getting ready to head out to sea and I didn't want to miss them. To miss him.

'Stop,' I said, as we reached the corner. Kyla bumped into me because I'd stopped dead and she wasn't expecting it.

'Alice,' she complained again, but I shushed her.

'Look,' I whispered, peeking round the wall. 'Look.'

'What am I looking at?' Kyla squashed herself up behind me and glanced over to the men. 'Ropes and baskets and nets are all I can see.'

'No,' I said, pointing. 'Him.'

Loading some baskets onto the boat was him. Lachlan Murdoch. The man I had fallen in love with. Not that he knew it, of course. I wasn't even sure if he knew my name.

Kyla breathed out in appreciation and I bounced on my toes, pleased that she was seeing what I was seeing. 'Nice view,' she said.

I clutched her arm. 'He is very handsome.'

'And strong.'

I followed her gaze to his broad chest, straining against his shirt as heaved the net on board the boat. He wasn't much older than me. I knew he was about the same age as Kyla. But though I often felt like I was still a child, Lachlan was a grown man.

'Is this what you wanted to talk to me about?' Kyla said. She sounded amused.

'I can't stop thinking about him. It's like an illness.'

'Maybe your ma can give you a potion for that.'

'Kyla.' I gave her arm a thump but I was laughing. 'Honestly, he's got me in such a state. I can't think properly. I can't eat. All I think about is Lachlan.'

'And his arms around your body,' Kyla said, her dark eyes dancing with mischief. 'Pulling you close to his hard chest . . .'

'Stop it,' I groaned. 'I told you because I thought you would be helpful. But this is not being helpful.'

'You want me to help?' she said. Her tone was teasing and it made me nervous. 'I'll help.'

She ducked under my arm and with a swagger, she headed towards the men.

'Kyla, come back,' I hissed from my hiding place, but she ignored me. After a moment's hesitation I scurried after her. 'Kyla, what are you doing?'

'Going to talk to him.'

'I don't know him.'

'Not yet,' she said with a grin, looping her arm through mine. 'Come on.'

Together we walked along the cobbles at the edge of the harbour. I felt my cheeks flaming, but Kyla chattered away about Gregor Kincaid, and the changes he was making at the big house.

'Make it look like we're not paying him any attention,' she said in an undertone. 'They love that.'

It was as though she was talking a different language. Who loved what? I had no idea. But I smiled and nodded as she jabbered on. Then suddenly, Kyla stumbled and let go of my arm. She threw me off balance on the bumpy stones and I staggered too – right into the arms of Lachlan Murdoch.

'Sorry, sorry,' I muttered.

'That's all right.' He was holding me round the waist, but now he let me go. 'It's very uneven here, you need to watch your footing.'

'I will,' I said, looking down at my feet. My heart was thumping.

'This is Alice,' Kyla said.

'I know.'

My cheeks were burning. All I could think was that he knew my name. Lachlan knew who I was.

'I'm Kyla.'

'I know that, too.'

'You know everything.'

I looked up. Lachlan was smiling at us both, as though he

knew exactly what we were doing. Kyla held his gaze boldly. She had always been more confident than me; even when we were wee girls she was in charge. She wound a strand of her thick, dark hair around her fingers and laughed. 'We have to go now,' she said to Lachlan. 'I've got to get back to work.'

'At the big house?'

'You really do know everything.'

Lachlan just smiled again. Then – oh my goodness – he glanced at me and gave me a little wink. My legs went weak and I thought I might faint dead away right there on the fishing nets.

'Come on, Alice.' Kyla tugged my sleeve and I followed her like a wee lamb. When I looked back over my shoulder, Lachlan was watching us go, his smile wide.

We sauntered casually round the corner and then without speaking, both of us hitched up our skirts and ran. We headed for the churchyard, clambering over the wall as we'd done when we were girls, and then collapsing in giggles onto the rain-soaked grass.

'He knows my name,' I gasped, clutching Kyla's arm.

'He does.' I was grateful Kyla didn't point out that he'd also known her name and where she worked.

I lay back on the grass, ignoring the damp seeping into my clothes. 'He's perfect,' I said, looking up at the sky, which was turning a deep purple as night approached. 'A perfect man.'

'No such thing.' Kyla propped herself up on her elbow and looked at me. She looked very pretty with her hair tumbling over her pink cheeks and her dark eyes sparkling. I often wished I looked like her. I was thin and hollow-cheeked with sallow skin and hair that didn't tumble so much as just hang limply. 'Enjoy him,' she said, sounding older than her years. 'But don't waste too much time on him. Men are never worth the bother.'

41

Chapter 6

Tess

Present day

I loved my work at the Haven. It was really hard, and sometimes I needed to go for a walk along the beach afterwards instead of going straight home, hoping the wind from the North Sea would blow away the awfulness of the stories I'd heard. But it was so good to be doing something 'real'. Something that made me feel like I was helping, instead of making everything worse.

It was really cold as I walked to work. September was almost over and autumn had definitely arrived. The trees were already bare, thanks to the gales we'd been having, and I could barely remember what the sun looked like. But I felt happy. It had been a good week. The cottage felt like home now, Jem was clearly settling into school and was working hard. I even liked having a cheerful neighbour in Eva, who I'd not spoken to since she came for tea, but who waved to me from her window almost every day.

This had been a good move, I thought for the first time since we'd fled Edinburgh. It felt as though everything had slotted into place suddenly. That instead of being us running away from home, it was a positive act of finding new friends and interesting work and being happy at school. I lifted my chin and smelled the salty tang of the sea. I felt free. I almost felt happy.

The Haven was a low, shabby, 1980s building at the side of a primary school. I buzzed in through the gate with my security pass and then again at the front door.

In reception was a woman in a nurse's uniform – one of the health visitors who ran baby clinics, I assumed. She was leaning over the front desk, chatting to Mandy, the receptionist. Another woman, who I knew worked at the local college and who came to the Haven to teach computer courses and things like CV writing and interview skills, was pinning notices on the board.

'Morning!' I called as I came in.

The nurse smiled at me. 'It's wild out there, isn't it?' she said. 'You've got an advantage, with your hair so short – mine was blown all over the place when I came in. I had to borrow Mandy's brush and try to untangle it all.'

I caught Mandy's eye and smiled. She didn't smile back, just watched me ruffle my hair. Feeling slightly uncomfortable at the scrutiny, but not wanting to show it, I put my hand to my head and grinned. 'I'm still getting used to it,' I admitted. 'I used to have it longer. It's a bit chilly round my neck.'

'Lucky you've got your lovely scarf,' the nurse said.

'My sister knitted this,' I told her, unravelling it so I could show her. 'She's really clever with her hands and she chose the wool . . .'

'You're in the little room at the end,' Mandy said abruptly, before I could carry on. She held out the laptop I used when I was at the Haven and I took it. She gave me a small, tight smile. 'It's a bit cold in there, because the door's broken. I've got a guy coming to mend it at lunchtime but I can find a heater if you need one.' She made it sound like finding me a heater would be an enormous task so I shook my head.

'No need. I'm sure it'll be fine.' I nodded to the nurse and the woman from the college who was standing back to admire her noticeboard and wandered along the corridor to find where Mandy had put me today.

The Haven was a hub for support focused on women and families so there were all sorts of things going on there every day from parenting classes and AA meetings to a sexual health clinic in the quiet area they used for medical appointments, and cookery lessons in the little kitchen. But Mandy called all the shots. It was Mandy who topped up the teabags and filled the printer with ink, and Mandy who booked the rooms.

And, I thought, as I opened the door to the tiny room she'd allocated me today, Mandy almost certainly didn't like me.

The room she'd put me in for today was more of a cupboard, with a small desk and two chairs and an empty bookcase. There was a door at the side, which led to the car park. Its handle was broken and it wasn't properly closed; instead it was held shut – almost – by some string wrapped round and round between the handle and the frame. A small but persistent draught was blowing through. With a sigh, I shifted the desk along a bit, moved my chair out of the breeze, then I sat down and logged in to the computer, ready to get to work.

I gave general legal advice to clients at the Haven. That morning I had two women who wanted to know about their rights after a divorce, one who was in dispute with her employer over holiday pay, and another who was having trouble with a neighbour. Nothing too taxing, but it was nice to hear about people's lives and their normal everyday concerns. Things I could help with. Problems I could solve. It was non-stop all morning and I just kept going, answering questions, calming worries, giving advice. It felt good.

By two o'clock I was starving. I had a break between appointments so I shoved a sandwich into my mouth and stood up to stretch my legs, looking out of the window at the rain-lashed car park.

There was a thump and the door to my office flew open. A man stood there, holding a toolbox. He looked startled when he saw me.

'Sorry, I didn't know anyone was in here. Mandy at the front desk said it was all right to come through.'

Surprised, I swallowed a lump of sandwich without chewing properly and immediately choked on it. I felt my face growing purple and tried not to panic.

'Shit,' the man said. He bounded across the room to my desk, picked up my water bottle and handed it to me. 'Drink this,' he said.

Gratefully I slurped a few mouthfuls and to my relief felt the sandwich dislodge itself.

'All right?' the man said. 'Can you breathe or do I need to do the Heimlich manoeuvre?'

I smiled at him. 'I'm fine now,' I said, feeling a bit embarrassed. 'Thank you. No need for manoeuvres of any kind, Heimlich or otherwise.'

He smiled back. He was handsome, but in a very different way to Alistair, who was chiselled and groomed. This man had longish scruffy hair, stubble and ripped jeans. 'Thank god for that,' he said. 'Because I don't know how to do it.'

I chuckled. 'I'm okay, no need for any medical procedures. Are you here to mend the door?'

'I am. Is that okay?'

I checked my watch. 'I've got about half an hour before my next appointment, is that long enough?'

'Should be.' He looked at me with curiosity. 'You look familiar. Have we met?'

I ducked my head, hoping he didn't know me from the endless news stories that had used my profile picture from LinkedIn. I thought I must look very different sitting here in my jeans and jumper, with my newly short hair.

'I don't think so,' I said, looking down at my notebook. 'Unless you've seen me around here? I've been at the Haven for a few weeks.'

'Oh, that must be it. I'm always in and out, doing jobs for

45

Mandy.' I looked up at him, and he gave me another broad grin. 'I'm Rory Baxter.'

'Tess.' Did I imagine it or did his eyes widen, just a fraction? But no, perhaps I had imagined it because his smile didn't falter. 'Tess Blyth,' I added, just to be sure.

'I'll crack on, then. If that's okay?'

'Absolutely fine. I'll just get on with some paperwork for now.'

He took his toolbox over to the door and got to work. I transferred some notes I'd made about today's visits from the scribbles on my notepad to my laptop. Rory took the door off, sending the wind whistling through the tiny room, and I wrapped my scarf round my neck and went to make a cup of tea while he worked. When I came back, with just five minutes to go until my next client arrived, he had fixed the door and was packing up his tools.

'All done,' he said, standing up.

'It's already much warmer in here, so thank you,' I said. I took my scarf off and draped it over the back of my chair. Rory smiled and I thought how good-looking he was. Like a Hollywood version of a handyman. He put his hand in his pocket and pulled out a business card, which he put on the table. It had his name on it and a mobile number. 'Mandy said you've just moved in. So if you need any carpentry doing, give me a shout.'

'Thank you.' I didn't need anything doing in the cottage, and I couldn't afford to pay anyone to do it even if I did, but I took the card anyway, though it made me uneasy to know he and Mandy had discussed me.

'Maybe you're handy with a drill yourself,' Rory said, looking at me appraisingly. 'You look the sort.'

'Actually, I'm not bad.' It was the truth. I'd got quite good at DIY since we'd moved. It was amazing what you could do when you had to. 'I watch YouTube videos to show me what to do.'

Rory sighed dramatically. 'I wish people would stop doing that. It puts me out of work.'

'Maybe you should do your own videos,' I suggested. 'You'd be great. You've obviously got the expertise and . . .' I looked him up and down with a critical eye – clearly I'd learned something from being married to Alistair all those years and hearing about who was good on camera. 'The right look.'

'What does that mean?' Rory glanced down at his ripped jeans and flannel shirt.

'You look like how people imagine a carpenter to look. Like Matthew McConaughey.'

He laughed loudly and I felt strangely pleased that I'd amused him. 'Maybe I will,' he said. He leaned over the desk and shook my hand. His fingers were warm and rougher than Alistair's and I liked the way they felt in mine.

'I'll see you around,' he said.

The room felt a bit emptier when he left.

Chapter 7

Honor

1661

We were wrong about the storm. It had not passed us without trouble. It had simply been biding its time, waiting out at sea to come to shore, bringing high winds and pelting rain.

Alice and I wrapped up in old capes that had belonged to my John, oiled with linseed to keep the sailors dry, and hurried outside to see to the animals.

We weren't farmers and we didn't have many creatures but there were chickens for eggs, two goats for milk who I cursed every time they got into my herb garden but for whom I had a strange fondness, and we kept a pig each year for meat. And we had several cats who invited themselves in and who Alice looked after.

'This is awful,' Alice shouted over the wind as we pushed the goat-shed door closed with some difficulty. It kept getting caught in the strong gusts and creaking on its hinges.

I leaned into the wind and with a groan the door pushed into place. Alice shot the bolt across. 'It's one of the worst storms I've seen,' I agreed. I stood for a moment, listening. The crashing waves were deafening and I could taste salt on my tongue. I felt a small twist of fear that the sea could come over the wall and up into our cottage. That had never happened before but I knew that just because something hadn't happened, that didn't mean it never would.

'We need to put everything upstairs,' I said. 'In case the waves get too big.'

Alice looked at me, her pale face fearful in the gloomy evening. 'Do you think the sea could come in the house?'

'It never has before, but it could. I've never seen waves as big before. Not even . . .' I stopped before I said not even before the night her father drowned.

Alice stood for a second, her head tilted upwards. I could see the rain soaking her skin but she didn't flinch. Then she nodded. 'We should move everything that's precious.'

We didn't have much in our little cottage, but together we shifted my favourite chair up the narrow stairs, my little keepsake box where I kept the caul Alice had been born in, and all my records, bundles of paper from years of healing and mixing tinctures and finding out what worked and what didn't. I didn't want to lose them to the swirling sea, should it come into the house. We carried boxes of tinctures and dried herbs up the stairs, and stacked them in my room. Then, when everything was safely upstairs, I took the capes Alice and I had been wearing and carefully wrapped the bundles of paper inside, just to be doubly sure they would be protected from the weather.

Exhausted, we fell into our beds where I slept immediately, despite the howling wind.

I woke with a start a few hours later. One of our cats was sitting on my chest, looking at me with her unblinking green eyes.

'What is it?' I said to her, still half asleep. 'What's happening?'

The cat gave a small meow and then jumped down onto the floor and padded out of the room. I sat up, wondering what she wanted. Probably hungry, I thought. The cats certainly knew their own minds. The wind had died down but I could hear the rain hammering on our roof and something else in the distance. Hooves? And shouts. Was that what the cat had heard?

I slid out of bed, cursing under my breath as my bare legs met the cold air in the bedroom, and quickly pulled on the clothes I'd been wearing that evening. Then I went downstairs where the floor was damp with flood water, just as there was a loud, frantic banging on our front door.

In two strides I was there, flinging it open to see the laird – Gregor Kincaid – and his brother Davey. Immediately my heart began to pound. Was this it? Was this him come to throw me in jail on some unfounded accusation of witchcraft?

'Widow Seton,' the laird said. He didn't wait to be invited in, simply walked past me, dripping rainwater and adding to the puddles already on the floor.

'Yes.' I tried to keep my voice steady. I didn't want him to see that I was afraid of him.

'We have a sickness in the house and need your . . .' He paused, glancing at his brother.

'Assistance,' the younger man said. He sounded tired and scared. 'We need your help.'

'What's wrong?' I was alert now, thanking the cat – wherever she was – for waking me ahead of the banging on the door.

'Sickness,' Gregor said again, impatient. He was obviously as scared as his brother, but reacting differently.

'Who is ill?'

'My wife,' said the laird. 'And my mother.'

Davey spoke, his jaw clenched. 'And my son. And his tutor.'

'What is wrong?'

'They are hot to touch, but shivering. Coughing. Barely awake.'

'Any swelling?' I asked, my mind racing. Could this be plague? Our town had escaped the worst of it so far, but it was unpredictable. And fast. 'Lumps in their armpits or neck?'

The laird shook his head. 'I don't think so.'

That was a relief, but it didn't mean this wasn't serious.

'I may not be able to help,' I said honestly. My skills were more in tending wounds and delivering babies. I could deal with shivers and runny noses, but if this was plague then I knew there was little I could do.

The laird took a step towards me. I was a tall woman but he towered over me and his shoulders were wide. I shrank against the wall, suddenly afraid he would lash out at me but his brother put a hand on his shoulder, calming him. Holding him back.

'Please,' Davey said, his voice cracking. 'Please do what you can.'

Flooded with sympathy for this man who had so much to lose, I nodded.

'I need to collect some things, and tell my daughter where I'm going,' I said. 'Stay here.'

'Bring your daughter,' Gregor said. 'She will be useful.'

I paused on the bottom step. 'I'd rather not.'

'But she is your assistant?'

'She is.' But I didn't want Alice to be near the big house if the plague was there. I couldn't say no for myself, but I didn't have to expose her to the danger.

Davey reached out and put his hand on my arm. 'Please, bring her. We need all the help we can get.'

I didn't say yes or no, but hitching my skirt up, I raced upstairs. Alice was already up and dressed – she had heard me talking. She was crouched on the floor, unwrapping my notes. I dropped a kiss on her head as I passed.

'Is it plague?' she said, fear in her voice.

'It could be,' I said. 'Though they have no swelling. But it sounds bad.' I began gathering tinctures, something to stop the sweating, something else to ease the cough. Alice collected everything I handed her in two large baskets.

'I will come,' she said firmly.

'No.'

'I can help.'

'It's not safe.'

'If it's safe for you, it's safe for me.'

'That's not true.'

She shrugged. 'Maybe not, but I'm coming.'

I looked at her. She was so defiant. So sure of herself. And eventually I nodded. 'Fine.'

'Ma,' she said as I put the last bottle in the bag, 'what if we can't save them?'

'Then they will die.'

Alice lowered her voice. 'And what if the laird blames us? I don't trust him, Ma. What if he uses this against us?'

The thought had occurred to me. I looked at my daughter's worried face and tried to smile. 'What choice do I have?' I said in a whisper. 'He wants me to come and I can't say no. We must pray that my treatment works.'

Alice closed her eyes briefly and then she nodded. 'We should go.'

Together, we ran downstairs to where the Kincaid brothers were already waiting in their carriage. 'Come on,' the laird shouted as we approached. 'Come, quickly.'

The horses were swift through the rainy night. As we sped towards the big house, I questioned the brothers about the illness.

'When did it start?'

'Just this morning,' Davey said, looking bewildered in the light from the candles that lit the inside of the carriage. 'They sickened so fast.'

'Has anyone new visited the house? Could they have brought the illness with them?'

'My son's tutor. He has been away. His father died . . .' He trailed off and I exchanged a look with Alice.

'We need to cover our mouths with scarves before we enter the house,' I said. 'We do not want to breathe bad air.'

There was a snort from the laird. 'Bad air?' he said. 'You're talking nonsense, woman. Your independence has gone to your head.' He turned to Davey. 'I told you this was a stupid idea. Women like her can't be trusted. It is against the natural order of things to have a woman without the guidance and protection of a man. A woman left to her own devices will cause chaos. This is not bad air. It is a judgement from God on the town that has made you its burgess.'

Alarmed by his outburst I looked to Davey for help. He put a hand on his brother's arm to calm him. 'Maybe you are right,' he admitted. 'But let us take no chances. We have sickness in our house and Widow Seton is the only person who can help us.'

Gregor looked bullish, but he also looked scared. I felt sorry for him suddenly. I knew what it was like to be frightened for the one you loved.

'I can help,' I assured him, hoping I was right. There was a pause, and then Gregor nodded. Heartened, I continued. 'If I am to help, you must do what I say. No arguments.'

'We will,' said Davey. The laird didn't speak but I took that as agreement.

Alice was quiet in the seat next to me, sliding slightly on the shiny wood as the carriage bumped over the uneven roads. Now she spoke.

'Sir?' she said. 'You have a servant in the big house. Kyla? Is she sick?'

The laird glanced at her, surprised, as though he'd forgotten she was there. 'The servants are all well,' he said. 'I fear this is a curse, brought by them as some sort of trick.'

'Gregor,' his brother said sharply. 'You are being ridiculous. You must calm down. You can do Isobel no good in this state.'

I felt Alice relax beside me, but I was tense with nerves. I was fearful of what we would find at the big house and scared of the laird's reaction if we couldn't help. And if it was plague, what then? The illness spread so easily, I didn't want Alice to get sick, or myself. What would become of her if I were to die?

We arrived at the big house and the laird was out of the carriage before the horses had properly stopped. He was fast on his feet for such a big man, hurtling into the house and calling for us to follow.

'Wait,' I called. 'You should cover your face.' But Gregor had gone. I helped Alice tie a scarf around her mouth and she helped me. Davey had already pulled his own scarf over his face. He picked up one of our baskets and chivvied us along out of the carriage.

'Who became ill first?' I asked.

'Isobel,' Davey said. 'And the tutor – Magnus. They are both suffering greatly.'

'And your mother is sick, too?'

'She is, but not so badly.' A ghost of a smile passed his lips. 'She is made from strong stuff.'

'And your son?'

Now Davey gave me a look so full of despair that I feared he was going to drop to his knees and weep. 'Christy,' he said. 'He is 12 years old.'

He led the way into the house. 'Tell me about his illness,' I said, as Alice and I followed. We were in a wide echoing hall, but I didn't care about the fancy surroundings.

'He is too weak to eat or drink. He can't speak. He just tosses and turns and cries that he is cold, though his sheets are wet from sweat.'

My mind was racing. Isobel, the laird's wife, had become ill first so she should be my priority, but my maternal instinct was to go to the boy.

'Alice,' I said, 'go to Christy and keep him cool. Ask a servant for cold water to bathe him. I will be there as soon as I can. Give him two drops of this on his tongue.' I reached into the basket and pulled out a small bottle of concentrated catnip – a strange choice for a remedy but one I had found worked well for children who had a fever.

'Show her where to go,' I said to Davey. 'I'll go to Isobel.'

'Hers is the room at the end of the hall,' he said, already halfway upstairs with a pale-faced Alice following.

I hoicked my basket up on my arm and ran up the stairs in their wake, and along the hall to the end. The door to Isobel's bedchamber was open and I went straight in, not bothering to knock. Gregor was sitting by the bed, and under the covers was his wife, so pale she could have been dead already.

Slowly, I walked towards her. Gregor looked up at me, his face stricken. 'Help her,' he said.

There was a shadow in the room, like a low cloud. I couldn't see it exactly but I knew it was there, and I knew what it meant. Gently I leaned over Isobel. Her breathing was uneven and raspy. There was nothing I could do for her now, but how could I tell the laird? With shaking hands, I took a bottle of white willow bark from my basket and moistened her lips with the liquid. She opened her mouth slightly as I did so, but I knew it was a reflex; there was no hope for this woman.

'Magnus is dead.' A voice at the door made us look up. It was Kyla. She was dressed in a long black dress with a white cap on her head. She didn't acknowledge me though I'd known her since she was born. Instead she glared into the room. 'You are too late.'

I swallowed. 'You must burn his clothes,' I said, hearing the tremor in my voice. 'And his sheets. Straightaway. Cover your mouth and nose when you go in his room. If you don't, the sickness will spread.'

Kyla hesitated. I understood why. It sounded like hocus pocus, but I had been healing people for a long time and I knew what precautions to take.

'Do as she says,' Gregor said. He sounded weary. 'We do not want any more sickness in this house.'

He looked up at me. 'Now save my wife,' he said.

Chapter 8

Alice

We worked all night, my mother and I. Dashing from room to room, tending Lady Isobel, and young Christy and the laird's mother, Lady Kincaid.

Just before dawn, I went to find Ma, who was in Isobel's bedchamber. The laird was asleep with his head on his wife's bed and his hand on hers, and I entered quietly so as not to disturb them. The room seemed misty, as though it was cast in shadow, even though the sun was beginning to rise. I frowned at Ma and she gave me a small shake of her head. Lady Isobel was not long for the world.

'How is the boy?' she whispered.

'He's no worse but I don't think he is over the fever yet,' I told her. 'Ma, what will we do if he dies? If he and Lady Isobel . . .'

Ma shushed me, looking over to where the laird sat. 'I can't save Isobel, but we can help the boy,' she said. She bit her lip. 'I need your help.'

Together we slipped out of Isobel's room and down the corridor to where Davey was pacing his son's bedchamber. There was a misty pall to this room too. Perhaps not as dark as in

Lady Isobel's but the sight frightened me. Did this mean the lad would die, too?

'He's struggling to breathe,' Davey said as we entered. 'I tried to sit him up but it's not helping.'

Ma went to the boy, whose breathing was shallow and gasping, and gently pulled him upright and forward, leaning on her. He looked floppy like one of my old dolls and it made me scared. 'Support him like this,' she told his father. Obediently, Davey did as she asked and immediately the boy's breathing eased slightly.

A howl from down the hallway made me jump. Ma looked sick.

'My brother?' Davey asked, his eyes wide.

Ma didn't speak, just nodded. 'I should go to him,' she said. 'You can use pillows to prop Christy up. If you help him stay upright, it will help him breathe.'

Looking worried, she left the room. I began rearranging the bolsters and pillows.

'Sir?' We both looked up. Kyla was there. She gave me a tiny smile and then turned her attention back to Davey. 'Your mother is awake and asking for you.'

Davey's expression cleared and he looked relieved for a moment, then he looked back at his son and frowned once more.

'Go,' I said. 'I can stay with him for a few minutes until you return.'

'Thank you.'

He kissed his son's head, where the blond curls were stuck to his skin with sweat, and went to find his mother. I marvelled at a God who would spare an old woman, and take a young bride and an innocent boy. Perhaps this was nothing to do with God, I thought. I looked at Christy again, his breathing laboured and his face pale. And that awful shadow hanging over the room. 'Fight,' I whispered. 'Fight with everything you have.'

Not really knowing what I was doing, nor why, I put my hand on his forehead, and closed my eyes, willing my energy into him, hoping he could feel the strength I was trying to pass to him.

I wasn't sure how long I stayed there but slowly, I felt the boy's breathing become deeper and more even. I opened my eyes. His cheeks, which had been pale, had more colour.

'Come on, Christy,' I said quietly.

Perhaps it was just the dawn breaking, and the sun rising over the sea, but the room lightened. The shadow lifted. I looked at Christy, where he lay on his pillows and to my relief saw he was sleeping peacefully.

'What did you do?' Kyla was standing beside me, her face drawn with tiredness. I started. I had forgotten Kyla was there. She looked straight at me and I saw fear in her eyes. 'What did you do?'

'Nothing,' I said hurriedly. 'I did nothing. My mother gave him a tincture to break the fever and it has worked. That's all.'

Kyla shook her head. 'You put your hand on his forehead and he slept.' Her voice was small and trembling. 'The room lightened.'

I went to her and touched her arm gently. 'Kyla, you need to rest. You're exhausted. The dawn has broken, that's all. The sun has come up and the storm has passed. Christy is recovering and you should sleep.'

She looked at me, but she didn't speak. She just turned and left without a word. I felt a flutter of fear. Had I done something? No. Like I'd told Kyla, it was Ma's tinctures that had helped, not my touch. I was tired too.

'He sleeps?' Davey appeared at the door.

'His fever has broken and he's breathing more easily.'

He leaned against the doorframe, weak with relief. 'Thank God.' 'Your mother?'

'She is asking for food,' he said with a small smile. 'She will be fine.'

I hardly dared ask about Isobel, but I had to know for sure. 'And your brother's wife?'

Davey shook his head. 'Your mother is washing the body.' 'Your brother . . .'

'He's angry now, but he will understand there was nothing your mother could do.'

There was a pause. I wanted badly to run away. To turn on my heels and run down the stairs and out of the big house and back home. But there was work still to be done.

'We need to change Christy's sheets,' I said. 'And burn the ones on his bed. Though his fever has broken he could still spread the sickness.'

'I'll ask Kyla to do it.'

'I can do it,' I said. I didn't want to see Kyla.

'You should go home and rest. You've been awake most of the night.'

'Our house is flooded,' I said, suddenly remembering.

'Then stay.'

'No,' I almost shouted. I didn't like this house with its high ceilings and too many rooms. I didn't like the laird, nor his bullish mother, nor their silent servants. Not even Kyla. I thought about the way she'd looked at me and shivered.

'Can you lift Christy?' I asked Davey. 'If you lift him, I can change the sheets without disturbing him.'

'There is linen in the dresser, there,' Davey said. He got to his feet and I found fresh sheets and blankets in the drawers.

'Be careful with him,' I warned as Davey went to pick up his son.

Davey gave me a withering look. 'I'm his father,' he said. But there was no irritation in his voice. Just fondness and pride.

'Ma says the sickness can stay in the sheets and in their clothes,' I said. 'I don't know if it's true but I've learned to do as she says.'

'Your mother is a clever woman.'

'She is.'

I pulled the sheets from the bed and quickly replaced them with clean ones and a warm blanket. Davey put Christy down and the little lad snuggled into his bed. I tucked him in and Davey sat down next to him, stroking his head.

'What should I do with the linen?'

'I believe your mother has arranged for it to be burned,' Davey said. 'I can smell the fire beneath the window. Perhaps you can take it down on your way out?'

I went to the window and looked out. I could see a fire burning fiercely and a man turning it with a long pole. Kyla stood nearby. As I watched, Gregor appeared. He walked over to her and they spoke. They both looked emotional. Upset. Understandable, of course, because Lady Isobel was dead, but I felt that flutter of fear again. What was Kyla saying? Whatever it was, Gregor was listening intently.

'Alice?'

Davey's voice made me start. 'Sorry,' I said, still looking at Kyla. 'I'll take the sheets now.'

'I like the view from this window,' Davey said. 'You can see the sea.'

'And our cottage,' I said, hoping the animals hadn't been disturbed by the storm.

'What is between your cottage and our estate?' Davey asked.

I turned to him. 'Nothing,' I said. 'It's our land. We have animals and my mother's garden.'

'You have a lot of land.' Davey looked impressed.

'My father was a shrewd man.'

There was a slightly awkward pause. I wasn't sure what to say or why he was interested in our land. I picked up the bundle of bed linen. 'I should find my mother.'

'Of course.' He looked at Christy and then up at me, and I saw his eyes were full of tears. 'Tell her thank you.'

Chapter 9

Tess

Present day

The weather was getting worse. There was a storm approaching which, Jem told me with undisguised glee, was called Storm Alice.

'Like our witch,' she said. 'Alice is coming to bring thunder and lightning and chaos.'

'And delayed trains,' I said, weary at the thought. 'What are you up to for the rest of today?' It was Saturday afternoon, so we didn't have anywhere to be. 'Are you seeing Cassie?'

Jem looked at her feet. 'Not Cassie, no. She's going to her granny's.'

'Do you want to come and help me? I'm going to Asda.'

Jem's cheeks reddened. 'Actually, a friend from drama has asked if I want to watch the film of *Macbeth* together.'

I looked at her carefully. She was blushing. 'A new friend?' I said casually.

'Yes.' She swallowed. 'Callum.'

Ah ha! That's why she was blushing. 'He's in the play with you, is he?'

'Hope so, we don't have our parts yet.' She gave me a little shy smile that made my heart swell. 'It won't just be me and him. There are some others coming.'

'Is he nice, this Callum?'

She flushed again. 'Yes,' she mumbled. 'Funny.'

'Good-looking?'

'Muuum.'

'I'm glad you're making friends,' I said, meaning it. 'Boys and girls.'

She grinned at me. 'Me too.'

I gave her a quick hug. 'Have fun.' Then the nerves took over. 'If anyone says anything you don't like or anything happens that you're not comfortable with, call me.'

Jem tutted but I wasn't finished. 'Text me when you're on your way home and I'll come and meet you.'

She rolled her eyes and I felt a bit bad. 'There are some of those posh chocolate biscuits in the cupboard. Why not take them with you to share with your friends?'

'I will.' She grinned again and I thought for the millionth time how well she had handled all the changes in her life.

Jem dashed off upstairs to get ready and I gathered all my empty shopping bags and headed outside. As I walked down the path, I heard a tapping on the window next door. Eva stood there, beckoning to me.

I went to her and she opened the window. 'Are you okay?' I asked. She looked a bit pale. Less vibrant than she'd been last time we'd met.

'I'm fine, darling,' she said. 'Just having a bit of a bad day with my arthritis. It's easing up now, but I saw you with your bags and wondered if you're going to the shops, could you get me a few bits?'

'Of course,' I said. 'What can I get you?'

'I've got a list.' She disappeared from the window and came back with a piece of paper covered in beautiful handwriting.

I scanned it – it was just basics and a bottle of gin. 'No problem at all,' I said, hoping she'd give me the money for her shopping. I didn't want it to be awkward and have to ask for it later. But Eva had that organized too.

'This should cover it,' she said, handing me two twenty-pound notes.

I slipped the money into my pocket and zipped up my coat because the wind was getting stronger.

'Back soon.'

As I wandered round the supermarket, I felt a bit odd. I was thrilled to bits that Jem was finding her feet in North Berwick. She was already as thick as thieves with Cassie, and now she had a new group of friends from the play too. But she was still my baby and to hear her talk about a boy made me realize she was growing up. Urgh. In some ways I wished she was still little so I could just keep her with me and know she was safe forever. But, I told myself, she was happy and that meant I was too. Of course, I was still dealing with the things Alistair had done – I'd been having counselling when we were in Edinburgh which had helped me but I hadn't found a new therapist. And I wasn't sure I could afford it anyway. But now we were away from all the memories, I could start to move on. At least, I hoped so.

It was busy in Asda, so it took me a while to get the things I needed and the bits Eva had asked for, but I got it all eventually. I unloaded all my own shopping first. It was quiet in the house without Jem there and I kept jumping when the wind blew and made things thud or bang. I'd never minded being on my own before – I relished it sometimes – but things had changed. Plus I'd made the mistake of reading one of the books about witches that Jem had brought home from the school library, and that together with the noisy weather, meant I was a bit spooked.

So I didn't argue when I took Eva's shopping round and she offered me a cup of tea and a biscuit. She looked much better than she had earlier. She said her arthritis was easing and she thanked me for getting the food she needed. She showed me her knuckles which were lumpy and swollen but, she said, better than they had been.

'I have learned that when it bothers me, it goes away again quickly if I rest,' she said. 'But if I soldier on, then it just gets worse.'

'There's a lesson there for all of us.' I smiled at her. 'Shall I make the tea?'

Eva came into the kitchen with me and directed me to the right cupboards to find teabags and some pretty cups with matching saucers, and a plate to put biscuits on. I liked that she had a particular way of doing things; it reminded me of my granny. Then I carried our tea on a tray through to the table in the leaded window bay at the front of the house where Eva said she liked to sit and watch the world go by.

'So what's new with you?' she asked. 'Have you settled in?'

'We have,' I said. 'Jem's very happy at her new school.'

'You were worried that she wouldn't be?' Eva asked astutely. 'You sound surprised.'

'She had a bit of trouble at her last place. There were a few personality clashes.' That was an understatement but I didn't want to go into too many details.

'But she is making friends. I've seen her with a girl with curly hair.'

'Cassie,' I said with a smile. 'She seems lovely. And Jem's doing the school play which is giving her lots of other new friends. There's even a boy she likes.'

'How old is your Jem?' Eva asked, taking a biscuit from the plate on the table.

'Fourteen,' I said. I chose a chocolate digestive and broke it in half, carefully catching the crumbs in my hand and putting them onto my saucer. 'I'm pleased. She's making lots of friends. It's good.'

Eva looked at me sharply. 'Feeling a bit lonely?'

I rolled my eyes. 'Yes,' I admitted. 'Isn't that silly?'

'Silly, but understandable.' She took a delicate sip from her mug. 'You're a team, I think. You and Jem.'

I nodded. 'My divorce wasn't easy.' I chose my words carefully. 'We are a bit bruised from it all. Jem doesn't see her dad now.'

Eva nodded, thoughtfully. 'It's hard when our children want to untie the apron strings.'

'It is.'

'Perhaps you need to make some friends here. Or even find yourself a boyfriend.'

'I don't think so. It's still very raw.'

Eva scoffed. 'I'm not saying get married, just go out, have some fun. Live a little.'

I swallowed my biscuit. 'Maybe.' But I didn't really mean it. I liked living quietly, just the two of us. And perhaps I didn't have much of a social life, but that was fine. Better than fine. 'Maybe I'll get a cat,' I said.

Eva rolled her eyes. 'That's not what I meant.'

'I know.' Feeling her piercing eyes on me, I changed the subject. 'Perhaps I could join a running club. I used to be a member of one in Edinburgh.'

'Or perhaps we should go for a drink,' Eva said.

I shrugged. 'Yes, that would be nice. One day next week, maybe?'

'What about now?'

'Now?'

'Why not?'

I thought about it, and couldn't think of a single reason why not. 'Go on then,' I said, amused by Eva's directness. I was going to enjoy having her as a neighbour, I thought.

We wrapped up in our coats and scarves and with Eva holding my arm, we walked down the street to the pub on the corner. My phone beeped as Eva shut the door behind us. It was Jem saying Callum's mum had ordered a load of pizzas for them and she'd be home later. I sent her a thumbs-up and a reminder to ring me when she wanted to come home.

The pub was called The Anchor. It was warm and cosy, with a real fire and stripped wood floors. The boss, who was chatting to some men at one end of the bar and watching the football on the TV in the corner, greeted Eva like an old friend when we walked in. We settled ourselves at a table close to the fire, where the wind rattled the windows and made us glad to be safely indoors.

I went to the bar to get the drinks and while I was waiting to be served, I saw the man who'd mended the door at the Haven the other day – Rory. He was standing slightly to the side of the group of men watching the football, with them but not quite. I paused, not sure if he'd remember me and whether I should say hello, and then he glanced up and grinned broadly.

'Hello,' he said. Then he frowned. 'Are you here to see me?'

I laughed because it was such an odd thing to say. 'Like a crazy stalker?' He looked alarmed and I laughed again, more nervously this time. Gosh, I was out of practice when it came to small talk. 'No. I'm with my friend.' I gestured with my thumb over my shoulder to where Eva sat, scrolling through her phone and looking just like Jem even though she was about seventy-five years older than my teenage daughter.

'Oh,' he said, looking sheepish and a bit awkward. 'Sorry.'

'Don't be.'

'What can I get you?' the barman asked, and in relief I turned to place my order. When I turned back, Rory was chatting to one of the other men, his gaze firmly on the TV screen.

I took the drinks back to Eva who gave me a knowing smile. 'Handsome,' she said. 'And looking at you.'

'Is he?' I looked over to Rory and met his gaze which made me blush. I gave him a small smile and he smiled back.

'I think I am not the only one who's pleased you moved here,' Eva said triumphantly.

'Cheers.'

Chapter 10

Jem

I woke up with a start, my heart pounding. It was dark in my room so I knew it hadn't been my alarm that had roused me.

Sitting up in bed, I felt for the switch on my bedside lamp and turned it on, squinting at the clock. It was 4 a.m. and outside the storm was hammering at the windows.

'Storm Alice,' I whispered in glee. I loved that this weather was named after the girl who I now considered to be 'my witch'.

The rain sounded like marbles pelting the roof because it was so heavy. That must have been what had woken me, because my bed was under the window and it was loud. Even though my bedroom was at the back of the house, I could hear the waves crashing outside and I wondered if the water had ever come as far as the cottage. Probably not, I thought. There was a thick sea wall between the cottage and the waves now, though perhaps back in the days before it had been built, it might have got a bit soggy. I knelt up at the window and peered out, into the night. I couldn't see much, just the rain splattering the glass and the tree in the neighbour's garden bending in the wind. Somewhere I could hear a bell ringing. Was it the church? Could the wind be strong enough to ring a big church bell? I opened the window and leaned out, trying to work out where the sound was coming from. Straightaway my face was wet from rain, and the wind was so strong it took my breath away, whipping my hair across my damp skin. That had definitely been a mistake. The bells were coming from the harbour, I thought, not the church. I pictured the little boats that sheltered there. I thought I remembered seeing some of them with bells. Shivering I tried to pull the window shut – it took a bit of effort because the wind was blowing and keeping it open – and as I yanked it, I heard a pitiful meow from somewhere below, round the side of the cottage. I gasped. Surely there wasn't a cat outside in this weather? With a final thud I shut the window, slid out of bed, shivering in the cold, pulled on my dressing gown, pushed my feet into my slippers and headed downstairs to investigate.

Without turning on the light – I didn't want to disturb Mum – I found my coat on the hook at the bottom of the stairs by the front door then I went into the kitchen and out into our little backyard, closing the door carefully behind me so it didn't get blown off its hinges.

It was wild outside. I was soaked through in seconds, the rain seeping into my pyjama bottoms and drenching my slippers. I wiped my face with my sleeve, but it was so wet it made very little difference.

And there was the mewing again, a tiny sound over the crashing waves and howling wind.

'Here kitty,' I said. Scrunching my face up against the rain, I went around the side of the house where the bins were, and called again, making a kissing sound with my lips. 'Here puss.' But there was no sign of the cat. Perhaps I'd imagined it. Maybe I had still been sleepy, half dreaming?

Suddenly, there was a huge crack and a groaning sound. The ground beneath my feet seemed to shake and then there was the noise of breaking glass and falling rubble. Instinctively I crouched down where I was beside the wheelie bin, protecting my head with my arms. 'Shit,' I breathed, feeling my legs trembling. 'Shit.'

Eventually, the noise stopped, and I stood up cautiously. I was fine. Nothing had fallen near me. Lights were going on, illuminating the yard and as I skirted back round the side of the house to where I'd just been, I could see what had happened. The huge tree in Eva's garden had fallen, demolishing her conservatory. Our house had escaped the worst of it, except for one large branch which had broken off and gone through my bedroom window.

Shocked, I darted back inside and upstairs.

'Jem!' Mum was shouting, her voice tight with tears. 'Jem!'

'I'm here,' I called. She whirled round where she stood at the door of my room and grabbed me, pulling me tightly to her.

'Oh my god,' she said. 'I thought you were in there.'

Over her shoulder, I saw the devastation that had once been my room. My bed was hidden under the heavy branch, and there was broken glass everywhere. My legs started shaking again and I clung on to Mum. 'I was outside,' I said.

She held me at arm's length and looked at me. 'You're soaking wet,' she said. 'What on earth were you doing outside?'

'I heard a cat.'

She shook her head and then squeezed me tightly again. 'Thank goodness,' she muttered into my wet hair.

'We need to check that Eva's okay,' I said. 'The tree has totally wrecked her conservatory.'

'Shit,' said Mum. 'Get yourself dry. I'll go and check on her.'

'No, I want to come.'

Mum didn't argue and I was glad. We went downstairs and out the front and knocked on Eva's door. It was still dark but there were lights on in lots of the houses and car alarms going off.

'What if she's asleep?' I said.

Mum made a face. 'I doubt that.'

Eva opened the door wearing a pair of men's checked pyjamas and some fluffy slippers. Mum and I swapped smiles.

'The tree has come down and my conservatory is no more,' Eva declared without saying hello. She looked quite pleased about it. Maybe she just enjoyed the drama.

'The tree has come down and my bedroom is no more,' I told her.

She gasped, her hand to her chest, and looked at me in horror. 'But you are not hurt?'

'I wasn't in there.'

She gathered me into her arms and squeezed me tight. She smelled like face cream. 'Thank goodness.'

'Eva, why not come through to ours and we can all sit down together and work out what to do?' Mum said.

So we all trooped back to our house. I went into Mum's room and dried my hair and put on a pair of her old gym leggings and a big jumper, while she put on jeans. Eva had got dressed too. Mum made coffee for everyone – even me though I didn't like it very much – and we watched it get light and the damage outside begin to show itself.

'I hated that conservatory,' said Eva looking out of the back window. 'But what a mess.'

Mum sighed. 'I don't know where to begin with clearing up. I suppose I should phone the insurance company.'

'I bet they're super busy already,' I said.

'Perhaps we should take some photographs,' Eva suggested. 'Before we begin the clear-up?'

'Of course,' Mum said, looking impressed with Eva's presence of mind.

We spent a while taking pictures on our phones from every angle, then we wrapped up warm and went outside into the blustery morning and took photos outside too. Then we clambered over what was left of the fence and did the same in Eva's garden, while she shouted commands at us through the window.

'You need to go inside,' she called. 'I'll come round the front way.'

Inside, Eva's house was completely fine, except for the back window and doors that had led into the conservatory. They were shattered and the wind was whistling through. It was freezing in there. Eva swore under her breath in German. I liked the way it sounded and made a little note in my head to get her to teach me.

Through the shattered glass, we could see Eva's neighbour from the other side. He was in what was left of his garden, looking at the fallen tree in despair.

'What a nightmare,' Mum called to him.

He came over, looking fed up. 'I know you didn't like your conservatory much, Eva, but this is a bit of an extreme way to get rid of it. Is this storm your doing? Are you some sort of weather witch?'

We all laughed and Mum and I exchanged amused glances.

'Cheeky,' said Eva, but she was smiling. 'I wouldn't have made such a mess of it all.'

'Your house must be freezing because of the broken windows,' the neighbour went on. 'Mine is too. I've already rung round a few people to get them to come and board it up but everyone's busy – not surprisingly.' He looked up at my bedroom. 'You'll need someone too.'

Mum looked thoughtful. 'I might know someone who can help.' She screwed her face up, like she was trying to remember. 'Where did I put it?' She patted the back pocket of her jeans and looked pleased. 'Here.' She pulled out a business card. 'Rory Baxter? Have you tried him? He's a carpenter.' Her cheeks were a bit pink, but maybe it was just the wind.

'I can call him, if you like?' she said to the neighbour. He said he would, so Mum took Eva back to ours and went to ring this Rory bloke. I went upstairs to look at my room. It was a school day, but I didn't know if I had to go, or if I could even get to my uniform or any of the books I needed.

It really was freezing in my bedroom. The wind and rain were howling through the broken glass and there were shards all over

71

my duvet. The photographs of my old friends from Edinburgh that I'd carefully stuck behind my headboard had blown from their fixings and were strewn everywhere. The pretty pale pink wallpaper I'd chosen was soaking and already starting to peel. It was horrible. My wardrobe, though, was unscathed and my desk had escaped most of the damage too. Looked like it would be a school day for me after all. Rolling my eyes, I plodded to my wardrobe and pulled out the clothes I'd need for that day, took them into Mum's room and dropped them on the bed. Then I went back to my room to get my books. I paused for a second, looking at the shattered window and split frame. And then something caught my eye – a bump in the bricks around the window. Had something fallen from the tree and wedged itself in the stonework?

Carefully, I pulled up the duvet, gathering most of the broken glass in its folds, and clambered onto the bare mattress so I could look more closely.

It was a little earthenware container, about the size of my hand, set in a gap between two of the stones that surrounded the window. It had been covered over by the wooden frame which had split. Intrigued, I pulled away the rest of the wood, and tried to pull the little container out. It wouldn't budge, so I found a pair of scissors on my desk and started chipping away at the soft stone with the blades. It didn't take much before I'd loosened it enough to get it out. Brushing away the dust I'd made, I wiggled the container a bit and it came free.

I held it up to the light. It wasn't pottery, as I'd thought. It was just really dirty. It was a grey-green glass bottle with a narrow top and fat bottom and it was sealed with a cork and a wax lid. I wiped it with my thumb. There was something inside but I couldn't see what it was. It reminded me of something. What was it?

I looked round my room, hoping to dislodge the memory and my eye fell on the pile of books about witches that I'd taken out of the school library. That was it.

I put the bottle on my desk and leafed through the books until I found what I'd been looking for. It wasn't exactly the same as the picture I'd remembered but it was close enough. A small container, tightly sealed and hidden somewhere in a house – the one in the book had been found under a fireplace. I read the caption and shivered with excitement tinged with a tiny bit of fear.

'It's a witch bottle,' I said out loud, picking it up again. 'A witch bottle.'

Chapter 11

Tess

'Mum!' Jem came thundering down the stairs, making my heart pound. I was on edge. I couldn't believe what had happened – there was so much mess to clear up and I kept thanking my lucky stars that Jem had got out of bed just minutes before the tree fell. If she'd been in bed when the window shattered . . . well, it didn't bear thinking about. I would have to find the cat that she'd got up to find and give it a special treat to say thank you.

Now I turned to see her bounding down the stairs, beaming from ear to ear.

'Look!' she said, waving something in my face. 'Look what I found.' She held up a small, dirty glass bottle with a wax seal.

'What is it?'

She grinned. 'It's a witch bottle,' she said triumphantly.

'A what?'

'A witch bottle. It was under the window frame in my room. I only found it because of the tree.'

Intrigued, I took it from her, turning it over in my hand. 'What's inside?'

She shrugged. 'Don't know. I need to look it up properly. Cassie's mum might know who to ask.'

'Oh god, it's a school day,' I said, suddenly remembering. I gave her back the bottle. 'What time is it? Lord, it's almost eight. You need to get dressed.'

'Or I could stay here and help clean up?' Jem said hopefully.

'That's very thoughtful of you but no, you need to go to school.'

'Worth a try.' She grinned at me again. 'Eva might need me? Where is she?'

'Gone back to bed,' I said. 'Her actual house is fine, apart from the broken window at the back. She said she'd keep the living-room door shut until it's boarded up and get some sleep.'

Jem nodded. 'I'm glad she's okay.'

'Me too.'

'I've put all my stuff in your room. Is it okay to put my uniform on in there?'

'Course it is,' I said, looking down at myself. I was all dusty from clambering about over the debris in the garden. 'I suppose I should have a shower, too, before this Rory gets here.'

'He's coming then?' Jem said as I shooed her upstairs and followed myself.

'He is. He says he can board up your window and make sure it's all safe and watertight until a glazier can come out. And he's going to do the same for Eva.'

'He sounds nice.' In my bedroom, Jem carefully put the grubby bottle on my dressing table, then she pulled off her dusty clothes and headed – totally unselfconsciously – into the bathroom where she turned on the shower.

'He is nice,' I said honestly, as she closed the door. 'Don't be too long in there. I need to shower too.'

While I waited for her to come out, I sat on my bed and examined the witch bottle. It had a design in the glass, but I couldn't see what it was because it was encrusted with grime and dust. It needed a wash before Jem took it to show Cassie's mum. I held it up to the light, trying to see what was inside, but I couldn't tell. It wasn't liquid, though – I could feel whatever it was rattling around against the glass.

'What were witch bottles for?' I asked Jem as she came back into the bedroom, wrapped in my towel and started pulling on her uniform without bothering to dry off properly.

'Don't know,' she said. 'I'll take some pics of it and have a look online.'

I gave her a hug and smoothed her hair away from her face. 'I'm so glad you went to find that cat,' I said.

She made a face. 'I know, right? I keep thinking about what could have happened if I'd been in bed.'

'Don't.' I shuddered.

'I hope the cat's all right,' Jem said. 'I never actually saw it so I thought maybe I dreamt it.'

'I saw a cat out there the other day. I'll keep an eye out.' I looked at the clock next to my bed. 'You need to go. Take some money out of my purse and get some breakfast on the way. Come straight home.'

'I will.' She kissed me on the cheek. She danced off down the stairs, slamming the front door behind her. I checked my face in the mirror, considering putting on some make-up to look more presentable when Rory arrived. Then I changed my mind. Who cared what he thought of me?

I had a quick shower and put on a scruffy old sweatshirt that I wore when I was painting or gardening, and some jogging bottoms. I was supposed to be working in Edinburgh today, but I rang young Mr Langdown and explained what had happened. He was very sweet – as he always was – told me to take the day off, and even said if I had any trouble with the insurance company to let him know.

Rory had said he was very busy, obviously, so I wasn't sure when he'd turn up. To distract myself, I set about clearing up in Jem's room. It was such a mess – broken glass everywhere.

Her curtains were torn and the walls wet from the rain that had blown in. Her mattress was wet too. I stood in the centre of the room, looking around in despair. My poor girl had put up with so much and now this. She'd had a big bedroom in our house in Edinburgh with a huge wardrobe, an en-suite bathroom and a double bed. Her room here was tiny. She had a single bed, a little wardrobe, some bookshelves and a desk. But she'd worked really hard to get it how she wanted, forcing herself to be positive and even joking that it was better than her old room because if she finished the book she was reading when she was in bed, she could get a new one from her shelf without getting up. She had been so brave through all the shit, and I was fiercely proud of her. But now this had happened and I couldn't stand to think of her having to be brave again.

Jem had already gathered her duvet up, taking most of the broken glass with it, so I shoved it into a black bin liner. Maybe we'd go to the shops after school and buy a new one. I could put it all on my credit card and just cross my fingers and hope the insurance company covered it. It would be worth the risk to make sure Jem didn't have to go without.

I vacuumed up the rest of the glass and took down her torn curtains, bundling them up in a bin liner too. Then I carefully took the photos and pictures from her wall and laid them on her desk, weighing them down with a pot of pens. We could print them out again, I thought. And I'd seen some nice pictures on Etsy that she might like. We'd make her bedroom better than it had been before.

Completely exhausted, I sat down with a thump on to the floor. I didn't miss Alistair himself. Not really. Sometimes I missed what we'd had, years ago, when he'd been an aspiring TV reporter and I'd been working all hours as a duty solicitor. But I didn't miss what he'd become – arrogant and self-obsessed. Our marriage had been off for years, really. Not surprising when I thought about what he was up to when he wasn't at home. We barely saw each other and when we did spend time together it was at events or awards ceremonies – all for show.

I did, though, miss having someone there to share things with and now I felt that more than I had for ages. The responsibility of having to deal with all of this – making sure Jem was all right, re-doing her bedroom, getting the paint brushes out again, dealing with the insurance company, getting quotes for repairs – weighed heavily on my shoulders. It was okay for bloody Al, I thought wildly and fairly illogically. He'd just sodded off to prison. It was me who had to pick up the pieces of our life. Me who'd had to sell the house and find somewhere new to live, and a new job, and a new school for Jem. Prison was a breeze compared to all that.

I found myself crying, angry tears that felt warm on my cold cheeks. I wiped them away, annoyed. I didn't let myself cry very often because I knew self-pity got me nowhere. And actually back when the first allegations came out, I had realized quite quickly that if I started crying, it was hard to stop.

'Come on, Tess,' I said out loud, shivering in a blast of cold air through the broken glass. 'We need to get that window sorted out.'

I went into the bathroom and washed my face and then I put on some make-up to try to make myself look a bit better, after my little cry. Finally, I went downstairs to put the kettle on. As I got a mug out of the cupboard, there was a knock on the door and there was Rory.

'I heard you had a broken window,' he said cheerfully. Then he looked at my face – clearly still a bit blotchy – and winced. 'Rough morning?'

'Pretty shit.' I stood back to welcome him in. 'Cup of tea?'

Chapter 12

Tess

With Rory in the house, I felt better, as though I didn't have to face everything on my own. He cheerfully rebuilt Jem's window frame and boarded up the broken window, but didn't cover over the hole where I assumed the witch bottle had been.

'I can put some filler in there, if you like?' he said.

I shook my head. 'Could you just leave it for now?'

He gave me a quizzical look but he agreed. Then he checked the wall and told me it was stable and the branch hadn't done too much damage – much to my relief.

'I can recommend a local glazier,' he said, standing back to admire his handiwork. 'Maybe a couple actually because there are broken windows all over the place and I think they'll all be busy.'

It was warmer in the room already, now the wind wasn't coming in, though obviously it was very dark. I switched on the light.

'I wish I could just click my fingers and have it all sorted out,' I said. 'It's a bit overwhelming.'

'It's hard when you're on your own,' he said sympathetically. 'I remember after my divorce being paralysed with indecision in B&Q when I couldn't decide which wallpaper to buy for my living room.'

I looked at him sharply. I hadn't said I was single. He obviously realized what he'd done and looked sheepish. 'Sorry, I just assumed . . .'

'It's fine,' I said. 'I'm divorced too. It's just Jem and me here.'

'I should go,' he said, slightly awkwardly. 'I need to see your neighbour too.'

'I really appreciate you coming out so fast. If you give me your bank details, I can transfer the money,' I said, pulling my phone from my pocket.

But Rory shook his head. 'Nah, don't worry. I'll drop an invoice in later on.'

He grinned at me and I felt a tug of something – attraction? It had been a long time since I'd felt that. Perhaps it was just gratitude. I prided myself on being independent and capable but sometimes it was nice to have someone else lend a hand.

'Do you have to rush off?' I said suddenly. 'Eva was taking a nap so she might not be awake yet. And I don't know about you, but I've not eaten today and I'm starving. Fancy some lunch?'

He hesitated, and I thought he might say no, but then he smiled again. 'Yes please. If you're sure.'

I had some part-baked rolls in the freezer so I put those in the oven and warmed up a carton of soup. Then I laid it all out on the kitchen table with some cheese and Jem's favourite ham – I'd have to get some more later – and we tucked in.

Rory was good company. He was a little prickly but he was funny and smart and interesting. We mostly talked about our jobs. I tensed, hoping he wouldn't ask what my ex-husband had done. He asked a few questions about my work at the Haven instead.

'They do really good work there,' he said. 'It's important.'

He sounded very forceful. I wondered if the Haven had helped him – or more likely someone he knew, as they mainly helped women. 'They do.'

'And you work there for free?'

'Yes, it's voluntary.'

He seemed surprised by that and I felt the need to explain. 'I'm trying to . . .'

'Trying to?'

I shook my head. I'd been about to say that I was trying to make amends. For all the awful things Alistair had done. For believing him. For writing that stupid tweet. But nice as Rory was, I didn't want to get into that. So I just smiled. 'Trying to be a good person.'

I ate some of my soup, to give myself time to think, then I changed the subject. 'How long have you been a carpenter?'

'Not long,' he said. 'About five years. I was an accountant for years.'

I made a face and he laughed. 'I know. Not the most exciting job. But it paid the bills.'

'What made you decide to change career?'

He paused, looking thoughtful. 'Michelle – my ex – and I broke up, and things got a bit on top of me there for a while.'

I felt a surge of sympathy for this quiet, quirky man. 'Divorce is tough.'

'I'd always been good at woodwork at school, and I'd done lots of jobs as a hobby. Building fitted wardrobes and that.'

'A good choice, then?'

He looked straight at me, his eyes dark. 'It wasn't really a choice, but it's worked out okay.'

I hadn't finished my soup, but I wasn't as hungry as I'd thought I was.

'Do you have children?' I asked, putting my spoon down.

Rory made a face. He tore a bit from his bread roll, scattering crumbs across the table and as he did so, he knocked over his glass of water. It spilled across the table and splashed onto the floor, soaking my own roll and dripping onto my lap.

'God, I'm sorry,' he said.

I jumped up and found some kitchen roll to mop it up. 'Don't worry, it's only water,' I said. 'No harm done.' Rory wiped up the spill on the table and I dabbed my trousers and dried the floor. Then he gave me a slightly awkward smile. 'Thanks for lunch. Now I should really go next door and check your neighbour's window.'

I went with him to make sure Eva was all right. She was absolutely fine. I stayed with her while Rory boarded up the back window and gave us the names of some glaziers, and we had yet another cup of tea and chatted some more as Rory worked. There was a moment, when I took his empty mug to wash it up and save Eva the bother, when our fingers touched and I felt that little pull of attraction towards him again. I pushed it away. I didn't want a new man. Even if he was handsome and funny and handy, and absolutely nothing like Alistair.

When Rory had finished, I was saying goodbye to him from my own front garden just as Jem and Cassie came tumbling down the road.

'Cassie wanted to see the tree,' Jem announced, throwing her bag past me into the hall.

'Hello, Miss Blyth,' Cassie said.

'Oh, Cassie, call me Tess,' I said. I couldn't get used to being Miss Blyth again after so long as Mrs Robertson.

Cassie grinned at me and I smiled back. I liked this new friend of my daughter. She was boisterous and funny and very supportive of Jem, unlike the girls at her old school. 'How was school?'

'Boring,' said Jem. She held out her hand to Rory. 'I'm Jemima,' she said. 'Everyone calls me Jem. And this is Cassie. You must be Rory.'

Looking vaguely taken aback, Rory took her outstretched hand and shook it. 'Nice to meet you, Jem. I've boarded up your window.'

'Thank you.' She turned to me. 'Is my bed wrecked?'

I screwed up my face. 'I've binned the duvet and your curtains. I thought we could go out to the shopping centre in a while actually. Get some new ones?'

'Cool.'

'Would you like to come, Cassie?'

'Can't,' Cassie said. 'I'm at my dad's tonight. We're having pizza and film night.'

'What are you watching?' Jem asked.

Cassie shrugged. 'It's Thea's turn so something rubbish.'

'You don't live with your dad?' Rory said.

'No.' Cassie exchanged a look with Jem that said 'weirdo'. 'He and my mum split up.'

'You must miss him.'

'See him all the time,' she said. 'More than when they were married.'

'Can I go and look at my room?' Jem interrupted.

'It's not great, so brace yourself,' I warned. 'Just pop up, get changed out of your uniform and we can head to the shops.'

The girls dashed off. 'Thank you again,' I said to Rory. 'I really don't know what I'd have done if you hadn't been around to help.'

He ducked his head, looking embarrassed by the praise. 'Pleasure,' he muttered.

Jem and Cassie came thundering back down the stairs. Jem was wearing jeans and a hoodie now. I turned to look at them and then turned back to Rory, who was watching our front fence swaying in the wind.

'What?' I said.

Rory didn't need to reply. Instead we all looked on in silence as ever so slowly, the middle panel of the fence creaked loudly and fell over, hitting the grass at the front of our house with a small sigh.

'Shit,' I said.

Behind me, Rory put a hand on my shoulder. It felt nice. 'I'll fix it,' he said.

'Oh, Rory, you've already done so much.'

'Honestly, it'll take me ten minutes. I've got some offcuts in my van. Though it'll be a different colour so you'll need to paint the whole thing when it's done. You go to the shops and I'll have it sorted long before you get back.'

'Really?'

'Really.'

I turned round and smiled at him. 'Thank you.' Something passed between us, a connection that made me shiver. 'I owe you one.'

'I'll remember,' he said.

'Make sure you do.'

'Muuuum,' Jem moaned, breaking the moment. 'Are we going? Can we drop Cassie on the way?'

'Yes,' I said, flustered all of a sudden. 'Let's go. Grab a coat, Jem, and I'll get my keys.' I ran around finding my handbag and phone and car keys.

'You're absolutely sure?' I said to Rory, who was already examining the hole in the fence.

'I'm sure,' he said. 'Go. Shop. Have fun.'

'Thank you.' I squeezed his – impressively firm – arm. 'Honestly, I really appreciate it.'

'Any time,' he said. He winked at me and for a second I felt a little bit giddy. And then I beeped the car to open the doors and the moment was gone.

Chapter 13

Honor

1661

Alice and I slept like the dead after our night at the big house. She'd been quiet on the way home and thoughtful. She only said she was pleased the boy had pulled through, and didn't mention anything else. We checked on the animals, who thankfully were all fine after the storm, and then fell into bed.

She was still quiet when we woke a few hours later. We had some food and then Alice said she was going for a walk on the beach. I didn't argue. She obviously had something on her mind and there was no doubt that last night had been hard. I was so sorry I'd not been able to save the tutor, nor Isobel. I felt her death weighing heavily on me. A young woman taken too soon would always bring sorrow, but I also worried that Gregor Kincaid would blame me. I knew he didn't like me. Didn't trust me. He hadn't wanted me there last night and had only come through desperation and fear. And I'd let him down and given him another excuse to make accusations against me.

I watched Alice from the window as she left our cottage and

walked down towards the harbour. She liked watching the fishing boats, I knew. I thought she was soft on one of the fishermen though she hadn't said anything to me. I just had a feeling. Her shoulders were slumped and I hoped a walk would cheer her up.

I sat down at our table and spent the next hour or so writing up my records from last night. I had given the boy a different treatment – a stronger catnip tincture than I'd used before – so I was pleased it had done the trick. But the treatment I'd given Isobel hadn't had an effect. I thought she had been too far into her illness and my treatment too late, rather than it not working. But I wanted to write my notes and get it all straight in my head. Different doses for different people was a delicate art and I needed to be careful.

I'd almost finished when there was a knock at the door. Davey Kincaid was there, looking a different man from the pale-faced worrier he had been the previous night.

'Widow Seton,' he said politely. 'May I come in?'

I did not like being called Widow Seton. I objected to existing only in addition to my dead husband, beloved as he had been to me. But I didn't argue. I simply said: 'Call me Honor.'

Davey looked strange in the cottage in daylight in a way he hadn't when he'd come calling in a panic in the middle of the night. He was tall and well fed and his clothes were bright. I was proud of our home, but suddenly seeing it through his eyes, I felt uncomfortable.

'Can I offer you a drink?' I said politely, hoping he'd say no.

'No, thank you.'

I let out a breath of relief.

'I wanted to come and tell you how grateful I am for your efforts last night,' Davey continued. He looked ill at ease, too, I noticed. He held his hat in his hand, turning it around and round in his fingers. 'If Christy had . . .' His voice cracked and he stopped talking.

'How is he this morning?'

'Sleepy and weak, but on the mend,' he said. 'I really thought we were going to lose him.'

'And your mother?'

'Bossing everyone around from her bedchamber.'

I swallowed.

'And your brother?'

Davey shifted on his feet. 'Sad,' he said. 'And angry.'

'I am sorry I couldn't do more to help Isobel.'

'She went downhill very fast,' Davey said. 'I know you did everything you could.' He paused. 'Gregor often opts for anger over other emotions. He is angry now but soon it will become sadness. I'm sure of it.'

I nodded, unconvinced. Gregor was looking for reasons to discredit me, and I knew his dislike would not be tempered by my failure to save his wife.

Davey put a hand on my arm, reassuringly. I looked down at it in surprise. I'd not been touched by another adult in a long time. 'I want you to know that I am grateful, no matter what Gregor says.'

I felt a tiny shiver of fear. What did he mean by 'no matter what Gregor says'? Had Gregor been saying that it was my fault Isobel had died? I wanted Davey to go, to leave me to my notes and my thoughts, but instead he looked like he had more to say.

'I know Gregor can be brutish.' He paused. 'He is my brother and underneath it all he does have a heart. He always looks out for me.'

Again, I was not persuaded. I remembered Davey following his brother around like a lamb when we were children. And I remembered the stories about Davey's fondness for cards and his foolishness with money, and not for the first time, wondered if his wealthy brother had paid his debts.

'Thank you for coming,' I said, hoping he'd take the hint and leave. But he cast an eye around Thistle Cottage.

'This is a lovely home,' he said.

I almost scoffed. It was so different from his own house that I didn't believe for one moment that he thought it was lovely. 'Thank you,' I said.

'You have plenty of land.'

'I have enough.' I was firm.

'Your husband ensured you were taken care of.'

'He was a good man.'

'Evidently.'

Davey looked round once more, his gaze falling on my records. 'These are yours? These notes?'

'Yes.' I felt as though I was being inspected. 'Actually, I was just writing up everything I used last night when you arrived, so if you'll excuse me . . .'

'You keep notes on your treatments?'

'It's useful to be able to look back at what I used, when.'

'You can read and write, then?'

'Yes.'

'May I?' He didn't wait for my reply, simply began leafing through my notes. I watched, wondering what he was looking for. But it seemed he was simply interested in what I'd written – pausing every now and then, reading a sentence or two out loud under his breath, nodding, and occasionally shaking his head.

'This is extraordinary,' he muttered. 'Such detailed descriptions.'

Despite myself, I was flattered by his interest. Other than Alice, there was no one I could share my findings with.

'I keep a note of everything, no matter how insignificant it may seem at the time,' I told him. 'Sometimes it helps in the future.'

He looked at me. 'You are a woman of science.' His expression was full of wonder and I felt a flush of pride.

'I am a widow with a working knowledge of plants,' I said modestly.

He looked down at the open page. 'I've never seen anything like this before.'

'Women have been doing this for generations. I learned from my mother, and she learned from hers. And not just in my family. Women across Scotland do the same. We have cared for the people of this town for hundreds of years. We deliver babies and dress wounds and cure ailments . . .'

'And banish the plague.'

'I don't think it was the plague,' I admitted. 'I have tended to plague victims and they rarely recover as your son did, nor only suffer mildly like your mother. I've been comparing symptoms in my records.'

'So not the plague, then? Something else?'

'That's my thinking. Though I don't know what. The speed of their illness was nothing I've seen before.'

Davey looked impressed. 'You do a wonderful job.'

'I do the same as others,' I said briskly, thinking of the other women I knew who also made medicines from plants, or cared for women in childbirth, or helped the dying to be comfortable. 'The only difference is I write it all down.'

'I've read Culpepper,' Davey said. 'I believe your research is just as good.'

I hadn't read Culpepper. I didn't know what it was. So I just smiled. 'You're interested in medicine, then?'

'I am.' Davey nodded vigorously. 'Fascinated. I would like to study more, but Gregor wants me here.'

'Do you always do as he tells you?' I was teasing, gently, but Davey looked stern.

'I do.'

There was a pause.

'Perhaps you could do both,' I suggested.

'I worry I'm too old now, for learning. I should leave that to Christy.'

'We're always learning,' I said. 'Don't give up so easily.'

He smiled at me and I thought how nice-looking he was. Tall and broad-shouldered. Strong. My thoughts surprised me. The only man I'd ever looked at in that way was my John. I felt my cheeks flame. Davey held my gaze for a second and then dropped his eyes back to my records.

'I have friends at Edinburgh University who would be interested to see these books. They could learn so much from you.'

'I don't think so.' I laughed, though I didn't think it was funny. This was my work. My learning. I didn't want to share it. I went to where he stood and took the book from him, shutting it and then holding it tightly to my chest. He looked amused. 'You're right,' he said, though I'd not spoken. 'Guard this knowledge, Honor. It is your future.'

Or my undoing, I thought.

'I'll not keep you any longer,' Davey said. He put his hat on and made for the door, just as Alice came in.

'What are you doing here?' she said.

'Alice!' I was shocked by her rudeness.

She looked unrepentant for a second, then her face softened. 'How is Christy?'

'He is doing well, thank you. I came to tell your mother how grateful we are for your help.'

'Please wish him well.' Alice looked uncomfortable but I didn't know why.

'I will indeed. You are welcome to visit him whenever you like.'

Alice gave him the ghost of a smile and Davey turned his attention to me. 'I have very much enjoyed seeing your work,' he said. 'Perhaps I could come again and you could tell me some more about what you do?'

'I would like that,' I said honestly. I was pleased to have someone so interested.

With another smile, Davey let himself out of the door and we heard his footsteps recede.

'Why so rude?' I asked my daughter, starting to tidy away my notes.

She glowered at me. 'I don't trust the Kincaids.'

'I have no time for Gregor, but Davey seems pleasant enough.'

'He is in his brother's pocket and too interested in your land,' she said. 'That's why he wants to visit, and why he is being kind.'

'He is interested in medicine, not our land.'

She made a disbelieving sound deep in her throat. 'That's what he wants you to think.'

'What's wrong?' I said. She wasn't usually so prickly and I was worried about her.

With a sigh, Alice sat down on her favourite chair by the fire. 'Nothing,' she said. She looked up at me. 'Do you think your tincture cured Christy?'

'What else could it have been?'

She shook her head, and looked despairingly up at the ceiling. 'It couldn't have been anything else. But there was a shadow in the room, and it lifted.'

'That happens.' I'd been present at many deaths and many near deaths, and I'd seen that shadow many times.

Alice sighed again. 'Kyla saw.'

'She saw the shadow?'

'Not exactly. She said the room got lighter.'

I felt the hairs on the back of my neck stand up. 'What did you say?'

'I told her it was the dawn.'

I nodded. 'Was it the dawn?'

Alice looked at her feet. 'Maybe.' She swallowed. 'But then I saw Kyla talking to Gregor. And I was worried she might have said it was something else. Put ideas in his head, perhaps? Made him think it could be . . .' She swallowed. 'Witchcraft.'

My head rang with the word, but I swallowed down my fears and forced myself to smile at Alice. 'Nonsense,' I sang. 'They were probably talking about Isobel, or about Lady Kincaid. Nothing to worry about. Christy is well, and so is his grandmother, and we should be glad.'

Alice looked at me, her eyes roaming my face, looking for any sign that I was lying. I kept my gaze steady. 'Now, are you hungry? What would you like to eat?'

I got up and busied myself by the stove, putting on a pot of water to boil for vegetables, and unwrapping some cheese. I turned away from Alice as I worked, hoping she couldn't see how much my hands were shaking.

Chapter 14

Alice

I had said the word out loud and now it echoed around the house. Ma was talking but all I could hear was 'witchcraft'.

I was afraid. And I felt silly to feel afraid. But I couldn't help it. Because I kept thinking about Granny telling me that babies born in their sac, like I had been, were special. That we had otherworldly abilities. Things not of heaven or earth, she used to say. And it sounded ridiculous. But the fact remained that I had put my hand on Christy's head, and he had recovered.

Ma was skilled with plants and herbal remedies. I didn't want to take that from her. There was every possibility that it was her treatment that had pulled Christy back from the brink.

And yet . . .

I was on edge and though I was hungry, I found I couldn't eat much. Ma watched me silently, but she didn't complain when I left half my bread and most of my vegetables.

'I am still tired from being up at the big house,' I said. 'I think I'll go to bed.' It was early but it was already getting dark. 'Do you need help with the animals before I go?'

Ma shook her head. 'I can do it.' Her brow was furrowed in concern. 'You get some rest.'

She pulled on her cloak and went outside to see to the goats and shut up the chickens. When she was gone I darted to the cupboard where she kept her dried herbs, plants and oils, as well as the little bottles and mixing bowls she used for making her tinctures. Ma collected glass bottles and pottery containers wherever she found them, because they were useful for her work. Now I found a small green glass bottle with a tiny cork, and put it into the pocket in my skirt. Then, as an afterthought, I added a little squat earthenware pot, and a similar tall, slim bottle.

With them all safely stored and hidden from view in case Ma came back inside, I took a candle and ran upstairs to my room. I had a table by the window, with a jug and bowl for washing, and space to write. I pushed the bowl aside and sat down, laying out my containers on the surface.

I was only 16 but I knew there had been witch-hunts for years in this part of Scotland. Since back before Ma was born, there had been accusations and wild imaginings of devilish acts. Whispers, gossip and fear were everywhere – and so were witch bottles.

I had seen them before, these tiny charms. Women used them to protect themselves against attacks – physical attacks, of course, but also from bad energy directed at them. Malicious rumours, or nasty whispers.

It was risky. Because owning a witch bottle was physical, undeniable proof that you believed in its power. And that was enough – more than enough – to put you at risk of accusations of witchcraft.

I sighed. I was going round in circles, here. If I had some sort of ability then Ma and I were at risk. I shook my head. This was silly. I had no otherworldly skills. That was just stories my granny had told me.

But the truth was, we were vulnerable anyway. Ma being a burgess, being able to read and write, having the knowledge she had, all worked against her anyway.

And if there was any chance – however small – that I could protect her, then shouldn't I do it?

Feeling faintly ridiculous, I stared at the containers I'd taken from Ma's cupboard. Could I write some charms that would protect Ma and me and hide them in these bottles? I thought about the stories my grandmother had told. And then I thought about how I'd put my hand on Christy's head and pushed my energy into him, and how the room had lightened. I made a decision: I had to do what I could – no matter how silly it all sounded.

I'd been busy earlier. I'd gathered some prickles from a thistle plant in the garden and plucked a few hairs from Ma's cloak, which I'd wrapped in a cloth from the kitchen and stashed in my pocket. I pulled it out and opened it up. The prickles and the hairs were still there. Now I pulled a few strands from my own head and put them in the cloth too.

I wasn't sure what to do next. But after a moment's thought, I took the glass bottle, uncorked it, and carefully pushed the hairs and the prickles inside.

Would that do? I had no idea. It was just silly superstition. A child's game. But I knew it was said that the prickles were supposed to trap any ill will. And the hairs would make sure we were the recipients of the protective charm. It didn't seem enough.

I had no paper – Ma guarded what she had very jealously as it was expensive and hard to come by – but I had a prayer book. Now I took it from my shelf and very carefully first folded a strip from the edge of the page, and then tore it, almost shocked by my own daring.

I had a tiny ink pot on my desk – a gift from Ma on my last birthday. I never used it really as it was too precious, but now I took my quill, opened the pot and dipped it in. And very slowly and deliberately, I wrote: 'Protect us.' I looked at the tiny slip of paper once more and added: 'Honor Seton and Alice Seton.'

Being very careful again, I tore off the rest of the strip of paper, leaving just the little scrap I'd written on, then I rolled it up and tucked it inside the bottle too.

'Protect us,' I said aloud. The candle flickered, though I couldn't feel a draught in the room. I pushed the little stopper into the top and then picked up the candle and dripped wax over it, sealing everything firmly inside the bottle.

'Good,' I said, feeling more at ease than I'd felt all day. 'That's done.'

I sat there for a little while, on the rickety stool that Ma told me my father had made when she was expecting me, drumming my fingers on the rough wooden tabletop. I had two more bottles. I could put them back in Ma's cupboard. Or . . .

I picked up the squat earthenware container, turning it round and round in my hands. And then suddenly, I fumbled and dropped it, and it split clean in two on the floor.

'Stupid Alice,' I muttered to myself, listening to hear if Ma had heard. But no, there was no sound from downstairs. She must still be out with the animals.

Only one bottle then. And the protection was done. I felt safer already. Was it possible that this was working?

So perhaps I could use this other bottle for something else. Something different.

I picked up my quill and smoothed out the rest of the paper I'd torn from my prayer book. Then I wrote 'Lachlan Murdoch.'

Was that enough? Perhaps I should be more specific. After all, I had no hairs from his head to focus the charm. So, feeling a little flutter in my stomach I added: 'And Alice Seton.'

And then, bolder now, I wrote: 'Alice Murdoch.'

I liked how it looked, so I wrote it again. And then again. I filled the little scrap of paper with the name I hoped would be mine one day. It looked so nice, I thought.

'Alice?' Ma called up the stairs. 'Are you in bed? Could you come and get your blasted cats away from the chickens.'

Startled, I quickly rolled up the piece of paper and dropped it into the tall, thin earthenware bottle. 'One minute,' I shouted back. 'Just coming.'

I knew I absolutely had to hide these bottles. I'd put our names on them, after all. If anyone were to find them . . .

No. They had to be kept out of sight. I looked round my room for inspiration and my gaze fell on the small window. It had a wooden sill that didn't quite fit in the frame – I think my father had cut it too small and never fixed it. Now I lifted it up and peered underneath. There was a little hollow in the stone, just big enough for the bottles. With a grin, I put first the tall, thin bottle, then the glass one carefully inside, stacked one on top of the other, and pushed them down a little, so they could hardly be seen. Then I dropped the wooden sill back down again.

I had no idea if these silly charms would do any good. If I was being completely honest to myself, I thought they probably wouldn't do anything at all. But I was afraid of what had happened in Christy's room, I was wary of what Kyla had said to the laird, and I was scared about Davey Kincaid's interest in my mother. I was just a girl, with no authority or agency, and I had done the only thing I could to look after my family. I just had to hope it would work.

Chapter 15

Tess

Present day

The next day I called young Mr Langdown again and took the day off. I wanted to help Eva clear up, and paint the fence, and generally just get things sorted after the storm. Jem's window was being mended later too so I had to be at home for the glazier.

First I went to the DIY shop at the edge of town to buy some paint for the fence. Rory had done a good job of fixing the hole, but as he'd said, the wood he'd mended it with didn't match so I needed to paint the whole thing.

The storm had cleared now, leaving the sky blue though the temperature had dropped. October was just a few days away and the air smelled of approaching winter. I liked it. I wrapped up warm and headed off to the shop. As I was queuing to buy the paint, balancing the pot and some brushes in my arms, I spotted Mandy, the receptionist from the Haven.

'Hello!' I called. She looked over at me and waved – friendly enough – but she didn't stop for a chat.

By the till was a rotating rack of cards. At the top was one with a picture of a black cat on it. On a whim I picked it up and added it to the shopping on the conveyor belt. The picture had made me think of how Rory had chuckled when I told him the story of Jem searching for an invisible puss that possibly saved her life.

'We don't know if there ever was a cat,' I'd said. 'Jem thinks she might have dreamt it. But whatever happened, I'm grateful to that mysterious moggy.'

'Perhaps it was a ghost cat, come from another realm to warn Jem of danger,' Rory had added gleefully.

'A witch's cat from the seventeenth century,' I had suggested. And I'd told him about how our cottage had once been home to witches. 'Jem's doing a school project on them,' I'd explained. 'She'll have to add in a bit about how their cat still lives here, more than 400 years later.'

'It's like a Stephen King novel,' Rory had said, shuddering. 'What's that one about the demon cat? *Cujo*?'

I'd laughed. 'Cujo is a dog.'

I thought vaguely that I could send him the card to say thank you for helping with the window and fixing the fence. Though I wasn't sure how I'd get it to him, as I didn't know where he lived. The invoice he'd posted through the door didn't have an address on it.

Paint bought, I headed home and spent an enjoyable morning sloshing it about. When I'd finished, I stood back to admire my handiwork. It wasn't half bad. And it really brightened up the front of the house. In fact, now the fence was gleaming white, it made the front door look a bit tatty. Perhaps I should paint that too?

But that was a job for another day. The glazier had messaged to say he'd be a couple of hours, so I had time to drop in and see Eva and check she was all right.

As she opened her front door, a van drove past and honked its horn loudly. Rory. He stuck his hand out of the window and waved, and Eva and I both waved back cheerfully.

'Nice man,' Eva said with approval. 'Come in, Tess.'

Her back garden was a mess – full of bits of conservatory. But her back window had already been mended.

'Apparently,' she said, 'I am a priority because I am elderly.' She looked quite pleased with herself.

I tried not to laugh, but I failed. 'What are you going to do about the conservatory?'

'I've got a chap coming to dismantle what's left and take away all the debris and then I might put a patio in. Perhaps in the spring.'

'Sounds lovely,' I said. 'You could get some pots and put strawberries in them.'

As we talked about the ideas for Eva's garden, I realized I was looking forward to seeing it. I clearly saw Thistle Cottage as home now. The thought made me smile.

Eva looked tired and when I commented that she seemed in need of a rest, she agreed.

'I might go and sit down. Put the kettle on, Tess, will you?'

I busied myself in the kitchen, making tea and finding biscuits. I put them on a plate the way Eva liked them and took them through to the other room. Eva was on the couch, eyes closed. I felt a surge of alarm.

'Eva?' I said.

She opened her eyes. 'Goodness, I'm tired today,' she said.

'Are you still catching up after the storm, or are you ill?'

She gave me one of her cheeky smiles. 'I think I'm a little bit hungover.'

'Eva Greenbaum,' I said, laughing. 'What were you up to last night?'

'I had a couple of friends over last night for a few sherries,' she said. 'We were chatting until gone midnight.'

'Early night tonight then,' I said, mock-sternly.

'It's important to live a little,' she said to me, equally sternly. She patted my knee. 'That Rory is a nice man. Handsome too.'

'He is.'

She gave me a sideways glance.

'Why are you blushing?' She frowned at me. 'Or is it a hot flush? Are you menopausal?'

'Eva!' I couldn't help giggling at her bluntness.

'Do you like him? Rory?'

I rolled my eyes good-naturedly. She didn't let anything get past her. 'No,' I said. 'Well, yes. There's something there,' I admitted.

'Sexual tension,' Eva said in a manner more like Sid James than an elderly woman.

'No.' I could feel myself blushing again. 'I just think he's nice, that's all. My divorce was very recent, Eva. I'm not sure I'm ready for a relationship.'

She shrugged. 'I think you deserve to have some fun.'

I laughed. 'Maybe.'

'No *maybe*. You should put yourself first for a change.'

I shook my head. 'Nope. Jem comes first.'

'Well joint first, then.'

I leaned back against the squishy sofa. 'Perhaps.'

'You should ask Rory for a drink.'

'Absolutely not.'

'Dinner then?'

'Eva,' I said, half laughing, half horrified. 'Were you like this when you were younger?'

'Like what?'

'So bold.'

Eva laughed. 'Oh, *liebchen*, I was much, much bolder.'

'I am not going to go and ask Rory out,' I said firmly.

'We'll see.' Eva folded her hands in her lap primly. 'I'm going to have a snooze. Could you turn the telly on before you go?'

I was being dismissed, it seemed. 'Sleep off the hangover?'

Eva snorted and I laughed as I turned on the telly and gave her the remote control. I liked her enormously. I was very glad she was my next-door neighbour.

As I put on my coat, the newsreader on the TV reported on a

politician who'd been accused of bullying his staff. Eva groaned. 'They're all as bad as each other, these men,' she said. 'This one, and that awful chap who did the animal programme, and the one from breakfast telly.'

I froze, halfway through tying my scarf. Eva was watching the television screen but it seemed to me she was unnaturally still – as if she was waiting for me to react to what she'd said.

With a considerable effort, I pulled a disgruntled face at her, holding tightly on to the ends of my scarf. 'They're all nasty pieces of work,' I said vaguely and honestly. 'Must go.'

I scurried down her path, and on to the pavement and stopped in horror as I looked at my newly painted fence. Where it had been bright, shimmering white, it now dripped with red paint.

'Witch!' someone had daubed across it in large letters.

I put my hand over my mouth, shocked at how brutal the word looked in the blood-like paint. My heart thumped painfully in my chest and I felt slightly light-headed. Did someone know who I was? I'd been called 'witch' a lot when the social-media hate campaign was at its height. Witch and hag and harridan and old bag and dried-up old crone and that was just the less-awful insults.

I took a few deep breaths, gulping for air, trying to steady myself. This was nothing to do with me, I thought rationally. We knew everyone called our cottage the witch's cottage. Cassie had even told us cheerfully that people used it as a landmark when they were giving directions: 'Go past the church, and the witch's cottage and then turn right . . .'

This was just kids having a laugh, I told myself. Playing a Halloween prank a few weeks early. This wasn't personal.

I touched the W with the tips of my fingers. Damn, it was dry already. Whoever had done it must have got busy as soon as I went into Eva's house. We'd not noticed anyone outside, but we had been at the back of the house for ages, looking out into the garden and talking about her plans for it. There was no chance of washing it off now it had dried on, and another coat of white paint wouldn't cover that deep red colour. I looked at my watch. I had a little while before the glazier arrived, and Jem came home from school. I didn't want her to see this – it had been a strange, unsettling couple of days and this would just make things worse. I would go back to the DIY shop now, buy some dark brown paint and cover it over. And I'd add a load of extra sweets to the online shopping for the local kids at Halloween. Seemed it would be a good idea to keep them on our side.

Chapter 16

Jem

Mum had been really generous, buying me a new duvet, and new sheets. I felt a bit bad because I knew we didn't have loads of money, but she told me it was fine and that I wasn't to worry. I did though.

In the end I slept in her room that first night, because it was so dark in mine with the board up – normally the street lights from the path along the back of our house, and the lights that illuminated the church, shone through my window at night. It was really cold in my room, too, and noisy . . . and I had to admit I was a little bit scared as well. I was much happier spending the night in Mum's bed with her, like I did when I was little and Dad was away working.

But tonight Cassie was sleeping over because her mum had a work thing, and Mum had draped a thick blanket over the boarded-up window to keep the warmth in, and found a load of lamps from all over the house, so instead of being cold and dark, my room felt warm and cosy. Mum had been a bit odd when we got home, slightly on edge. But it had been a hard week, I supposed.

Cassie and I were planning a *Pitch Perfect* marathon, but first Cassie wanted to examine the witch bottle and see where I'd found it.

'There's definitely something inside,' Cassie said, holding it up to the light.

I bounced on the bed on my knees. 'Blood, maybe,' I said with relish. 'I looked it up. Blood, or wee or hair.'

'Urgh.' Cassie dropped it and I caught it before it hit the floor.

'Careful. It's like 400 years old. It's actual history.'

'Ohmygod,' Cassie said, clasping her hand to her mouth. 'I totally forgot to tell you.'

'What?'

'Mum spoke to one of the historian peeps at her work and she's an expert in witches and she'll be in the museum tomorrow if you want to pop in after school with the bottle and she says she's dying to see it.' Cassie parroted the whole message without taking a breath.

'Cool,' I said. 'Will you come with me?'

'Course. Show me where you found it.'

'It was under where the tree had split my window ledge.' I crawled across my bed to the window. 'Here. See this wee hole?'

Cassie pulled her phone out of her pocket and turned on the torch, shining it into the space. 'There's something else in there.'

I felt a flutter of excitement. 'No way? Another bottle?'

'Maybe.'

I shoved Cassie out of the way and looked myself. 'It doesn't look like a bottle, because it's not got the waxy seal.'

Cassie leaned against me. 'It is a bottle. It's just not glass.' She looked at my hands. 'You've got skinnier fingers than me. Try to get it out.'

She held the phone so the light shone down into the hole and I saw she was right. It was another bottle, wedged firmly into the small space. I tried to get my fingers down the side, but I couldn't squeeze them in.

'I need something to kind of lever it out,' I said, looking round my room for inspiration. 'Ooh what about a ruler?'

I got the ruler from my desk, jammed it down the side of the bottle and promptly snapped it in half as I tried to wiggle it about. 'Nope.'

Cassie giggled. 'What about a spoon? Or a knife?'

'Excellent idea.' I jumped off the bed and ran downstairs to the kitchen. 'Found another bottle,' I shouted to Mum as I passed her in the living room. But she was on the phone and she didn't seem to hear. I grabbed an ice-cream spoon – the sort with a long handle and a small bowl – and a knife and ran back upstairs again.

'Right, try to get the spoon down the side, then maybe you can sort of get it under the bottle and pull it up,' Cassie said.

I eased the spoon into the hole, wiggling it round until I thought it was underneath the bottom of the bottle. 'Got it,' I said. I levered it up and the bottle moved. 'It's coming,' I said.

'Give it a bit more oomph,' Cassie advised.

I pushed down on the handle of the spoon firmly and the hole gave way. The bottle catapulted out of its resting place and flew across my room where it hit the wall with a loud crack.

'Oops,' I said.

'That's 400 years old,' Cassie said sternly. I gave her a good-natured shove and slid off my bed to go and inspect the damage.

This bottle was a different shape from the first one. It was tall and thin, but Cassie had been right that even though it didn't have the waxy seal on it, it was definitely a bottle. It was made from some sort of brown pottery and it was on my bedroom floor, cracked in half. 'Oh shit, I've totally smashed it,' I said. I bent down to pick up the two pieces and a roll of yellowed paper came out. 'Cass, there's something inside.'

Cassie sat down next to me on the floor and I moved one of the lamps to give us more light. Then very, very carefully, because it was 400 years old after all, I unrolled the tiny strip of paper.

There was writing all over it. Tiny, old-fashioned writing. 'God it's so hard to see,' I complained. Cassie found a magnifying glass app on her phone and together we peered at the writing.

'It's Lachlan!' Cassie shouted in triumph, making me jump. 'Look! That's a big loopy L. It says Lachlan. Like the funny-looking lad in fourth year.'

I squinted at the writing. 'Yes,' I said. 'Lachlan Murdo?'

'Murdoch,' said Cassie.

I looked at her, impressed. 'You're good at this,' I said.

She shrugged. 'My dad's writing is terrible. I've had years deciphering birthday cards and notes he's written.'

I clutched her arm. 'Alice,' I said. 'The name above it is Alice Seton – the witch.'

'Nice.'

My hands were tingling as I pointed to the other names written over and over on the little slip of paper. 'Alice Murdoch,' I breathed. 'She's written Alice Murdoch again and again.'

Cassie let out a bark of laughter. 'Because she fancies him,' she said in delight. 'Alice Seton fancies Lachlan Murdoch and she's practising her married name.'

'Oh my god, this is amazing,' I said, laughing too. 'She's just like us. She fancies a boy and she's just like us, only 400 years ago.'

'Have you written Callum's name on a piece of paper?' Cassie said with a sly glance at me. 'Have you written Jemima Stokes over and over, in case you ever get married?'

'Shut up,' I said. 'Like you haven't written Max's name on your maths book.'

'I haven't,' Cassie said in outrage. We both collapsed in giggles again and I wondered if Alice Seton had had a best friend who she could laugh with about Lachlan Murdoch. I hoped she had.

'Do you think she was killed?' I said suddenly, my laughter stopping as the thought occurred to me. 'Do you think Alice was killed for being a witch? They did horrible things to them. Burned them and tortured them.' I felt upset, which was ridiculous considering even if Alice had lived to a ripe old age, she'd still have been dead for hundreds of years.

'The woman at the museum might know,' said Cassie. 'I hope they didn't hurt her, though. I feel like she's our friend.' She looked up at the ceiling. 'Alice, if you can hear us, we're your new besties.'

She was joking but I felt a bit spooked. I shivered. 'God, I hope she can't hear us,' I said. Then I added: 'Sorry for breaking your bottle, Alice.'

Cassie put her arm through mine. 'Shall we go downstairs and show your mum what we've found?'

'Good idea.'

Mum had finished her phone call and she was thrilled by our find. She gave me a plastic folder to put the slip of paper in to keep it safe, and we put that and the pieces of bottle, and the first bottle, in a little cardboard box. She said she wanted to come to the museum too, which I was quite pleased about. And then we ordered pizza and we all watched *Pitch Perfect* and *Pitch Perfect 2*. Eventually, Mum went to have a bath and Cassie and I watched *Pitch Perfect 3*, and all the spookiness of thinking about Alice disappeared.

When Mum had finished her bath, she came downstairs in her pyjamas and dressing gown and asked if we'd like a hot chocolate. Cassie and I had stuffed our faces with popcorn and pizza but we still nodded.

I went into the kitchen with Mum to see if she needed a hand, and as she was warming the milk – in a pan on the hob because she said that was better than in the microwave – and I was leaning against the back door and not really helping at all, I heard the mewing again.

'Mum,' I said. 'It's the cat. Cassie, listen.'

Cassie came into the kitchen holding her stomach. 'I've eaten too much popcorn,' she complained. 'Hmm, that hot chocolate smells delish.'

I laughed. 'Shush a minute. I want to listen.'

We all stayed quiet and there was the mewing again. Delighted, I clapped my hands. 'I knew I hadn't imagined it.'

I opened the back door and went out into the side return of the house. 'Here kitty,' I called into the darkness. 'You saved my bacon. I need to repay you.'

I felt something nudge my leg and there was a little black cat, weaving around my ankles. I bent down and picked it up. It didn't struggle, just sat contentedly in my arms.

'Hello,' I said. The cat purred loudly. 'Look.' I went into the kitchen and showed the little animal to Mum and Cassie. 'I've got a new friend.'

'She's so sweet,' Cassie said, stroking the cat's head. The cat nuzzled her hand.

She was sweet. If she was a she. I wasn't sure how you'd know. 'Can I keep her, Mum?'

Mum frowned. 'Oh, Jem, I don't know. She must belong to someone?'

'She's not got a collar,' Cassie said.

'See, she's not got a collar. Please?'

'You can't just adopt a cat,' Mum said. 'It's stealing.'

'Our old cat was really greedy and kept going in other houses and eating their cat food,' Cassie said. 'We only found out when one of the other owners put a paper collar on him with a message on it. You could do that.'

'Brilliant!' I said. 'We could ask if she belongs to anyone and then we'll know for sure.'

Mum knew when she was defeated. She smiled. 'Fine,' she said. 'Let's find some paper.'

She got a notepad from the drawer and ripped a long strip, which reminded me of Alice's note. Then she wrote:

This cat has been to visit us. If she belongs to you, please text and let us know.

She added her phone number and then I held the cat's head still while she fastened the paper collar round her neck and stuck the ends together with some Sellotape. I kissed the kitty's little pink nose and put her back outside where she mewed sadly.

'I know,' I said. 'But go and explore and come back again if you want to live here.'

The cat gave one last little mew and then wandered off into the darkness of the garden.

'I hope she comes back,' I said. 'She's lovely.'

Chapter 17

Jem

Mum put her head round my bedroom door the next morning.

'Are you awake?' she whispered.

I sat up and looked at Cassie, who was stirring in her sleeping bag on the floor in the light from the landing – it was still really dark in my room because of the board over the window. 'We are now.'

'There's a surprise for you in the kitchen.'

'Is it the cat?'

'Come and see.'

I slid out of bed and gave Cassie a kick. 'Cass, the cat's back.'

She stuck her head out of the sleeping bag and gave me a sleepy smile. 'Cool.'

We both ran downstairs in our pyjamas and there was the cat, still wearing her paper collar, wolfing down a tin of tuna Mum had put on a paper plate on the floor. 'She came back,' I said, delighted.

'She did.'

The cat looked up and mewed and I bent down and scratched her head. 'Can we keep her? She obviously wants to live here.'

Mum sighed dramatically but I knew she didn't mean it. 'I think we should take her to a vet and make sure she's not microchipped, but yes, we can keep her if she doesn't belong to anyone else.'

'She's a witch's cat,' Cassie said with a gleam in her eye. 'Black with green eyes.'

'All cats have green eyes, don't they?' said Mum. 'Not just the ones who belong to witches.'

'Do you know that black cats are always the last ones to be adopted at shelters because people think they're unlucky,' I said. 'But I think she's lucky because if it wasn't for her, I'd have been squashed under that tree branch.'

'Maybe we should name her Lucky,' Mum suggested.

I looked at the cat. 'No, she doesn't look like a Lucky. She needs a witchy name.'

'Alice,' said Cassie.

'God no, I don't want to make the real Alice angry,' I said with a shiver.

Cassie laughed. 'What about Hazel? That's a good name for a witch.'

'Or Sootica? From that book you liked when you were little?' Mum added.

The cat had finished her tuna and was nudging me with her nose. I picked her up. 'What's your name?' I said. The cat stared at me unblinkingly with her green eyes.

'What's Hermione's cat called in *Harry Potter*?' Cassie said. 'Thea would know. She's bloody obsessed.'

'Crookshanks. But he's a boy.'

'Oh well.'

'How about Hermione?' Mum said. 'She's clearly very clever, like her namesake.'

'Hermione,' I said. The cat purred loudly. 'I love it. Hello Hermione.'

'Let me take some pictures,' Cassie said, pulling out her phone. 'She's totally Instagrammable.'

'Just the cat. None of Jem,' Mum warned.

'Muuum. Cassie uses so many filters I'd be unrecognizable anyway.'

'It's fine,' Cassie said. I'd told her about Mum's obsession with the evils of social media and she had been totally cool with it, but I was still a bit embarrassed. 'Take one of me, Jem.'

She took Hermione from me and held her up, pouting for the camera. I took a few pics, and she did her thing, adding hearts and filters on top of filters until she was happy. Mum looked on, frowning. 'Cassie, you're much more beautiful in real life than in these pictures,' she said.

Cassie grinned. 'There are two versions of me – the Instagram/TikTok me and the real me,' she explained. 'I don't let one affect the other.'

'As long as you don't compare the real-life you to the social-media version of everyone else,' Mum warned. 'That's when it gets tricky.'

'I'm too clever for that,' Cassie said and Mum laughed. 'Actually, we should post about the witch bottles,' Cassie added. 'There's a local residents' group on Facebook that my mum is on. Perhaps we could ask if anyone knows anything.'

'Are you on Facebook?' I said doubtfully. 'I thought that was for old people.'

'Oh yes, it totally is,' Cassie said. 'I'm not on it.' We both looked at Mum and she pretended to look shocked.

'What?' she said. 'I'm old so I must be on Facebook?'

'Are you?' I doubted it, given how much she hated social media and not surprisingly, Mum shook her head.

'I'm not.'

'I'll ask my mum to post something about the bottles,' Cassie said.

Mum frowned but she didn't say no, which I was pleased about. 'You need to get dressed, girls, because it's a school day.'

Cassie and I ran around like mad things, getting showered and dressed, and fussing over Hermione, who followed us upstairs, until we were ready to go to school with the first witch bottle I'd found tucked safely in my bag, wrapped in one of Mum's dusters.

The day dragged but eventually we got out. Unlike most days, we didn't hang around and chat with our friends; instead we went straight to the museum.

It was right in the centre of town, not far from the place where Mum volunteered, and next to the library. Mum met us outside, because she wanted to know about the bottle too. At least, that was what she said. I knew that actually she was nervy about me meeting strangers. Cassie knew everyone in the museum, and soon we were sitting in a large room full of books and pictures and filing cabinets, with a woman called Heather. She was wearing lots of bright knitwear, a matching woolly hat, and had her nails painted vibrant purple, and she was almost speechless with joy when I got the witch bottle out of my bag. We'd left Alice's love note and the broken bottle at home; I felt that was a bit too private to share.

'Oh my goodness,' she said. 'May I?'

I shrugged and she picked it up, turning it over in her hands. 'This is wonderful. Where did you find it?'

'It was sort of buried in my window frame,' I told her. 'A tree broke the window in the storm and we found it.'

She nodded. 'They were often in frames, or under fireplaces, or over doors,' she said.

'What were they for?' I asked.

'Protection.'

'From witches?' Mum said, puzzled. 'But the witches lived in our house. At least that's what we've heard. Honor Seton and her daughter Alice.'

Heather went a bit red with excitement. 'You live in the witch's cottage? By the sea?'

'We do. Thistle Cottage.'

'It's one of the oldest houses in the town, you know?' Heather said. 'So I'm not surprised there was a witch bottle there.' She turned the bottle round in her fingers. 'As far as I know, women would use these bottles to protect themselves from attacks.'

'Women?' I said. 'Witches?'

Heather shrugged. 'There's no such thing as witches.'

I sighed. 'So what—'

'These bottles were a superstition. Like not walking under a ladder.'

'Black cats being unlucky,' said Cassie with a grin.

'Crossing your fingers when you don't mean what you're saying,' said Mum, winking at me. I always did that when I promised I was going to tidy my room, or that I'd absolutely done all of my homework.

'Exactly,' Heather said. 'The women would make a bottle as a sort of lucky charm, to "catch" the bad luck that was coming their way.'

'We found Honor Seton's name on a list of accused witches,' Mum added.

Heather nodded, her face serious. 'There were several witch-hunts round here. Hundreds of women – and a few men – put to death.'

'So maybe Alice was worried that would happen to her and her mum?' I said, feeling so sad for poor Alice. 'Maybe she wanted to keep them safe.'

'Perhaps.'

'Did it work?' Cassie asked. Her eyes were huge. 'Did Alice and Honor get put to death? Or did the bottle protect them?'

'Well, the ironic thing is, making a bottle like this would be considered proof that the woman was a witch. Anything ungodly like this would have been enough. Later on, people who were frightened of witchcraft adopted the superstition themselves and used witch bottles to protect themselves from spells. But at the time your Alice was around, making a bottle like this was a risky move. She must have been desperate.'

'Do you think they were killed?' I said. I felt close to tears which was a bit silly.

'I don't actually know,' Heather said. 'But I can certainly try to find out for you. It's for a school project, is it?'

'We need to find lessons from history that we can apply to the present day,' Cassie parroted.

'Witch-hunts are perfect for that. All this "be kind" stuff that's around right now? If only it had existed back then.'

'How do you mean?' asked Mum. She leaned forward in her seat, looking straight at Heather.

'Most of the witch-hunts started as whispering campaigns,' Heather explained. 'Rumours about women who were doing things in a different way.'

'Casting spells,' said Cassie but Heather shook her head.

'Not as such, though that would have been some of the charges put against them. They could have been early pharmacists, using herbal medicines to cure people of common ailments. Or midwives, delivering babies. Or sometimes they were just women who had money of their own and a bit of independence. They were always regarded with suspicion.'

Mum shivered and I edged my chair closer to hers. 'So they weren't actual witches?' I asked.

Heather laughed. 'Of course not. There were no witches back then, just as there are none now. It was more like a social contagion. People accusing other people before they could be accused. Pointing fingers. Spreading rumours. Nasty gossip.'

'We could totally link that with the present day,' said Cassie, who was busy typing everything Heather was saying into her phone. 'It's basically school life.'

Mum looked a bit pale. 'Are you all right?' I asked.

'Fine.' She gave me a tight smile. 'It's just not very nice to hear about these poor women, is it?'

'It was a dark time,' Heather agreed. 'Shall I find you some books that might help with your project?'

'Yes please,' I said. 'We need all the help we can get I reckon. Don't you think, Cass?'

Cassie didn't answer because she was taking a selfie by a shelf filled with books that looked hundreds of years old. I laughed. 'She agrees,' I said.

Mum pushed her chair back. 'I think I might run to Asda and get some cat food, if you're all right here?' she said.

I gave her a questioning look. We'd agreed we were both going to get cat stuff together. But she didn't look like she was enjoying this very much, so I didn't argue. 'See you at home then?' I said.

Mum thanked Heather, said goodbye to Cassie and me, then picked up her bag and hurried out of the room without looking back.

When we had bags full of books, and Heather had promised to find out all she could about the Setons, Cassie and I went for a hot chocolate at the centre's café.

'So, your mum was totally weird there, right?' she said when we'd sat down.

I made a face. 'She was. Not sure why.'

'Really?' Cassie looked at me, her eyes roaming my face.

I winced. I'd not mentioned our life in Edinburgh much, and I'd never told Cassie why we'd moved. But maybe it was time to be honest. If she didn't want to be friends with me afterwards, then perhaps she wasn't the girl I thought she was. I took a deep breath. 'If I tell you something, will you promise not to freak out?'

'Okaaaaaay.'

'And if you don't want to be my friend once I've told you, could you please just be honest and not pretend it's all fine and then ghost me?'

'Jem, what is this?'

'Promise?'

'Yes, I promise.'

'And please don't tell anyone else what I tell you. Well, maybe your mum. But no one at school . . . please.'

'Jem.' Cassie looked straight at me, serious for once. 'You're my BFF. Nothing you can say will change that.'

I thought perhaps she was wrong but I smiled. 'Okay. Well, do you remember Alistair Robertson? The breakfast television presenter?'

'Vaguely,' said Cassie. 'Wasn't he some sort of perv? Did he go to prison?'

I nodded. 'He did. He went to prison for sexual assault and attempted rape.'

'Urgh. What's that got to do with you? He didn't . . .' She grimaced. 'Hurt you?'

'No,' I said quickly. 'No, he didn't. Not in that way.' I took another breath. 'He's my dad.'

Cassie's jaw dropped. 'Shit, Jem,' she said. 'Shit.'

'I know.'

'There was a lot of stuff said about him, and my mum, online when he went to prison. Some of it was accurate. Lots of it wasn't. It was weird. Mum got a lot of the blame even though she didn't have a clue what Dad was doing.'

'That's why she's funny about social media,' Cassie said.

'That's why.'

'Shit,' Cassie said again. 'That's rough.'

'It wasn't nice. It's why we moved. There was a lot of gossip, online and in real life. Mum got death threats. Rape threats. They put our address on Twitter and told people to go round. They took photos of me going to school and posted them online. Mum was scared all the time. So was I. We had to sell our house. And I had to leave my school.' My words were tumbling over each other. I'd never really spoken about all this with anyone except Mum. And I never wanted to worry her by telling her how awful I'd found it all. 'Mum wanted to get away from it all, but not go too far, because my grandparents are in Edinburgh, and my dad's got a brother who's really nice – much nicer than my dad – and I've got cousins and stuff. And we'd lost so much

117

that she didn't want to lose anything else . . .' My voice cracked and I stopped talking.

Cassie got up from her seat and for a horrible moment I thought she was going to walk out and leave me sitting alone at the café table like a lemon. But she didn't. She came round to my side and put her arms round me. 'Mate,' she said. 'Poor you.'

I thought I was going to cry and I didn't want to. 'Don't be nice,' I growled.

'No wonder you're such a freak,' Cassie said cheerfully. 'Shall we get some biscuits to go with our hot chocolate?'

Chapter 18

Tess

I had expected Jem to be chatty and enthusiastic after her trip to the museum but she was a bit subdued. The little cat – Hermione – was investigating the kitchen and Jem sat down on the floor so she could stroke her.

'Oh, Jem, it's freezing on those tiles,' I said. 'Bring her into the living room where it's warmer.'

Obediently, Jem scooped up the kitty and we went into the other room. Hermione padded around on her little paws, getting her bearings. Jem and I watched like indulgent parents.

'Did you get her a proper collar?' Jem asked.

'I did, but I think we should wait until we get her checked at the vet, and find out if she's microchipped,' I said.

Jem rolled her eyes. She was being very odd. Prickly. I sat down on the sofa next to where she was on the floor, and played with her ponytail.

'Is everything okay?' I said. 'Did you find out anything else interesting at the museum?'

'Heather's going to try to find out what happened to the Setons,' she said.

119

I tugged her hair gently. 'What's up, Jem?'

She looked up at me, and I thought she might be about to cry.

'I told Cassie,' she said.

'Told her what?'

'About Dad.'

'Oh, Jem.'

She scrambled to her feet, and stood in front of me, bristling with sadness and defiance and teenage indignation.

'She's my friend.'

'I know.' I wanted to reach out to her but she was so nervy I thought she might bolt upstairs if I touched her. So instead I just said: 'What did she say?'

Jem gave a tiny smile. 'She wasn't bothered.'

I relaxed a fraction. 'Good.' I patted the sofa cushion next to me. 'Sit.'

Reluctantly, Jem perched on the edge of the settee and I pulled her into my arms, where she stayed stiffly but didn't wriggle away. 'I know Cassie's your friend and she seems absolutely lovely, but can you trust her not to mention this to anyone else?'

'She promised.'

'A proper promise or one of yours?' I teased, crossing my fingers and waving them in front of her face.

'A proper one.' Jem was too cross with me, with her dad, with the situation, to respond well to teasing. I put my hand down and squeezed her a bit tighter. 'I understand why you told her, sweetheart.'

'I just didn't like having a secret.'

'I know.' I paused. 'I love that you've settled in so well here and that you've made friends. I was just thinking earlier that we made a good decision when we chose to move here.'

'But?'

I sighed. She knew me well, my daughter. 'But we still have to be careful.'

'But—'

I stopped her before she could protest. 'But nothing. Your dad did a very bad thing. Lots of bad things. And people are angry because they felt like they knew him. They trusted him and they liked him.'

'I liked him.'

My heart tightened and I pulled her closer to me again. 'I know, sweetheart. So did I. And some of those people think I should be punished for what he did as well.'

'Because of your tweet.'

I stared at her. I'd never really known how much Jem had taken in what was going on, but I realized in a flash how naive I'd been. She had a laptop and a phone and those girls at her school – Madeleine and her hangers-on – would have made sure she knew the details. Now I nodded. 'Because of my tweet.'

'I reckon some people would have had it in for you anyway,' Jem said astutely. 'Because women are always blamed for what men do.'

'Where did you hear that?'

She shrugged. 'We had an assembly on victim blaming. It's true.'

'I suppose it is.' I kissed her head. 'But whatever the reason, there were a lot of angry people and they wanted to frighten me, and they succeeded. Perhaps they wouldn't ever have gone through with their threats, but I don't want to risk finding out how serious they were.'

Jem nodded. 'I know what they did,' she said. 'I know about them posting our address online and the pictures of me and stuff.'

'God, Jem.' I was appalled that she'd been sitting on all this knowledge and never spoken to me about it. 'God.'

'I'm not scared,' she said. 'Because you're here. And I know you'll look after me.'

'I will.' I felt the weight of that responsibility pressing down on me. 'We just have to be a bit careful about who we tell, Jem.'

'I know.'

'Don't tell anyone else. Not unless we've talked about it first.'

'I'm not going to announce it in form time, if that's what you're worried about.'

'Just, remember that not everyone's as nice as Cassie,' I said, thinking how sad it was that Jem had to learn these lessons when she was still so young.

'I will,' she said. 'I promise.'

She waggled her fingers in front of my face to show they weren't crossed and I laughed, glad that the moment of tension between us had gone. It felt very important to me that Jem and I were united. If we didn't have each other, then I thought everything might just fall apart.

Chapter 19

Alice

1661

I wanted to see Kyla. Even though I'd made the bottle with the little protection charm inside, I was still worried about what she might have been saying to Gregor that awful night at the big house. Emotions had been running high then, and everyone had been sad about Isobel's death and worried for little Christy. Now things had calmed down, I wanted to see her and talk to her and put my mind at rest. After all, we'd been friends since we were wee girls, running around on the beach and collecting shells. We'd laughed and cried together, and teased each other, and told each other our secrets. The way she'd looked at me when Christy started to recover – fearful and wary – was simply because of the illness in the house. That was all.

'I'm away to see Kyla,' I told Ma, a couple of days after I'd made the bottle. I'd thought Kyla would come to me and ask if I fancied a walk to the harbour, or perhaps our paths would have crossed when she was doing chores. But she hadn't appeared, so I thought it was time I ventured to the big house to see if I could find her.

Ma was arranging her bottles, frowning slightly as she counted.

I wondered if she'd realized there were some missing; it was time for me to go before she asked what I'd done with them.

'Where are you going?' she said, not looking at me but still glaring into her cupboard.

'Not sure,' I lied, hoping she would assume I was meeting Kyla at the beach. Ma wouldn't want me going to the big house even though Kyla worked there. It wasn't somewhere you went without being asked.

'Be back by dark.'

I nodded. The nights were longer now, and without actually agreeing to do it, Ma and I had somehow fallen into a routine of being warm inside, with the bar across the door and the animals all shut up, by the time darkness fell. It felt safer that way.

Outside it was freezing. Winter was coming early this year. I pulled my cloak around me and put the hood up over my cold ears, glad of the warm wool. It was a gloomy day and I saw some houses had candles lit already even though it wasn't much past lunchtime.

I walked up the road to the big house. I wasn't completely sure why I'd chosen to go that way – it was much quicker cutting through the fields at the back of our house – but I sort of felt as though I shouldn't sneak up to the house. That seemed wrong somehow, as though I was doing something that I shouldn't be doing.

The big house had a long approach, and as I trudged up I felt as though it was watching me. How silly. The windows were blank, like unseeing eyes. I thought I saw movement in one of the upper floors, but perhaps I was mistaken.

I didn't go to the front door, of course. I knew my place. Instead I went round the side and rang the bell at the kitchen.

The cook answered. She stood there, in her funny white dress, and looked at me without recognition.

'Yes?'

'I'm Alice Seton,' I said, folding my hood back so she could see my face. 'I'm looking for Kyla.'

The woman ran her eyes over me, head to toe and back again. Her lip curled slightly and I wondered if the servants at the big house had been talking about us.

'Is Kyla here?'

She shook her head. 'She's busy.'

'I understand, but could I see her for just a minute? It's important.'

'She's not here.'

'Where is she?'

The cook rolled her eyes. 'She is working.'

'Fine,' I said. 'Please tell her I called.'

The woman had closed the door before I'd even finished speaking. But as she'd told me Kyla was too busy to see me, I'd seen her gaze shift to the barn at the opposite side of the yard. Kyla must be in there, I thought. No doubt she'd been sent to collect some milk, or eggs, or something else. The cook had obviously been worried she would emerge just when I was standing there and make her look silly.

'Thank you,' I called through the kitchen door. 'I'll just go home then.'

There was silence.

Pulling my hood up again, I headed for the barn. I hesitated at the doorway as my eyes adjusted to the gloom inside.

It wasn't a large barn. There was a pen with a cow in it, lying down. She looked at me with large brown eyes as I approached. It was hard to see inside so I stood on one of the rungs of the fence and peered over. No sign of Kyla in the pen. Though she was scared of our goats so I doubted that she'd be comfortable around this beast.

I sighed. Clearly I'd got it wrong and Kyla wasn't here after all. Ah well, I'd try again tomorrow.

I jumped down and turned to go, but as I did, I saw a bucket made from a half barrel, full of milk next to the pen. I touched my hand to the liquid. It was warm – so obviously hadn't been there long. Kyla had been told to come and collect the milk then, just as I'd suspected. But where was she?

'Kyla?' I said quietly, feeling a bit nervous suddenly though I didn't know why. I picked up the milk. 'Kyla? It's Alice. I've got the milk for you.'

A sudden movement at the end of the barn caught my eye. I walked forward a few steps to where there were some hay bales stacked and there was Kyla.

She was lying back on the hay, her skirt rucked up around her waist, her eyes closed, cheeks flushed, and an expression of pure ecstasy on her face. And on top of her, his torso bare and Kyla's hands gripping his broad back as he thrust into her, was Lachlan Murdoch.

'Ohhh,' I said aloud. Kyla opened her eyes, and gave me a defiant glance and then she pulled Lachlan's chest down on top of her, writhing underneath him as though she was putting on a show. Which, in a way, she was.

I had no idea why I stood there, hand gripping the pail of milk, but I couldn't move – couldn't tear my eyes away from the sight of my oldest and dearest friend and the man I thought I loved.

Lachlan gave a shuddering moan and collapsed on top of Kyla, laughing into her neck. She kissed him and then, over his shoulder, looked at me again. This time she gasped as though she'd not seen me before. But I knew she had.

'Oh my goodness, Alice,' she said, scrambling out from underneath Lachlan's large frame. She pulled her skirt down over her legs, faking modesty now while Lachlan sat up, slowly and languidly, pulling on his shirt.

I glowered at Kyla. 'The cook will be waiting for your milk,' I said. I gestured angrily with the bucket and some of the liquid sloshed out and spilled onto the floor.

Immediately a rank, sour smell rose up, catching in my throat and making me gag. Kyla stood up.

'What have you done?' she said.

Hurt, I stared at her. 'What have I done? You knew how I felt . . .' I looked at Lachlan but somehow he didn't seem so handsome now. His face was gaunter than I remembered, more rat-like, and his shoulders didn't look so wide and strong. His mouth had a mean thinness and his eyes were narrow. 'Never mind,' I said. 'It doesn't matter.'

The smell of the milk was stronger, hanging heavily in the air and coating my nostrils. I tried not to breathe in too deeply.

'What have you done?' Kyla said again. She looked frightened. Her eyes wide and fearful. 'Alice . . .'

She looked down at the bucket and I followed her gaze. The milk had separated into a greyish thin liquid with lumps of fatty curds floating on top.

Shocked, I let go of the handle and the pail fell on to the floor of the barn, spilling across the cobbles in lumps. The sickening smell of the sour milk was unbearable. I covered my mouth with my hand and Kyla did the same. Lachlan didn't – after all, he spent all day around the stench of fish – but he looked rattled.

'Did you do this?' he said to me. 'Did you sour the milk?'

'No. Of course I didn't. It was sour already.' I answered quickly but even as I said it, I was wondering if that was true. Had the milk been sour when I picked up the bucket? Surely I'd have smelled it when I bent down to see if it was fresh?

'You soured the milk,' Lachlan said.

Kyla shook her head, joining in. 'You did this.'

'I didn't,' I protested. 'How could I? It's not possible.'

Lachlan picked up his shirt and with his trousers still not fastened properly, he almost ran out of the barn, without looking back. Kyla turned to me, her face twisted with fear. Or was it hatred? I couldn't tell.

'Get away from me,' she hissed.

I backed away on trembling legs. 'Kyla,' I begged. 'I didn't do this. You know me.'

But she didn't listen. 'Get away,' she said. 'Witch.'

127

Chapter 20

Honor

I was shutting up the goats for the evening, stroking their soft heads and enjoying them butting my hips gently in the hope of some treats, when I heard running footsteps coming through the field, making me jump.

'Alice?' I called. My voice sounded shrill. It was getting dark and it was hard to see who was approaching. I wiped my clammy palms on my skirt. 'Alice?' I was jumpy and out of sorts; hearing someone thundering towards me wasn't helping my nerves.

'Ma?' she said and I breathed out in relief. But then she appeared, her hair wild and her face streaked with tears and my heart thumped again.

'What is it, Alice?' I said, grabbing her as she slumped against me, breathing heavily. 'What's happened?'

'Oh, Ma, I'm so sorry. I'm so sorry.' She was gulping for air, sobbing and shaking. I took her shoulders and shook her roughly.

'Alice, you need to stop this,' I said sternly, as though she was a wee girl and I was giving her trouble for being cheeky or stealing some cheese. 'Stop it right now.'

That did it. She stopped sobbing and stared at me with wide eyes. 'I'm sorry,' she whispered this time.

I put my arm around her and gently led her inside. 'Come on now, I'm sure it's not as bad as it sounds,' I soothed.

Alice sat down at the table and put her head in her hands. 'I fear it's worse.'

I opened a cupboard and bent down, reaching right to the back until my fingers found a bottle of whisky. One of my John's friends had brought it when he came to tell me John had drowned. Good for shock, he'd said. I hadn't drunk it then partly because I already knew John had perished – had woken in the night with a dull certainty that I'd never see my love again – and partly because Alice had been turning and spinning in my belly and I hadn't wanted to numb that feeling.

But now I pulled the cork from the bottle and sloshed the liquid into two mugs. I sat next to her, as close as I could, and pushed one of the mugs towards her. 'What happened?'

'I went to find Kyla,' she said. She took a breath. 'She was in one of the barns at the big house. With Lachlan Murdoch.'

'The fisherman?'

Alice bit her lip. 'I liked him,' she whispered. 'Kyla knew that.'

I felt weak with relief. So just a silly quarrel over a man, then. Nothing sinister. I looked down at the whisky in my hands and marvelled at how I'd over-reacted. But I took a sip anyway, wincing as the liquid burned my throat and warmed my stomach.

'You can't trust that girl,' I said, as I'd said a thousand times.

Alice looked straight at me. 'I know,' she said. 'I can't trust her.'

I took another swig of whisky because Alice had never agreed with me before. 'There's more?'

Alice nodded. 'I had picked up a bucket of milk, from the barn. And after I saw them together, there was this awful smell.'

'What kind of smell?'

'Sour milk.'

'The milk was off.'

129

'But it hadn't been before,' Alice said. 'I didn't smell it when I picked it up.' She picked up her cup and drank half of it straight down without flinching. 'I made it sour.'

'No.'

'That's what Kyla said.' She breathed in a long, shuddering breath. 'And then she called me a witch.'

The word rang out in our little house, bouncing off the walls and echoing all around the rooms. Or was that just how it felt? I shook my head vigorously. 'Kyla is hitting out at you because she knows she's done wrong. She betrayed you and she feels guilty and she wants you to feel as bad as she does.'

Alice didn't speak so I carried on. 'The bucket was dirty. That's the only explanation. You know how careful we need to be when we milk the goats. A stupid girl like Kyla wouldn't know that. Her head's empty and she's taking it out on you.'

'But, Christy . . .' Alice began.

'Christy was a very lucky boy,' I said firmly. 'My treatment caught his sickness before it could get a grip on him, like it did his poor mother, God rest her soul.'

'Kyla talked to Gregor.'

'Gregor is a bully and too interested in money, but he's not stupid,' I said, wishing I believed the words I was saying. I picked up Alice's empty mug. 'You have had too much of this whisky and you're speaking nonsense.'

'Do you really think so?' Alice looked desperate for reassurance.

'I know so,' I said. But I was lying.

*

Alice slept in my bed with me that night. She curled up with her head on my chest, though she was as tall as me now. I listened to her breathing and stroked her hair and didn't sleep so much as a wink. How had it come to this? I wondered. How could we be so safe one minute and then in such danger the next, simply because an old man had died and his son didn't think I should have that which my own husband had left me? Because he didn't want a woman getting in the way of his plans to become even richer at the expense of other men's livelihoods. None of it made sense to me.

I felt anger bubbling inside me as Alice slept. How dare that silly Kyla break my girl's heart and then make such dangerous accusations? Despite what I'd said to Alice, I knew Gregor Kincaid would seize on any excuse to get rid of us from our land. I stood in the way of his plans to dredge the harbour because of my concerns for the fishermen. And I stood in the way physically, too. If he took our land, he'd have a clear route from his house to the sea, instead of having to go along the road. I knew he was an ambitious man. He had made a great deal of money during the war, selling weapons to both Cromwell's Army and the Royalists from what I could understand. And I knew he wanted to trade with the colonies. Having my land would make that easier on a practical level and not having to worry about my vote could give him the go ahead for his plans. We were vulnerable and I didn't know what we could do to protect ourselves. My books and my bottles and my tinctures were all enough to be used as evidence of witchcraft if Gregor pointed the finger. The very fact that I could read and write would be seen as suspicious. That we lived alone, with no man to protect us, was enough to raise an eyebrow. That I had my own money could be seen as ungodly. Everything we did could put us in danger.

I slept eventually, fitfully, and with unsettling dreams. When the sky finally began to lighten, I slipped out of bed and got dressed quickly because it was very cold. Then I went downstairs and out into the garden. In one of our sheds were some old wooden boxes. Crates that had once held vegetables or other deliveries, that my John had kept because he liked to use the wood for other things. Some of them were open topped but I knew there were a couple that had lids and that was what I wanted. I found two, right at the back, and pulled them out. They were of similar sizes, solid wood with tightly fitting tops. Perfect.

Back in the house, I filled one box with all my bottles, only keeping a few of the most common tinctures out in case anyone needed anything. Then I wrapped all my books in the oilcloth, just as I'd done when the house flooded, and put them into the other box.

Creeping up the stairs, I peeked round the door to check Alice was still sleeping. I didn't want her to see what I was doing and worry. But she was still dead to the world – that whisky had done the trick.

Back outside, I took a shovel and dug a hole, not far from the back door of the cottage. Into it I placed the box containing my books, and then the box with the bottles, and covered them both with earth. The sound of the soil hitting the wooden lid reminded me of my John's funeral and I felt a deep sadness. One of Alice's cats was sitting beside the hole, watching me with her green eyes as I filled it in. As I replaced the last bits of soil, she got up and came over to me rubbing her soft body against my ankles. I knew she just wanted food, but it was still a comfort. I bent down and rubbed her ears and she purred loudly. It suddenly struck me that even having all these cats about the place could look suspicious. I'd heard tales of women being regarded as witches because they kept one pet, let alone all the animals that lived around our house. But there was nothing I could do about that. Alice loved the cats and I would never make her get rid of them.

A loud knock at the front door made me jump. I leaned the shovel against the wall of the cottage, and went inside to see who was visiting.

It was Davey Kincaid, one hand against the doorframe, his hat in the other. I looked at him in horror. Why was he here? Was he spying for his brother? Trying to find something that could incriminate us?

He straightened up when I opened the door and looked at

my alarmed face with worry. 'I thought you might be pleased to see me,' he said. 'But obviously not. I'm sorry to startle you.'

I closed my eyes briefly, trying to collect myself. 'I wasn't expecting a guest so early in the morning,' I said.

Davey hit his forehead with the heel of his hand. 'I am an early riser and I always forget that not everyone is the same.'

I laughed, despite my shock at his arrival. 'It's fine,' I said. 'I was awake and busy anyway.' I stood back from the door. 'Please come in out of the cold air.'

He followed me inside and immediately he looked at the cupboard where my books and bottles had been.

'What?' I said, seeing his quizzical glance.

He made no comment and I was glad. It was better unsaid.

'I thought you might like to come for a walk on the beach with me.' He twisted his hat in his hands, as he'd done before. I thought perhaps he did it when he was nervous or unsure and I quite liked it.

'A walk?'

Davey ducked his head, looking uncertain. 'I enjoyed speaking to you the other day,' he said. 'I would like to talk to you some more.'

I felt an odd sensation, familiar but long forgotten, as he smiled at me. 'What do you say?'

I knew I should say no, but instead I nodded. 'That would be nice.'

I went to fetch my cloak and put it on and my boots. Davey went outside to wait for me.

'Ma?' Alice stood at the top of the stairs.

'I'm going for a walk.'

'With Davey Kincaid?'

I didn't know she'd seen him. 'Yes.'

'His brother hates you,' Alice said. 'He hates us. Do not be fooled by Davey's good looks and kind nature.'

'He's not like his brother.'

133

'Isn't he?' Alice narrowed his eyes. 'How do you know?'

I didn't know. I just had a feeling. So I shrugged. 'The goats need feeding,' I said.

Outside the cold air took my breath away, and the wind was sharp on my cheeks. But it was good to be out in the bracing sea breeze.

The waves were grey today, reflecting the gloomy sky as they crashed onto the wet sand. We walked along, away from the harbour. I thought it might be awkward but it wasn't. Davey was chatty and interesting, telling me how well Christy was recovering, and how his mother was causing problems, trying to run the household from her sickbed.

I told him about Alice's cats and how we were over-run but she refused to turn any stray away.

'She is kind-hearted,' he said. 'Like you.'

'I'm not always kind.'

He looked at me with a serious expression in his eyes. 'I believe you are.'

'My John was the best man I ever knew,' I said, tearing my gaze away from him and looking out at the fishing boats coming into harbour after a night's work. 'He would never put himself before others. Always helped anyone who needed it. He made me a better person and I try to be like him.' I paused. 'I have a skill that can help people and I try to use it as much as I can, but now I fear I should stop, at least for a while, in case it puts Alice and me in danger.' I frowned. 'So you see, I'm not as kind-hearted as you think I am.'

We had reached a point where we could go no further on the sand because there were rocky cliffs tumbling down to the sea. Davey stopped walking and turned to me. 'That's why I wanted to see you today, to warn you,' he said.

I felt cold fear dripping down my back. 'Warn me?'

'My brother is not a nice man, but Isobel always smoothed his rough edges. Now she is dead and he is grieving, and . . .' He paused. 'He blames you.'

I nodded. 'I know.'

'He is looking for any way he can get you and Alice to leave town. I'm trying to keep him in check, but I know him, Honor. He is single-minded and he is ruthless.' He took both of my hands in his. 'Just be careful, please.'

'How can I be careful?' I snapped. 'He is choosing to focus his sadness on me, because I am the only thing standing in the way of his ambition. Not because I have done wrong.'

Davey didn't let go of my hands, despite my cross tone, and I was pleased. 'I know,' he said. 'I just meant to say, please don't give him anything he can use against you. You saving Christy's life has already rankled him. And I've heard him talking about how strange it was that Christy lived while Isobel died.'

I let go of his hands. 'And what do you say?'

Davey blinked at me. 'What?'

'What do you say, when he's dripping poison about my daughter and me? Do you tell him he's wrong?'

The waves crashed at the foot of the cliff and sprayed my face with salt. I turned away but kept my eyes fixed on Davey.

'I . . .' he began.

'You don't speak up in our defence?'

Davey sighed. 'It's complicated.'

But I didn't want to hear it. 'Your brother is a bully, Davey Kincaid, but you are a coward and I believe that is worse.'

I turned to go, not wanting to spend any more time with this man, but he took my hand and stopped me.

'I am in Gregor's debt,' he said.

I lifted my chin and looked at him. 'How so?'

'When we were both young men, after the war, he was well regarded by Cromwell's men.' He gave a small smile. 'And, indeed, by those planning uprisings.'

I shrugged. 'The only cause Gregor is committed to is himself.'

'You're right,' Davey said. 'But that aside, he worked hard and made a great deal of money by being neither one nor the other.'

'This has nothing to do with your cowardly behaviour.'

'But it does,' Davey said. He pushed his hat up his forehead slightly. 'Because while he was working, I was playing.' He looked out over the grey sea, where a single boat bounced across the waves. 'It was a strange time,' he said. 'Soldiers everywhere, uncertainty, whispers.'

'You were in the Army?'

He shook his head. 'I did a bit of this and a bit of that. And mostly I gambled. Late nights playing cards with soldiers. Chasing each loss by playing another game.'

'You were married then?'

'I was. But I would go for weeks without going home to Marion.'

'And Christy?'

'He was so small then, and not as interesting as card games.'

He turned to look straight at me. 'I'm not proud of myself, Honor. I wasn't the same man then.'

'How does Gregor fit in to this?'

'He helped Marion. Checked in on her. She was living with her parents then. Her father was in the Army and he liked Gregor.' He smiled that little sad smile again. 'Me, not so much.'

'I don't blame him.'

'When Marion died, her father was going to take Christy to England. Send him to school. Gregor dragged me out of a card game one night. He literally took me by the collar and pulled me from the table. He paid my debts – and I owed some bad people, Honor. People I never want to see again. Gregor forced me to see what I was about to lose. He said Christy was a Kincaid and that I couldn't let him go.'

'And you listened?'

Davey shrugged. 'Eventually. It wasn't easy. But I stopped gambling and I brought Christy home. Because of Gregor.'

'How much did you owe?'

'Enough to keep me in Gregor's debt for a long, long time.'

'And that's why you won't stand up to him?'

'If it was just me,' Davey said. 'If I only had to think of myself, then I would. But I fear he could cast me out of the house and send me away, and keep Christy as his heir.' His voice cracked. 'I couldn't bear to lose my son.'

I reached out and touched his fingers momentarily. 'I understand.'

'Just . . . don't give him anything else to use against you, please.'

'I think it's already too late for that.'

Chapter 21

Tess

Present day

'I've got an idea,' I said to Jem at the weekend.

She was sitting at the kitchen table wearing a unicorn onesie and staring blearily into a bowl of cereal.

'Is it to go back to bed?'

I laughed. 'No, and if you're tired you should have gone to bed earlier instead of staying up watching Netflix. You knew you had a rehearsal today.'

She rolled her eyes at me. 'What's the idea then?'

'It's October now, right?'

'Riiiight.'

'And this is the witch's cottage, right?'

'Get to the point, Mum.'

'I think we should decorate the house for Halloween.'

'Already?'

'Why not? It'll be fun.' And, I couldn't help thinking, if you can't beat 'em, join 'em. I hoped that the writing on our fence had been a silly prank and if so, I wanted to show whoever had done it, that I was in on the joke. That we loved the fact our cottage had once been a home for witches, and we were going to make the most of it. I pushed away the fear that the graffiti had been aimed at me. No one knew who we were. No one cared. That was all in the past, and I wanted to think about the future.

'When you say decorate . . .'

'I mean, let's go all out,' I said. I'd not been sleeping very well so I'd had lots of time to think about it. 'We can go to that big cash and carry place and get loads of stuff. They've got fake gravestones and skeletons and all sorts. We can do spiders' webs on the windows, and prop a broomstick up at the front door.'

'We could make a cauldron,' said Jem looking more awake finally. 'And each evening when it's getting dark we could put some tea lights inside so it glows.'

'Nice.'

Jem was grinning. 'Cassie says everyone makes a real effort at Halloween here. She said some of the houses have themes like *Stranger Things* or *Nightmare on Elm Street*. And there's a big Halloween party at school too.'

'Sounds fun.'

'Can we go and get the stuff this afternoon?' Jem said eagerly. 'After my rehearsal?'

'If you like.'

'Amazing.' She stood up and put her bowl on the side, next to the dishwasher. I glared at her.

'Sorry,' she sang. She opened the dishwasher and shoved the bowl inside before shutting it with her unicorn-clad bum. 'I promise I'll remember next time.'

But as she sashayed away, she made sure I saw her fingers, crossed behind her back. I laughed as she disappeared up the stairs, practising her witchy cackle as she went. Jem had been given the part of one of the three witches in *Macbeth*, as well as various other roles including being a soldier covered in foliage marching from Burnham Wood to Dunsinane. I was pleased she was involved in the play, but I had to admit, hearing her rehearsing her screech in her bedroom didn't help calm my nerves, which were still frazzled after discovering the graffiti.

Once Jem had headed off to school, where the rehearsal was taking place even though it was Saturday, I was at a bit of a loose end. It was cold outside, but sunny, so I thought I might go for a walk along the beach. 'Blow away the cobwebs,' I said out loud, mimicking Jem's cackle. God, I was losing my marbles. Perhaps Eva was right and I did need more of a social life. I wasn't sure how you were meant to make friends as a grown-up. I didn't really see much of other Haven staff during the week, because we were all shut in our own little rooms, seeing our own clients. And we were always so busy that there wasn't time to chat. In fact, the only person I saw regularly at the Haven was Mandy, who'd made it clear she wasn't keen on making small talk with me at work, let alone inviting me to join her social circle. I didn't have a baby group to go to, or school gates to chat at. Maybe I needed a hobby. I should definitely find out if there was a running club. Or yoga classes perhaps. That could be something to do.

I wrapped up, with my scarf round my neck, and wandered off towards the sea. The beach was just a stone's throw from our house, so I was there in no time. It wasn't busy today. There were just a few dog walkers standing in a group chatting while their mutts ran in and out of the waves, and a couple of hardy parents with little ones, huddled in their coats and watching their children digging in the sand.

I walked all the way along, as far as I could go to where there was a crop of rocks. I'd heard there had once been cliffs there that had tumbled into the sea. Now there was just a rocky barrier that stopped me going further. It was nice there, with the smell of the salty air in my nostrils. My cheeks were rosy with the wind and I was warm despite the cold weather. The birds overhead swooped and swirled on the thermals and out at sea I could see a huge oil tanker slowly making its way north. I liked it here. I liked living by the beach.

I turned back and walked along the way I'd come, considering taking off my shoes and socks and dipping my toes in the water. But then I thought about how cold it was and changed my mind.

As I reached the stairs back up to the street a shout made me look around. And there, coming along the street from the direction of our house, was Rory.

'Thought it was you,' he said as he reached me. 'Been for a walk?'

'Making the most of living by the sea,' I said.

'Clears the head, doesn't it?' He nodded vigorously. 'I like to get out every day.'

He was wearing jogging bottoms and a fleece with a padded gilet over the top. He looked sporty and full of health.

'Have you been running?' I said, wondering if he was in a running club. But he shook his head.

'I just like to walk. I find I see more when I'm walking. I like watching the birds and the boats and the colours in the sea.'

I was amused and impressed. He didn't seem the poetic type. 'It's easy to miss things when you see them every day, isn't it?' I said. 'I used to work in an office that had the most wonderful view of Edinburgh Castle, but I kept the blind shut most of the time.' I frowned now, wondering why I'd done that.

'Well, it was good to see you,' Rory said.

I thought about going back to my empty house, and on a whim I said: 'I was going to grab a coffee. Fancy joining me?'

Rory tilted his head and looked at me. 'I don't drink coffee.'

My cheeks flamed with humiliation. 'Not to worry,' I said awkwardly. 'I'll head off then . . .'

'But I'll come for a cup of tea,' Rory added quickly. 'That would be nice.'

I was relieved and pleased. 'I like the café beside the sea-life centre,' I said. 'Shall we go there?'

'"Then lead on, Macduff",' he said.

'Jem's doing *Macbeth* at school,' I said as we walked away from the beach.

'I was rubbish at Shakespeare.' Rory gave me a little wonky smile. 'I was rubbish at most things at school.'

'Except woodwork, presumably,' I pointed out and he laughed. 'Except that.'

I got the drinks and we sat down and chatted about the town mostly. I told him about our plans to decorate the house for Halloween and he told me more about the houses that went all out for the festivities.

'One year, one of the houses down the far end did a *Jaws* theme. It honestly had a shark sticking out of its roof,' he said, with a chuckle. 'And another one just had a silhouette of a woman in a rocking chair in the window, like *Psycho*.'

'How creative,' I said. 'We were planning on classic Halloween stuff. Gravestones and witches and ghosts.'

'Sounds perfect.'

'Actually I should go,' I said, checking the time on my phone. 'Jem will be home from rehearsal soon. Thanks for this though. It was nice to get out. I don't know many people here yet.'

'Maybe we could do it again sometime?'

I stood up and pulled on my coat, wondering if he meant as a date or just as friends. Urgh, this was awkward. 'I'm, erm . . .' I said. *Nice one, Tess.* 'I mean, I've not really dated anyone since my divorce. I'm not sure I'm ready for anything . . .'

'Oh, gosh, me neither,' Rory said, standing up too. 'I'm busy with work and happy as I am. I just enjoyed your company and thought we could hang out again sometime.'

He looked straight at me, and I felt a stirring of something deep inside. 'I had a nice time,' I said. 'It would be good to do it again.'

Rory leaned forward and kissed me on the cheek. It was strange, I thought, being so physically close to a man again. But I liked it.

'You've got my number,' he said. 'Give me a call.'

'I will.'

*

142

I wandered home feeling quite pleased with myself. I'd made a friend, I thought. Well done me.

But my thoughts trailed off as I reached our house and saw something outside.

'What's that?' I said out loud. I tutted. Had Jem started the decorating without me?

A little pissed off that she couldn't have just waited and wondering where she'd got the decorations from, I hurried over to the cottage and stopped with a gasp at the front gate.

Hanging from the front porch was a life-size model of a witch – complete with pointy hat and black and purple striped tights. Around her neck was a noose and she dangled in a grimly realistic fashion, toes scraping the ground as she swayed in the wind.

'Urgh,' I said aloud. 'Too much, Jem.'

Feeling a bit silly, I edged round the horrible creature and opened the front door. 'Jem!' I shouted. There was no reply. I put my bag down and went into the living room. 'Jem?'

Back in the hall, I called up the stairs, but the house was quiet. 'Weird,' I muttered. I went back outside and stared at the hanging witch. Somehow she looked even creepier now. I shuddered.

'You couldn't wait?' Jem appeared behind me on the path.

I turned, revealing the witch in all her glory. 'What's this?'

Jem made a face. 'Urgh, Mum. That's awful.'

'You didn't do this?'

'No.' She hitched her bag up her shoulder. 'Didn't you?'

'No. Of course not. It's horrible.'

'So if you didn't put it up, and I didn't put it up, who did?'

I felt sick. Was this another message after the graffiti? Someone had called me a witch in horrible red paint, and now they were showing what happened to witches? My hands were sweaty and I wiped them on my jeans, trying to keep calm. 'Maybe it's a prank,' I said, staring at the macabre model.

Jem grinned. 'OMG I bet it's like a thing.'

'What kind of thing?' My voice sounded quivery to my own ears and I hoped Jem hadn't noticed.

'Like because this is the witch's cottage, all the goths and weirdos come here round Halloween and do creepy stuff.'

I breathed out in relief. That actually made perfect sense.

'Remember there's that tiny witch memorial near Edinburgh Castle?' Jem said. 'Heather at the museum told me that people leave wee offerings there for the women who died. Maybe this is similar.' She looked up at the swinging witch. 'A slightly gruesome tribute.'

I felt dizzy with relief. Of course! Of course this wasn't personal. 'I think you might be on to something there, Jemima,' I said. 'Though I'd rather they'd have left some thistles or something. What kind of weirdo would think this was appropriate?'

She shrugged. 'There's loads of kids like that at school,' she said, examining the witch's legs in her stripy tights. 'They like hang out in the graveyard and listen to the worst music.'

'Do you think they would be offended if we took her down?' I said laughing. I felt a bit hysterical now I could believe that this wasn't another death threat. 'I can't have her swinging in front of our door until Halloween – it's weeks away.'

'We can move her,' Jem said. 'Make her part of our decorations. We can have a witch theme.'

'Good idea. Shall we head out to the shop then? Get some more bits?'

Even though Jem's theory had reassured me, I suddenly wanted to be away from this swaying mannequin.

'Let's go,' Jem said. 'I've got some really good ideas.'

Chapter 22

Tess

'Have you seen my scarf?' I asked Mandy. 'I think I must have dropped it when I came into the office this morning.'

'Your stripy one?' she said. 'No, I haven't.'

I sighed. I loved that scarf. I hoped I'd just forgotten to pick it up from the coat hook that morning. 'It must be at home,' I said, frowning because hadn't I been wearing it on the way to the centre that morning? Or was that last week? I couldn't remember now.

'I hope it turns up,' Mandy said. 'Are you all right locking up? I need to dash off.'

'Course.' I waved her off and went back to my office for another look. But even though I checked in all the drawers, and in my filing cabinet, and down the sleeves of my coat, my scarf was nowhere to be found. Now I thought about it, I was sure I'd been wearing it that morning, because hadn't Mandy mentioned it when I came in? That had definitely been this morning because I remembered her saying it was very cheerful for a gloomy morning – it had been chucking it down with rain and, in fact, still was – and I'd thought she was being uncharacteristically chatty. So where had it got to? Perhaps one of my clients had accidentally picked it up.

Feeling glum, I put on my coat and my hat because it was very cold outside and trudged towards home. I'd promised Jem that we would finally decorate the house for Halloween that evening. We'd been putting it off because of the weather but October was already almost a week old, lots of houses around us had their decorations up and we thought we would just have to do it, whatever the weather.

I wasn't feeling it really. I felt like my life had been taken over by witches. Jem's project, and Hermione the cat – who was a sweet little thing but, even so, decidedly witchy – Jem's school play and of course our unexpected guest. We'd pulled down the witch from the porch and sat her on the little cast-iron bench that the former owners had put in the front garden.

I crossed the road outside the centre and walked along the road through soggy fallen leaves. It wasn't late – just past 5 p.m. – but it was quiet. Everyone was at home, staying out of the cold, drizzly evening. Goodness, I was feeling sorry for myself and I had no reason to feel so glum, not really. This evening would cheer me up, I thought. We were going to put up the decorations, then watch *Hocus Pocus* for the millionth time.

My phone rang and I pulled it out of my bag, hoping it wasn't Jem telling me she'd been held up with another rehearsal or had decided to go round to Cassie's instead. But to my surprise it was Rory's name on the screen.

'Hello,' I said.

'Hi,' he said. 'How are you?'

'Bit grumpy actually,' I said.

'Me too.' Rory sounded quite pleased. 'It's so miserable and grey.'

'I can't believe how dark it is already,' I agreed. 'I've only just finished work but it feels much later.'

'Are you home already?'

'Almost. Just walking past the church.'

'Ah.' He sounded disappointed. 'I was going to ask if you fancied a drink. I was supposed to be meeting a friend in Edinburgh but he's not well.'

'I see, I'm your second choice, am I?'

Rory chuckled down the phone. I liked the sound. 'Not at all.'

'I'm really sorry, I've promised Jem we'll do our Halloween decorations this evening.'

'Well I definitely can't get in the way of that,' Rory said. 'Enjoy yourself and we'll catch up later.'

I hung up just as I reached the front door. Jem was inside taking off her coat.

'You're back late,' I said.

'I had to stay behind to look for my tie.'

'Oh you've not lost another one? Did you find it?'

'Nah, but I bet bloody Rosie Richards picked it up after games. She's so dozy. I'll get it back off her tomorrow.'

'You've got a spare in your wardrobe,' I said. 'Ready for the decorations?'

'Definitely.'

Jem and I had a lovely evening, decorating the house, eating the sweets I'd bought for guisers and trick or treaters, laughing and making each other jump. We positioned the witch – Winnie, Jem called her – next to the cauldron Jem had made from cardboard covered in silver foil. We hung black nets over the windows, and then we carved pumpkins with the silhouettes of witches and put them outside with candles flickering. It looked amazing and Jem was thrilled.

'I'm taking some pics to send to Cassie,' she said. 'She can put them on her Instagram.'

'Just the house, no selfies,' I warned. Jem rolled her eyes but she obeyed. She was a good girl. I snapped my own photo and sent it to Rory.

Sorry I couldn't do a drink, but we spent our time wisely.

He texted back immediately.

It looks awesome! Can't wait to see it IRL.

147

'Who's that?' Jem asked when my phone beeped. For some reason I felt a bit odd about telling the truth, but equally unwilling to lie, I said: 'Rory. You know, the guy who mended your window?'

Jem gave me a sharp look. 'Why are you texting him?'

'I bumped into him the other day and we had a coffee together. Just as friends,' I added quickly, seeing her face cloud over.

She shrugged. 'It's fine, Mum,' she said. She grinned. 'I saw him at school today actually. Think it was him anyway. He was doing something to the cupboards in the science lab.'

'That sounds like something he'd do. He's definitely kept busy doing jobs all over the place.'

'I don't mind, you know,' Jem said, dangling a jelly worm into her mouth.

'Don't mind what?'

'If you want to go out with him. He's kind of hot for an old man. Like Harrison Ford.'

'Jem,' I said, embarrassed but laughing despite myself.

'I just think you could do with some fun.'

'I think you're right,' I agreed. 'But I'll stick to making friends for now.'

*

I felt much less gloomy the next day. Jem skipped off to school wearing her spare tie and full of chatter about the play and all the other dozy things Rosie Richards had done.

Meanwhile, I had the day off. Rory and I had messaged already that morning. He said he was busy working just outside town, and asked what I was up to.

Shopping for Eva, I typed as I rooted around for another scarf in the back of my wardrobe.

He replied with a little emoji with a halo.

Ah, there was my other scarf. I yanked it free from where it had wound itself round one of my running trainers. It wasn't as nice as the one my sister had made but it was better than having a cold neck.

Believe me, I'm no angel, I wrote, adding a winking emoji. Was that flirting? Was I flirting? This was all new to me. When Alistair and I had got together, mobile phones were still enormous and text messages had to be typed by pressing each number on the keypad about five times. Any winking we'd done was in person.

I'd like to see your devilish side, he shot back.

I read the message, feeling my cheeks flush. What did I say to that? I just sent back a devil emoji.

My phone beeped again almost straightaway.

I enjoyed our coffee, fancy dinner one evening? When are you free?

My stomach turned over with nerves. He had definitely said he only wanted to be friends, hadn't he? Mind you, Jem was right. He was 'hot'. God, I was so out of practice with this sort of thing. I had nothing on any evening, but I didn't want to be too keen.

How about next Friday?

That gave me just over a week to prepare.

Perfect, Rory replied immediately.

I sent back a thumbs-up. Then I noticed the time on my phone, and rushed downstairs to get Eva's shopping before she headed off to play bridge with her friends.

It was dark again when I came home, weary after a day on my feet. I'd met Cassie and Jem on the way so there were three of us heading back to the cottage, Cassie leading the way because her legs were the longest.

As we got close to home, she stopped suddenly and shrieked. I jumped and Jem let out a little gasp, but Cassie was jumping up and down in excitement.

'Oh my god, I love it,' she exclaimed. 'You guys have done such an amazing job. Jem, you should totally be an interior designer or something. You're so creative.' She bounced up the path to the tiny front garden, Jem and I following.

149

'I love the skeletons,' Cassie called over her shoulder. 'That's so funny.'

I looked at Jem and she looked at me and we both hurried up the path to where two fake – I assumed – skeletons sat propped up against the house. Their bony faces glowed in the light from the streetlamps. Wrapped around the neck of one of the skeletons was my missing scarf, while the other wore Jem's school tie.

'Oh my god,' I breathed. All the hairs on the back of my neck were standing up and for a horrible second I thought I was going to throw up. 'Breathe, Tess,' I told myself. 'Breathe.'

This wasn't a goth paying tribute to a long-dead witch. This wasn't a Halloween prank or a ghoulish game. There was absolutely no doubt in my mind that this was personal.

'Mum?' said Jem in a small voice.

I felt for her hand. 'It's just a joke,' I said. I tried to sound reassuring and calm, though I felt anything but. 'Let's go inside.'

I bustled the girls into the house and upstairs to do their homework. Then I went to the window and looked out. The skeletons sat there, staring out to the street with their hollow eyes.

'Just a joke,' I said again. But I didn't believe it for one minute.

Chapter 23

Jem

Mum was properly freaked out by the skeletons, I could tell. It was a bit weird, that one was wearing her scarf and the other had my tie on. I guess dozy Rosie hadn't picked it up by accident, after all. I couldn't actually work out how it had got from school to my front garden and that was making me feel unsettled.

Cassie, though, thought it was all a laugh. 'I'd love to know who put them there.'

'Do you think it was someone from school?' I said, thinking about my tie.

'Nah.' She shook her head and her curls bounced. 'Has to be some of those emo students from the college or somewhere. Some freak who's obsessed with witches.'

I grinned. 'We're obsessed with witches.'

I flopped onto my bed, where Hermione was curled up, fast asleep. I rubbed her head and she opened one eye and looked at me, unimpressed, then shut it again. 'Did you see who left the skeletons, Hermione?' She snored on and I lay down next to her so her face was close to mine. I'd been surprised by how much I loved this little cat. I'd never really been one for pets – I'd mostly ignored the cat Mum and Dad had had when I was younger and I'd not been bothered when she got ill and had to be put to sleep. Hermione, though, was so sweet-natured and followed me round like a shadow. Plus, even though I didn't know for sure it had been her mews I'd heard on the night of the storm, I felt like she'd saved me.

'Show me your costume for the disco,' Cassie said.

The big Halloween disco was still two weeks away but it was all anyone was talking about. I was feeling a bit weird about it. I knew Callum from the play was going and I liked him a lot. I sort of wanted to see him there but then I worried that I'd do something wrong or say something silly or he'd turn out not to like me in that way after all, even though Cassie swore he did.

'I hate my outfit,' Cassie said, lying back on my bed dramatically.

'No you don't, yours is perfect.' I'd seen Cassie's dress – made by her mum – and it was amazing. Long and sleek and black. 'It makes you look about 21. So sophisticated.'

'Really?'

'Really.'

She smiled. 'Show me yours.'

I jumped off the bed and pulled my costume from my wardrobe. Mine was less Morticia Adams and more Harley Quinn. Not nearly as elegant as Cassie's but much more me. It had a short, sticky-out black skirt with lots of bright pink netting underneath, and the top was black satin. I had black and pink stripey tights to wear with it – not unlike the ones worn by the witch mannequin that had turned up in our garden – and my big black boots.

'Ohmygod, I love it,' Cassie squealed. 'That's amazing. Did your mum make it?'

'Nope,' I said proudly. 'I did. Eva helped me. Remember her? Our next-door neighbour. She's got a sewing machine.'

'Awesome.'

'Callum's going as Harry Potter,' I said, giggling because Callum had messy hair and glasses and looked just like the famous wizard.

'Well, of course he is.' Cassie gave me a sly look. 'Maybe he'll whisper love spells into your ears.'

'Cass,' I groaned, feeling my cheeks flame.

She picked up my pillow from my bed and cuddled it. 'Ohh, Jemima, Expecto patronum,' she said in a soppy voice. 'Oh, Callum, expelliarmus.'

Giggling, I snatched the pillow from her and whacked her. 'I heard Max is going as Donald Trump.'

'No!' Cassie looked horrified. She'd had a crush on Max for ages and she was convinced the disco was going to be the night he finally noticed her.

'Yes!' I was triumphant. 'But I've heard he's a great kisser. The best. Bigly.'

Cassie collapsed in laughter and I flopped over onto my stomach, thinking about the disco. I was really looking forward to it, and not just because Callum was going – though that was quite a big part of it. I just really wanted to have some fun and hang out with Cassie and the other girls from school. Even dozy Rosie. And this weekend, I'd been invited round to Cassie's on Saturday. It was her mum's birthday and her family were having a party. Cassie had been allowed to invite loads of people from school and it sounded really fun.

We did some French homework – Cassie was much better at languages than I was so she helped me with mine – and then Mum shouted upstairs that it was time to take Cassie home.

'It's still early,' I moaned but Mum had her determined face on and I didn't want to argue.

We dropped Cassie off, and then Mum went to the McDonald's drive-through on the way home, which never happened and made me suspicious.

Sure enough, when we were back home and I was stuffing fries in my mouth and picking the gherkins out of my cheeseburger, she dropped the bombshell.

'I spoke to Granny when you were upstairs with Cassie,' she

said. 'She's free this weekend so I thought we'd go and stay. We can leave first thing in the morning.'

I stopped chewing and stared at her. 'Not this weekend,' I said. I took a slurp of milkshake, thinking she'd got confused. 'I've got a rehearsal tomorrow and then Cassie's party. Do you mean next weekend?'

Mum scrunched up the paper from my burger and put it in the bin, not looking at me as she said: 'No, I thought we'd go tomorrow.'

I threw down my burger in disgust, not hungry anymore. 'Mum, no!'

'Granny would love to see you.'

'Is this about the skeletons? Why are you so freaked out?'

'It's not about the skeletons,' Mum said, but she was clearly lying because she still wouldn't look me in the eye.

'Ohmygod, what is wrong with you?' I said. 'It was a joke, obviously.'

'Not a very funny joke.'

'So? It doesn't mean we have to run away to Granny's. What about Hermione?'

'We can ask Eva to feed her.'

I threw my head back in despair, thinking of all the time I wouldn't spend with Callum and the fun I'd miss at Cassie's party. 'I'm needed at rehearsals.'

'I'm sure they'll be fine without you, Jem. We can play *Macbeth* with Granny.'

'Jesus,' I said. 'I'm not 5 years old, Mum.'

'We'll have fun. We can watch some old films and snuggle up on the sofa.'

'I don't want to snuggle anywhere,' I shouted. 'I want to go to Cassie's party and have fun like a normal teenager.'

'Jem . . .' Mum began but I was so angry I didn't let her speak.

'You were always on at me to make friends and now I have and you're not letting me see them,' I wailed. 'You are literally ruining my life, Mum.'

154

'Don't be so dramatic, Jemima,' she snapped. 'It's just a party.'

I stood up so I was facing her, feeling rage burning in my belly. 'I hate you,' I hissed.

'Well, I love you,' Mum said calmly, which only made me feel even more annoyed. 'And that's why I have to protect you.'

I let out a frustrated groan. 'This is totally unfair. I know Dad is a shit, and I know you're sad, but it's not my fault.' I was shouting but I couldn't help it. 'I don't see why I should pay for his mistakes. He's the bloody grown-up.'

Mum looked like she was going to cry but it didn't stop me being cross. 'Jem, I was wrong to try to shield you from what was happening when we were in Edinburgh. You're old enough to understand and I want to be honest with you now . . .' Her voice quivered and I suddenly wanted to cry, too. 'I'm just worried someone's worked out who we are.'

She looked so worn down and sad, that my anger suddenly vanished like a puff of smoke. 'I don't hate you,' I whispered. 'I had my fingers crossed behind my back when I said that.'

'I know.'

'I just really want to go to the party.'

'I know that too.'

She walked out of the kitchen area and into the living room where she sat down heavily on the sofa. Seeing an opportunity, Hermione jumped up onto her lap and Mum gave a small smile.

'She's such a sweet cat,' she said. I left my cold burger and fries on the worktop and went into the living room too.

'I really don't think this is personal,' I said. 'Everyone knows our house is the witch's cottage and there are loads of weirdos who do this sort of thing. Cassie reckons it's one of the emo students from the college.'

'Does she?' Mum looked thoughtful.

'She's going to have a trawl through social media and see if she can find any pictures, or work out who's done it some other way.'

'She's a good girl.'

I grinned. 'She's the best.'

Mum rested her head on the back of the sofa, stroking Hermione, who looked very pleased with herself. 'You're probably right,' she said. 'It's just a prank.'

'So we don't need to run away?'

'I suppose not.' Mum sighed. 'I'll ring Granny and tell her. Maybe we can go next weekend.'

'Thank you, thank you, thank you,' I said. I threw myself onto the sofa and hugged her hard. 'Know what? I bet these weird pranks happen here every year. It's probably a thing.'

'You could be right there, Jem.' Mum looked thoughtful. 'Eva didn't seem to know anything but she did say the people who lived here before us kept themselves to themselves. I've got their contact details, maybe I'll email them just to check.'

'Do it now,' I urged. 'Put your mind at rest.'

The doorbell rang loudly, before Mum could reply. 'I'll get it,' I said.

To my surprise, it was Rory.

'Hello, Jem,' he said. He held up a pile of pizza boxes. 'I was just passing and thought I'd see if you guys were hungry.' In his other hand he held a bottle of wine. 'Or thirsty.'

I grinned at him, thinking about my discarded McDonald's on the kitchen counter. 'Muuuum!' I shouted. 'It's Rory. He's got pizza.'

'Come in,' Mum called. When Rory and I went into the living room, she was standing up and she'd taken her hair out of its ponytail and fluffed it up with her fingers. *Nice work, Mum*, I thought. She definitely seemed to have a crush on him, which was sort of weird. I wondered if she worried about what to say to him, like I worried about what to say to Callum.

'I thought I'd wander past to see the decorations,' Rory said. 'But then I thought, why not pop in. I hope I'm not intruding.'

'Not at all,' Mum said. 'Especially not when you bring wine and food.' She smiled at him, and I thought how nice it was to see her looking happy. 'I'll get some glasses and plates.'

'You really don't mind?'

I eyed Rory carefully. He seemed to like Mum, too. I wasn't sure how I felt about that, but I knew I liked pizza and I'd hardly eaten any of my burger, so I smiled at him. 'Sit down,' I said. 'Watch out for Hermione.'

Mum put some plates on the coffee table and two wine glasses, and handed me a can of Diet Coke. 'Jem and I were just talking about the additions to our decorations,' she said as if it was no big deal.

'Additions?'

'The skeletons – did you notice them?'

'I did,' Rory said. 'Nice touch. I liked the school tie round the neck. Bored to death in a lesson, were you?' He grinned at me and I smiled back less than enthusiastically at his lame joke.

'The other one's wearing Mum's scarf,' I told him.

'Spooky. Whose idea was that?'

'That's just the thing,' Mum said, concentrating on laying out the plates. 'We don't know.'

'You didn't put them there?'

'Nope. Mum was totally freaked out.'

'You were?'

Mum looked a bit sheepish. 'Not totally,' she said, backtracking now Rory was there.

Rory made a face. 'It's a bit weird,' he said. 'Seems personal, because they're wearing your stuff. Like a threat.'

I felt a shiver down my spine. 'It's just a joke,' I said firmly. 'Actually, I need my tie for school. I got paint on my other one in art. I might go and get it.'

I dashed off outside and pulled Mum's scarf and my tie from round the necks of the skeletons. I couldn't really imagine why we hadn't done that in the first place. Suddenly they looked less scary and more like silly Halloween decorations and I felt a bit foolish for being spooked.

Inside, Rory was leaning forward to open the boxes of pizza. 'I just got margheritas because I thought everyone likes those.'

'We do,' said Mum, gazing at Rory in a way that made me want to be sick.

'I'm not that hungry actually,' I lied, feeling my mouth water as the smell of the melted cheese hit my nostrils. 'I might give it a miss.'

Mum gave me a sharp look, which I ignored.

'Halloween's nearly over anyway,' I said, fake cheerfully. 'Everything will be back to normal in a couple of weeks.'

Chapter 24

Tess

I hated rowing with Jem, and I was a little ashamed that she'd seen me so rattled, but as I sat and ate pizza with Rory, I felt the stress easing. Jem didn't seem to be upset – not now I'd seen how silly it was to run away. Though she didn't eat any pizza. Mind you, we'd been to McDonald's so perhaps she genuinely was full up. It was also quite nice to spend time with Rory. I was glad he'd popped round on the off-chance.

It was still early when Jem said she was knackered and was off to bed. I gave her a suspicious glance, because she's always been a night owl. Was she making herself scarce so I could spend some time with Rory? But she gazed back at me with innocent eyes so perhaps she was just tired. She trotted off upstairs with little Hermione following behind.

'She loves that cat,' Rory said, watching them go.

'She does.' I waved the bottle of wine at him. 'Top-up?'

'Thank you.'

I poured us both more wine. 'I'm glad you came over,' I said. 'It's been quite a week and it's nice to chill out and not have to cook.'

'I just thought it was ages until we were having dinner and it might be nice to catch up.' He raised his glass to me and grinned as he held my gaze for a long moment. Again I felt that fluttering sensation in my stomach and I pulled my eyes away from his, hiding my embarrassment by swigging my own glass.

'Jem's a great girl,' Rory said.

'We have our moments,' I said. 'It's not all plain sailing.'

'I wish . . .' he began then stopped talking.

'You wish?'

He looked thoughtful and more than a little sad. 'It's funny how things work out, isn't it?'

I wasn't sure what he was trying to say. He'd never actually told me if he had children, but I had assumed he didn't. Now I wondered. Perhaps he'd not seen his children since his divorce. Or he'd had a child who'd died? Or experienced some other heartbreak. I didn't want to push him to talk about something he wasn't comfortable with, so instead I just smiled.

'Life's what happens when you're making other plans,' I said.

Was it my imagination, or had Rory moved a little closer to me along the sofa? I was very aware of him, suddenly. I could feel the warmth of him.

'I've had a lovely evening,' he said.

'Me too.' I swallowed. With surprise, I realized I wanted him to kiss me, but I was also scared that he might try. I felt the tension crackle between us like static electricity, and then Rory shifted along a tiny bit and stood up.

'I should go,' he said.

I felt relieved and disappointed at the same time.

'Busy weekend?'

'I've got a job tomorrow morning, and I'm meeting some friends in Edinburgh to watch the football later on.' He put on his coat. 'What about you?'

'Jem's got rehearsal tomorrow morning and then her friend Cassie is having a family party in the evening. I've been invited too, actually.'

'Sounds wild,' he said, drily.

I chuckled. 'I've not been very sociable since we've lived here and I wasn't sure at first if I would go. But Eva says I should live a little.' I didn't want to say that I was also nervous about being alone in the house.

Rory nodded. 'What's the worst that can happen?'

I shuddered inwardly, thinking of the skeleton wearing my scarf. But outwardly I just smiled. 'Shall we catch up after the weekend?'

'I'd like that.' He leaned towards me and kissed me on the lips. A chaste kiss, but it still had an immediate effect on me, sending blood rushing to my cheeks and making my stomach flip with desire.

I watched him saunter off down the road, then I went over to where Jem had dropped her tie and my scarf when she took them off the skeletons. I picked them up and threw them both in the washing machine. I felt vaguely foolish but I didn't know where they'd been.

I was still wide awake so I got my laptop from my work bag and opened it up, scrolling through my emails to find the correspondence I'd had with the previous owners of our cottage. Then I wrote a quick note, telling them how well we'd settled in, mentioning the storm and what had happened to Jem's window and the conservatory next door. Finally I added: *We discovered our house is known locally as the witch's cottage – much to Jem's delight. And we wondered if that's the reason we keep coming home to find Halloween decorations outside.* I described the witch and the skeletons and then finished by saying: *Jem thought that perhaps this is a thing that happens every year, so we wondered if you'd had the same when you lived here?*

Satisfied that my daughter was right and that this was a regular happening, I shut my computer and went to bed.

*

I was going to Cassie's family party mostly because Jem was full of chatter about Callum, and a boy called Max that Cassie liked – though Jem didn't think much of him – and her friends from the play, and lots of them, including Callum, were going to be at the party.

'Muuum,' Jem warned, as we got ready to leave. 'Please don't embarrass me.'

She was wearing skinny jeans and a drapey black T-shirt and Converse. I wasn't sure she was dressed up enough for a party, but I didn't say anything because I was just glad she wasn't wearing an outfit like the ones I'd seen some of the girls from her school wearing.

I didn't really have any party clothes either. I'd sold most of my fancy outfits when Al and I had divorced. They'd paid for quite a lot of the furniture for the cottage, in fact. So I just put on black trousers and a thin black jumper, blow-dried my hair properly for once and pulled it into a low bun, and accidentally put on quite a lot of make-up.

'Have a I been a bit heavy-handed with the eyeliner?' I asked Jem.

'You look like you're doing a tango on *Strictly*,' she said, looking at me with a critical eye.

I shrugged. 'That wasn't what I intended, but I'll go with it.'

Jem giggled. 'Are you ready?'

'I'll just get my bag, and the bottle of wine.'

I felt stupidly nervous on the way to the party, like I was the teenager and Jem was the grown-up. Cassie's mum – Andrea – opened the door and I gave her the little gift bag I'd brought, containing some fancy soap and hand cream and a birthday card and she beamed at me.

'Thank you so much,' she said. 'It's lovely to meet you, finally. Cassie's told me lots about you. Come on in.'

Jem had said that Cassie's house was welcoming and I saw what she meant. Within seconds, I was in the warm lounge, glass of wine in my hand, being introduced to Andrea's friends.

'I know you,' one woman said, smiling broadly. 'You work at the Haven.'

'Just a couple of days a week.'

'You helped my sister get her deposit back from her landlord.'

I frowned, thinking. 'Claire?' I said. 'Lived in a flat over a shop?'

'That's the one. She was in a bad way,' the woman explained to the other people nearby. 'She'd been suffering from depression and she wanted to move, but she couldn't until she got her money back. I'm not sure what would have happened if she hadn't.'

Ah, now I remembered the details. 'Is she on the mend now, Claire?'

'Getting there,' the woman said. She stuck her hand out for me to shake. 'I'm Sally, by the way. My daughter's at school with Cassie and your Jem.'

'Pleased to meet you,' I said.

An older man touched my arm gently and I turned.

'Sorry to interrupt,' he said politely. 'I wanted to say hello. I'm Sidney. I believe we are mutual friends of Eva Greenbaum.'

I was delighted. 'She lives next door to me,' I said. 'She's wonderful.'

'She thinks the same of you. She's told me how helpful you are and that she values your company.'

'She's a good friend,' I said. 'How do you know Eva?'

'We play bridge,' he said. Then he leaned towards me and added: 'That's what we tell people we're doing, but actually we drink whisky and put the world to rights.'

'That sounds like a lot of fun,' I said. 'And very Eva.'

I was just thinking how nice everyone was and how silly I'd been to worry, when in walked Mandy from the Haven. She gave me a small, thin smile, and I saw her huddled in the corner with Andrea, both of them talking intently and not looking up.

What were they saying? I wondered. Were they talking about me? And then I caught myself being so very self-involved that even Alistair – who was the king of narcissism – would have been

163

impressed. I was being ridiculous. Of course they weren't talking about me. Why on earth would they be?

I got myself another glass of wine, and found Callum's parents, who were both teachers and so nice that I stopped worrying that Callum could be the wrong boy for Jem and started hoping they'd get married one day.

We played some silly games, and ate the delicious party food Andrea had prepared. I drank more than I'd intended – not too much but just enough that my worries about the skeletons seemed to disappear. Cassie's brother Drew put on an excellent playlist that he'd prepared and everyone danced – Sidney even tried to teach me how to tango, though he didn't have much luck because I was definitely not *Strictly* material, despite my eyeliner. It was just a lovely evening, even if Andrea didn't have much to say to me after Mandy had arrived – Mandy barely acknowledged me at all.

Jem and I walked home, much later than I'd expected, arm in arm.

'So you think Callum's nice?' she said. 'Really?'

'He seems lovely.' Callum had struck me as being very sweet, quite geeky and clearly smitten with Jem, which endeared him to me. 'Is he your boyfriend now?'

'No,' she said, burying her face in my shoulder as we walked. 'But I'd quite like him to be.'

I tousled her hair. 'Just spend some time together and see what happens.'

'Is that what you're doing with Rory?'

'Jem!'

'I meant it when I said I don't mind, you know,' she said. She stopped walking and looked at me, her pretty face serious. 'I do understand that Dad isn't a good person, but you are, Mum.'

'Oh, Jem.' She was so young to know about the awful things grown-ups did to each other. 'He let us both down.'

She bit her lip. 'I'm just saying, you should be happy, Mum.'

I gave her a hug. 'How did you end up so mature and thoughtful?' I said.

'Absolutely no idea,' Jem said cheerfully. 'My parents are both total screw-ups.'

We started walking again, both laughing. And then, as we approached the cottage, the glow from the streetlights shining on the white walls, my heart lurched with fear.

'What the . . .'

'Mum? What is that?' Jem sounded very young as we both stared at the outside of our home. Its white frontage was splattered in dark red blood – across the windows, all over the brickwork and window frames. It looked like a crime scene.

I felt dizzy and put a hand on the front gate to steady myself. 'I don't know.' I looked at Jem. 'Stay here.'

She stood on the pavement, while I went up the path to the house. As the breeze blew I got a whiff of paint and, flooded with relief, I put my hand out to touch one of the splatters. 'It's paint,' I said over my shoulder. 'Red paint.' Just like the graffiti, I thought to myself.

'Shit, I thought it was blood,' Jem said, coming to stand next to me. We both stared up at the cottage wall. 'What a mess, though, Mum.'

'It's a disaster.' I felt close to tears as I looked at the devastation, the paint starkly contrasting with the bright white walls. 'Why would anyone do this to us?'

Chapter 25

Honor

1661

Little Annie Marsh was sick. Her mother, Ebba, arrived at my back door, looking pale and worried. She looked round to check no one could see her before she came inside.

'I know Christy Kincaid got better because you helped him,' she said. 'Can you help my Annie?'

'How long has she been ill?'

'Since last night. It happened so fast.' Ebba bit her lip. 'I know that's not good.'

'Fever?'

'Yes.'

'Is she awake?'

'Not really.'

I remembered what Davey had said about being careful not to give Gregor anything he could use against us, and feeling villainous, I shook my head. 'I don't think it's a good idea.'

'Please.' Ebba's eyes filled with tears. 'She's my only child. Please help her.'

My heart twisted. How could I be so selfish? I could help this little girl and there was me worrying about my own safety. I felt ashamed.

'I can give you a remedy for her – the one that helped Christy.'

'Would you?' Ebba said.

Fortunately, I hadn't hidden all my tinctures. I quickly made a small bottle with the same ingredients I'd given Christy – catnip and some thistle extract. I hoped it would do the trick.

'You need to cover your mouth when you're helping her,' I told Ebba as I worked. 'Give her clean blankets – do you have clean blankets?'

She shook her head, looking embarrassed, and I opened one of our cupboards and gave her some of mine. 'Here. Burn the ones she's been sleeping on. And the clothes she was wearing. You need to get rid of the sickness before it finds someone else.'

Ebba shifted uncomfortably and I understood. 'Stay there,' I said. I ran upstairs to the trunk in Alice's room and found an old dress she had grown out of, and a clean nightgown. I gave them to Ebba too. 'Alice is too big for these now,' I said. 'But they'll be fine for Annie. Here's the remedy. Drop it into her mouth as soon as you get home. Air the room if you can. Keep the door open, even if it's cold.'

'And this will help her?' Ebba gripped the bottle tightly.

'I can't promise,' I said. 'It depends how deeply the sickness has taken. But we will pray that we've acted fast enough.'

Ebba took my hand. 'I have no money,' she said.

'I don't want anything.'

She looked relieved. 'One day I will repay your kindness.' She slipped out of the back door and vanished into the garden. It made me feel uneasy that people weren't happy to be seen at my cottage anymore.

And yet, people still came to ask for help. Not long after Ebba had gone, I was called to assist a woman who was giving birth. I didn't know her – she lived right at the edge of town – but her husband, a harried-looking fellow with bright orange hair and a kindly manner, said one of the fishermen he worked with had told him to call for me. It was a long and difficult birth – I felt awful for the poor mother who was exhausted – but eventually their baby boy arrived, hale and hearty with a shock of orange hair like his da.

'You did this,' the father said, his face etched with tiredness and shock, but happy too. He pushed a coin into my hand. 'This is all I can afford.'

For a second, I thought about taking his money. After all, who knew what was going to happen and I had a strong sense I should be getting ready for harder times. But then I shook my head. 'Keep it,' I said. 'Buy something for the bairn.'

The father looked over to where his wife was sleeping, her baby in her arms, and smiled at me. 'You are a good woman.'

I nodded my thanks, and hoped others felt the same.

This time it was me who slunk out of a house. I liked this family with their bright hair and sweet manners and I didn't want to bring trouble to their door. Was this what we had to do now? Sneak around like thieves in the night? I didn't even know where Alice was. She was being so strange lately, and I wondered what she was up to.

Once I was on to the main street, I could relax a bit. There were enough people around that no one paid any mind to me. I pulled the hood of my cloak up and walked fast, hoping I would blend into the crowds. And it seemed to work, because no one looked at me twice.

But then I saw the minister. He was standing beside the gate to the kirk, waiting for someone, perhaps? But as I approached, I caught his eye and I saw terror grow on his face. He was scared of me, I realized with a mixture of amusement and concern. He really was frightened. He clutched his chest with his hand and turned on his heel to hurry back inside the church. I walked on by, trying not to think about what he must have heard about me to make him react in such a way.

I let myself into the cottage. 'Alice?' I called. Where was she? I didn't like to think of her being out around town when people were being so odd. 'Alice?'

'She's not here.'

I whipped round to see Alice's awful friend Kyla standing in the middle of the room.

'What are you doing here?'

She shrugged. 'I came to see Alice.'

'I don't know where she is, so you can leave.' I narrowed my eyes at her. 'She won't want to see you. She told me what you did with Lachlan Murdoch.'

'Did she tell you what she did when she saw us?' Kyla asked. Her expression was defiant.

'There was nothing to tell.'

'But things have got worse.'

'What things?' What was Kyla saying? All this talking in riddles and sneaking around was making me want to scream with frustration.

'All the milk is sour. No matter which cow is milked, we cannot drink it.'

'That's nothing to do with Alice.'

'Isn't it?' Kyla looked angry but there was something else in her eyes – fear? 'The milk is sour and the chickens aren't laying.'

'Your cows must have a disease,' I said bluntly. 'I've seen it in our goats. I do not know about the chickens, but it's unlikely it's caused by anything my daughter has done.'

'I saw it with my own eyes,' Kyla said. 'I saw the milk sour.'

'Did you?' I said calmly. 'Or is that just what you thought you saw?' I stood aside and opened the door. 'Please leave.'

'The other servants are blaming me,' Kyla said in a hurry. 'They are blaming me for everything. They say I am impure and immoral.'

I gave her the ghost of a smile. 'They're not wrong.'

But Kyla lurched forward and held on to my arms desperately. 'It's worse than it sounds.'

169

'How can it be worse?' I snorted.

'Cook said it's my actions that have caused the animals to sicken. She even said it was my fault that Isobel died because I brought evil into the house.'

'That's silly talk.'

'I know that,' Kyla wailed. 'But I am frightened because she took her stupid, unproven worries to the minister.'

I thought about the minister's face when I walked past and I went cold. 'What have you done, Kyla?'

'Nothing.'

I shook her hands off my arms and gripped her shoulders instead. 'What have you done?'

'The minister came to the big house and he said unless I told him who was really to blame, then he'd have to tell the laird it was my doing.'

'And who did you tell him was at fault?'

Kyla didn't answer, and full of rage I yanked her towards me. 'Who did you blame?'

'Alice,' she whispered. 'I told him it was Alice.'

I let go of her arms and she stumbled away from me.

'You stupid, selfish, dangerous girl,' I hissed.

'It was Alice,' she said, back to defiance again. 'I saw what she did when Christy lived, and when the milk soured. She is the one who's dangerous, not me. And I need her to lift whatever enchantment she's cast.'

'There are no enchantments,' I said in despair. 'Alice is just a girl, same as you, and Christy got better because I helped him. This is not her fault.'

'If Alice can lift the charm, and the cows and chickens go back to normal, then no one will point any fingers anymore.'

I shook my head, feeling completely at a loss. 'Kyla, she can't lift the charm because there is no charm.'

Kyla stared at me sullenly. 'The minister will tell the laird what Alice did,' she said. 'What you both did.'

I leaned against the wall, all fight gone. 'The laird hates me.'

She shrugged. 'Won't make any difference then, will it?'

I pushed open the door and shoved her out onto the path. 'Get out,' I said. 'You are not welcome here.'

'Ma?' Alice was hurrying along the street towards us. 'Kyla? What's this?' She and Kyla stood facing each other, like cats about to fight. 'What's going on?'

'I came to ask you to lift the enchantment,' Kyla said.

Alice looked blank. 'I don't know what you mean.'

'Kyla, you need to leave,' I said.

Alice gave her former friend a look of such disgust that less defiant girls than Kyla would have withered. I felt a flicker of pride in my daughter, whose heart had been broken but who wasn't hiding away or moping. She pushed past Kyla, but as she did, Kyla grabbed her arm and something fell from Alice's cloak.

Quick as a flash, Kyla pounced on it and held it up to the light in triumph. 'This is it,' she sang, peering at it carefully and nodding. 'This is the proof.'

Alice made to grab whatever Kyla held but Kyla darted out of reach and finally I saw what she had taken. It was a small bottle – one of mine, I assumed. But that proved nothing, surely? It was just a tincture.

Kyla held the little glass phial in her thumb and forefinger and thrust it in my face. 'See?' she said. And at last, with a sinking heart, I did see. It wasn't a tincture. Inside the glass as it caught the light, I could see that it wasn't liquid inside. It was a witch bottle. Silly, superstitious nonsense as far as I was concerned and not the sort of thing I'd ever been interested in doing. But it was – indeed – the evidence Kyla had been seeking that would stop any suspicion falling on her and instead point the finger directly at me and my daughter.

'Give Alice the bottle,' I said, trying to stay calm.

Kyla, playing like a fool, showed me her empty hands. 'I don't have it.'

'It's in your cloak,' Alice said. Her voice was dull.

'I don't know what you're talking about,' Kyla was crowing. I wanted to grab her by the scruff of her neck and shake her until the bottle fell out of her cloak, but I knew that wouldn't help.

I snorted and without looking at Alice, I turned and walked inside the cottage. That then, was that.

I sat down at the table and put my head in my hands, not even looking up when I heard Alice sit down opposite me. What on earth were we going to do now?

Chapter 26

Tess

Present day

Because it was Sunday the next day we had to leave the splatters all over our lovely whitewashed cottage walls for a whole day and two whole nights before we had any chance of getting it painted over. I called lots of house painters the day after the party when my nerves were still jangling and I was strung out with lack of sleep and the after-effects of all the wine I'd drunk, but none of them would come out at a weekend without me paying over the odds, which was fair enough.

With a bit of help from Jem – who was as nervy as I was – I managed to wipe the splatters off the windows using turpentine, soapy water and a lot of elbow grease. As we scrubbed, I kept going over and over it in my head. Who could have done this?

Mandy had been late to the party, my wild mind told me. Perhaps she'd been late after splattering paint all over our house because she didn't like me? But no. That was a ridiculous idea. It was just kids. Bored, Halloween-obsessed kids.

On Monday I told young Mr Langdown a fib and said that I

had to wait in for someone to come and fix our boiler so I had to work from home. I felt odd about telling the truth, as though saying out loud that someone had covered our house in blood-like red paint would make it seem worse than it was. Though I wasn't completely sure how it could be any worse. Luckily, he was very sweet.

'Well isn't it marvellous we have all this technology now that allows us to work virtually,' he said, sounding much older than his forty-odd years. I agreed that it was very useful and promised to make up any hours I missed that evening.

Jem, who'd been so positive and upbeat about the other happenings, barely spoke the day after the party, and was still quiet and pale at breakfast on Monday morning.

'I don't think I should go to school,' she said.

'Sweetheart, you have to go to school.'

'I don't want to leave you on your own.'

My heart twisted with love for her. 'I'll be fine,' I assured her. 'Honestly. This is just a silly Halloween prank, that's all.' My words sounded hollow and unconvincing and Jem looked up at me, her eyes huge in her pale, worried face.

'Do you honestly think it was just a prank?' she said, pushing away her half-eaten cereal.

'Honestly,' I lied. But I couldn't meet her gaze and I knew she didn't believe me.

Jem glanced over to the back door, where she had filled Hermione's bowl with food. 'Where's the cat?'

'I've not seen her this morning. She'll be back when she's hungry. You know what she's like – she's an explorer.'

Jem gave me a tiny smile. 'She is.'

I was on my laptop, trying to find a local company that might be able to come and repaint the front of the house with short notice. Now I picked up my phone and dialled the number of the first company on the search results that I hadn't yet called. 'Have you got everything you need for school?'

She nodded as there was a ring on the doorbell. 'I'll get it,' she said.

I heard her chatting as I left a message for yet another painter, and ended the call. Then Jem reappeared in the kitchen with Callum in tow.

'I told Cal what happened,' she said, looking pleased. 'So he came round because he thought we could walk to school together, in case I was spooked.'

'That's so kind of you, Callum,' I said, touched that while Jem was looking out for me, someone had her back, too.

'It's worse than I thought it would be,' he admitted. 'I didn't realize it would be all over the house.'

'Oh yes, all over,' I said grimly. 'We got most of it off the windows but I'm trying to find someone who can paint over it. It's proving a bit tricky.'

'My uncle's a builder,' Callum said. 'He probably knows someone. Want me to ask him if he can call in a favour?'

I could have kissed him, but I thought Jem wouldn't be impressed. So instead I just grinned at him. 'Yes please.'

Callum sent a message to his uncle explaining what had happened and giving him my number, while Jem found her school shoes and put them on. 'Can you message me when Hermione's home?'

'Of course.' I kissed her goodbye and watched her and Callum walk down the road together. They weren't holding hands, but they were close together. It was sweet. He was a nice lad.

Once she was away, I sprang into action, taking down all our Halloween decorations and shoving them in bin bags in the front garden. They were all splattered with paint anyway, and I had to admit I was completely over Halloween. I thought I might just take everything to the tip because I wanted rid of it all.

My phone rang as I was wrestling the skeletons into the bags and I paused to answer, hoping it was a painter. But it was just a spam call asking if I'd been in a road accident. I blocked the number and carried on, though by the time I'd got four bin bags full of spookiness, I'd had several more similar calls which frustrated me so much I considered turning my phone off. But then I might miss a call from a painter. Grrr. I felt like screaming. Or crying. Or running away. Or all three, actually.

With all the decorations down, I stood back and looked at the pile in the garden. My car was only small, but I thought it would all fit if I put the back seats down. The only trouble was, my car was parked right down the end of the road. Parking was at a premium in town and the last time I'd been out in the car, I'd not been able to get a space nearby. There was a spot outside now, though, so I thought I'd go and get the car and bring it closer, rather than lugging all the decorations along the street. My phone rang as I went and I answered it with an impatient sigh.

'Yes?'

'Hear you're looking for a painter?'

It was Callum's uncle. Embarrassed that I'd assumed it was another spam call, I explained what had happened and I was relieved when he said he could send 'some of his lads' later that day. I even managed not to gasp out loud when he told me roughly how much it would be, despite giving me mate's rates.

Relieved that something was finally going my way, I thanked him and rang off.

But when I reached my car, my heart sank again. Someone had dumped the remains of a kebab on the bonnet. I could see some mushed-up meat and pitta bread, and scattered fries all over the car, and the discarded paper bag they'd been in a little way along the road. But though that was unpleasant, it wasn't the worst of it. Oh no. The worst of it was that the seagulls had been feasting on the abandoned food. Feasting and pooing, all over my car. It was covered in streaks of bird waste, squashed kebab, and lots of little scratches where their claws had marked the paintwork. One large, fat gull stood on top of the roof, a long chip in its beak, staring at me.

'Get off!' I shrieked, waving my arms and the gull rose up on its huge wings, still clutching the fry.

'Shit,' I said. My phone rang again and I shouted: 'Oh sod off!' as an elderly man walked past and looked at me disapprovingly. 'Sorry,' I muttered. And then I burst into tears.

Still sobbing, I jerkily moved the car from one end of the road to outside our house, parking it extremely badly and trying not to look at the crime scene that was the front of the cottage.

As I shifted the rubbish bags from the front garden to the boot of the car, wiping away my tears and sniffing, Eva appeared at her gate.

'*Liebchen*,' she said with concern, coming straight to me and taking me in her arms. She was so petite I towered over her, but I still found her embrace a comfort. 'What's happened?'

'It's out of control,' I wailed, gesturing vaguely at the house and the mess all over my car.

Eva nodded. She turned and went back into her house, without saying a word, and then she re-emerged with her handbag on her arm, wearing her coat and boots. She shut the front door behind her.

'Where are we going?' she said.

I gave a little surprised laugh. 'The tip,' I said. 'And probably the car wash.'

'Right then.'

She got into the passenger seat and sat there like the queen, with her handbag on her lap. I slammed the boot shut and got in too.

'Now,' Eva said. 'Tell me all about it.'

It was easier talking in the car. It was a trick I used with Jem sometimes when there was something awkward I wanted us to talk about; the lack of eye contact made the words less of struggle. But I still wasn't sure where to start.

'I know who you are,' Eva said. 'If that makes it simpler?'

I kept my eyes fixed on the road ahead. 'Who I am?'

'I know you were married to that man. The breakfast presenter.'

'Shit,' I breathed. 'How long have you known?'

'Since you moved in. I recognized you straightaway.'

'I thought I was in disguise,' I said.

'It's not a very good disguise,' Eva pointed out. 'All you've done is cut your hair.'

Despite the horrors of the day, I laughed. 'And changed my name.'

She snorted and I laughed again.

'Do you think everyone knows?' I said. 'If you knew as soon as I arrived?'

'I don't,' Eva said.

'But—'

'I am an old woman with too much time on her hands and a grubby habit of starting each day by reading the *PostOnline*'s sidebar of shame,' Eva said. 'If I was busier and less interested in the entertainment pages, I'd never have paid you any attention. People are generally more worried about their own lives than anyone else's.'

That was reassuring. I sighed. 'We've had a few other things happen,' I admitted. 'It's not just the paint. There was the weird hanging witch outside our front door, and the skeletons wearing my scarf and Jem's tie. And someone graffitied "witch" on our fence, too.'

Eva was quiet for a moment. I glanced at her. She was biting her lip and looking out of the side window, deep in thought.

'I think that people focused their anger on you,' she said eventually. 'They were angry with your husband but they blamed you.'

'They did.' I took a deep breath. 'We had some trouble in Edinburgh. A lot of trouble. Awful stuff on social media and in real life. Threats.'

'And so I think that perhaps you should go to the police,' Eva said gently.

The thought had occurred to me. 'I thought about ringing the family liaison officer who helped us in Edinburgh.' I indicated to turn into the tip. 'But I was worried she might just think it's all a silly practical joke?'

'I doubt that,' said Eva. 'If you ask me, this is beginning to sound personal. And with your history . . .'

'I don't want to panic Jem. Having the police come into our home and go through our belongings was awful. She had nightmares for months. I don't want to trigger anything.'

Eva sighed. 'I can understand that. But I am afraid for you.'

'I'm afraid for me too,' I whispered. 'It's starting to feel like a . . .' I trailed off.

'A witch-hunt,' Eva said.

*

We spent the morning at the tip, and then the car wash, and got home at the same time as the painters arrived.

Eva squeezed my arm. 'I'll leave you to it,' she said. 'But please do as I said.'

I nodded and kissed her cheek as the painters got out of their van and looked up at the cottage.

'Jeez,' the boss said, staring at the mess across the front of the house. It was a sunny day and it looked even worse in the bright light. 'Looks like something out of CSI.'

'I know. It's awful.' My voice wobbled as I spoke and I blinked away more tears.

He gave me a sympathetic smile. 'Bloody kids, eh? Don't you worry. We'll get this sorted.'

'Cup of tea?' I croaked, still trying not to cry.

There was a chorus of 'yes please' as the other men gathered round, shrugging on their overalls. There were three of them, and the boss, and I was reassured that they would do a good – and quick – job. I knew I couldn't live with the horrible splatters all over the house. I would get it sorted and I would worry about the money later. Forking out for the damage to Jem's room, and now this paint job, was going to leave me short. I was hoping the insurance for the storm would come through any day and I still had a credit card for emergencies. I would crunch some numbers and cross my fingers that everything would work out.

I made the tea, noticing with a small flicker of worry that Hermione's food hadn't been touched, then handed it out to the painters, and settled down in the living room with my laptop to catch up on my work.

It took me ages to log in. My computer was running very slowly and I couldn't work out why. I got there eventually though and cracked on, listening to the men's conversation outside and hoping they would finish before it got dark.

The afternoon passed quickly and I was surprised when Jem got home, with Callum behind her.

'They've almost finished,' she said, gesturing to the men outside. 'Looks much better.'

'Thanks to Callum.' I smiled at him. 'Good day?'

Jem shrugged. 'Same as usual. Where's Hermione?'

With a start I realized I'd still not seen her. 'She must be outside somewhere,' I said. 'Maybe hiding from all the activity. Give her a shout.'

'I'd have thought she'd be hungry by now,' Jem said, her brow furrowed.

'Unless she's caught some mice.' Callum grinned.

I was still focusing on my screen. I hit return and groaned as the little disc began to spin. 'Not now,' I begged.

'What's the problem?' Callum said, sitting down next to me.

'Callum's a total computer nerd,' Jem said cheerfully. 'He'll fix it.'

Was there anything this boy couldn't do?

I handed him the laptop. 'It's been so slow all day.'

Callum started typing away, frowning at the screen. I got up and stretched, enjoying the sensation in my back, which was aching after my exertions carrying all the bags to the tip. Jem went out in the garden and I heard her calling for Hermione.

'Here.' Callum held the laptop out to me. 'All done.'

'Really? That was quick.'

'You had loads of spam downloaded from emails. I just deleted it all.'

'I've had lots of annoying phone calls today too,' I said. 'I must have had my details sold on by some dodgy company.'

Callum nodded. 'It's irritating.'

'She's not out there,' Jem said, coming back inside. 'God, it's freezing outside. I hope she's okay.'

'I'll get off then.' Callum stood up, looking a bit awkward. 'See you tomorrow, Jem.'

Jem went with him to the front door, and I heard them saying goodbye.

'Homework,' Jem shouted to me as she thundered up the stairs. 'What's for dinner?'

Christ, I'd not even thought about food. 'Something from the freezer,' I called back, hoping there was something in there. I really didn't want to have to get a takeaway and spend more money I couldn't afford.

My email was pinging madly as all the messages that had been backed up arrived. I clicked on my inbox and found a reply from the McKinleys – the people who'd lived in the cottage before us. I scanned down to the part of Mrs McKinley's email I was most concerned with:

We knew that everyone called our house the witch's cottage, but I can't say we ever had any pranks played on us at Halloween. At least, nothing that stands out. We had trick or treaters, of course, and the little ones coming guising. But nothing unpleasant.

I shut my laptop firmly. It was nice that she'd replied so fast, but knowing they'd never had any trouble didn't make me feel better.

'All done,' one of the painters said, putting his head round the door.

Feeling worn out, I went to admire their handiwork. I had to admit they'd done a good job. There wasn't a hint of red splashes anywhere. I got their payment details and dragged myself back inside to pay them online.

Jem was still buried in her books, and it was almost five o'clock, so before I changed my mind, I found the number for the family liaison officer – Jacqui – and rang her. A man answered the phone.

'Family liaison.'

'Is Jacqui there?' I asked, stumbling a little over the words because I had expected her to pick up the phone.

'She's away on holiday,' he said. 'Florida, the lucky thing. Can I help you?' He sounded nice, with a warm voice. But I couldn't bear to explain everything that had happened before and everything that had been going on recently. So instead I just said I'd call Jacqui when she was back and hung up without even leaving my name.

I felt a bit unsettled, like a safety net I hadn't even been aware of had been taken away. Perhaps a glass of wine would help? I wandered into the kitchen in search of booze and found nothing. I was staring into the bare fridge, hoping a chilled bottle of Sauvignon might appear by magic, when the doorbell rang.

Standing on the step looking slightly awkward, was Andrea – Cassie's mum. She was holding a bottle of wine and when I opened the door she grinned. 'Peace offering,' she said.

Confused, I stood back to let her into the house. 'What on earth for?'

She thrust the bottle at me. 'I think I was a bit funny with you at the party. I wanted to explain.'

'I was actually just hunting for some wine in the kitchen,' I said. 'Fancy sharing this with me?'

Andrea looked relieved as she followed me into the living room. I opened the wine and poured two glasses, then we sat at the table. I wasn't sure what was going on, but there was no denying Andrea had been less chatty after Mandy had arrived – that had been very noticeable. I thought about how easily Eva had recognized me and wondered, with a prickle of unease, if that was why Mandy clearly didn't like me, and why Andrea had been a bit 'off'.

Forcing a smile, I put the glass down in front of my visitor. 'What's up?' I said.

Andrea put her fingers on the stem of the glass but she didn't drink. 'I didn't know you worked at the Haven,' she said, looking down at her hands. 'It took me by surprise when Mandy told me.'

I raised my eyebrows. 'It's not a secret.'

'No, of course not,' Andrea said. 'I just . . .' She sighed. 'My divorce was quite tricky.'

'I hear you,' I said, swigging my own wine. But Andrea shook her head. 'I was an idiot,' she said. 'I did lots of things I'm not proud of, including packing the kids up and taking them to France without telling my ex where we were going.'

'Ah.'

'Believe me, being woken up by a strict gendarme knocking on your door with an arrest warrant isn't fun,' she said.

I gave her a sympathetic smile, thinking how clearly I could imagine that scenario.

'Anyway, that was more than ten years ago,' Andrea went on. 'We've worked it all through and things are civil. But I got a lot of help from the Haven. Financial support, and legal advice, and I still have counselling sometimes. That's how I know Mandy.' She rubbed the back of her neck. 'I was just a bit worried you might hear it all from someone there.'

I was horrified. 'God, no,' I said. 'Never. We never talk about clients like that.'

'I know that really,' Andrea said.

Andrea drank some wine and I reached out and patted her hand, feeling relieved that this was about her and not me. Perhaps Eva had been right that people were too busy with their own shit to worry about mine.

We finished our glasses as I made dinner, and then Andrea had to go home. The rest of the evening passed in a flurry of finishing off my work, and helping Jem with her French homework, and when I finally fell into bed I lay awake for ages worrying about money and wondering if I should ask Mr Langdown for more hours. I could perhaps work one of the weekend days at the Haven instead, or do a couple of evenings. It wouldn't be easy but I could definitely do with the extra cash.

I drifted off in the wee small hours and it felt like about ten minutes later when my alarm woke me. Jem was similarly grumpy when we met downstairs.

'Hermione still isn't here,' she said. 'I don't understand it. She always sleeps on my bed. You need to look for her while I'm at school.'

'I'm working today. I can't take another day off. Mr Langdown is understanding but even he has his limits.'

Jem slumped over her breakfast. 'I just hope she's not got into trouble,' she said darkly.

'She was managing fine by herself before you adopted her,' I pointed out, draining my coffee mug and pouring myself another. It was that sort of day. 'She'll turn up. Come on, eat up. We need to get out of here – I want to catch the early train.'

We both darted around collecting bags and homework books and bottles of water, and then Jem opened the front door and screamed so loudly that my ears rang and my heart nearly leapt out of my mouth.

'Mum!' she shrieked.

On the doorstep, placed neatly in the centre of the mat, was Hermione's little pink collar.

Jem threw herself into my arms. 'Has something happened to her?' she sobbed.

'Not necessarily,' I said. 'This might not even be her collar. Perhaps she managed to get it off somehow – she's not used to them, is she? And someone just came across it and remembered seeing Hermione at our house and returned it.'

184

Jem wiped her eyes, looking very young. 'Do you think so?'

'Hermione is a streetwise, sassy kitten,' I said. 'She'll show up when she wants.'

'What if she doesn't?'

I felt sick, thinking about that possibility. I picked up the collar and put it on the shelf by the front door. 'She'll come back,' I said, far more confidently than I felt. I adopted a fake cheery voice. 'How many things is this now? I think we've definitely had more than three lots of bad luck, haven't we? We're due something good.'

But Jem was staring at the tiny lawn in the front of her house. 'Mum?' she whispered. 'I'm scared.'

The green grass was brown in patches, where someone had obviously poured something – weed-killer, perhaps, or bleach? And the patches spelled, clearly and obviously, the word 'WITCH'.

Chapter 27

Alice

1661

I had made a terrible mistake with the witch bottles, I could see that now. The ones I'd made and hidden in my window frame hadn't worked, and the third one – one I'd made after the incident with the milk and had intended to hide in our fireplace – had made things worse. And now Kyla had it and would no doubt use it against me and Ma. I knew the Kincaids were looking for any chance they had to discredit my mother. Gregor wanted to dredge the harbour and allow bigger ships in, and the way he saw it, my mother was the one standing in his way. I knew that wasn't true, of course. But the men in the town would support Ma as long as she was there, and then switch allegiance at the drop of a hat if it served them well to do so. I knew that. I couldn't even blame them for it.

But add Gregor's dislike of Ma to his grief for his wife and these whispers of witchcraft, and there was an easy way for him to get rid of Ma and get what he wanted.

'I'm sorry,' I said to Ma. She was still sitting at the table with her head in her hands. 'I didn't mean . . .'

Ma looked up, her eyes red-rimmed. 'I know,' she said. She put her hand out to me and I went to her and crouched down next to her. 'I know.'

'What can I do, to make it right?'

She shook her head. 'Nothing.'

'No.' I was firm. 'The Kincaids are bullies and they do not like that you are a burgess with your own money.'

'Just Gregor,' Ma said. 'Not all of the Kincaids.'

I thought she was being blind to Davey's true nature because of his handsome face and broad chest, but I didn't say so. Instead I just took her hands. 'Ma, you can't just let this happen.'

Ma reached out and cupped my face. 'I have lived through many winters,' she said. She sounded as though she wasn't really speaking to me. 'I've seen this many times. These whispers and rumours can die away, or they can take on a life of their own, twisting and turning through the town. We need to see which this will be.'

'If it dies?'

'Then we can carry on with our lives here.'

I was almost afraid to ask. 'And if it doesn't?'

Ma swallowed. 'We should be ready to go.'

'Go where?'

She shrugged. 'North? It is safer in the Highlands.'

'What about the cottage? And the cats?'

'We can find a new cottage, and new cats.'

'I like it here.'

'Alice, it doesn't matter where we are. Our home is you and me, and that's all that matters.'

But I knew she was lying. Ma loved it here too. She loved the sea and the taste of salt on her lips and the sound of the crashing waves. Sometimes I would catch her, eyes fixed on the horizon, staring out across the grey water and I knew she was thinking about my father. He was here, in the calling of the gulls and in the wind that bounced across the shallows, and clouds that

187

gathered in the evening sky. She wouldn't want to leave him. Not unless she had to.

'I don't want to leave,' I said.

Ma shrugged. 'If Gregor is determined to push us away, then he will. Perhaps it's easier just to let him win.'

I had never heard her so defeated. Never. I stared at her in despair.

She kissed my forehead gently and then pushed her chair back from the table and got up, slowly and heavily. My mother wasn't old, by any means, but just now she looked like my grandmother had before she died; worn out and weary of the world.

'I'll go and feed the chickens,' she said.

'I'll come and help. I just need to do something.'

I waited for Ma to go outside, and then I picked up the cat that had somehow found its way onto my lap and kissed her little furry nose. 'I'm going to make this better,' I said.

The cat jumped down from my arms and I headed for the front door, away from the chickens and Ma. I pulled on my cloak, put up the hood and went outside into the chilly air. The clouds were hanging low over the sea, and I thought we were in for some bad weather. The wind was sharp on my cheeks and I could taste the salt, bitter on my tongue. A storm was coming.

With my head bent against the wind, I hurried along the street towards the big house. I was planning to go to the Kincaids and plead our case. If I spoke to them, reminded them that Ma had saved Christy's life, and that of their mother, I was sure they would understand how good she was. How clever she was, and how vital to the whole town her skills were.

But in speaking out for Ma, I was going to have to point the finger at Kyla. She may have been my oldest friend but she'd made it clear she would betray me without so much as a second thought. Whether it was rolling in the hay with the man I had told her I was in love with, or using my own silly superstitions against me, it was obvious she didn't value our years of friendship.

I felt anger and betrayal burning inside me, red and simmering and ready to burst into flames. I was going to take that anger and I was going to use it against Kyla. I was going to show the town, and the Kincaids, that she was the one who had caused the milk to sour and the chickens to stop laying. She was the witch. And if the town's eyes were on Kyla then surely Gregor's campaign against my mother would have to stop?

I knew Ma had spoken sense when she said Gregor wouldn't give up until he won, but still I thought this might buy us some time. Let us come up with another way to fight his plan for the harbour, without fearing for our lives.

I quickened my steps, eager to get to the big house as soon as I could. Kyla had my witch bottle on her. I knew that. I'd been foolish to take it from my room and carry it with me but I felt it gave me comfort. But that was of no consequence now. She had it and that was that. So I was going to tell Gregor and Davey that I'd seen Kyla with a witch bottle, chanting an incantation. And later I might find myself in the church, and tell the minister about my fears. I knew this would be a lowdown and nasty way to defend my mother's honour but I didn't care. I was scared and I was angry and I wanted to make it right.

This time when I approached the big house, I didn't go round to the kitchen door. Instead I walked right up the wide path that led to the front of the impressive building, just as we had on the night the sickness had arrived.

Christy Kincaid was sitting at the top of the steps, leaning against the stone wall. He had a large, leather-bound book on his lap and he was reading it intently. He looked up as I approached.

'Hello,' he said. 'I remember you.'
I smiled to see him there. He was pale and still a little scrawny, but he had colour in his cheeks. 'Hello.'

'Have you come to see Kyla?'

I shook my head. 'Not today. It's your father and your uncle that I wanted.'

Christy made a face. 'They're arguing.' He looked very sad and I felt sorry for him. 'Always arguing. That's why I come outside to read. It's more peaceful.' The sound of raised voices drifted round the side of the house and he rolled his eyes. 'Most of the time.'

'What are you reading?' I was intrigued by the thick book he was holding. It didn't look like something a boy should be interested in.

'Court reports,' said Christy. His eyes shone. 'Every time something happens in a court, someone makes a note of it. They write it all down.'

I thought that sounded dreadfully dull, but my eyes were drawn to the pages Christy was turning. I stepped closer to him so I could see it properly.

'Everything that happens?' I asked.

'Trials, decisions, verdicts . . .' Christy's eyes gleamed. 'Punishments.'

I shivered though I wasn't sure why.

'Do you want to borrow it?' He shut it with a thud and held it out to me. 'I've got another volume.'

I did not want to borrow that huge, dull book but somehow I found myself nodding. 'Yes please,' I said. I took it from him. 'Thank you.'

The voices were louder now; I turned to look.

'They're in the garden,' Christy said with a sigh. 'You can go round.'

He got to his feet, less energetically than a 12-year-old boy would usually, but with enough vigour that I was heartened to see how well he had recovered.

'Thanks for the book,' I said.

'Keep it.' He gave me an odd look. 'It might be useful one day.' And then he slid through the half-opened front door and disappeared inside.

The voices were louder still. I stopped, listening to what they said. It was the Kincaid brothers, arguing, I knew that. But I wasn't sure which one was which.

'You are blinded by your own avarice,' one man was saying. He sounded frustrated.

'And you are blinded by a pretty face,' said the other.

Very quietly, I walked towards the side of the house, keeping close to the thick walls, and peered round. There was a neat garden on that side, with a carefully tended lawn and some flower beds. I thought Ma would like to see those – she could grow all sorts of interesting plants there, because it would catch the morning sun and be sheltered from the wind.

I shook my head, that wasn't important now. Edging forwards a bit more, I looked round properly. There, sitting on a stone bench, was Gregor Kincaid. He was a large man anyway and he looked bigger than normal on the small seat. He had one arm spread along the back of the bench, and his legs were spread wide, so he took up the whole chair, even though it was designed for two people.

His brother, Davey, was pacing up and down in front of him, gesturing with his arms. He too was a big man, tall and broad, but less imposing than the laird. Right now, though, his face was red with anger and his voice was raised. It was no wonder I'd heard them shouting.

'All you care about is money,' he was saying. 'Lining your pockets with gold.'

'Lucky for you that one of us cares about it,' Gregor hissed. 'Because you would have gambled away our fortune. Thrown it down on card tables or pissed it up against the wall each night.'

There was a pause and Davey rubbed his face. He looked . . . what was the word? Anguished, that was it. Anguish was the only way to describe his expression.

'You are a disgrace,' he said softly. 'Imagine what our father would think to see this.'

'Our father is not here.' Gregor sounded amused, which only served to infuriate Davey more, because his face went even redder. 'And if he was, how do you think he would feel about your friendship with Widow Seton?'

191

At the mention of my mother's name, I froze, shrinking back into the shadows at the edge of the house.

Davey kicked a stone, sending it skittering towards me. 'This problem with the harbour is of your making, Gregor,' he said. 'Your greed is responsible and you are the one who needs to sort it out.'

'Oh, I will sort it,' Gregor said. The self-satisfactory tone to his voice made me shudder. 'I am sorting it. Widow Seton will help me.'

My blood ran cold. What could he want with my mother?

Davey was thinking the same. 'What do you want with her?' he said.

'Allegations have been made against her and her daughter, and as the laird it is my responsibility to put them to her.'

'Allegations?' Davey's voice was disbelieving and I felt a bit of hope. Perhaps he was on our side. 'What sort of allegations.'

'A serving girl has told me of disturbing deeds,' Gregor said. He didn't sound disturbed. In fact, he sounded cheerful. It was me who was crouching close to the ground, trying to control my breathing and hoping I wouldn't cry out in fear, because I was too late to help my mother. The men were quiet, Davey had stopped his pacing and was staring at his brother.

'I can't ignore the claims she has made, Davey. If I were to let them go, then I fear we would be the ones to pay the price.'

I gripped the wall to steady myself, concentrating on the feeling of the rough stone beneath my fingers, hoping it would stop my rising panic.

'Gregor . . .'

'Davey, think of Christy, and our mother. We cannot expose them to danger.'

There was silence again. Davey muttered something under his breath and I stayed where I was, my mind whirling as I thought about what options I had, now Kyla had told Gregor about me, the lies she'd told.

192

Wildly I wondered if the things Kyla had said really were untruths. I had put my hand on Christy's head and watched him recover. The milk soured when I was angry. What if the things Kyla was saying were true? I was beginning to doubt myself.

'We need to take action,' Gregor urged his brother.

I knew I had to do the same. But what could I do? Could I run now, to the minister? And hope my own allegations would counter Kyla's? I wasn't sure my trembling legs would carry me.

'What are the claims?' Davey asked. 'How do you know this girl is telling the truth?'

'She has spoken to the minister and given him the evidence.' Gregor paused. I thought he sounded triumphant and that made me even more afraid. 'Evidence she has found of witchcraft.'

My legs gave way beneath me and I slumped on to the cold stony path at the side of the house, shaking like a rabbit who had seen a fox. What could I do now? Kyla had made her allegations and we were in trouble. The foxes were the Kincaid brothers and my mother and I were the rabbits. The hunter and the prey.

'Gregor,' Davey said. 'This is serious. You know what will happen if you call in the witch finder. This isn't a game. You have seen what's been happening all over the lowlands?'

'I know.'

Everyone knew. Not a week went by without hearing news of another town being visited by the witch finder. But he had so far stayed away from our wee corner of the coast.

'Is this serving girl trustworthy?' Davey asked. He still sounded angry and I didn't understand why.

'She is a good, hardworking girl, loyal to God and the king.'

That meant nothing, I thought. People swore loyalty to whatever church, whatever king, whatever laird, they had to, to survive.

'To be within the law, you need to see Widow Seton to put these charges to her, before anything else,' Davey said.

Gregor gave a bark of laughter that made me jump but clearly Davey wasn't joking because his brother gave a snort, got up

193

from the stone seat and brushed down his trousers. 'We shall go together.'

Davey muttered again and this time I thought he was swearing. 'Fine.'

I knew that whatever happened I had to stop them going to my mother. If they didn't give her a chance to answer to the allegations, then they couldn't go any further – at least that was how it was supposed to work. I had to stop them seeing her face to face, so we had more time to make a plan. An escape plan, I realized with a heavy heart. It seemed leaving was the only thing we could do now.

But how could I prevent the Kincaids from going to my mother? If only the storm I'd seen gathering over the sea would arrive. The sky was darkening, and the wind was cold, but would it be enough to stop them? I gazed up at the clouds, wishing the rain would at least arrive.

Gregor and Davey were also looking at the heavens and debating the best way to get to my mother's cottage. Should they walk? Or should they take the carriage?

A clap of thunder overhead made my heart thump heavily. I screwed up my eyes and clenched my fists and wished with all my heart that the storm would be a bad one. Bad enough to stop them leaving home. I felt spots of rain on my forehead and without opening my eyes, I raised my face to the sky. 'Come on, storm,' I thought to myself. Was it my imagination or were the raindrops getting larger?

'Carriage,' Gregor announced. I opened my eyes to see him set off round the building, away from where I was hiding, with Davey following. Their boots splashed through the puddles on the path because the rain was pouring down now.

I scurried round to the front of the house, waiting for them to come out in the carriage, still hoping for the storm to pick up. One of the servants appeared, holding two of the Kincaids' horses by the bridle. The rain really was hammering down now and one of the horses was tossing his head, clearly unhappy about being out in the nasty weather. As Gregor and Davey appeared, both wrapped in their cloaks and wearing hats, there was another enormous clap of thunder, a spark of lightning lit up the trees lining the drive, and the horse – spooked – reared up on to his hind legs, sending the groom sprawling on the ground. With a loud whinny of fear, the horse raced away down the drive towards town. The other horse, also skittish, ran in the opposite direction, leapt over the wall close to where I was hiding, and was gone into the woods behind the house. I watched in disbelief as the groom scrambled to his feet and Davey and Gregor both shouted instructions that were whipped away from their mouths by the howling wind. The groom raced down the drive, after one of the escaping horses, while Davey pulled his hat down over his ears and headed into the woods. Gregor rolled his eyes and disappeared into the warm, dry house.

I waited for a while, feeling my cloak get heavy with rainwater, and my hair soak my back, and then – satisfied the Kincaids wouldn't be going anywhere for a while – I set off for home.

Chapter 28

Jem

Present day

As soon as I saw the letters on the grass outside our front door, I said I didn't want to go to school. I was scared and I didn't want Mum to be alone. But Mum made me go. She drove me herself and waited outside the gates until she saw me walk in. She said she was going to work because she was afraid if she took many more days off, the Langdowns would sack her. I thought the Langdowns were very lucky to have her, and they knew it, but I didn't argue. And I felt better knowing she was going to work rather than being on her own at home. Nothing could happen to her there. Could it?

I'd messaged Cassie to tell her I was running late, so as soon as I got into the classroom, she was there waiting for me.

'What's happened?' she said, obviously clocking my face, which I couldn't seem to twist into a smile, no matter how hard I tried. 'What's wrong?'

But I was so late that I couldn't tell her then, because it was already time to go to French. 'I'll see you at lunch,' I said. 'On our bench.'

I found it hard to concentrate in lessons. My thoughts kept coming back to those brown letters on our little front lawn, and Hermione's pink collar on the doorstep. I wanted to go home and check if she was there, but I knew if I did, someone from school would phone Mum to find out where I was, and I didn't want to add to her worries.

At lunchtime, I hurried outside to the far end of the benches where we ate when the weather wasn't bad. They were quiet at this time of year with most people preferring to stay inside, but Cassie and I liked to sit on the bench at the end, which was under the sloping roof and sheltered from the wind. Sitting on the table, with his feet on the seat and a book on his lap, was Callum. My heart thumped when I saw him. He looked so sweet sitting there, concentrating on his reading. Sweet and also hot. He looked up as I got near and grinned.

'I saw Cassie in science and she said something was up.'

I dumped my bag on the ground and climbed up so I was sitting next to him. 'Literally, everything's gone wrong,' I said.

Callum opened his mouth and I knew he was going to tell me that I was using literally wrong, so I nudged him. 'I mean it, literally everything.'

'Start from the beginning.'

'No, wait,' Cassie appeared, holding a can of Diet Coke and balancing a plastic lunchbox on top of a pile of books. 'Wait for me.' Awkwardly, she elbowed my leg. 'Sit down properly or we can't all fit.'

Callum and I jumped from the tabletop and sat down next to each other again, on the seats this time. Cassie emptied her arms onto the table, plonked herself down opposite us and started rearranging the books and her lunch. 'What's going on, Jem? Are you all right?'

I looked at her lovely, concerned face, and at Callum's worried frown, and I suddenly felt like I was going to cry.

'I'm fine,' I said in a funny, tight voice. I swallowed and tried again. 'I'm fine, honestly. There's just been some weird stuff happening.'

'The skeletons?'

I nodded. 'And more.'

Quickly, I explained about the word in the grass, and Hermione disappearing and then her collar being on the doorstep.

'Mum was really rattled,' I said. 'She's so edgy anyway, after the witch and then skeletons showing up, wearing our stuff. And now this . . .' I felt my voice tighten again. 'I'm scared something's happened to Hermione.'

Cassie reached across the table and squeezed my arm, and I felt Callum's hand sneak into mine. I gave them both a weak smile.

'This doesn't feel like a Halloween prank anymore,' I said.

Cassie's eyes widened. 'What are you saying?'

'That it could be personal.'

'Why would anyone want to do nasty stuff to you and your mum?' Callum asked. He pushed his glasses up his nose. 'You're really nice.'

'Thank you,' I said and he reddened slightly.

'I mean, you're not bad people.'

'Ah.' I pressed my lips together. 'Not everyone would agree.'

'What? Why not?' He looked alarmed.

I looked down at my knees, thinking about how Mum had reacted when she found out I'd told Cassie about my dad. But I trusted Callum and it was hard to explain what was going on without him knowing the whole story. I glanced at Cassie and she gave me a tiny, encouraging nod. 'You know Alistair Robertson?' I said to Callum.

'The TV presenter?'

'That's him.'

'Isn't he in jail?'

'He is,' I said. 'And he's also my dad.'

Callum's jaw dropped. 'But your name's Jemima Blyth.'

'It is now. Mum went back to her maiden name after they got divorced and I wanted to be the same as her. But my name used to be Jemima Robertson.'

'He did some bad shit.'

I almost smiled at Callum's turn of phrase. 'He did.'

'But your mum didn't.'

'No, but lots of people blamed her. They said she knew what he was like, or that she'd driven him to it. She sent a tweet she shouldn't have sent and it all went crazy. There was some awful stuff on social media. That's why she won't let me have Instagram or TikTok.'

'Man,' Callum said. 'That's tough.'

'So that's why I'm worried it might be personal,' I went on. 'We're not hiding, but Mum doesn't go around shouting about who my dad is.' I felt tears behind my eyelids again. 'This was supposed to be a new start. I don't want to move again.'

'No,' Cassie said firmly. 'You're not going anywhere, we need you here.'

I sniffed. 'Thank you. It just all seems a bit hopeless.'

'Nothing's hopeless,' Cassie said. 'We'll get this sorted out.'

'What can we do?'

'Tell the police?' Callum suggested.

I shrugged. 'We had a family liaison officer in Edinburgh. She was nice. I could ring her?'

'Do that.' Callum pushed my phone towards me. 'Do you have her number?'

'Yes.'

'Do it now.'

'Shouldn't Mum call her?'

'Maybe but so what?'

I found the number in my contacts and hit the green button. But it rang out.

'Voicemail,' I said, listening. My heart sank as I heard Jacqui's familiar voice telling me she was away until the middle of November. I ended the call without leaving a message.

'Holiday,' I said.

'Ohh, where has she gone?' Cassie said. I looked at her and she made a face. 'Not important.'

I played with my phone. 'I think the North Berwick police will just think it's kids,' I said. 'There must be loads of this stuff going on at this time of year. Especially round here where everyone gets so into Halloween.'

We all thought for a moment and then Cassie sat up straighter, looking excited. 'We can solve the crime,' she said. 'We can set up a stakeout, or do some other detective work and work out who's doing this.'

'We're not the Famous Five, Cassie.'

She made a face. 'I know that, but think about it. We've got Callum's geek brain for tech, you're sharp as anything and you're good at puzzles, and I know just about everyone who lives here. Surely together we can work it out?'

'And then we can go to the police,' Callum said. 'Because we'll have evidence.'

Cassie rolled her eyes. 'Yes, whatever.' She picked up her own phone and started scrolling, her fingers moving fast. 'I'm just searching for any mention of North Berwick on social media,' she said. 'There's loads of local accounts. Someone might be talking about it.'

'Aren't they mostly tourist stuff?'

'Some of them. But there's gossip, too. My mum's on the Facebook group and I've seen people share stuff on Insta.'

Callum and I exchanged a smile. Cassie's social-media expertise was proving useful for once.

'Shiiiit,' she breathed, staring at her screen.

My stomach lurched. 'What?'

Cassie put her phone on the table and pushed it across so Callum and I could both see the screen. On a group called North Berwick Gossip there was a post that read: 'Missing: Jemima Robertson, aged 14. Last seen in North Berwick East Lothian.' It had been shared hundreds of times.

'What is this?' I said. My voice sounded shrill. 'What does this mean?'

'I don't know,' Cassie whispered.

Underneath the writing was a picture of me from my old school, wearing the horrible maroon uniform I'd hated, and staring at the camera without smiling.

'That's from my old class photo,' I said. 'How did they get that?'

'How many kids in your old class?' Callum asked.

'Twenty-two.'

'That's a lot of people who could have shared that picture somewhere.'

I felt hot and cold and sick all at once. 'But I'm here,' I said, pointlessly because obviously I was here. 'Why would anyone say I was missing?'

'I don't know.' Cassie took my hand and I gripped it gratefully.

I swallowed. 'What if it's a warning?' I said. 'A threat?'

'No,' Callum said. 'Surely not?'

'In Edinburgh, people took photos of me and posted them online,' I said. 'People do really weird, scary stuff, Callum.'

'We should tell your mum.'

'No.' I was firm. 'No way. She's on the edge. She can't know about this.'

'But . . .'

'No,' I almost shouted. 'We will deal with this ourselves.'

Callum shook his head, but he didn't say no. I scrolled down the post. Lots of people had commented when they shared it, all over the country. 'Shared Southampton,' I read, wondering why anyone from the south coast would bother. 'Shared Newcastle. Shared Glasgow.' My heart was thumping and I had a funny taste in my mouth like I was going to throw up. 'It's everywhere,' I said. And then I realized that whatever sicko had posted this had used my old name. This time I did heave, turning away from Cassie and puking up into the bin next to our table.

'God,' I heard Cassie say. She shoved her can of Diet Coke into my hand. 'Drink some of this.'

I took a massive gulp, swilled it round my mouth, and then spat it out. 'Thanks,' I said, holding the can out to Cassie.

'Ewww,' she said. 'Keep it.'

'It's someone who knows who we are,' I said. 'It's their creepy way of telling everyone where we live.'

Callum was staring at the post on Cassie's phone, his mouth in a tight line, typing furiously. 'There,' he said. 'I've reported the post. I ticked the box that said it was fake news.'

'Will they take it down?' Cassie said.

He shrugged. 'No idea. But it's not just on Facebook, it's all over every platform.'

I buried my face in my hands. 'Maybe I was wrong. Maybe I actually should tell my mum.'

'Yes,' said Callum definitely, as Cassie, just as firmly, said: 'No.'

'Which?'

'Let's do our own digging first,' Cassie said. 'Maybe it's just someone wanting to spook you.'

'Ha,' I said, though it wasn't funny. 'They've succeeded.' I threw my head back in despair. 'But Mum would freak out. She'd make us go and stay with my granny. She might even make us move in with her.'

'You'd miss the Halloween disco,' said Cassie.

'And the play,' Callum added.

I nodded. 'Okay, let's see if we can find anything out before we worry Mum.'

Callum didn't look sure, but after a bit of hesitation he nodded.

'Where can we start, though?' he said. 'The post was anonymous.'

'I don't know,' I wailed. 'I just want to do something. Maybe I should say I'm ill and just go home?'

'We've got rehearsal,' Callum reminded me and I groaned, even though I enjoyed our school play preparation.

'You've just got to get through that and history,' Cassie said.

'I suppose we can do our project in history so it's interesting enough to distract me,' I said.

'I've got games, count yourself lucky,' Callum added with a shiver, looking out at the muddy field.

The bell rang and we all jumped even though we were used to it.

'Fine,' Cassie said with a sigh. 'I wanted to do a stakeout, but we can go and read some history instead.'

Callum laughed. 'Are you going to be okay?' he said seriously, staring into my eyes. I felt a bit giddy and I wasn't sure if it was because of the throwing up or how close he was to me. But I nodded. 'I'm fine.'

'Good. I'll see you at rehearsal.' He stood up and squeezed my shoulder, then he picked up his bag and wandered off, looking less than enthusiastic about an afternoon of rugby.

'He is so nice,' Cassie said as we watched him go. She made a face. 'He's nicer than Max, isn't he?'

'Max is a douchebag,' I pointed out. 'Everyone's nicer than he is.'

Cassie groaned. 'You're right,' she said. 'Why do I even like him?'

'Beats me.' I was still shaky but I was feeling slightly better. It felt good to have Cassie and Callum on my side. 'Come on, we don't want to be late for history.'

We spent the first bit of the lesson going over what we'd learned about the witch-hunts and then Miss McGinty said we should start to look at how we could learn from the past and apply it to life today.

'How can we learn from an old prison?' I heard someone complaining and I grinned at Cassie.

'We totally chose the right topic. Everyone's doing the jail.'

'We'll be Miss McGinty's favourites forever,' she said, looking pleased. 'Right, so I was thinking, remember how Heather said the witch-hunts started with rumours?'

I nodded. 'People accusing everyone else.'

'So it's kind of like gossip at school, isn't it? Last year, I swear there was a rumour going round that Michael Malone has six toes on one foot.'

I giggled. 'Does he?'

'I don't think so. But everyone believed it. He was called Mickey Six Toes for months.'

'It's like the stuff with my dad,' I pointed out. 'That gossip went round school in a flash. And every time someone passed it on, there were more and more rumours added to it. Some of it was true, but loads of it wasn't.'

'We can't put that in our project though. We don't want to start gossip about you here, too.'

I stared at Cassie. 'This is just like Honor and Alice,' I said.

'Erm, yes. That is literally the point of our project, Jem.'

'No, I mean the stuff that's been happening to Mum and me. Spreading lies. Sharing a photo that could mean people recognize me.' I paused. 'Calling us witches.'

'Shit,' Cassie breathed. 'You're right.'

I drummed my fingers on the desk. 'Maybe if we find out more about what happened to Honor and Alice, it'll help us work out who's doing this to me?'

'I don't see how.' Cassie looked sceptical.

'I can't think what else to do, Cass,' I said. 'Someone's spreading stuff about me on social media, like someone spread rumours about Alice in real life and like the girls in my old class talked about me, too.' I looked at her pleadingly. I felt so helpless and researching the Setons was the only thing I could think of doing. 'I don't want it all to fall apart again.'

She linked her arm through mine. 'Shall we go back to see Heather? Tomorrow, maybe? She said she was going to find out more for us.'

'That would be good.'

'Cassie and Jemima, are you researching or gossiping?' scolded Miss McGinty.

'Bit of both, Miss,' said Cassie cheerfully and I laughed, feeling more positive now I had a plan.

*

After school and the rehearsal, I raced home, wanting to see Mum and make sure she hadn't stumbled upon the weird post online.

I flung open the door and there was Mum in the living room, sitting next to Rory on the sofa. They were both looking at Mum's laptop and they were quite close together. I scowled. 'Is Hermione home?' I asked, throwing my coat on the sofa. 'Has she eaten her food?'

Mum made a face. 'She's not been back as far as I can tell.'

'Oh no.' Suddenly everything that had happened that day felt too much to deal with. I just wanted to cry and cuddle my mum but stupid Rory was there.

'I'd really hoped she would come home,' I said, focusing on Hermione because she really was missing, unlike me. 'What if something's happened to her?'

'It is quite a busy road,' said Rory. I glared at him.

'She's not been run over, has she? Because her collar was on the doorstep. Unless it just magically flew off when the car hit her.'

'Jem,' said Mum, warning me not to be rude. 'Rory was just trying to help.'

'Sorry,' Rory muttered.

'Cats do sometimes wriggle out of their collars though,' Mum said. 'Especially ones like Hermione who might not be used to wearing them. Maybe we just didn't do it up tightly enough.'

'Maybe,' I said, doubtfully.

'We'll find her, sweetheart. How about we go and have a look now? Perhaps she's got stuck somewhere.'

'Aren't you busy?'

Rory shut the laptop. 'All done,' he said.

'Rory's put up one of those CCTV doorbells,' Mum said. 'So we can see if anyone comes up to the house.'

'That's actually a good idea,' I said.

'Thank you.' Rory looked pleased with himself. I wasn't sure about him. But perhaps that was just the way he looked at my mother. I turned back to Mum, thinking about the horrible post.

'We could make some lost cat posters for Hermione, maybe? We could put them on lampposts along the road.'

'Okay.'

Rory was gathering his stuff together. He kissed Mum on the cheek a bit awkwardly and I noticed that Mum's cheeks flushed. 'I'll message you later.'

'Right,' Mum said as he walked down the path. 'Let's find this cat, shall we?'

Chapter 29

Tess

Rory had turned up on my doorstep like a knight in shining armour. Or a knight with a bar of chocolate and a CCTV doorbell to be precise.

He'd called me when I was on my way home from work – a bit early, thanks to Mr Langdown's seemingly never-ending tolerance – to see if I fancied a drink.

'No,' I said. 'I can't. I have to go home.'

'What's up?'

Hearing his friendly concern made my stoicism crumble and I burst into tears. Sniffing and sobbing my way through my story about weed-killer graffiti, and the missing cat.

'What did school say?' Rory asked when I paused for breath.

'About what?' I blew my nose, grateful that the train was mostly empty and there was no one to overhear my tales of woe.

'About Jem.'

'What about Jem?'

'Going missing.'

'Jem's not missing,' I said. 'It's her cat. Jem's cat is missing.'

207

There was a crackly pause as the train went under a bridge. 'I misheard you,' Rory said. 'I'm sorry.'

'Don't be,' I tried to laugh but it came out a bit squeaky and odd. 'I'm glad it's this cat and not my daughter.'

Rory hesitated.

'How are you?' he asked. 'Really?'

'Really? Pretty terrible. This doesn't feel like someone playing a Halloween trick because witches once lived in our cottage.'

'No,' Rory said thoughtfully. 'It feels . . .' He trailed off but I knew what he had been about to say.

'Personal,' I said. 'It feels personal.'

'Do you have any enemies?' He gave a little chuckle, because normal people didn't have enemies, did they? But I did.

'Tess?' Rory said, because I'd gone quiet. 'Do you have any enemies?'

I wasn't sure where my friendship with Rory was going, and I knew that if things progressed then I'd have to tell him the truth about my divorce and my ex-husband eventually. But for now, I didn't want to drag it up again. So I mimicked his little laugh. 'Enemies?' I said. 'Only Jem when I make her do her homework instead of watching make-up videos on YouTube.'

'What about work? You're a lawyer, after all. Have you crossed paths with any criminals? Sent anyone to prison?'

I shuddered at the mention of prison but I forced myself to keep my voice light. 'I work for a firm of family solicitors, Rory. The most dangerous thing in my office is the photocopier.'

And then the train went through a tunnel and we got cut off, and I thought I would call him once I got home.

But instead, I'd not long taken off my coat and put on the kettle, instead of opening a bottle of wine because it was only just after four, when he knocked on the door.

'Shit,' he said when I answered, not even bothering to say hello. 'It's worse than I imagined.'

I looked past him at the lawn, where the 'witch' seemed to be becoming more obvious with each passing minute, though the thistles still looked strong and straight. 'I guess the weed-killer is still working. At least it'll be dark soon.'

'Who would have done this?'

I threw my hands out in a 'no idea' gesture. 'I'm going round and round in circles,' I said. 'I even wondered if Cassie's mum could have done it. She was here last night.'

'Cassie's mum?'

'I know,' I groaned. 'It's ridiculous.'

'Not least because weed-killer takes a few days to work,' Rory said. 'This could have been done any time in the last few days.'

'Brilliant.'

Rory gave me a sympathetic grin and held out his hands. He had a large bar of chocolate in one, and a box in the other. 'Brought you these,' he said.

'Oh my god, you're an angel.' I gestured for him to come inside. 'What's in the box?'

'Doorbell.'

I frowned. 'We've got a doorbell.'

'CCTV,' he said. 'Might make you feel a bit safer.'

'Thank you.' I was genuinely touched by his thoughtfulness. 'I'll see if Callum can set it up for me.'

'I can do it,' Rory said. He seemed eager to help. 'I can do it now if you like? Do you have a drill?'

'In the cupboard under the stairs. But only if you're sure you have time?'

'Course I do.'

'Then thank you,' I said again. He really was a treasure. 'Cup of tea?'

'Great.'

Rory had the camera up and running in no time. He showed me where the pictures would be on my laptop and said there was an app I could put on my phone, too. So I could get an alert when someone came up the path.

'Big Brother is watching you, eh?' I said. 'This really is helpful, Rory. Fancy another cuppa to celebrate?'

'Sure,' he said. I picked up his mug and my own and went into the kitchen where I rinsed them out and refilled the kettle and switched it on. Then, as I turned round to get the teabags from the cupboard, I almost walked into Rory, who'd followed without me realising.

'Oh, sorry,' I said. He was very close to me in the small kitchen.

'I was just going to give you this – thought you might fancy some with your tea?' He handed me the bar of chocolate, but he didn't move away. In fact, he possibly came a little closer. Our torsos were close enough that I could feel the warmth coming from his body. I felt a flutter of nerves in my stomach.

'Tess,' he said.

I looked up at him and he leaned in and touched his lips to mine. At first it was a soft kiss but he wrapped his arms around me and pulled me closer and increased the pressure. I was still holding the chocolate which made things a bit awkward, and he was the first man I'd kissed since Alistair, which was strange, but I tried to relax into it, because he was very handsome and he smelled good, and there was a definite feeling of longing inside me – something I'd almost forgotten existed. And hadn't Eva told me to have some fun? This was definitely fun.

But it was no good. I couldn't quite let myself go. I pulled back and Rory looked disappointed.

'Sorry,' he said, running his fingers through his hair. 'I didn't plan that. I really did come round to bring the doorbell.'

I smiled. He was very sweet. 'Don't be sorry. It just took me by surprise a bit, that's all.'

He still had his arms around me and I felt a bit flustered. Glancing at the clock on the wall, I grimaced. 'Jem will be home any minute,' I said, putting my hand on his chest and wriggling out of his embrace.

'Could we park this? Not forever, I promise. Just for now.'

He reached out and touched my cheek. 'Of course.'

And then, of course, ridiculously, I felt disappointed and a little guilty as though I'd led him on, which I hadn't. It was years since I'd been in the dating game and I didn't have a clue how to play it. The day I'd met Alistair, I'd just had my hair cut into a 'Rachel' – that's how long ago it was. I was very out of practice.

With hands that trembled the tiniest bit, I made more tea while Rory leaned against the worktop and watched me. I felt his eyes on me as I moved around the kitchen and I quite liked it. It had just been the wrong moment, I told myself.

As I handed him his mug, he grinned. 'We've got our dinner date to look forward to, if you're still up for it?'

I'd forgotten all about it in the drama, but now it seemed like something nice to look forward to – and perhaps with my glad-rags on and the right atmosphere, I'd feel more ready for romance.

'I am still up for it,' I said. 'And I am looking forward to it.'

And so we sat together and ate some chocolate and drank our tea, while he showed me the fancy things our new doorbell could do, though I still felt slightly awkward. Then Jem came home and I was – I had to admit – a tiny bit relieved that I had an excuse to leap up from the sofa and comfort her when she was upset about Hermione.

'We'll find her, sweetheart,' I said, feeling terribly guilty that I'd been snogging in the kitchen when I should have been worrying about the kitten. 'How about we go and have a look now? Perhaps she's got stuck somewhere.'

But we had no luck. Jem and I spent ages in the back garden, calling for Hermione. We went to all the neighbours and asked them if they'd seen her, but none of them had. And when we got home, the 'witch' on the lawn in front of the house was even more vivid, glowing in the light of the streetlamp in the gloomy evening darkness.

Jem looked at it and gave a sigh. 'I can't believe we have to look at this every day,' she said.

'Why don't you make some lost cat posters?' I said. Jem shivered and I gave her a nudge towards the front door. 'Go on, you're freezing. Get into the warm. I've got an idea.'

Right at the back of our little back garden was a pile of paving stones, obviously left over from when the McKinleys had redone the patio. I'd seen them when we were looking for Hermione, having never really noticed them before. I put on my gloves and then heaved them one by one, round the side of the cottage and out to the front, where I – quite clumsily because they were heavy – dropped them with a thud on to the lawn, covering over the 'witch' but leaving gaps for the occasional clumps of thistles to poke through. There were eight slabs, and when I laid them out with gaps in between, they covered the whole lawn so perfectly it almost looked as though they were supposed to be there. Maybe I could put a couple of pots out there in the spring. That might be nice.

The CCTV doorbell was glowing blue in the darkness and I smiled to myself, reassured that it was doing its job. If anyone decided to play any more Halloween tricks, they'd be captured on video.

I gave my newly paved front garden a final approving look, then I went back inside to make dinner – locking the door firmly behind me – feeling happier and safer than I'd done for days.

Chapter 30

Alice

1661

I arrived home from the big house soaking wet from the rain and burning with rage.

I was angry all the time at the moment. It was really unlike me – I'd always been content to wander through life, following my mother's lead, or letting Kyla drag me into her mischievous schemes, but no more. Now I felt like one of my cats when they were ready for a fight. Hissing and spitting, my back arched and my hair standing on end. I didn't want to leave, and I didn't want my mother – and me – accused of being witches when we were guilty of nothing more than being women who were not dependent on a man. At least, Ma was. My own guilt was less clear cut. Rationally I knew that Christy had recovered because my mother had healed him, that the milk was sour because the cows were ill, and the storm had been coming long before I'd spied on the Kincaid brothers, but right at the back of my mind there was a small, nagging doubt that perhaps – perhaps – they'd happened because I'd wanted them to. And I quite liked it.

My mother was in the kitchen, making something to eat, and she stared at me as I entered, dripping water on to the stone floor.

'Where have you been?'

I thought about telling her what I'd seen, and heard, and how the Kincaids were plotting against us, but I'd not worked out what to do yet, and I didn't want to worry her. Instead I just shrugged. 'Went for a walk, but I got caught in the storm.'

'You must be freezing,' she said, and her look of concern made my heart twist with protective love for her. 'Come here.' She threw her shawl around my shoulders and wiped my damp face.

'Go and get into some dry clothes, and then come and sit by the fire to get warm. I'll heat up some milk for you.'

'Thank you,' I said.

We passed a quiet evening, Ma and I. We sat beside the fire. I had hung my wet dress up and it steamed in the warmth, making the room feel heavy and cosy. Ma passed the time writing in her records and reading through some notes. I wound some wool, ready to knit into a shawl for the colder months.

From the outside, it must have looked like a quiet, peaceful scene. But inside my anger was still smouldering.

It burned away inside me all evening, and while I slept, and when I woke up the next morning, it was still there, scratching at me, reminding me that while we may be pretending all was peaceful, the Kincaids were plotting to send us fleeing – or worse.

And then the rain stopped, and Davey Kincaid arrived at our door.

I was upstairs when he arrived, but I recognized his voice immediately and the anger surged through me again like the waves in a storm.

I hadn't intended to confront him, but almost before I realized I was moving, I was running down the stairs to face him.

'What do you want with us?' I demanded.

'Alice, please,' my mother said, but Davey looked sheepish.

214

'I do not wish you any harm, Alice,' he said.

I laughed in his face, a sharp, barking laugh. 'You are lying.'

'No.'

'I heard you,' I hissed. 'You and that lying, deceitful brother. I heard you plotting against us.'

Davey's face was pale in the dim hallway. 'I don't know what you heard, but it certainly wasn't a plot against you and your mother.'

'Your brother told you of allegations that had been made against us.'

My mother gasped and shrank back against the wall, and I cursed myself for not telling her the truth about where I'd been yesterday. She shouldn't be hearing all this for the first time in this way. But now I'd started, I couldn't seem to stop.

'He told you that Kyla had made accusations against us, and that she'd given the evidence to the minister.' I took a breath. 'And you were on your way to put the allegations to Ma when the storm came.'

Davey's eyes widened. 'You were spying on us?'

'I'd come to tell you that Kyla was not trustworthy.' I tossed my hair. 'But you've obviously made your mind up about her if you're here.'

Ma was looking shocked but, I had to admit, not surprised. She'd been expecting something like this, I knew.

'Kyla is a troubled soul,' she murmured, almost to herself. 'She is never happy. Always wanting what someone else has.'

'She is a liar,' I spat. 'Like the Kincaids.'

Davey flinched, but I thought I saw a flash of annoyance in his eyes. 'Gregor is . . .' He paused. 'He loved his wife deeply and he is heartbroken.'

I scoffed but Ma nodded. 'She was a good woman.'

'Gregor has always been focused on wealth. It's what drives him. But Isobel was always there to give him something else to think about. She softened his edges, made him more likeable. With her gone, he has no one to be good for.'

'He's grieving.' Ma looked sad, but I shot her a disgusted look. How could she be so nice about this?

'He's grieving, and he's got nothing to lose,' Davey said. 'And I fear that makes him dangerous.'

It was my turn to wince. 'What will he do?'

'He wants to make these allegations and he believes he has proof.'

'There is no proof,' Ma said, her voice firm. 'Because the allegations are false.'

Davey held her gaze and for a second I felt something unspoken pass between them. 'I know,' he said eventually. 'But I fear he will take them to the town council.'

Ma shrugged. 'Let him do his worst,' she said. 'I am a burgess and I have voting rights.'

Davey bit his lip. 'Is that enough?'

'I believe it is.' Ma gave him a sly smile. 'It was enough to vote down his proposal to dredge the harbour.'

'What about you?' I asked shortly. Davey looked at me as though he had forgotten I was there.

'What about me?'

'You are also a burgess, with voting rights,' I pointed out. 'But you always back up your brother. You voted with him on the harbour. Will you stand with him against us?'

There was a pause. I felt it hang heavy in the room.

'No,' Davey said hesitantly. 'At least, not if I can avoid it.'

I raised an eyebrow but I said nothing.

'I am on your side,' Davey went on. 'You can trust me. But these things are complicated and often it is better to be quietly in opposition, than confront them.'

I snorted.

'You may think that I am working against you, but I urge you to understand that I am not,' Davey said. Once more he wasn't talking to me, just to Ma. He looked earnest, but I didn't believe anything he was saying. 'Things are more complicated than they seem and I need to think about Christy.' He took Ma's hand in his and I snorted again. 'You must know that I think you are a clever woman doing an important job,' he said to Ma. 'And you should be celebrated for it, not criticized.' He took a deep breath. 'I am going to the beach. I will be there for a while, walking and thinking. If you care to join me, I would enjoy your company.'

I gave a loud sigh, but Ma was looking at him in a way I'd never seen her look at anyone before. He had bewitched her, I thought in disgust. Charmed and enchanted her into thinking he was a good man, using his sweet words and his handsome face.

Davey put his hat on and gave Ma a little bow. A bow. 'I hope I will see you shortly,' he said.

Ma and I watched him walk down the road towards the beach in silence. Ma shut the door and looked at me. I couldn't read her expression, which was unusual. Was she annoyed with me? Disappointed? Upset? Scared? I had no idea. And so, unsure of the best way to react, I chose to attack.

'Do not trust that man,' I snarled. 'Do. Not.'

Ma pushed past me and went to stand by the fire, warming her hands. 'I know people, Alice. Wasn't I right about Kyla? And Davey Kincaid is a good man.'

'You aren't thinking straight,' I said. 'Your head is turned by him.'

Ma hissed through her teeth. 'I'm no fool, Alice Seton. I've known the Kincaids a long time and I know Davey is worth ten of his brother.'

'You are acting like a fool.' It felt as though I was the mother and she my wayward daughter. Everything had been turned upside down since the sickness came to the big house and I didn't like it.

I glared at Ma where she stood by the fire, and was it my imagination or did the flames suddenly jump higher in the grate? She saw it too, because she turned to me, looking at me with narrowed eyes.

'Rumours are rife,' she hissed. 'There are whispers in the street when I walk by. I have to scurry into people's cottages because no one wants to be seen with me. Everyone is scared, and scared people do dangerous things. We have to be careful and having Davey on our side will work in our favour.'

I threw my head back in despair. 'Davey is not on our side.'

Ma caught my arms and pulled me to her. She clasped my face in her fingers. 'Trust me, Alice,' she said. 'Davey Kincaid has his own demons to fight. But I would never lie to you and I know he is a good man. I truly believe that if things go too far he will stand up for us if Gregor makes these allegations.'

'If you believe that, then you are a fool,' I said in a dull tone. 'I know Davey likes to gamble. He is as driven by money as his greedy brother and you should not expect him to stand up for you.'

Ma looked surprised when I mentioned gambling. Perhaps she had hoped I didn't know about Davey's misdeeds. But we were not the only people that the town liked to gossip about. I wondered if Davey had told her about his old life, drinking and spending someone else's money. The thought of them huddled together, exchanging chit-chat, sickened me.

'You said you wanted to run away.'

'Maybe we won't have to.'

'Do you really believe that?' My eyes searched her face. I wanted to trust her, I really did.

She nodded, slowly. 'I do.'

But I did not.

Chapter 31

Jem

Present day

I was worried that everyone at school would have seen the missing person appeal online and worked out who I was.

'Just lie,' Cassie said. 'Say it's not you.'

I made a face. 'Do you reckon?'

'People believe anything,' she said, as Michael Malone walked past. She held up six fingers and raised an eyebrow at me. I smiled. Maybe I could just brazen this out?

I walked into my French lesson and straightaway Mia, one of the girls I knew from the play, thrust her phone into my face.

'Ohmygod, Jem, have you seen this?'

I knew immediately what it was. Sure enough, there was the social-media post claiming I had gone missing. My younger face stared out at me.

'Woah,' I said, crossing my fingers behind my back. 'That girl looks a bit like me.'

At my old school we'd had to tie our hair back every day so in the picture I had a tight ponytail. The rules weren't so strict in my new school, so I tended to wear my hair down with a stretchy headband holding it off my face, or sometimes – like today – I'd plait the front to hold it back.

'She looks exactly like you,' Mia said, frowning. 'Is it not you?'

'No,' I scoffed, glancing at Cassie. 'I'd never wear my hair like that. It's so lame. And urgh, check out that uniform.'

'It's grim, isn't it?' Mia said with a giggle.

'Totally grim.'

And that's what I did every time someone asked me about it. I just straight up lied. I said it wasn't me, that it was an amazing coincidence that she looked like me and was also called Jemima. Cassie pointed out all the completely fake differences between me and the girl in the picture. 'Jem's hair is much wavier,' I heard her say. 'And her nose doesn't have that bump in it. And her teeth are straighter. Also,' she added, 'our Jem is right here, you weirdo.'

I even heard Callum telling someone that it must be to do with weird social-media algorithms matching faces and first names and going wrong.

'It's quite sinister what they can do,' he said, with his brow furrowed as he looked at the phone being brandished by Micah, the captain of the rugby team. 'They literally know everything about us. I'd delete all your social media if I were you.'

By the end of the day, I was exhausted with all the lying and making up excuses, but we seemed to have pulled it off.

'They'll all be talking about something else by tomorrow,' Cassie said. 'And no one's made the connection between the name on the missing poster and your dad.'

'I guess,' I said.

We were walking out of school, bags slung on our shoulders weighing us down because we had so much homework.

'Jemima?' I looked round to see our form teacher – Miss Lenihan – calling me. 'Can I borrow you for five minutes?'

220

I glanced at Cassie and Callum who both shrugged. 'You go home,' I said. 'I'll message you later.'

'Sure?' said Cassie and I loved her for looking out for me.

'Sure. No idea how long I'll be, and you've got all that science homework to do.'

Cassie made a face, but she nodded. Callum gave me a little grin. 'Later,' he said. They both wandered off and I went over to where Miss Lenihan waited.

'Come into the classroom,' she said. I went in and she shut the door and perched on her desk while I sat on a chair.

'Have you seen this?' she said, picking up the tablet she used for teaching. Suddenly my face was on the whiteboard at the front of the room, the old Jem with her stupid ponytail and ugly uniform looking at me sternly from the fake missing person appeal.

I made a face and she looked sympathetic.

'I know that Robertson was your old name,' she said. 'Your mum explained it all when you joined us.'

I went cold. 'Does everyone know? All my teachers?'

'Just me, and Mrs Ahmed.' Mrs Ahmed was the teacher who did the pastoral care. 'And the head, of course.'

So it wasn't all the teachers gossiping in the staff room then. I tried to smile but I couldn't.

'This is just a stupid joke,' I said. 'But it's not very funny.'

'Are you all right?'

'Sort of.'

'What does your mum say about this?'

'She doesn't know,' I said. My voice was quiet.

'Would you like me to call her?'

'No.' I was firm. 'She really worries about me. This is nothing, Miss. No one's bothered.'

Miss Lenihan looked concerned and I felt sorry for her. She was really young and new to the school and she probably didn't want to have to deal with something like this. Which was good news for me.

'We had loads of stuff like this happen before and honestly we found it was best to ignore it and it would go away.'

'But . . .'

'It'll already be way down everyone's news feeds. If we make a fuss about it, it'll just bring it to people's attention.'

Miss Lenihan leaned back on the desktop, tapping her toes on the floor as she thought. Then she nodded. 'I'll do a deal with you,' she said. 'I won't do anything about this now, but only on the condition that if anyone gives you hassle about it, or you're worried or upset, you come straight to me.'

'Sounds good,' I said, weak with relief that she wasn't going to call Mum.

'Is it a deal?'

'It's a deal.'

I grabbed my bag and scurried off out through the quiet corridors and through the deserted playground feeling antsy. I kept thinking people were looking at me as I walked towards home, wondering if I was the girl from the appeal. I walked past a man on a bench, his head bent as he scrolled through his phone and caught his eye accidentally when he looked up just as I glanced in his direction. He blinked at me, and turned his focus back to the phone. I ducked down a side road and hurried away. Had he been looking at the post just as I walked past or was I imagining his expression of surprised recognition?

I scuttled down the little lane I'd walked down. This was a longer way home but it was much quieter and better than having to walk past lots of people. I considered going into a shop and buying a hat or a pair of sunglasses but that wouldn't help much.

And then I stopped outside a hairdresser. I had birthday money in my account. Perhaps I could spend it now? My hair was long – right down my back almost to my waist. It had a nice natural wave to it which stopped it looking so mousey. When I had time, I curled it more with my straighteners.

What if I cut it all off? Or dyed it? Or both?

Without stopping to think, I pushed open the door to the salon and went inside to see if they could fit me in.

*

Just over an hour later I left with my hair swinging round my face. I had a fringe and a wavy short bob. A French bob, the stylist had called it. I didn't care what it was called, I just knew it made me look very different from the picture on the poster. Also I liked my fringe, and the way my shorter style made my hair even wavier than before. I felt lighter and less like I wanted to hide away. I stopped outside the salon window to take a selfie, pouting for the camera, and I sent it to Cassie. Then, wondering what Mum would think of my new 'do, I headed for home.

At the end of the street was an empty shop that was being done up, and parked outside was Rory's van. I saw him going in and out of the shop, putting some bits of wood and tools into the back of the van. Maybe I should go and say hello, I thought. I'd been a bit rude the last time I saw him.

I crossed the road, and walked along to where the van was parked, one of its back doors open. Rory had gone – presumably inside to get more of his stuff, so I stopped on the pavement to wait for him to come out again.

The wind blew across my bare neck and I shivered. I'd have to get a scarf now I had short hair, I thought. Maybe Auntie Rachel could knit me one like my mum's.

Rory's van had those back windows that were mirrored on the outside but normal glass on the inside, so I wandered over to look at my reflection in the closed door. I liked my new hair a lot. It made me look older. Sophisticated. Or perhaps not sophisticated but definitely more mature.

I turned my head, admiring my side view and then through the open door, my eye was caught by something in Rory's van.

Tucked into the edge, beside a toolbox, was a pile of rags. And the rag on top was covered in red paint. It looked as though someone had cleaned a brush or their hands on it.

My heart pounding, I edged a bit closer. It looked just the same as the red paint on our house. I reached out, planning to take the cloth, but then a burst of laughter from the closed-up shop made me stop. Rory was coming, chatting over his shoulder to a man inside the store. Quick as a flash, I grabbed the rag and shoved it into my bag, then I slid round the side of the van door, ducked my head down, and ran.

*

Mum wasn't home when I got back. I paced the living room backwards and forwards until she opened the front door.

'Mum!' I said before she'd even taken her coat off. She looked at me, and I couldn't help notice the dark circles under her eyes and how her hair hung limply round her face. But she smiled broadly when she saw me.

'Look at your hair!' she exclaimed. 'When did you do that?'

'Total spur of the minute,' I said. 'They wanted models,' I added, thinking the white lie would stop her asking more questions and mean she didn't worry about how much it had cost.

Mum span me round so she could see it from all angles. 'I love it,' she said. 'You look so grown up.'

'Sophisticated?' I said hopefully.

'Definitely.'

'Let me just go and get changed and then I'll get dinner on,' Mum said.

'I'll do it. Shall I just make some pasta?'

'Perfect.' Mum gave me a kiss. 'Thank you.'

She went upstairs, hauling herself up on the bannister. She was so worn out, I thought sadly. Working and worrying about money and me and the horrible things that kept happening. I had definitely made the right decision not telling her about the social-media post claiming I was missing.

When she came down, I had the pasta bubbling on the hob and I'd poured her a glass of wine.

'This is lovely,' she said gratefully.

'I need to tell you something,' I blurted out.

She looked at me, her face pale and I felt awful. 'I think Rory's the one who's been doing all the horrible stuff to us.'

Mum frowned. 'Jem, I really don't think . . .'

'Look.' I pulled the paint-stained rag out of my bag and showed it to her. 'I found this in his van.'

She took it, still frowning. 'What is it?'

'It's proof that he splattered our house with the red paint.'

'Is it?'

Oh my god, why was she being so slow? 'Yes,' I said impatiently. 'Look. There's red paint all over it.'

'And white paint,' Mum said. 'And black paint.' She turned the cloth round in her hands. 'And a bit of blue, too.'

I looked. She was right, the cloth did have lots of different colours on it. I'd only really paid attention to the red.

'Jem, Rory's a carpenter,' she said. 'He must paint lots of things. Doors and cupboards and all sorts. This is probably just a rag he uses to wipe his brushes on. It doesn't prove anything.'

I felt totally embarrassed. 'Shit,' I said under my breath.

'Jemima.'

'Sorry.'

Mum sighed. 'Sweetheart, I know things have been difficult but honestly, you can't go around accusing people in this way. Rory's set up our CCTV for us, hasn't he? Why would he do that if he was the one tormenting us?'

That was a good point. I looked at my feet. 'I just have a feeling about him, that's all.'

'I'm not in a relationship with him, if that's what you're worried about.'

225

'Urgh, no, Mum,' I said. 'That's not it at all.'

She seemed as though she didn't believe me, but she didn't push the point, much to my relief. Instead, she looked at the cloth again. 'Did you take this from Rory's van?'

I nodded, ashamed.

'Did he see you?'

'No.'

'Well let's get rid of it shall we?' She bundled it up and shoved it into the kitchen bin, pushing it down so it was hidden and I smiled. Mum had my back, I thought. Even when I leapt to silly conclusions and stole bits of rag from her friend's van. For a second I thought I might tell her about the appeal online, but then I changed my mind.

'I think the pasta's ready,' I said. 'I hope you're hungry, I made loads.'

Chapter 32

Honor

1661

I had made Davey's case as forcefully as I could. Alice seemed reassured but the air in the cottage was still heavy with tension. The fire was burning furiously in the grate and the smoke filled my nose and throat.

'I'm going to the beach,' I said.

She looked at me and nodded. 'I thought that you would.'

I wasn't sure how we'd ended up here. Alice and I had always been so close. Two parts of the same whole, I always thought. And yet we were sniping at each other and arguing. It was clear she didn't trust Davey, no matter what she said, and that meant she didn't trust me, either.

And did I trust her? I looked at the flames licking the stone fireplace and shivered despite the warmth in the cottage. It seemed I did not.

Without saying another word, I pulled my cloak over my shoulders and went outside, feeling Alice's eyes following me as I went.

Her gaze wasn't the only one on me as I walked towards

the beach with my hood up. I felt people looking from their windows, or standing still as I passed, watching me go. Several people hurried inside and shut their doors, making me want to run after them and beat my fists on the wooden entrances and shout that I wasn't dangerous, that they didn't need to fear me. I was unsettled and unhappy when I got the beach and saw Davey right at the far end by the rocks, where we'd walked before.

It took me a while to reach him; striding over the soft sand was hard on the legs, and when I arrived he looked worried.

'You came,' he said. 'I thought you would stay with your daughter.'

'Alice is confused and scared and hot-headed,' I said, though as I said the words I thought that she had never been hot-headed before. This was new. 'She'll calm down.'

Davey took my hand and I let him. His fingers were soft – my John's hands had been rough and calloused after years working on the boats. I had always liked the feel of John's skin on mine, but I found I liked Davey's too. It felt soothing.

'Honor, I promise that you can trust me.'

'I know.' I looked him straight in the eye and saw no deception there. I hadn't lied to Alice when I said I could read people – it was true. I knew when people were up to mischief, or plotting against others, or lying about where they'd been. I'd never been wrong. And I knew without a shadow of a doubt that Davey was a good man.

Comforted by my own convictions, I smiled at him. 'How is Christy today?'

'Giving Gregor cheek, and tormenting the servants,' Davey said with an indulgent smile. 'He is almost back to full strength.'

'It may take a while,' I warned.

'He is impatient to get back to learning, but of course, we lost his tutor too and finding a new one is proving difficult.'

'People are often nervous about a house where sickness has been,' I said. I'd seen that before. 'But once they realize that you are all well, they will return.'

'I hope so,' Davey said. 'I can't keep teaching him because he already knows more than I do. I imagine you find the same with Alice. Is she a willing pupil?'

'She has been until now,' I said thoughtfully. I sat down on a smooth rock and looked out to sea. 'But I think she is more talented than I am.' I felt a prickle of fear as I thought about Alice glaring at the fire and the flames jumping. But didn't fires ebb and flow like the waves, depending on the fuel they were burning and the breeze? It was more likely a draught from the chimney that sent the flames leaping, than Alice's anger.

'You are real assets to the town.'

I laughed, but it wasn't with humour. More disbelief, thinking of the way the people had reacted as I'd walked by. 'I don't think so.'

'You are a burgess,' Davey pointed out.

I nodded. 'That's true. But only because my John made it so.'

'He was a clever man.'

'Clever, yes. And he was quiet and thoughtful, and very kind,' I said. I felt a sudden twist of missing my husband so piercing that I gasped and Davey took my hand again.

'I know how that feels,' he said. 'I miss my Marion in that way. Suddenly and without warning. Though in my case I feel guilt that I wasted the little time I had with her.'

I gave him a weak smile. 'My John has been gone almost seventeen winters,' I said. 'And still I see him sometimes when I walk past the harbour. Or I hear him shout my name.'

'I see Marion in Christy.' Davey pulled his feet up under himself and rested his chin on his knees like a schoolboy. 'Sometimes when he looks at me in a certain way, I am made dizzy by how much he reminds me of her.'

'Does he miss her?'

Davey shrugged. 'He was only small when she died. But he says he remembers her – the way she laughed, and a song she would sing him at bedtime. He remembers the way she stroked his hair.' He swallowed. 'When he was sick, he called out for her and I was so scared . . .' He fixed his gaze on the horizon. 'I was so scared he could see her, and she'd come to fetch him from heaven. I wished she would come for me too.'

Gently, I tucked my hand under his arm, hoping to give him reassurance. 'I felt like that when John died,' I said. 'I wanted to die too. But I was expecting Alice and she brought me such hope. If I didn't have her, well . . .' I trailed off.

Davey turned to look at me. 'We have both known heartbreak,' he said.

'Show me someone in this town who hasn't.'

He nodded. 'You are an astonishing woman, Honor Seton,' he said.

I felt my cheeks redden. 'I am just a woman.'

'You can read and write,' he said. 'You know more than most apothecaries and physicians about illnesses and how to cure them. You have brought up your daughter alone, and given her the knowledge you hold. And you stand firm at the town council as a burgess, even when faced with . . .'

'Even when faced with your brother.'

'Stay strong, Honor,' he said. 'Gregor is angry now but he won't be forever.'

'I am afraid,' I blurted out. Until I said the words I hadn't really understood how I was feeling. But now I knew that the unsettled, shaky sensation that was stopping me eating, and causing me to pace the floor all night instead of sleeping, was fear. It was the same as I'd felt when John had gone to sea for the last time. I'd known – just known, somehow – that he shouldn't go, and that if he did I would never see him again. But I'd not said anything, just let him walk out of the door and leave me forever.

'I am afraid,' I said again.

Davey put his arm around me and pulled me close to him. I leaned against him, drawing strength from his presence. 'Don't be.'

'Gregor is dangerous,' I said. 'Alice told me what he said, what he is accusing us of. And Kyla . . .' I spat out the name. 'She is protecting herself by attacking us.'

'I know all this.' Davey frowned. 'Gregor understands how serious this is.'

'Does he?' I didn't believe him. 'Rumours don't go away, Davey. They grow and they grow. Already people are running into their houses when they see me coming. It just takes one whisper in the wrong ear and there will be a witch-hunt on our doorstep.'

'Gregor wouldn't do that,' Davey said, but he didn't look convinced. 'He wouldn't take it so far.'

'He is blinded by his love of money.'

'Even so, he's not a bad man. He cared for me when I was at my lowest. I don't think he would go as far as to call in a witch finder.'

'It might not be down to him.' I took a deep breath. 'You know how it works. We've all seen it before. People make accusations against others so there are no fingers pointed at them.'

Davey squeezed me tighter. 'Your voice carries weight in this town.'

'That's not enough.' I felt weak with frustration. 'Because I am a woman and my voice isn't as loud as a man's.'

'Isn't it?' He turned to me again. His face was very close to mine and I didn't pull back. 'Any accusations would need to be made firstly at the town council before they go to the assizes.'

I winced at the mention of the assizes. Surely things wouldn't go that far? But Davey hadn't finished. 'And you will be at the town council, Honor, because you are a burgess. You will be there to refute the allegations and people will listen.'

'Do you really think they would listen?'

'They listened when you spoke out against Gregor's plans,' he said.

'Because they affected the whole town.'

'So does this,' he said firmly. 'Because without you . . .'

'Without me?'

He grimaced. 'Our children will die, and our babies will be born sleeping, and our elderly will weaken.'

'They won't see it that way, not if they're scared. Because speaking out for me will mean they are accused too. The stakes are too high.' Almost without thinking, I leaned my forehead against his. 'Alice and I will leave,' I said. 'Tonight.'

'No.'

'Perhaps we could borrow one of your horses? It would help with the journey.'

'No,' he said again. 'Please, Honor. Please don't leave.'

I moved away from him and stood up on the sand, throwing my arms out in despair. 'What choice do we have? If we go, we can start again in the Highlands, where we don't have to look over our shoulders all the time. Where we don't have to be afraid, all the time. There is nothing left for us here.'

Davey stood up too and came to stand by me. 'There is me,' he said. He gathered me into his arms and kissed me. At first I wriggled, thinking I should stop his embrace and he leaned back, his eyes searching my face. 'Honor?' he said. There was a short pause, and then it was me who pulled him close and kissed him, deeply and for a long time.

When we finally broke apart, Davey smiled. 'I didn't invite you to the beach so I could do that,' he said. 'I wasn't planning it.'

'Me neither,' I said. 'But I'm glad it happened.'

Davey laced his fingers through mine. 'Could we do this again, do you think?'

'Kiss?'

He grinned. 'Spend time together. I like being with you.' He pushed a strand of hair away from my face and looked at me. 'The love I had for Marion will never go away and the guilt I feel about the way I treated her will never fade. But that doesn't mean I shouldn't be happy. I want you to stay.'

I nodded, understanding exactly what he meant. 'John and I were together for many years, from when we were little more

232

than children,' I said. 'Every day was like an adventure and we grew up together. But he is gone, and I think now, after so long alone, I would like someone to grow old with.'

We gazed at one another, both of us in wonder that after sadness we had found happiness, and then I spoke: 'We should keep this between ourselves for now. No one heeds know. Not yet. It's still new and we are just beginning to know each other. Your brother would not be happy. And let's not forget that Alice is being odd, and things in the town are . . .' I searched for the right word. 'Difficult.'

'I believe you're right,' Davey said. He gave me another kiss and I leaned into him, enjoying the solidity of his body. 'Just us for now.'

'I should go,' I said with regret. 'I need to check how Alice is.'

'Let's walk separately.' Davey looked positively gleeful, like a schoolboy playing a prank. 'So no one knows we have been together.'

And so, we headed back towards my cottage, on opposite sides of the street, with Davey a little ahead.

As we passed the harbour and turned inland, I saw a messenger approach Davey. It was the lad who always came to tell me when an unexpected town council meeting had been called. I felt a shiver of trepidation. Was there a meeting? And if so, why?

Davey stopped to talk to the messenger and I continued walking, more slowly than I had been, on the other side of the street. Out of the corner of my eye, I saw Davey nodding. He gave the messenger a coin, and carried on without so much as glancing back at me.

The messenger looked over at me, meeting my gaze, and I stopped walking, expecting him to come and speak to me now. But instead he pulled his hat down over his eyes, turned and hurried away. That was odd. Again I felt that shiver. Was there a meeting then that I was not to be told about? I would never have known had I not been with Davey at the beach, because it was clear the messenger was not here for me. I resolved to go to the hall that evening to see for myself.

Chapter 33

Tess

Present day

All my senses were jangling all the time. I felt as though I was on high alert constantly, jumping at every noise. Checking outside when I drew the curtains at night. Jem's little cat hadn't come home and she was devastated. I found myself hoping the kitten had simply wandered off somewhere, as cats liked to do, rather than something awful happening to her. But the untouched bowls of food in the kitchen added to my unease. The blue glow of the CCTV doorbell gave me some comfort but the initial feeling of security soon wore off.

As Halloween got nearer, I got jumpier because I was expecting another nasty prank. I thought there might be another spooky surprise waiting when I came home. More graffiti perhaps, more seagulls divebombing my car, or something else that was more awful than anything that had gone before.

But nothing happened.

'I'm on edge,' I told Eva one evening, a couple of days before Halloween.

She gave me a sympathetic look and handed me a gin. 'I'm not surprised, darling.'

I took a mouthful of my drink and winced as it hit my throat. Eva was rather generous with her measures, that was for sure. 'I'm watching everyone all the time, wondering if they were the ones who splattered our house, or wrote "witch" on our lawn.' I took another swig and gave a dry laugh. 'Jem's exactly the same, which makes it harder to deal with. She stole a cloth from Rory's van because it had red paint on it.'

Eva raised an eyebrow. 'That is a bit suspicious.'

'It would be if it was only red paint,' I said. 'But it was covered in all sorts of colours, and he's a bloody carpenter.'

'Fair enough.' Eva gave me a sly look. 'Have you seen much of him?'

'Rory? Not at all actually. He messages every now and then, but he's been busy.' A sudden picture of Rory kissing me in the kitchen popped into my head and made me blush. 'We're meant to be having dinner tomorrow, though.'

'Good.'

'I'm thinking about cancelling.'

'Don't be so silly, *Liebchen*.'

I groaned. 'I'm not in the right headspace for a date. And I don't want a new relationship. It's way too soon.'

'I can understand that,' Eva said, looking thoughtful.

We were sitting in Eva's living room. Jem was at Callum's – she said he was helping her and Cassie with their witch project, which sounded implausible to me because as far as I knew Callum wasn't even in their history class. But she'd sent me a picture of them together when she arrived, so I knew she was there safely and I wasn't worried. I liked her friends and I knew they'd look out for each other.

Now a noise outside made me jump and I got to my feet and wandered over to the front of the room, pretending to casually glance out of the window. Eva watched me, her brow furrowed with concern.

'You really are nervy.'

Checking once more to make sure there was no one outside I turned to her. 'I'm a wreck, Eva.'

She patted the sofa next to her and I sat down, finishing off my gin.

'I even suspected Andrea for a second, did I tell you that?'

'Cassie's mother?'

'That's the one. I thought she might have been the person who put weed-killer on the grass because she'd been to visit the night before I noticed it.'

'But you don't think that now?'

'No.' I sighed. 'Not really. I just don't trust anyone.'

'Even me?'

I smiled at her. 'I trust you,' I said.

*

I was at the Haven the next day. Mandy was her usual cheery self in the morning, barely looking up when I came in. She'd put me in the little cupboard of an office again but I actually didn't mind too much. I was getting used to it, and it was much warmer in there now the door had been mended. It was another busy day and I spent ages with one client who wanted help filling out some forms for a school appeal for her son. Once they were all done, I needed to make a copy for my files so I left her in my cupboard and went to the photocopier, which was in a little room behind Mandy's reception desk. Mandy wasn't there – she must have popped to the loo or to make a drink – so I sidled past and into the copier room. It took me longer than I expected to do what I had to do because there was a paper jam and I had to fart about taking the trays out and pulling bits of paper from the depths of the machine, but eventually I got it sorted, made the copies I needed to, and emerged – triumphant – from the copier room.

Mandy was sitting at her desk, her back to me. She was

browsing social media and as she scrolled down her feed I saw, or at least I thought I saw, a photograph of Jem. It was blurry because it was blown up, but it looked familiar. She was looking straight at the camera and wearing her school uniform from her last school.

'What's that?' I said.

Mandy jumped and hit her keyboard, and the picture disappeared.

'Was that a photograph of my daughter?'

She spun round on her chair and looked at me. Her face was pale and there were two red spots on her cheeks. 'No,' she said. 'Why would I be looking at a photograph of your daughter?'

'It looked like her.'

Mandy lifted her chin. 'I've only met your daughter once.'

'You don't remember her?' I could feel adrenaline pumping through me. I wanted to grab Mandy and shake her and demand to know why she had a photograph of Jem on her screen. I stared at her and she stared back at me, defiance in her eyes.

'No.'

'Let me see,' I said. 'Let me see your screen.'

Mandy turned round and bashed her keyboard to wake up her computer. Her background was a school photograph of a little girl with reddish blonde hair. Younger than Jem and wearing a different uniform. Was that the picture I'd seen? Why would I mistake a photo of a little girl who looked nothing like Jem, with one of my daughter? I really was losing my marbles.

'Did you manage to get that copied?' My client had obviously got bored waiting and come to find me.

'Yes,' I said, flustered. 'Sorry.'

Mandy had opened a spreadsheet and was concentrating on it very deliberately. I looked at the back of her head and then forced my attention back to my client. 'Let's get this sorted, then,' I said.

*

I didn't usually take a lunch break when I was at the Haven. I used the time to catch up on paperwork from my clients and get ready for the people I was seeing that afternoon. I had to be a jack of all trades when I was there and I was learning about parts of the law that I'd not even thought about since university. I needed that time to swot up before my next client blindsided me with a difficult question.

Today, though, as soon as my last client of the morning left, I took out my phone and called Andrea. Her phone rang and rang without going to voicemail. I tried a few times and then I gave up. Instead, I pulled on my coat and hurried along the road to the museum. I wanted to speak to Andrea and I hoped she would be there. The sea wind whipped my hair around my head and stung my eyes but I didn't care. I just wanted some answers.

Fortunately, Andrea was in the shop, arranging a display of scarves. She took one look at my face and looked worried. 'What's happened?' she said. 'Is it the girls?'

Now I was there, I wasn't sure what to say. I just shook my head. 'They're at school,' I said. 'Nothing's wrong. I've been trying to call you.'

'My phone's not working because I dropped it in the sink. I've had no messages, no email, nor internet. What a nightmare.'

I looked at her helplessly, trying to decide how to ask the questions I wanted answers to but not knowing where to begin. Andrea, realizing I was worried about something, turned to the woman who was working with her. 'I'm going to take my lunch now.' The other woman nodded and Andrea took me by the arm and steered me towards the café where she sat me down, plonked a cup of coffee in front of me and then sat herself, with her arms folded.

'Spill,' she said.

I took a breath. 'How well do you know Mandy?'

Andrea looked surprised. She'd obviously been expecting me

to say something else. 'Quite well,' she said. 'We're not best mates, but I've known her for years.'

'Do you trust her?'

'She wouldn't work at the Haven if she wasn't trustworthy.'

'Yes, but do you trust her?'

'I do.'

Andrea looked straight at me. Her curly hair was pulled back with a bright scarf – like the ones she'd been arranging in the shop – and her skin was clear with just the tiniest hint of wrinkles round her eyes. I knew she was older than me, but she didn't look it, especially now with my hair tangled by the wind, my make-up running and my face puffy with lack of sleep.

'Why?'

I rubbed my forehead. 'She doesn't like me.'

Andrea grimaced, but she didn't argue, which made me more confident I was right. 'You knew this?'

'She mentioned you,' Andrea said carefully, swilling her coffee round in the cup.

'What did she say?' I was jiggling my leg up and down nervously.

Andrea sighed. 'We know who you are.'

I leaned forward and rested my forehead on my hands. 'How?'

'Mandy followed your husband's case quite closely,' Andrea said looking wretched. 'She recognized you almost as soon as you started work.'

The smell of my coffee was making me feel sick. I pushed the cup away quite violently and some of the liquid splashed onto the table. 'Why did she follow it?' I didn't want to know the answer really, but I asked anyway. 'Did she have reason? Is she connected to one of . . .' I still found it hard to talk about my husband's victims. 'To one of the women?'

'Speak to Mandy,' Andrea said.

She got up from the table. 'I have to go.'

I watched her walk out of the café, wondering if she'd find a way to tell Mandy about our conversation. Shakily, I wiped up my spilled coffee with a paper napkin and then I got my phone out and called Lorna, the manager of the Haven. I told her I was ill and couldn't come back that afternoon and asked if she could rearrange my appointments. She agreed.

'You sound terrible,' she said. 'Get some rest.'

But I had no intention of resting. I needed to find out more about Mandy because I was absolutely sure she was the person who'd been tormenting us. And I wanted her to stop.

Chapter 34

Honor

1661

It was of little surprise to me that when I arrived at the meeting hall, the men of the town council were already there. Alice had – after some persuasion – come with me but she had stayed silent and sullen by my side as we walked through the streets.

As we approached the hall, we could hear the sound of men's voices. Not raised in anger, but more rumbling in agreement. It was dark outside, but the hall was lit with lanterns and we could see the glow round the doors and from the windows.

I exchanged a glance with Alice and in quiet agreement we both stepped forward at the same time and pushed open the wooden door.

Everyone in the room turned to look at us and I felt a moment of sheer fright. There were fifteen or twenty men – men I'd known all my life – but right then no one seemed familiar. They all looked at us – Alice and me – with hostility. I felt very strongly that we were intruding, that they didn't want us there. And once my initial nerves had subsided, that feeling made me more determined.

Alice, who had always been so outspoken and unafraid, shrank down behind me. 'We should leave,' she said in a quiet tone, but I shook my head.

'I am a burgess and this council should not be meeting without me,' I said. I didn't speak loudly but my voice seemed to carry over the heads of the men who stared at us.

Davey was there, to the side. He looked up and caught my eye and, remembering the feel of his lips on mine, I felt my face flush, and dropped my gaze. In the far corner of the room was a space at the table – my space. I tugged Alice's sleeve and I walked slowly, chin lifted, to the chair. Alice stayed where she was, hovering beside the door. She looked as though she was about to bolt and I knew I couldn't stop her running if she wanted to.

I sat down at the table, the legs of my chair scraping loudly in the quiet room, and looked round at the men. I knew them all. Men who'd fished alongside my John, whose babies I had delivered or whose wives I had helped to nurse a weak child. Men who had known me since I was learning to walk, or who I had known since they were squalling in a crib. Davey, of course. Gregor. The minister from the kirk. And one stranger.

He was sitting beside Gregor at the head of the table. While everyone else was stiffly upright, this man was leaning back in his chair, watching us all with sharp eyes. He was richly attired in a plain black velvet jacket and a soft hat and he looked as though he didn't belong here. As I watched him, he shifted slightly in his seat and Gregor took that as his cue to carry on speaking.

'As I was saying,' Gregor said, looking at me with a defiant expression. 'There have been some troubling stories told and I would be remiss if I did not investigate further.'

There was a rumbling of agreement as the men all nodded. I looked over to where Alice stood by the door, her eyes wide with fright and I felt my resolve harden.

'Forgive me,' I said. 'I was unaware this meeting was taking place and so I missed you explain the nature of these stories. Could I ask you to elaborate further?'

'At this point, I cannot,' said Gregor. 'I think the people of the town have all heard the whispers, but until we have more proof . . .' He emphasized the word 'more'. 'We should wait.'

He smiled at me, showing his teeth. Like a wolf baring his teeth at a lamb, I thought. I smiled back, hoping my eyes were as icy cold as his.

'Wise,' I said. 'It is important to be sure.'

Gregor gave me a small nod. 'Indeed. And to that end, may I introduce my friend, Malcolm Black.'

The velvet-clad man sat up straighter and, unsmiling, nodded a greeting to the room. And in that second I suddenly understood who he was. Because I had heard the name Malcolm Black before. I had heard it in huddled whispers and frightened rumours from travellers who had passed through nearby towns and seen him at work. I swallowed and looked over to Alice, who was slumped against the wall, white-faced, any last remnants of fight gone. She knew too, then. Knew that Malcolm Black was a witch finder. The most determined, pious, and – if the stories were to be believed – the most vicious witch finder in all Scotland.

'Malcolm Black,' I breathed.

At the head of the table, Malcolm Black stood up. 'This pestilence is infecting all of Scotland,' he said. He sounded as though he was confiding in everyone in the room. Taking them into his confidence, and sharing secrets. 'But I am here to tell you, you should not fear. For God is mighty and we shall seek these witches and find them.'

His voice was loud without shouting and the men in the room were all gazing at him. The way they looked at him filled me with terror, because I knew they were already in his thrall.

'The deacons and elders of the kirk will help me in my quest,' he continued. The minister preened like a peacock and I curled my lip in disgust at his pride. 'And I call on you burgesses to follow my lead and do what is necessary.'

There was a pause as the men all considered his words and for a second I felt a rush of hope. These were good men. They wouldn't do this witch finder's dirty work.

'I remind you,' Malcolm Black continued, his voice dripping poison, 'that in cases as serious as this, it is clear that if you are not working with us, you are working against us and you can find yourself facing the assizes. Therefore I assume you will all follow my lead.'

This time the men all nodded vigorously and I couldn't help but shake my head, disappointed in how easily they were recruited.

Now Malcolm Black looked directly at me. He put his hand flat on the table in front of him and I noticed how clean his fingernails were. How smooth his skin. I raised my eyes to meet his glare and almost winced when I saw the malevolence there.

'You are?'

My mouth had gone dry. 'I am Honor Seton,' I said. 'I am a burgess of this town.'

Malcolm Black scoffed. 'No,' he said.

'My husband John . . .' I began, but he waved his hand dismissively.

'No,' he said again. 'Did not John Knox warn of the dangers of women holding authority,' he said, talking to the men now, not me. 'Did he not say that women who have property or power are a danger to the social order?'

The men all murmured their agreement. I tried to catch Davey's eye, but he was looking at Gregor.

'The social order has been created by God,' Malcom went on. 'And if we try to change it, we will face his wrath.'

I cleared my throat. 'Be that as it may,' I began, 'I am a burgess.'

'No longer.'

'Gregor?' I said. My voice was shrill. 'Gregor, who is he to dismiss me?'

Gregor raised his head. 'He is the guest of the laird.' He gave me that wolfish smile again. 'And the laird also dismisses you.'

I looked round at the faces of the men, waiting for someone – anyone – to speak out. To say that I had been a burgess since my John had died. That I had worked hard for the town. But they stayed silent. I looked at Davey and he met my gaze and then dropped his eyes to the table. Weak, I thought. Him and me. I pushed my chair back with a squeak and stood up, knowing I was beaten.

Gregor watched me looking at his brother and like a cat pouncing on a mouse, he saw his chance. 'Mr Black, there has been talk in the town that Widow Seton is close to my brother, Davey Kincaid,' he said. The way he said 'close' made it sound sordid and sinful. 'And therefore I believe this is an opportunity to lay these rumours to rest. If Davey is indeed a friend . . .' He said 'friend' as though it was something amusing. I didn't think it was funny. 'If Davey is indeed a friend of Widow Seton then he should leave the meeting too. If not, then he is welcome to stay.'

No one moved. I took a sharp inward breath, hearing my own heart thumping. I had not expected the finger of suspicion to point at Davey so soon. I glanced at Alice, but she simply shook her head. And I waited, as time stretched to breaking point, for Davey to speak.

Eventually, Davey looked up. 'I know Widow Seton,' he said clearly. 'Of course I do. She is known throughout the town. But I am no closer to her than any man here.'

I breathed in again, his words hitting my heart like darts.

Malcolm looked at Davey through narrowed eyes. 'What is Widow Seton to you?' he said.

Davey glanced at me briefly. 'Widow Seton is nothing to me.'

There was a pause and then I pulled my shoulders up and, gathering every bit of courage I had, I walked slowly from where I stood at the table to where Alice stood. I took her hand and together we pushed open the doors from the hall and went out into the cold, dark night. We didn't look back.

Chapter 35

Tess

Present day

Rory cancelled our date. He sent a message saying he had some work in Glasgow for the next few days, so working long days and a tiring commute meant he wasn't going to be good company. He said he was sorry and he would see me soon. I read his text as I raced home in the afternoon after I'd met Andrea at the museum. I was relieved. I was not ready to be going on a date, and I had too much else to worry about.

I shoved my phone back in my pocket and kept walking, hunched down in my coat. When I arrived at the cottage, Eva was standing in the window of her house, looking out and she waved. I raised a hand to wave back and then, on a whim, decided to go in.

She answered the door, looking worried.

'Are you all right, *Liebchen*?' she said. 'You're . . .' She waved her hand in front of her face, telling me my make-up was a mess.

I shook my head. 'I think it's Mandy from the Haven,' I said.

'Who is?' Eva looked bewildered.

246

'Who's been doing all the horrible things to us.'

Without saying a word, Eva bustled me inside and shut the door behind me. I heard her slide the chain across and I was glad.

'Tell me everything,' she said.

So I explained about Mandy being rude and unpleasant to me, and seeing what I thought was a photograph of Jem on her computer screen.

'I don't trust myself any more though,' I said. 'I was sure it was Jem I could see on her screen. But when she showed me, it was a photograph of her niece.' I groaned. 'But I keep thinking perhaps she had two tabs open on her screen and just showed me what she wanted me to see.' It sounded ridiculous to my own ears but Eva was nodding like she understood. 'The thing I keep asking myself, is why she would have a picture of Jem?'

'That's the question,' Eva said.

'She knows who I am.' Eva looked alarmed and I nodded. 'Andrea told me.'

'Do you think she has an axe to grind?'

I shrugged. 'Maybe. I wondered if she had some connection to one of the women Alistair assaulted? Andrea wouldn't tell me, but it's possible.'

'Have you looked her up?' Eva asked.

'Looked Mandy up?'

'Online.'

I blinked at her. 'No, I've not.'

'Maybe we should take a look?'

I reached into my bag and took out my phone.

'Google her,' Eva said. 'What's her surname?'

'Leavis.' I typed it in.

There were a few profiles. A dog groomer from Norfolk. And a pouty 20-something from Indiana.

'Nothing,' I said, disappointed.

'What about the Haven? Does it have a page on there? She might be following it.'

I was impressed with Eva's knowledge of social media. I told her so.

'I'm old, Tess, not dead.'

That was me told, then. I searched for the Haven and found its website and then, as Eva had suggested, its Facebook profile.

And there, right at the top of its followers list, was Amanda Leavis. I hadn't even thought that Mandy would be a nickname.

I clicked on to her profile and waited for it to load.

'She's single,' I told Eva. 'Born in 1985.'

'Spring chicken,' Eva muttered. 'What's the matter?'

With shaking hands I turned my phone so she could see it properly. Because Mandy had shared a post that had Jem's face on it.

'What is this?' Eva said. 'Jemima isn't missing.'

It was one of those appeals, that you see all the time online, saying 'missing' along the top in red type. Beneath it was Jem's school photo – the one I'd seen Mandy looking at – and under that it said Jemima Robertson was missing. *Jemima Robertson.*

'Mandy didn't post this,' Eva pointed out. 'It's anonymous. Perhaps she isn't the person behind these pranks after all.'

I looked up at the ceiling, thinking hard. This was all so horrible. 'This isn't an appeal, it's a threat,' I said, my voice quiet and squeaky.

'You need to call the police.'

But I was a step ahead. I was already dialling the non-emergency number, even though it felt like an emergency.

A bored-sounding man answered my call. I tried to explain but there was so much to say and I kept getting my words muddled up.

'There's a fake missing appeal online?' he said. 'But your daughter isn't missing?'

'She's at school.' I was confident that if Jem wasn't there, the school would have phoned, and I liked the idea of her being safely in a lesson.

There was a pause at the end of the phone. 'So what's the problem?' the man said.

'It's a threat,' I said, frustrated.

'Sounds more like a practical joke to me.'

I wanted to scream but I didn't. I patiently spelled my name for the man and Jem's name, and explained that she went by Blyth even though her surname was Robertson. He said he would pass it on to the right department. Then I hung up and looked at Eva in despair.

'I don't know what to do,' I said.

She reached out and took my phone from me. 'Go and put the kettle on,' she said. 'I'll have a think.'

I checked my watch, thinking Jem would be leaving school soon. I thought I'd go and meet her, because I didn't want her to walk home by herself.

'Okay,' I said. 'I've got time for a quick cuppa.'

I made tea and when I came back through to the living room, Eva was holding my phone at arm's length, looking pale and worried.

'What?' I said, my stomach dropping as I saw her expression. 'Is there something else?'

She handed me the phone. On the Haven's page was a post – added by someone calling themselves User413. It had an old corporate photograph of me, from my LinkedIn page, which I'd taken down months ago, alongside a newer pic, snapped as I walked along the street by the beach, my phone clasped to my ear.

In shock I dropped the phone and it bounced on the carpet. I bent down to pick it up, and my legs gave way, so I sank onto the floor and stayed there instead.

Eva shifted along the sofa so she was next to me and put a comforting hand on my back. 'I know,' she said.

I forced myself to look at the post again. 'Tess Blyth, legal adviser at the Haven, North Berwick is the wife of rapist Alistair Robertson, who stood by him in court and blamed his VICTIMS for his abuse,' I read out loud, before letting out a small moan.

As I looked at the post, the number of comments underneath

was going up and up. People leaving shocked emojis. Others saying they would never use the Haven now and commenting that I was being paid from taxpayers' money, conveniently ignoring the fact that my work at the Haven was voluntary.

'She just gets to live her life, while the women he abused are suffering,' one poster said. 'It's not right.'

Bile filled my mouth and I took a deep breath, jabbing at the phone to shut the screen. 'It's never going to go away,' I said. 'Never.' Eva stroked my hair and I leaned against her legs, like a child. I was going to have to resign. I could see that. I would go in tomorrow morning and speak to Lorna, the centre manager, I thought. Apologize for all the trouble I'd caused. I didn't want to leave, but how could I stay now?

Feeling wretched, I wrapped up in my coat, pulled my scarf up over my chin and my hat down over my brows, and headed off to meet Jem from school. She was gratifyingly pleased to see me – she was nervy too, though she pretended she wasn't. She talked about her history project and said she and Cassie were planning to go back to the museum the next day to do some final bits of research.

Now the clocks had changed, it was almost dark by the time I got home. Jem needed a wee so she took my keys and ran ahead to let herself in while hating how jumpy I was, I hurried along behind her. I saw Jem run up the path and into the house and heard the door close. Everywhere was shadowy and still, and I longed for the long evenings of summer. They seemed very far away.

Suddenly someone loomed out of the darkness at me, right outside our house, and I shrieked.

The person yelped in fright. 'God, sorry, Tess, it's me.'

'Lorna?'

A car went past, lighting up the pavement and I saw it was indeed Lorna from the Haven, her hair hidden under a woolly hat. I laughed, the kind of laugh that comes from nerves, not

250

humour. 'I'm sorry to react like that, I wasn't expecting anyone to be outside the house.'

'Sorry,' she said again. 'I should have phoned.'

'I know why you're here,' I said. 'I was going to come and see you tomorrow.'

'Could we go inside, do you think?'

Feeling unsettled and uncomfortable, I led the way up the path and inside, noting the now familiar blue glow of the CCTV doorbell.

I offered to take Lorna's coat but she shook her head.

'No thanks,' she said. 'I won't keep you.' She looked terribly worried and her expression made my stomach churn. 'There was a post on our social media,' she began.

I nodded. 'I saw it.'

'We've taken it down now,' Lorna assured me. 'But it was shared quite widely before we got to it.'

I sat down heavily even though Lorna was still standing. 'Shit.'

'I know.' She sounded sympathetic but I knew what she wanted to hear.

'Consider this my resignation,' I said. 'I'm so sorry to bring all this to your door.'

Lorna shook her head. 'I'm afraid I won't accept your resignation.'

I stared at her. 'What?'

'I *am* going to have to ask you to take some time off,' she said. 'Just while we work out a way to get through this. But I don't need you to resign.'

Not yet, I thought. But I was grateful she hadn't sacked me outright.

'I'll be in touch,' she said. 'You know all of us at the Haven are very fond of you, don't you?'

That was rich. 'Does Mandy know . . .' I began.

'I'll tell all the staff tomorrow,' Lorna said.

I opened my mouth to say that this was all Mandy's fault and then shut it again. I had no proof of anything.

'Thank you,' I said politely. I let her out and then I sat back down, still wearing my coat.

'Fuck you, Alistair,' I hissed under my breath so Jem, who was thumping about upstairs, wouldn't hear. 'Fuck you.'

I sat there for a minute or two, and then I dragged myself upright again and took my coat off.

'Jem,' I called upstairs. 'I'm going to start dinner.'

'Be there in a minute,' she shouted.

My phone rang.

'What now?' I whispered, looking at the screen. It was Rory. I almost cancelled the call, but then desperate to hear a friendly voice, I answered it instead.

'Hello,' he said, sounding pleased I'd answered. His cheery tone lifted my spirits, the tiniest amount. 'I thought it was going to go to voicemail.'

'Couldn't find my phone,' I lied. 'Where are you?'

'Just leaving Glasgow. Thought I'd say hello.'

'Hello,' I said, much more cheerfully than I felt.

'Are you all right? You sound a bit stressed.'

Clearly I wasn't as good an actress as I thought. 'It's been a crappy day.'

'Tell me why.'

I paused. Should I tell him the truth?

'Tess?'

'I'm still here,' I said. 'Rory, have you heard of the television presenter Alistair Robertson?'

'Yes,' he said. He sounded far away, because he was driving, I supposed. 'Not seen him on telly for a while, though.'

'No,' I said. 'He went to prison.'

'Right,' Rory said. 'What's that got to do with your crappy day?'

I took a breath, readying myself to tell him, then changed my mind the very next instant. It seemed he was the only person in this town who didn't know the truth but I wanted to keep it that way as long as I could. 'I thought I saw him, that's all.' I laughed.

'In the McDonald's drive-through, would you believe? And then I thought I saw . . .' I searched my mind desperately for another infamous celebrity – anyone would do. 'Margaret Thatcher in Tesco. And Saddam Hussein walking on the beach.' I forced myself to laugh. 'I'm clearly losing my marbles.'

Rory was silent.

'Rory?'

'Sorry,' he said. 'Traffic. Can I call you tomorrow?'

A car horn sounded down the phone and I jumped. 'Of course, sorry for distracting you.'

'Bye, Tess.'

'Bye,' I said. But he'd already gone.

Chapter 36

Jem

By the time Cassie and I got a chance to go to the museum, I was as twitchy as anything. Hermione still hadn't turned up, and I was convinced someone had taken her. Mum was snappy and short-tempered, and she said she was taking some time off from the Haven. Which was weird. But she wouldn't talk to me about it.

School was dragging, and Cassie and I still hadn't done our history project. Somehow the appeal of writing about the witch-hunts had disappeared a bit now I was actually living in one. The only good thing was the Halloween disco which was just one day away now, but I was properly worried that with Mum so jumpy she'd turn around and say I couldn't go.

After school the day before Halloween, I met Cassie and Callum at the gate and we walked to the museum. Heather was waiting for us, looking just as enthusiastic as she had last time.

'How's the project going, girls?'

We both looked a bit sheepish. 'Slowly,' I admitted while we all sat down. 'We've not done much.'

'Well, perhaps this will inspire you,' she said, so eagerly I felt sad that I didn't find history as exciting as she did.

'What have you got?' Cassie asked. 'Did you find out anything about the rumours?'

'Yes and no,' Heather said. 'There's not many written records from the time, because not many people could read and write back then.'

'Alice could,' I said proudly. 'She wrote the little charm inside the witch bottle.'

'She did,' Heather agreed. 'That was really unusual for women at the time.'

I grinned.

'So what have you found?' Cassie asked.

'I went back through the council records,' Heather said, looking remarkably excited about trawling through endless boring documents. 'And I found a report of a town council meeting from when the witch finder arrived in town.'

I felt a little shiver down my spine as she spoke, imagining a man clad in black riding into town to seek out poor Honor and Alice.

She pushed a bound book towards us and we all looked down at the indecipherable writing and then back up at Heather.

'It's not easy to read,' she admitted. 'But basically it explains that Honor Seton was asked to leave the meeting.'

'Why?' I frowned. 'Because she was a witch?'

'Because she was a woman.'

'Uh-oh,' said Callum. Cassie gave him an approving glance and I was pleased. 'So women weren't allowed at these meetings then?'

'Ordinarily, no,' Heather said. 'But Honor Seton was different.' She grinned. 'I've done a bit of reading from records of other meetings, and it seems she was a burgess – a local councillor – at a time when women weren't even allowed to vote.'

I was confused. 'That makes no sense.'

'It was a legal loophole. Her husband was a burgess and when he died, he left his title to her.'

'Nice,' said Cassie.

'Except they threw her out of the meeting,' I pointed out.

'Well, she was a burgess for more than ten years as far as I can see from old records,' Heather said. 'I had no idea any women had taken on that role so early, so this is interesting for me, too.'

Callum was looking puzzled. 'So they let her do it for ten years and then decided to throw her out? What changed?'

'The witch finder?' I felt that shiver down my spine again. 'Was it because of him?'

Heather pushed another book across the table. It showed a little line drawing of a man in a black jacket with a large white collar, wearing a floppy hat and brandishing a stick.

'Malcolm Black,' she said. 'Scotland's most notorious witch finder.'

'Looks nice.' Cassie made a face.

'He was feared all over the area,' Heather said. 'He went from town to town looking for witches.'

'What, he just turned up?' Callum said.

'Normally in response to rumours of salacious activity.'

'So he turns up at the meeting and throws Honor out, just because she's a woman?' I felt personally attacked by the idea. 'Was that really enough to be suspicious of her?'

'John Knox . . .' Heather looked at us. 'You know who John Knox was?'

'Yes,' I said firmly, though I wasn't totally sure of all the facts.

Heather clearly cottoned on to my lack of knowledge. 'John Knox was a religious reformer from about a century earlier,' she said. 'He had taught that women with power were a threat to the natural order of things, so yes, Honor being a woman and a burgess was enough to get her thrown out.'

'Why didn't anyone stand up for her?' Cassie said, outraged. She had a very clear sense of right and wrong, which I loved. 'Why didn't anyone point out she'd been there much longer than he had?'

'I imagine that they all knew Honor was about to be accused of being a witch,' Heather said. 'And if they stood up for her, then that was as bad as being accused themselves.'

'That's not fair.'

'It's one of the reasons the witch-hunts spread so fast. Anyone speaking up was accused, and the only way to stop the finger being pointed at you was to accuse someone else.'

'God,' I said. 'That's exactly what happened with my . . .' I shut my mouth and stopped talking, not wanting to tell Heather about my dad. But Cassie nodded at me, understanding. It was so familiar. Mum had stood by Dad – at first – and that had been enough to bring the accusations down on her head. 'Things haven't moved on at all, have they?'

'Well, we don't put witches to death anymore.'

'Just make death threats instead.'

Heather gave me an odd look and Cassie jumped in. 'This is great for our project,' she said sweetly.

Heather beamed at her. 'I'm so pleased.'

'Is there any more about the rumours?' I asked.

'Not really.' Heather scanned the report in front of her. 'Just that there was some gossip about Honor being involved with a man called Davey Kincaid. He was a local bigwig. But he denied it and actually it seems he and his older brother, who was the laird, were behind the rumours about Honor.'

'Shit,' I breathed. 'So he was pretending to be Honor's boyfriend but really he was doing the dirty on her?'

Heather shrugged. 'We'll never know.'

*

'What are you thinking, Jem?' Callum asked as we walked home, laden with printouts and notes about Honor.

I made a face. 'I'm thinking that perhaps she trusted this Davey Kincaid and he used that against her.'

257

'Poor cow,' said Cassie. 'Men are the worst.' She stuck her tongue out at Callum and he shoved her good-naturedly.

'But it's the same, isn't it?' I said.

'What is?' Callum looked confused.

'Honor and her bloke, and Mum and Rory.'

'Is it?'

I stopped walking. 'Think about it. He's been sniffing around, making himself useful. Bringing pizza. Being all nice.' I spat out the word. 'Getting Mum to trust him.'

'He's being nice because he fancies your mum,' Cassie said.

I started walking again, faster this time because I was annoyed. 'It all makes sense,' I said over my shoulder to Callum and Cassie. 'He was even at school the day I lost my tie. We saw him, didn't we, Cass?'

'Well, we saw someone who could have been him,' she said doubtfully.

'And then it turned up round a skeleton's neck.'

'That doesn't mean anything,' Callum said. 'What else?'

I thought. 'The paint on the cloth in his van.'

Callum shrugged. 'It's all just circumstantial.'

'All right, CSI boy,' I said. 'I've just got a feeling about him, that's all.' I felt a bit deflated now. 'I'm not sure about him.'

'That's probably because he's doing it with your mum,' Cassie said. 'That's always weird.'

'Urgh,' I said. 'They're not doing it, Cass. They've not even been on a date.'

'They're doing it,' Cassie said with conviction.

'Stop it.'

'Doing it, doing it, doing it.'

'Cassie,' I said. But I was laughing too. She could always cheer me up.

Callum was walking a little way ahead of us, clearly uncomfortable with the discussion about my mother's sex life.

'Rory set up the CCTV, didn't he?' he said over his shoulder.

'Yes.'

'So why would he do that if he thought it would catch him doing something awful.'

'That's what Mum said,' I said reluctantly. 'Maybe it's not him after all.'

We'd reached the corner, where we all had to go our separate ways, so we stopped walking.

Cassie gave me a hug. 'I have to go because my dad's coming to pick us up,' she said. 'Message me later.'

She headed off and Callum grinned at me.

'Want me to walk you home? I could help you look for your cat again?'

'That would be good. Shall I ask my mum if you can stay for dinner?'

Callum gave me a broad smile. 'Great.'

I pulled out my phone and started typing a message to Mum as we walked towards our cottage.

'Don't ignore your gut,' Callum said suddenly.

'What?'

'If you've got a gut feeling about Rory, you shouldn't ignore it.'

'You think?'

He shrugged. 'Not sure. But I've read stuff online about instincts and how often it's you picking up on something, rather than some sort of sixth sense.'

'Sounds a bit weird.'

'Witchcraft,' he said with a grin. 'Maybe just keep an eye on him, that's all.'

Chapter 37

Honor

1661

I felt foolish. Foolish and ashamed and angry, and more than a little frightened. Alice was very sweet and didn't say that she'd warned me that Davey wasn't on our side, or remind me of all the times she'd told me not to trust him. Instead she held my hand as we hurried home through the cold evening air and deadlocked the door behind us.

'What should we do?' she said in a very small voice, once we were barricaded inside.

'We need to go.'

'But the cats . . .'

I pulled her close to me and held her tightly. 'We need to go. Tonight.'

'Where will we go?'

I was at a loss. Once upon a time the fishermen would have taken me where I needed to go – up the coast to Leith or even as far as Arbroath or Montrose. But I didn't want to ask them. If Malcolm Black was here for me – and I was sure he was – then anyone who associated with me would be guilty too. I thought of Davey denying me in the meeting and shuddered. I couldn't blame him for saving himself. Little Christy needed his father, and I would never expect Davey to sacrifice himself because we'd kissed once. It still stung, though.

'Ma?' Alice said again. 'Where will we go?'

'North,' I said, making my mind up on the spot. 'We'll try to get to Edinburgh as fast as we can. Walk tonight and perhaps hitch a lift with a farmer in the morning.'

'Is Edinburgh safe?'

I knew the witch-hunts were rife in the city, with women being tortured in the castle and their bodies thrown into St Margaret's Loch. But I also knew the narrow, cobbled streets and crowded town would be a good place to hide. I nodded. 'We can stay there a night or two and then move on.'

'I don't want to.'

I pulled her tighter to me again. 'I know.' I stroked her hair like I'd done when she was a tiny girl. 'But I need you to trust me and I need you to do as I say.'

Alice didn't speak.

'Alice?' I said. 'Will you do as I say?'

She raised her eyes to mine and, reluctantly, she nodded. 'I will.'

'Good girl. Now, come. We need to pack. Not too much because we need to carry our bags ourselves and too much weight will slow us down.'

I tugged her arm and she followed me upstairs. I took out the loose floorboard and chose some of my records and phials to take with us, leaving the rest with genuine regret. We took a few clothes and tied them into our spare cloaks so we could hang them from our backs.

'We can leave food for the animals,' I said. 'And set them free so they can go elsewhere when they're hungry.'

Alice was quiet. 'Alice, I know you're sad about leaving the cats, but they will be fine,' I said, tucking the ends of my cloak under each other and tying them securely. 'Cats are independent creatures.'

Again Alice didn't speak. I looked at her where she was kneeling on the floor, holding her own package in her arms. She was very still, her head cocked like she was listening, and her eyes were glazed as though she was looking at something far away.

'Someone's coming,' she said.

'No one's coming,' I assured her. 'It's quiet, listen.'

'Shhh,' Alice said forcefully. 'They're coming.'

I strained my ears, but I could hear nothing. Alice was still sitting, stock still, gripping her package. So I scrambled to my feet and went to the window. I lifted the latch and opened the small glass panel and leaned out. And there, over the wind and the crashing of the waves in the distance, I heard horses' hooves.

'They're coming,' Alice said again, more quietly this time.

I shut the window with a bang. 'Alice,' I said, rushing to her and holding her by the shoulders. 'Alice.'

She focused on me, looking for all the world like she'd just woken up. 'What?'

'They're coming,' I said urgently. 'You need to hide.'

'No.'

'You promised you would do as I asked,' I said desperately. 'You promised and now I'm asking.'

'Come with me.' She was crying now. 'Come with me, Ma. We can both hide.'

I took her face in my hands and wiped away her tears with my thumbs. 'If I come, they will look for us both. If you can hide tonight, you can leave before it gets light. Try to get on a cart – you're so slight you can easily secrete yourself in the back.'

'No,' Alice said again. 'I don't want to.'

The pounding of the hooves was getting louder. 'Alice Seton, you listen to me,' I said sternly. 'You need to go and hide immediately.'

Alice clung to me for a second. And then she got to her feet, still crying.

'Wait,' I said as she turned to go. 'Take this.' I thrust my own package at her. 'Take the records. You might need them. Hurry.'

'Ma,' she said.

'I know, my girl. I know.' I pressed my lips to her temple and then gave her a gentle push. 'You understand where to go?'

She nodded. She looked at me once more, her eyes huge in her white face, and then she turned and I heard her running down the stairs and out into the back of the cottage. I knew she would go to the goat shed. It was raised up from the ground, and there was space underneath. Impossible to see if you didn't know it was there, but it had been a good hiding spot when Alice was small and didn't want to do her chores or learn her letters.

I swallowed a sob, thinking about how perfect she had been as a little girl. How happy we'd been, just the two of us once my own mother had passed away. And how now my precious, clever, funny, quirky daughter would be all alone in the world. I hoped she would be all right. I thought she would because she was quick-witted and sharp, but she was kind – too kind – and people might take advantage.

Through the quiet streets outside I heard the horses come nearer. My heart was pounding in time to the rattling of their hooves.

'Stay strong,' I told myself aloud. 'Stay strong, Honor.'

I shook out my cloak and put it on, then slowly, concentrating on nothing but putting one foot in front of the other, I went downstairs to wait my fate.

I didn't have to wait long. Just a few minutes had passed when there was a thudding on my door and shouts from outside.

'Widow Seton,' a voice called. 'Open up, Widow Seton.'

I thought about running. I thought about turning tail and haring it out of the back door and across the fields. It was dark and I knew this countryside better than Malcolm Black, who wasn't even from these parts. I even knew it better than Gregor and Davey Kincaid who had never played outside as children, as I had. But I also knew they would follow with their horses – and their dogs – and I knew they would find me quickly and running would simply make me look guilty.

With supreme effort, I drew back the bolt on the door, and opened it. I expected to see the whole town council, with flaming torches and swords. But instead I simply saw Malcolm Black astride his horse, and Gregor Kincaid, who'd dismounted his own beast and was standing by my door, holding its reins.

'Widow Seton,' Gregor said as I opened the door. 'You are accused of witchcraft.'

I lifted my chin. 'I am entitled to appear at the assizes.'

On his horse, Malcolm Black tipped his hat up with the tip of his riding crop. I could see his ratty, narrow face in the moonlight. He gave me a nasty, mocking smile.

'I am authorized by the Privy Council witch-hunting commission to summon an assize,' he said. He sounded as though he had said these words many times before. 'The assize will be of no more than forty-five men, and there will be a jury of fifteen.'

'Men?' I asked.

Malcolm Black looked down at me, his expression unreadable. 'Pardon?'

'Will it be fifteen men?'

'It will.'

I nodded. As always it seemed it was men making decisions and women suffering for it.

'We will compile a list of charges, which will be put to you at the assizes. You will have the opportunity to confess.' He gave me a small, humourless smile. 'Or to answer the charges put to you. We will also allow you the chance to tell us of any other witches you may know of in the area.'

'Other witches.' I felt sick hearing those words. It was clear these men had already found me guilty and no matter what I said now, their opinion would not change.

'You are entitled to a lawyer,' Malcolm Black went on. 'Do you have the means to pay?'

I breathed in. I had never even met a lawyer. I knew fishermen and farmers and fathers and mothers. Not lawyers. 'I do not.'

'Very well.'

Something about the way the men were looking at me, as though I was already tortured, tried and convicted and on the way to the gallows, made my fear subside. Instead rage rose inside me.

'When is my trial to be?' I said.

Malcolm Black stared at me. 'Tomorrow.'

'Morning?'

'Yes.'

'Whereabouts?'

Gregor made a frustrated groan but Malcolm Black simply blinked and then said: 'At the meeting hall.'

'Then I will bid you goodnight, gentlemen,' I said. 'And see you in the morning.'

I made to push the door shut, but Gregor was too fast. He put his foot on the step. 'You'll come with us now.'

'Where to?'

'The jail.'

'I am not yet found guilty.'

Malcolm put his riding crop to my cheek. 'You will do as I say.'

I opened my mouth to argue and – swish – his crop whipped through the air and caught me across the face. Immediately my eyes watered with the sharp pain. I wanted to cry out but I would not give them the satisfaction of knowing I was hurt.

'Very well,' I said in a voice that shook more than I liked. 'I will come with you now.'

Gregor climbed up on his horse and then he leaned down and roughly dragged me up on to the saddle in front of him too, yanking my arm in its socket. This time I did cry out, with surprise and fear and pain. Gregor smacked me on the top of my skull with an open palm, making my head spin. Finally, with all my fight gone, my face bleeding from Malcolm Black's riding crop, and my vision blurred from the blow to my head, I slumped down onto the horse's neck. I would accept my fate, I thought. But I would not go quietly.

Chapter 38

Jem

Present day

Mum was really subdued when we got home. She said she'd been for a walk on the beach, which usually cheered her up, but she wasn't happy. She was nice enough to Callum and she pinched some of our chips but she was quiet and jumpy. I thought she was missing the Haven and I wished she would tell me why she wasn't working there anymore. I'd ask her again when Callum went home. Or maybe it was because Halloween was coming. I had to admit I was a bit nervous about that myself. I wondered if there would be another prank at the house. That picture of my face, saying I'd gone missing still lurked in the back of my mind and creeped me out a bit.

Callum and I spent ages in the garden looking for Hermione, but there was no sign of her. Eventually, when it was almost dark, I shook my head. 'I think I need to accept that she's wandered off,' I said. I felt like crying, which was totally lame. 'She must have gone to live somewhere else.'

Callum was standing next to me and now he put his arm round me and hugged me. 'Cats are bastards,' he said.

I laughed but then it turned into a sob halfway through.

'Don't cry,' Callum said. I buried my face into his shoulder and he wrapped me up in his long arms and held me tightly and it felt really nice. And then I looked up at him and he looked at me and he kissed me. And that felt even nicer.

After a little while we realized it was properly dark and very cold, so we went back inside. I couldn't stop smiling and I thought Mum would totally realize what we'd been doing but she barely looked at me. She just asked if we'd had any luck with finding Hermione and I said no.

Callum went home and Mum sat on the sofa, watching *Schitt's Creek* but not really watching it.

'I'm quite nervous about the play,' I said. I wasn't actually nervous as my parts were pretty small and I only really had one line, but I couldn't think of anything to say.

'You'll be great,' Mum said mechanically.

'Did you see Eva today?'

'Yes.'

God, it was like she was the teenager and I was the parent. She was really making me work hard to get some conversation.

'It's a shame you didn't go out with Rory tonight.'

She shrugged. 'Wasn't really in the mood anyway.'

'I don't think Rory's worth bothering about,' I said cautiously. 'You shouldn't let him upset you.'

Mum looked at me for the first time. 'He's not upset me.'

I bit my lip. 'Good.'

Mum got up and poured herself another glass of wine. 'Sorry, Jem,' she said, smiling. It wasn't a very genuine smile – it was all lips and no eyes – but I appreciated the effort. 'I'm just tired. Rory had to work tonight. I'm not sad that he cancelled.'

'I'd be sad if Callum cancelled,' I admitted.

She smiled again – more genuinely this time. 'You like him, eh?'

'I do.'

'He's a nice lad.'

I grinned. 'He's going as Harry Potter tomorrow.'

'Going where?' Mum looked blank.

I threw my head back dramatically. 'To the Halloween disco, Mum. It's literally all Cassie and I have been talking about for weeks.'

'Oh god,' said Mum, putting her hand over her mouth. 'I forgot about that.'

'There are teachers there so it's all safe,' I said firmly, anticipating her next move.

'Jem, I'm not sure . . .'

'It's fine.' I was going to that disco, whatever she said. 'You can drop me off and pick me up if that makes you feel better.'

Mum looked totally exhausted. She was all pale and thin and her face was puffy and saggy at the same time. She nodded. 'Okay.'

We both went to bed early. I curled up under my duvet, reading over the notes I'd made about Honor being sold out by her boyfriend back in 1661. I was more convinced than ever that Rory was behind the nasty stuff that had been happening, but I just didn't know why. And nor did I have any evidence.

*

The next morning, Mum and I had breakfast, and then I did my homework, quite half-heartedly because I kept thinking about the Halloween disco and how I was going to paint my face. I wanted it to be a bit like Margot Robbie as Harley Quinn. So I didn't pay much attention to the doorbell when it rang, because I was watching a make-up video on YouTube. But then I realized I could hear a man's voice and my ears pricked up.

Rory's here! I messaged to Cassie. *What shall I do?*

Nothing!!!!! came the answer. *Wait for me to get there. Coming now.*

She was on the doorstep within half an hour. I bounded downstairs to let her in.

'It's Cassie,' I sang, hearing Mum and Rory's conversation pausing to listen. I pulled Cassie upstairs. 'I told you that he cancelled Mum's date last night,' I hissed once we were in my bedroom.

'Guilty conscience.' Cassie nodded knowingly, peeling off her coat and hat. 'Couldn't face her.'

I made a face. 'But he's here now.'

Cassie shrugged. 'Do you still think he's the one who's been doing all the weird stuff. And posted that poster thing online?'

'I don't know,' I admitted. 'Not really, I suppose, if I think about it rationally. But Callum said I shouldn't ignore my gut. Maybe if I knew him better, I'd have a better idea.'

'Well, maybe we should find out more about him.'

'Sit him down and ask him loads of questions?'

'Not outright. We just need to charm him and get him to open up.'

'Okay.' I bounced on my toes. 'How do we charm him?'

'Just get him talking. We can chat to him and find out more about him.'

'Right,' I said. 'Let's go.'

We trooped downstairs and into the living room, where Mum and Rory were both standing up, and Mum was looking for her car keys.

'Are you going somewhere?' I said, panicking. 'Don't go.'

Mum gave me an odd look. 'I was just going to pick up those pots I ordered from the garden centre while Cassie's here with you. Rory said he'd help me plant them.'

I felt a little prickle of annoyance that she wouldn't let me stay at home by myself. I was 14 years old. I had a boyfriend. I was fine. I glared at her.

'That's a shame you're going out,' said Cassie.

'A shame?' Mum frowned.

'Because we were hoping Rory could help us,' Cassie said in

a hurry. She looked at me desperately and I racked my brains trying to think of a reason we needed to speak to him.

'With set design,' I blurted. 'We've got a bit of a crazy idea for the *Macbeth* scenery and I wanted his opinion on whether it would work. If you don't mind, Rory?'

'Of course I don't mind.' Rory looked quite flattered and for a moment I felt guilty about lying.

'Why don't you stay here and help the girls and I'll pick up the pots,' Mum said. 'It'll only take me half an hour and I'll feel better if they're not here on their own anyway.'

'Can you manage?' he said.

A shadow crossed Mum's face and I hid a smile. She didn't like her independent nature being questioned. Never had, even before Dad went to prison. It was one of my favourite things about her. 'I'll be fine,' she said. She put on her coat and pulled her car keys triumphantly from her pocket. 'Ah ha!'

'Have fun,' I said, eager for her to go. 'Can you see if they have any of that cat grass in pots? Maybe we could put some of that outside and tempt Hermione to come home?'

'Okay,' Mum said. She headed off, jangling her keys, looking more relaxed than she had for days.

'Cup of tea?' I said to Rory.

In the kitchen, Cassie and I huddled together. 'What are we going to say?' I murmured. 'I've got no set ideas.'

'Ask how to make that wood thing move,' she suggested.

I giggled. 'Burnham Wood?'

'That's the one. It moves, doesn't it? Ask him how to do it.'

'It doesn't really move – it's the soldiers in camouflage making it look like it's moving.'

'Oh.' Cassie looked disappointed. 'Ooh, I know. There's a picture inside the cover of our *Macbeth* books of the witches in some old production. And they're on like a floating platform?'

I nodded; I knew the picture she meant.

'Ask if we can do that.'

271

'Brilliant.'

I finished making the tea and took it through into the living room for Rory. Cassie sat down on one side of him and I sat on the other.

'We wanted to know if we could make a platform for the witches,' I said. 'Like on a pulley that lowers them down.'

Rory made a face. 'Is this play going to be in your school hall?' We both nodded. 'Won't work,' he said.

'Really?'

'Because there's a suspended ceiling.'

Cassie and I both looked at each other and then at Rory. 'Suspended what?' I said.

'Suspended ceiling. Look.' He picked up a pen from the coffee table and I handed him an envelope. Quickly, Rory sketched out an explanatory drawing. 'It's not a real ceiling, see? So you couldn't hang anything from it.'

'Oh,' I said, weirdly disappointed even though we'd only just thought of it. 'Never mind.'

Cassie was frowning at Rory. 'Have you been to our school?'

He grinned. 'Of course. I've been doing some work there.'

'In the science labs,' I said.

'Yeeees,' said Rory looking at me oddly. 'Did you see me?'

I nodded. 'Just wasn't sure if it was you, that's all.' I glanced at Cassie who gave me a small nod. So he could have taken my tie, then. And I knew he had done some work at the Haven so he could have taken Mum's scarf, too.

'Do you have to be checked?' I asked. 'To work in school?'

'Checked?'

'You know, to make sure you're not dodgy?'

'Make sure you're not a paedo,' Cassie added unhelpfully.

Rory gave her a hard stare. 'I've been working there for years,' he said.

'Means nothing,' I pointed out. 'You could still be dodgy.'

'They know me.'

272

'Yes, but how well do they really know you?' said Cassie. 'You could be anyone. Do the parents know they're letting any old bloke wander round the corridors?'

Rory looked pissed off. I quite liked it. 'I'm not any old bloke,' he said. 'I'm a parent. Or I was. My daughter went there.'

There was a small, slightly awkward pause. Rory drank some tea and I caught Cassie's eye behind his back, making a surprised face. Because I knew Rory was divorced but I was pretty sure Mum had never mentioned that he had kids.

'What?' Cassie mouthed.

'I didn't know you had a daughter,' I said, keeping my voice super casual. 'Mum never mentioned her.'

Rory shrugged, his expression guarded.

I wasn't sure what to say next, so I just jumped in with another question.

'Looking forward to Christmas?'

Rory laughed, looking pleased we'd changed the subject. 'It's a while off, yet.'

'It'll come round quick,' I warned, sounding like my granny, who was already claiming to be 'almost 80' when she was actually only 72. 'Will you be here for Christmas?'

'I've not made plans.'

'Will you see your daughter?' Cassie asked Rory.

'Not this year,' Rory said. His face darkened.

Cassie and I looked at one another. We'd obviously touched a nerve there.

'What's her name?'

'What does she do?'

Rory looked vaguely alarmed at all the questions. 'What is all this?' He sounded lighthearted but I thought he was still a bit cross.

'Do you see a lot of her?' I asked. It really was weird, I thought, that he'd never mentioned her before. Never talked about visiting.

Rory looked straight at me. 'Her mum and I were never great together,' he said. 'Off and on and then off again, you know

273

what it's like?' I looked back at him, feeling a bit odd. He was talking to me like I was an adult who understood the ins and outs of grown-up relationships. But I just nodded, not wanting to interrupt him. 'When I found out Michelle was pregnant, I was annoyed. Thought she'd done it deliberately.'

He leaned forward, elbows resting on his knees and I looked at Cassie over the top of his head. She made a face, clearly feeling as weird as I did at the turn the conversation had taken.

'But when she was born, I held her in my arms and I just felt this rush of love. And I knew I would never let anyone hurt her. It was up to me to protect her.'

I felt a lump in my throat because the person who'd hurt me more than anyone else in my life was my dad. He'd certainly never protected me, nor my mum.

'You sound like a really good dad,' I whispered, suddenly feeling awful that we'd quizzed him so hard. Rory looked round at me, as if he'd forgotten that I was there.

'I'm not,' he said fiercely. Then he smiled. 'But thank you.'

Mum's key in the door made us all look up. She came in, rubbing her hands. 'Bloody hell, it's freezing out there. Are you all okay?'

I grinned at her. 'Fine,' I said. 'We can't do the idea we had for the play, but that's okay. Rory was really helpful.'

'Good,' Mum said. She gave Rory an indulgent smile. 'Thanks for that.'

He stood up. 'Shall I help with these pots then?'

He and Mum went back outside to the car, and Cassie and I ran upstairs and watched from the landing window.

'What do you think?' Cassie said.

'I don't know, now.' I scratched my head. 'Because he's been working at school and at the Haven and he could easily have picked up my tie and Mum's scarf.'

'But he really loves his daughter.'

'Exactly.' I sighed. 'When he was talking, I wished my dad was more like him.'

Cassie gave me a little squeeze of sympathy.

'We should google her,' Cassie said suddenly. 'Google his daughter.'

'Ooh, yes.'

We went into my bedroom and I opened my laptop.

'Ah,' I said. 'We don't actually know her name.'

'Look up Rory,' Cassie suggested.

I typed in his name but all that came up was a Facebook profile with no picture, and some reviews about his carpentry work.

Cassie clapped her hands.

'My mum's been doing her family tree,' she said. 'She's found loads of old people's birth certificates and that.'

'So?' I said. 'You're not related to Rory. Are you?'

'No,' Cassie said tutting. 'I mean we could search for him on the website and find his marriage certificate. It would have his wife's name on it. And maybe we can find a birth certificate for his daughter, too.'

'Ohmygod that's brilliant,' I said. 'It's like actual detective work. What's the website?'

Cassie thought. 'Not sure,' she admitted. 'I really should have paid more attention when Mum was telling me about it.'

'Even just vaguely will do. We'll find it.'

It took us a few attempts but we got there in the end. Cassie guessed her mother's password far more easily than she'd guessed the name of the website and we typed in 'Rory Baxter'.

'When did your parents get married?' Cassie asked.

'2003.'

'Mine were 2002,' she said. 'Rory's roughly the same age, isn't he?'

I screwed up my nose. 'He's a bit older, I think. And his daughter's grown up, isn't she?'

'So if I do weddings from 1990 onwards?'

'That would work.'

She set the search terms, pressed return and there it was:

Rory Baxter and Michelle Hamilton, married at St Cuthbert's in Edinburgh, 15th May 1995.

'You are a genius,' I said, properly impressed at Cassie's detective work. 'You should be like one of those private investigators.'

She looked pleased. 'I actually might.'

'Now look for births,' I said.

Cassie set the search parameters and pressed return and there it was. Billie Baxter, born in Edinburgh in 1997.

'Billie,' said Cassie approvingly. 'Nice name.'

'So he's definitely got a daughter,' I said, thinking hard. 'Why would he be so secretive about her?'

'Perhaps they don't get on.'

I giggled. 'Perhaps he hung skeletons off her porch and called her a witch.'

'Google her,' Cassie said. I typed in Billie Baxter and nothing came up.

'Nothing,' I said. But then I had a thought. I used my mum's maiden name – what if Billie did the same? I deleted Baxter and typed in Hamilton, and this time the top result was a Facebook page. It was set to private but we could see the profile picture was of a very pretty young woman in her twenties, and we could see her location was Scotland.

'That could be her,' I said, turning the screen so Cassie could see.

'Click on it.'

I clicked through on to the profile. 'Ooh look, we can see her friends list.'

'See if there's a Michelle on the list who could be her mum.'

There it was – Michelle Hamilton. I clicked on that name and it brought up a picture of a woman a bit older than my mum, hugging someone that was clearly Billie, though her hair hid her face. 'Me and my girl,' the caption read.

'This must be her.' I was pleased.

But Cassie shrugged. 'Doesn't prove anything though, does it? None of this has anything to do with what's been happening here.'

'No, I suppose not.'

I looked at Billie's picture again. 'Could we message her?'

'Why? What would we say?'

'I don't know.' I sighed. 'Let's leave it for now. Look at this make-up video – I thought I'd try to do it for tonight.'

Chapter 39

Alice

1661

I did not want to leave my mother to face the Kincaids and Malcolm Black alone, but I had promised to do as she asked, and so when she thrust her package at me and told me to hide, I did.

I ran down the stairs and out the back door to the cottage, into our large garden. It was dark and I had no candle but I knew where to go. I felt the ground beneath my feet, welcoming me, and the cats' eyes shone in the moonlight and showed me the way. I reached the goat shed and threw myself on to the earth, then wriggled on my belly like a worm into the space beneath the wooden floor. There was a gap beneath the shed, large enough for me to fit in nicely. I used to play in there when I was a wee girl, hiding from Ma when she wanted me to practise my reading or help her with cleaning. If you knew it was there, you could see it, but the grass was overgrown and it was dark outside, so I thought I would be safe. When I was safely inside, two or three of the cats came and lay down by the gap, hiding it from view. I felt a rush of love for the creatures. I didn't want to leave them behind and I hoped that we wouldn't have to leave.

I heard the horses come nearer, then shouts and the sound of a sharp rapping at the door. I heard talking and the whistle of a riding crop through the night air and my mother crying out, and I wanted to go to her, to help, but I knew she would be angry. I tried to gather my rage, and focus on stopping the men – the way I had when I was at the big house listening to the Kincaid brothers – but I was too scared.

I listened as they took Ma away, and as the horses set off, I crawled out of my shelter, scurrying through the darkness with all senses alert in case anyone had stayed behind to look for me. I watched the horses disappear into the night – just two of them. When I'd felt the impending danger, I'd expected more of them. The men of the town council, led by Malcolm Black and the Kincaid brothers. But now I could only see two shadowy figures. There was Malcolm Black, his floppy hat silhouetted against the moonlight, and Gregor Kincaid with Ma sitting on his horse in front of him.

'Just the two of them,' I whispered to myself. That was interesting. In fact, it gave me a tiny glimmer of hope, like the soft light of dawn in the darkness. Malcolm Black's horse whinnied and, nervous, I scuttled back to the safety of the goat shed. I stayed there, hidden under the shed, until the sky began to lighten from murky black to deepest grey, and I heard the squawk of the seagulls and knew morning was approaching.

Ma had told me to leave. To hide myself in a cart leaving town and go north where it was safer. But I wasn't going to do that. I was not going to flee like a frightened rabbit and leave Ma to face whatever dreadful punishment Malcolm Black decided would suit her. No. Because I had read the book that Christy gave me. I had waded through the lines of dry and dull court reports, without even really knowing why. And now, because I had read the book, I had a plan.

But before anything else, I needed an outlet for my anger. I firmly believed this was Davey Kincaid's fault and I was going to make sure he knew he was to blame. I wanted him to carry Ma's fate on his back for the rest of his life. I wanted the guilt to weigh him down. And I was going to tell him that.

So, as the shouts of the fishermen coming home echoed through the quiet, early morning streets, I left my hiding place and ran upstairs to where I'd stowed Christy's book. Then I pulled my cloak around me, and walked across our garden, past the churchyard, and up to the big house. It was shrouded in darkness, the only lamps burning were at the front door and in the kitchen window. I would go round the back way, I thought. The back entrance would be open.

Sure enough, the door was not locked. A man – a servant judging by his clothes – slept in a chair by the fire, but he didn't stir as I walked past. I knew the layout of the house from the night the fever came, so I went out into the wide hall and up the stairs. It was still dark, but I didn't seem to need to light my way; I just knew where to tread. My footsteps were silent and no one was around as I made my way upstairs to Davey's room.

Outside his door, I paused for a second, wondering if he'd wake with a start and call out for help. I hoped not. I wanted to speak to him, not be dragged away before I got to say my piece.

Taking a deep breath, I turned the handle and went inside. To my surprise, Davey was not in the large bed, but instead standing by the window, looking out over the dark town and to the sea beyond. He turned as I entered and nodded to me, then focused his attention back on the view.

Nonplussed by his lack of reaction, I stayed where I was, unsure how to proceed.

'They have taken her to the jail,' he said, eventually, as though I'd asked a question.

'My mother?'

He turned properly now and looked straight at me. 'My brother and his witch finder, Malcolm Black, have taken your mother from her home and thrown her in jail.'

'Because of you.' My voice was clear and icy cold. I wanted my words to wound Davey like darts.

'No,' he said.

'They took her because of you. You are the one who asked her to come and care for Christy and you are the one who denied her at the council meeting.'

Davey's eyes narrowed and then he nodded. 'You are right to judge.'

'Because you are to blame.'

'I let her down.'

'Is there a difference?'

'Perhaps not.' Davey's shoulders slumped. 'But I did what I thought was best. If I had stood beside her at the meeting, then I would be in jail now, too.'

'Hardly,' I scoffed. 'Not when your brother holds the key. He bailed you out before and he'd do it again.'

'You know about that?'

I shrugged. 'Everyone knows about your gambling habit. It wasn't hard to work out the rest.'

Davey sighed. 'My brother despises me. He sees me as a cross he has to bear and he hates that I have a son and he doesn't. He'd see me hang without blinking and then he'd take Christy as his own.'

I stared at him. He was playing me for a fool, surely? Pretending to be on my side, then he'd call for his servants and before I knew it I would be in jail with my mother. But he sounded plausible. And I knew Gregor was cold-hearted and self-absorbed.

'Alice,' Davey said. He sounded desperate. 'You must believe me. I didn't want any of this to happen. I thought I could talk Gregor round, convince him that this wasn't the way to do what he wants.'

'What does he want?' I said, but I knew the answer.

'To dredge the harbour. He believes your mother is the reason no one approved his plans at the meeting.'

'No one wants the harbour dredged,' I hissed. 'Those plans are madness. They will make Gregor rich and the town poor because they will destroy the fishing trade.'

'I know.' Davey looked wretched. 'Gregor only sees money. I thought that when your mother came, the night of the fever, he might understand that she was a good person and change his mind about the plans . . .'

'You called on her deliberately?' I said, shocked. 'You brought her here to help you talk your brother out of his greedy plan?'

'No,' Davey shouted. 'No, not at all. I brought her here because my son was dying and I knew she was the only one who could help. But then Isobel died, and Gregor was so angry. She was the only one keeping his avarice in check. With her gone, he has nothing to lose. He hates that a woman stands between him and riches.'

'And Malcolm Black simply hates women,' I said, understanding.

My legs felt weak. Malcolm Black and Gregor Kincaid were driven by hatred and my mother was in their sights.

'They're going to kill her.'

Davey looked startled at my blunt words. 'I fear so.'

'And when they've killed her, they will come for me.'

'Yes.'

'You could call Gregor now. Tell him that I am here.'

'I could,' Davey said. 'But I won't. You must trust me, Alice. I'm on your side.'

I felt strangely calm as I looked at Davey carefully, closing my eyes so I could feel his emotions. Perhaps it was foolish, perhaps I was signing my own death warrant, but all I could sense within him was pain. I thought about Ma telling me that he was a good man, and I nodded slowly. Ma understood people – she had been right about Kyla, after all. It seemed she was right about this too.

Slowly, I opened my eyes. Davey was watching me curiously but with no malice in his expression.

'Do you trust me?' he asked again.

'Do you trust me?' I said. 'Because I have a plan but I need you with me.'

'I will stand beside you, Alice. If you stand by me.'

I nodded. 'I will. But know this, Davey Kincaid. If you betray me, I will bring down every plague, every misery, every sorrow on your head.'

Davey raised an eyebrow. 'Do not let Gregor hear your threats of witchcraft,' he said. 'He will assume you mean it.'

I took a step towards him. 'I mean it,' I said. Davey shrunk away from me and I grabbed his elbow and pulled him closer again. 'Don't test me, Davey.'

He held my gaze for a second or two and then he nodded. 'You are a terrifying enemy, Alice. I'm glad we are on the same side.'

I let go of his arm and stepped away from him, looking out at the town, which was beginning to wake up as dawn broke. 'We don't have long,' I said. 'The trial will begin shortly.'

Davey ran his fingers through his hair. 'What is your plan? Should we go to the jail? Can you do something . . .?'

'Shh,' I said. 'I am thinking.'

Davey clamped his lips together.

'There were fifteen or more men at the council meeting,' I began. 'Many men.'

Davey nodded.

'I don't remember the witch-hunts that happened before, because I was only young, but I do know that they spread like the fever spread through your household. I know that women confessed, or pointed the finger at others, and soon there were thirty or forty people accused. No one ever stayed quiet. It was accuse others, or be accused yourself.'

'I remember,' Davey said. 'Stories from Prestonpans and else-where. Like a plague ravaging these towns.'

'And yet, only Gregor and Malcolm Black came to take Ma.' I lifted my chin. 'And that is important.'

'I can help.' A small voice spoke from the door of the room and we both turned. There was Christy, his little face serious. 'I can help you,' he said again.

'No.' Davey went to his son. 'This is no fight for a child. Especially one who is still recovering from illness.'

But Christy scoffed. 'I'm fine. And I'm 12 years old and Alice is only a little older.'

'Christy . . .'

'I know what Uncle Gregor has done and I know why.'

Davey blinked at him. 'Really?'

'I know he wants to dredge the harbour.'

'How do you know that?'

Christy smiled. 'I am quiet and still and I listen when people don't think I'm listening.' I caught the boy's eye and gave him an encouraging nod. 'And I like Widow Seton and I want to help.'

Davey looked at me and I smiled. 'Seems to me we need as many people on our side as possible,' I said. 'But Christy's already helped, more than you know.'

Christy came properly into the room and I saw he was fully dressed, despite the early hour. 'Do you have the book?' he said.

'I do.'

'Did you read it?'

'I did.'

'I wanted you to read it, in case it was useful. Was it useful?'

'Yes.' I turned to Davey. 'We have an idea,' I said.

284

Chapter 40

Jem

Present day

I was very excited about the Halloween disco. Everyone at school had been talking about it so much and telling so many funny stories from last year's party that I was desperate to get there. But as I started to get ready, I did have a little gnawing feeling that I should mention Rory's daughter to Mum. Was it weird that he'd not mentioned her before? Or maybe he had and Mum just hadn't told me. It was no biggie, really. It was just niggling at me and I didn't know why.

I had my laptop in my room so I could watch the YouTube video for my make-up – my phone screen was a bit small. Now I opened it up and looked at Billie Hamilton's Facebook page again. Hmm. I picked up my phone and typed a message to Cassie.

Is it weird if Mum doesn't know that Rory has a daughter? Should I say something to her? I wrote. *Just to see if she knows?*

Definitely, Cassie replied.

And then before I'd even had a chance to respond, she sent another message: *No.*

Which?

I don't know!

Helpful.

Sorry.

I thought about it and typed again: *Do you think I expect all men to be crap because of my dad?*

Deep, but yes.

So I might be projecting?

Deeper. But also yes.

So should I say something to Mum?

I waited ages, watching the little dots bouncing while I put the finishing touches to my make-up, until finally her response came: *Yes.*

But it was already nearly seven o'clock and even though I'd done my make-up, I still wasn't dressed.

I'll speak to her tomorrow, I typed back to Cassie.

K, she replied. Then she sent a selfie. She looked amazing in her long, sleek witch's dress. She'd scraped her hair back into a bun and done loads of smoky eye make-up and she looked so sexy and grown up, I almost died of envy. I took a photo of myself – still in my dressing gown – but with my newly short hair curled wildly and with my Harley-Quinn-inspired face. I had put on sweeping pink eyeshadow and drawn a little heart on my cheekbone with liquid eyeliner.

OMG I love it! But HURRY UP!

Laughing, I jumped up and put on my dress. It wasn't as sleek as Cassie's but I loved the sticky-out skirt.

On our way, I typed. Mum was driving Cassie and me to the disco, and we were picking up Cassie on the corner.

I picked up my laptop and took it downstairs with me to charge. Mum was in the living room and she grinned when she saw me.

'You look fabulous!' she said. 'I'm sure Honor and Alice would be proud.'

I did a silly curtsy holding out my skirt, and then I put on my witch's hat that was on the sofa and got Mum to take a picture.

'We'd better go,' Mum said, looking at the time. 'Poor Cassie will be wondering where we are.'

As she looked – again – for her car keys, there was a ring at the doorbell. I was standing right there, putting on my coat, so I opened it. Outside was a woman, her face drawn and worried. She was clutching a brown folder. 'Is Tess here?' she said.

'Muuuum,' I shouted. 'It's for you.'

Mum came out into the hall holding her keys. She looked alarmed when she saw the woman, and then a bit cross. 'Mandy?'

'I'm so sorry to bother you,' the woman said. Her voice was shaky and all her words were tumbling over themselves because she was trying to speak quickly. 'I wanted to come to explain. To tell you why I did . . .' She trailed off. 'I want to explain,' she said again.

Mum stood up a bit straighter. She filled the hallway suddenly, like when animals make themselves look bigger as a defence thing. 'Mum?' I said, feeling nervous. 'What's happening?'

'Can you walk to school?' she said. 'Do you mind?'

I looked from the woman – who was still on the doorstep, sort of cowering against the side of the porch – to Mum. 'Will you be all right?'

Mum nodded. 'I will.'

'Okay then,' I said. I put my scarf on. 'I'll text when we get there.'

'Good girl,' said Mum. She was looking at me, but I could tell her attention was still on the scared-looking woman at the door.

'Are you sure you're okay?' I said. 'I can stay if you want.'

Mum looked at me properly now. 'You go,' she said. 'Have a brilliant time and send me lots of pictures.' She gave me a big hug and kissed me. 'Go on, Cassie will be waiting.'

I walked outside and the woman – Mandy – flattened herself against the wall as I passed. She was really odd. I didn't like leaving Mum alone with her. But I saw Eva's light was on and felt better knowing she was next door.

'Bye then,' I said to Mum. I had a really odd feeling, like something bad was going to happen. But then my phone beeped with another message from Cassie saying, *Where ARE you?* and Mum stepped back into the hall and said: 'Come in, Mandy.' And I felt a bit silly to be so nervous. I waved goodbye to Mum and hurried off along the road to find Cassie.

It was freezing and I'd forgotten my gloves, so I shoved my hands under my armpits and huddled down as I went. Just then I heard a car horn and my name being called.

'Jem!'

I looked round. Behind me, Rory was leaning out of his van window. 'Jem! Are you off to the disco? I'm heading up to the school to drop some stuff off. Need a lift?'

Maybe if I hadn't been so cold, I'd have said no. But my hands were numb, and I was still curious about Rory's daughter and I wanted to know more. So I gave him a beaming smile and ran to the van as he pulled over.

'Can we pick up Cassie?' I asked. 'I'm meant to be meeting her on the way.'

'Sure,' Rory said. I clambered into the passenger seat. 'Love the outfit. Is Cassie a witch, too?'

'She's a sexy witch,' I said. 'She wants to impress Max.'

'Boyfriend?'

'She wishes, but he's a douchebag.'

Rory chuckled. 'You've got the right idea, Jem. Stay away from boys.'

I laughed too but when I looked at Rory he wasn't smiling anymore.

'Cassie will be on the corner up here,' I said. 'Past the church.'

There were roadworks up ahead and a line of traffic stopped at temporary lights. Rory tutted at the cars and suddenly swung the van round and headed back the way we'd come.

'This'll be quicker.'

'Cassie's waiting,' I said. 'Back there.'

Rory pushed his foot down on the accelerator and the van speeded up. 'Rory, Cassie needs a lift.'

'We're not going to pick her up.'

'She'll be wondering where I am,' I said. My voice shook a bit and we were still travelling away from school. 'Rory, Cassie will be worried.'

He ignored me.

'Rory . . .'

'Do you know why I don't talk about my daughter?' he said.

Confused, I shook my head. 'No.'

'Because I never see her.'

'You don't?' My mouth had gone very dry.

Suddenly Rory banged his hands on the steering wheel, making me jump. 'No,' he said. 'I don't get to see her at all. She doesn't want to see me. And do you know whose fault that is?'

I didn't know what to say. I felt a sudden, weakening wave of fear. I wasn't even sure where we were now, but I knew we were nowhere near school, nowhere near Cassie and nowhere near my house.

'I want to go to the disco,' I whispered. 'Can you take me to school?'

'Do you know whose fault it is?' Rory said again.

'No.' My voice was very quiet.

'It's your mum's fault.'

Chapter 41

Honor

1661

I knew I was lucky I had been kept in North Berwick overnight and not been taken to a bigger town. Our jail had burned down after the last witch-hunt – many people claimed it wasn't an accident – and the new one had been built in a hurry and was much smaller. Malcolm Black had not been impressed when he slammed the door closed on my cell – shutting himself in with me.

'Where is the equipment?' he muttered to Gregor, who'd stayed on the other side of the bars. He was white-faced and looked tired. I hoped he was regretting taking things so far, but I doubted it. Gregor thought only of himself.

'We have nothing.'

'No pilliwinks to twist her thumbs?'

Gregor shook his head.

'No caspie claws?'

I winced at the mention of the vicious device used to clamp women's arms and crush their bones.

Again Gregor shook his head and Malcolm Black rolled his eyes.

'No matter,' he said. 'We will go back to basics.' He seemed quite pleased about it.

'I will leave you,' said Gregor.

'Could you write up the bill?'

A smile danced around Gregor's thin lips. 'The bill?'

'I fail to see why the town, or your good self, should pay for this woman's punishment,' said Malcolm Black. 'She is clearly a woman of means. She should pay.'

Gregor smiled properly this time. 'Indeed,' he said.

'Ten loads of coal for the burning and two barrels of tar.' Malcolm Black looked me up and down. 'She is not big, but it is good to have enough for unexpected events.'

I felt vomit in my throat and swallowed it down, wincing at the sour taste. I didn't want Malcolm Black to know I was scared.

'I will include your expenses,' said Gregor, and with a definite spring in his step, he departed. Even though I hated him, and knew he felt the same about me, I was still sorry to see him go. Without his presence there was just me, left in the tiny cell with the most notorious and most malicious witch finder in Scotland.

Malcolm Black bent down and felt the stone floor with the palm of his hand. 'It'll do,' he said, straightening up. 'Take off your dress.'

'No.'

He hit me so hard and so fast across the face that I didn't realize what had happened until I was sprawled on the floor. I felt blood trickling from my nose.

'Take off your dress.'

This time I complied, standing up shakily and noticing splatters of blood down my front from my nose. I dropped my dress on the floor and he kicked it into the corner of the room. 'Now the rest of your clothes.'

Shivering in the cold air of the cell, and from embarrassment, I did as he told me, trying to hide my modesty with my arms.

'Sit down.'

'The floor is cold.'

'Sit down.'

I realized what he had been doing when he felt the stones. He wanted me to be cold. He wanted me to suffer. He may not have had pilliwinks or caspie claws, but he was determined to hurt me, nevertheless.

'You have been seen in the company of the devil,' he said.

It was such an outlandish accusation that I laughed and immediately regretted it because Malcolm Black looked triumphant.

'You do not deny it?'

'Of course I deny it.'

'The minister is scared of you.'

'The minister is scared of everyone. He whispers his way through his sermons because he is so frightened of speaking in front of people.'

'You killed Isobel Kincaid.'

'I did not.'

'The laird has told me how you administered potions to make her sick.'

'Has he told you how I healed his mother, and his nephew?'

Malcolm Black's eyes narrowed. 'You do not deny killing Isobel?'

'I didn't kill her, I just wasn't able to save her. She had the sickness.'

'You have familiars.'

'I have cats.'

And so it went on. Malcolm Black would ask me questions and I would answer. He never tired. He never got bored. He didn't seem to feel the cold, wrapped as he was in a fur cape with his velvet hat on his head. Within an hour of being locked in the cell, I was shivering so violently that my jaw hurt and my teeth rattled in my skull. I sat on the freezing floor, hugging my knees to my chest and trying to stay warm, but it didn't make any difference. My breath came in irregular pants of cloudy air and my fingertips were blue.

Yet still Malcolm asked me questions.

I started to get confused, my head hurting from the cold as he twisted my words and fired accusations at me. I muddled my words, lost my train of thought, couldn't follow what he was saying.

'Isobel died in pain,' he said.

'She did.'

'Ah!' he said in triumph. 'You caused her pain.'

'No.' I held my head in my icy fingers. 'No.'

'You just said that you caused her to die in pain.'

Had I? I couldn't remember. I rested my head on my knees and closed my eyes. I was very tired now. I didn't know how long I'd been in the cell, but my head was so heavy and I was weak from shivering. Maybe I could just sleep for a minute and then I would be able to understand the questions Malcolm Black was asking.

'Wake up!' he bellowed. His face was close to mine as he crouched down to shout in my face. 'Wake up!'

By the time dawn broke, I just wanted the questions to stop. I wanted to sleep, and I wanted to be warm, and I cared about nothing else.

'Widow Seton?' Malcolm Black said. 'Do you confess?'

I was lying on the freezing floor, trying to keep my eyes open.

'If you confess, this will end.'

I moaned softly, at the thought of this being over.

'Do you confess?'

Somewhere, very far away, I thought I heard Alice. My little girl, calling me. 'Ma?' she said. 'Hold on, Ma.'

I lifted my head from the flagstones and listened.

'Widow Seton?' Malcolm Black said.

'Shhh.'

'Ma!' Alice called again. She wasn't here; she was in my head. In my heart. And somehow, knowing she was with me gave me strength.

'Widow Seton?'

I pushed myself upright on arms that shook and looked Malcolm Black straight in the eye.

'What?' I said.

'Do you confess?'

I gathered what little saliva I had in my mouth and spat at him. 'No,' I said.

Malcolm let out a roar of frustration and I think he would have hit me, had Gregor not arrived at that point.

'We are ready,' he said. He averted his eyes from my nakedness. 'The members of the assize are gathered in the meeting hall.'

Taking a deep breath and drawing all my strength, I stood up, facing the men unashamedly. 'Let's go,' I said.

Gregor turned away from me in disgust. His displeasure made me stronger. I pulled my shoulders back and lifted my chin.

'Get dressed.' Malcolm threw my dress at me and feeling like it was a victory of sorts, I tugged it over my head, grateful for its warmth.

With Malcolm in front of me and Gregor behind, I walked through town from the jail to the meeting hall. It wasn't far and it was still early morning, but the street was busy. People had turned out to see the witch stand trial, it seemed. I had expected jeers and taunts but the people were quiet. Heads bowed. I looked for Alice, worried that although she had run as I told her, she might not have gone far but instead stayed in town to see my fate. But I couldn't see her and I was glad. Perhaps she had made her escape already. Perhaps right now she was hiding in a cart, speeding towards Edinburgh. I hoped so. I didn't want her here, seeing this laughable trial.

Up ahead in the square I could see the barrels of tar and the piles of coal. I had already been found guilty, before my trial began. Perhaps it was hopeless, but I was going to keep fighting until the first flames licked my bare feet and the smoke singed my nostrils.

Inside the meeting hall, I was forced up two wooden steps to stand on a box. The crowds had followed us in, and now huddled together in silence as I stood, swaying slightly, in front of them.

I looked for Alice again and felt calmer – but disappointed too – when I couldn't see her.

'Widow Seton,' Malcolm Black began, 'you are charged with the following offences . . .'

He droned on, reading through the list of charges, which sounded more ridiculous the longer he spoke. That I'd danced with the devil on top of Berwick Law. That I'd killed Isobel Kincaid because I envied her youth and her handsome husband. I rolled my eyes at that one. That I'd conjured up storms and caused my John to drown. That I'd been seen speaking to demons who took the form of cats in my garden. That I had soured the milk and stopped the Kincaids' chickens laying. That was Alice, I thought. I felt a bubble of laughter in my throat and bit down on it. This whole situation was absurd but it wouldn't do to giggle. And really, there was nothing funny about my daughter being responsible – not that I really believed she was responsible – for the witchcraft I was now charged with.

'Ma?' I heard her voice in my head again. But louder this time. And when I looked up, there she was, pushing her way through the crowd, followed by Davey – and Christy – Kincaid.

My heart lifted in joy to see my daughter, and then crashed in fear as Malcolm Black stopped reading the charges and his gaze fell on her.

'Who do you think you are, intruding on this trial?'

Alice – my brave, beautiful girl – stood in front of him looking defiant. 'I am Alice Seton,' she said. 'And I have something to say.'

Chapter 42

Tess

Present day

Mandy was in a state. She looked like she'd been crying. She was holding on to a brown cardboard folder like it was a life raft and she was drowning. I wasn't keen on letting her in, but she kept saying she wanted to explain, and to be honest, I wanted to hear it. Wanted to hear why she'd tormented us the way she had.

So I said goodbye to Jem, and let Mandy into our house, hoping I wouldn't regret it.

She sat down on the sofa and looked at me. I stayed standing.

'I need to explain,' she said again.

'I'm waiting.' I was short with her. I wasn't sure what she could say that would make me excuse her behaviour.

'I spoke to Andrea,' she began. 'She said you'd been asking about me.'

I looked at her with a raised eyebrow. 'You know who my ex-husband is?'

'I do.' She looked straight at me with a hint of defiance in her eyes. 'I didn't write the post on the Haven's page. I know why you'd think it was me. But it wasn't.'

I didn't speak. It was clear she had more to say.

'I did share the fake missing appeal,' she went on. 'I knew it wasn't real and I shared it anyway.' She swallowed. 'I shared it from my personal account and from the Haven's.'

'Okay.'

'I've been so rude to you,' she said. 'And then Lorna said you'd taken some time off, and I realized it was probably all to do with me. And I felt so bad.'

I glared at her. 'Of course it was to do with you. How can you think otherwise?' Mandy winced. 'I've been so scared,' I said. 'Coming home each day, not knowing what treat you'd have left for me. What graffiti would be scrawled on our house today. What death threat would be lurking.'

'Death threat?' Mandy looked horrified. 'I've not sent you any death threats.'

'You didn't write "witch" on our fence?'

She shook her head.

'Or splatter paint across our walls?' I looked at her through narrowed eyes. 'I saw you,' I said. 'In the DIY shop. Were you buying paint?'

Mandy looked blank. 'No, I was buying some superglue to mend a picture frame that fell off my wall. I don't know what paint you're talking about?'

'You didn't steal my scarf and wind it round the neck of a skeleton?'

'Tess, please.' Mandy's voice wobbled. 'I don't know what this is, but I promise you, all I did was share the post about your daughter. And then as soon as I'd done it, I felt awful.'

I wasn't sure I believed her. None of this made any sense to me.

'Why did you do that?' I said, my tone harsh.

Mandy raked her fingers through her already messy hair. 'I wanted other people to know who you were.' Suddenly her voice

297

wasn't shaky anymore. Instead it was full of venom. 'I saw you living your life and I didn't think it was fair.'

I snorted. 'Believe me, none of this is fair, least of all people like you blaming me for my husband's crimes.' I looked at her with disdain. 'Why are you even here?'

'I wanted to explain.'

'You said that.'

Mandy breathed in deeply. 'Having you at the Haven brought back some bad feelings for me . . .'

I noticed her hands were shaking and felt unexpectedly sympathetic towards her. What wasn't she telling me? 'Andrea said you'd followed Alistair's trial quite closely.'

Mandy nodded. 'Because of this.' She leaned forward and opened the cardboard folder that she'd put on the coffee table. 'This is my file,' she said. 'From the Haven.'

Inside was a sheet of photographs of a much younger Mandy. There were close-ups of her face. And her neck, and her chest, and her legs. And in every picture she was battered and bruised. One eye was swollen shut. She had reddish-purple finger marks on her shoulders. A thick lip. What looked like a broken ankle. I winced and looked away.

'Did . . .' I caught my breath. 'Did Alistair do this to you?'

Mandy looked shocked. 'No,' she said. 'No, god. Not him.'

I felt myself sag with relief. 'Then who?'

'A music producer.' I sat down next to her on the couch and she looked at me. 'I was so young,' she went on. 'But I thought I knew it all, you know how young women are? I was a singer back then. Almost twenty years ago now. I'd done my time on a cruise ship. I'd done a summer in a holiday camp. And a season in the bars in Salou. I was ready for the big time. And this producer – Harry – he booked me as a session singer.' She looked a bit misty-eyed. 'It was amazing. I was living in London, sharing a flat with two other girls. Hanging out with boy bands. Partying hard.' She swallowed. 'Harry and I had an understanding. He liked me to stay behind after recording sessions, or go back to his room when we were away. You get the idea.'

I did. I felt sick.

'I knew if I said no, there would be no more work for me,' Mandy went on. 'But I hated him, Tess. I hated the smell of him, and the feel of him on me. I'd come home from work and shower twice or three times.' She shuddered. 'And then one day, I got talking to one of the singers I was recording with. And she offered me a spot on her tour. I was so pleased. I told Harry straightaway.' She made a face. 'But I was cocky, you know? Told him where he could stick his understanding.' She looked at the photographs. 'And he did that.'

'Fuck,' I said. 'Did you report it? Is he in prison?'

'No. I just ran away. Came home to North Berwick and gave up singing.'

My emotions were all over the place. Five minutes ago I'd been convinced she was the person tormenting us. Now I just felt so sad for her. I reached out and patted her arm. 'You don't have to talk about it if you don't want to.'

'No, I'm fine now,' Mandy said. 'Mostly fine anyway. But something about what Alistair Robertson did was so similar to what Harry did that it just kind of brought some memories back. And then Lorna told me you were coming to work with us – she didn't say who you were but I recognized you from all the newspaper stories.'

'That's why you didn't want me there.'

'I knew what you tweeted.' It was Mandy's turn to sound angry. 'I couldn't understand why someone like you would work in a place like the Haven.'

I put my head in my hands. 'I didn't mean that tweet the way it sounded. My daughter was being bullied at school and I was annoyed. It was aimed at the girls who were upsetting her. Not at Alistair's . . .' I swallowed. 'Women.'

Mandy stared at me. 'Really?'

'Really. I don't blame those women one bit. They're victims.'
I looked at her. 'Like you.'

'Survivors,' Mandy said. 'Like you.'

We looked at each other for a moment and I felt the tension lift.

'So you really didn't post that stuff about me working at the Haven?'

'Really didn't.'

'You didn't make the missing appeal post?'

'God, no. That's nasty. Really sinister.'

My head was spinning. 'And you honestly didn't do anything else? The weed-killer? Or kidnap Jem's kitten?'

'No.' Mandy frowned. 'Has someone been doing that stuff to you? Who would do that?'

'I don't know,' I said. 'I thought it was you.'

'I promise you, it wasn't.'

I looked straight at her, trying to decide if I believed her. And then the doorbell rang once, twice, three times. And someone hammered on the knocker.

Startled, I left Mandy on the sofa, and went to open the door.

Cassie and Callum stood there, both in their Halloween costumes and both looking a little bit worried. My heart dropped. 'What is it?' I said, panicking. 'What's happened? Where's Jem?'

Cassie's eyes were wide. 'I thought she was here?'

'She went to meet you.' My heart was thumping. 'She left ages ago. Have you not seen her?'

'She wasn't at the corner.' Cassie looked scared.

'Maybe you missed her?' But Callum shook his head. 'I was at school early so I walked to the corner to meet the girls,' he said. 'I'd have seen her.'

Cassie was breathless. She didn't wait for me to invite her in but simply marched into the cottage with Callum following. 'We've rung her loads of times but she's not answering.' She looked like she might cry. 'We got a bit frightened.'

'Because of the appeal?' I said shrilly. 'Because of that missing post online?'

'You know about that?'

'Yes I know.' I was furious suddenly. 'And so did you, apparently, but you didn't think to tell me about it?'

Cassie's eyes filled with tears and I felt bad. 'Sorry,' I muttered. 'It's not your fault, Cassie.'

Mandy stood up and put a steadying hand on my arm.

'Do you have any idea where she is?' she asked Callum and Cassie. 'Any idea at all?'

Cassie looked at me. 'You should sit down,' she said. 'You're really pale. And this might be a shock.'

I tasted bile in my mouth. 'What?' I said frantically. 'What shock?'

'We think she might be with Rory.'

My vision blurred and I sat down with a thump. 'She's not with Rory,' I said. 'Why would she be with him?'

'We don't know.' Callum sounded close to tears. 'But we think he was the one playing all the mean pranks on you.'

'Callum, don't be so stupid,' I snapped, knowing I was being unfair but powerless to hold in my anger. 'Rory's the one who set up the CCTV for me. Why would he do that if he was the person playing the tricks?'

'There haven't been any tricks at your house since then,' Callum muttered. I stared at him. He was right.

'Can I check it?'

I nodded wordlessly. Jem's laptop was on the side by the plug and Callum picked it up. He tapped a few keys and then asked for my password for the CCTV. I typed it in and he pressed return. Straightaway we could see our path and the little bit of pavement outside the garden.

We saw Mandy walking up the path and ringing the bell, and then Jem wandering off in her witch dress.

But that was all. No clues about where she'd gone.

301

'I still think it's Rory,' Cassie said. 'I think he's taken her some-where.'

'Stop it, Cassie,' I said sharply. 'This isn't a game.' Immediately I regretted it because once more she looked teary. I reached out and took her hand and she gripped my fingers.

'I just want to find her,' she said. 'She thought Rory was being weird and I'm scared she was right.'

I pushed my hair away from my face. 'I'll ring Rory,' I said.

'No, don't.' Cassie and Callum spoke in unison.

'I don't think you should warn him,' Cassie added. But I ignored her. I picked up my phone, found Rory's number and pressed the button to call. The phone rang out. I looked at the scared teenagers sitting there, in their Halloween costumes and felt weak with fear.

'Cassie, you're being silly,' I said. But was she? I wasn't sure anymore.

I shut the window on the laptop with the CCTV feed and then paused as I saw what was on the window behind it.

It was a Facebook page and it was on the profile of a young woman who looked vaguely familiar. Billie Hamilton, the name said.

'What's this?' I asked Cassie.

She looked shifty. 'Jem didn't tell you?'

'Tell me what?' I knew I was shouting but I couldn't seem to control my voice.

'She's Rory's daughter,' she said. 'We looked her up online because we thought it was a bit weird that he'd never mentioned her before.'

She and Callum both started to talk at once, but I wasn't listening because I was staring at the screen. Billie Hamilton? I felt cold, suddenly. Cold and weak. I tasted bile in my mouth and rushed into the kitchen and to the sink where I was suddenly and violently sick. I ran the tap to wash the vomit away, and cupped water into my mouth. 'Billie Hamilton,' I groaned.

The names of the women that had accused Alistair – the women he'd assaulted – were etched in my mind forever. Three of them.

Lana Montgomery. Katherine Arnold. And Billie Hamilton. Their names hadn't been reported in the press, of course. The women had been spared that and it meant Jem didn't know who they were. But I knew I would never forget them.

And now Cassie was telling me that Billie Hamilton was Rory's daughter?

'Are you okay?' Cassie had followed me into the kitchen.

'I need to phone the police,' I said wildly. 'Rory's got Jem.'

Cassie took a step away from me and I didn't blame her. I must have looked a state with my hair wild, and my face pale, smelling of sick.

'I'll get your phone.' She sounded scared and I wanted to reassure her, but I didn't have the words.

'Billie Hamilton,' I said. I heaved again and gripped the side of the sink tightly, staring down at the steel surface and trying desperately to think what I should do.

Cassie came back into the kitchen and handed me my phone. She was shaking.

'Ms Blyth?' Callum called from the living room. He sounded scared and shrill. 'I think you need to see this.'

Cassie – bless her – picked up a glass from the draining board, filled it with tap water and handed it to me. Then she took my arm, like I did with Eva when she was having one of her bad days with her arthritis, and helped me through to the lounge. I was glad of her support because I wasn't sure I could stay upright on my own.

'What is it?'

Callum had Jem's laptop on the coffee table, and he and Mandy were both staring at it with shocked expressions. Callum turned the screen slightly so Cassie and I could see it too. And there was Rory. He was in his living room, I assumed, but there was little to show it was a home. Just a plain beige sofa and white walls.

'What's he doing?' I asked.

'He's livestreaming.' Callum hit a few keys and Rory's voice filled the room. 'My name is Rory Baxter,' he said. 'My daughter was one of the women assaulted by disgraced paedo Alistair Robertson. I recently discovered that Robertson's wife Tess had moved to my hometown and I was disgusted that she could go on with her life like nothing had happened. I am here with Jemima Robertson, daughter of sicko Robertson and his whore wife. And she has something to say.'

His vile words felt like daggers on my skin. I put my hand to my mouth to stop myself crying out.

Rory reached out and moved the screen that was recording him, and suddenly I could see Jem. My lovely Jem. She was sitting next to Rory on the sofa, still wearing her witch costume, though her make-up was smudged and she'd lost her hat. 'Oh god,' Cassie breathed.

Jem was holding a piece of paper. Rory gestured to it. 'Jemima has a statement to read out,' he said. 'Whenever you're ready, Jemima.'

Chapter 43

Jem

Rory had driven right to the edge of town and then back again and parked outside a little row of shops near the leisure centre where I'd been swimming with Mum. They were all in darkness and closed up – it was the evening after all.

We got out of the van and he took my arm, obviously not wanting to give me a chance to make a run for it. Not that there was anything nearby really. Just a car park. Though I could see the roof of the leisure centre in the distance. I wondered how far away it was? That would be open, surely? There were probably some weirdos who wanted to spend Halloween night at the gym.

As we walked towards the shops, a group of boys – a bit older than me – ran round the corner, all wearing gruesome Halloween masks. They were shouting loudly and made me jump and then – ridiculously – burst into tears.

They'd obviously spooked Rory too because he tightened his grip on my arm and hurried me into a doorway at the side of the little parade of shops. Inside was a steep flight of stairs. He pushed me up and into the flat at the top, behind another door.

It was weird. There was nothing there to make it look like a home. There was a bookshelf with no books on it. An empty table. White walls and beige carpets. Like a holiday home.

'Do you live here?' I said, wiping my eyes with shaking hands.

Rory looked round like he was seeing the house for the first time. Then he nodded. 'I've not been here long. Had to sell my old place. When Billie comes home I'll get somewhere better. Somewhere with enough space for her too.'

'It's nice,' I said, trying to sound polite, but horribly aware that my voice was thin and frightened. My mind was racing. His expression had changed when he mentioned Billie. Should I ask him more about her? I didn't want to annoy him.

'I was going to wait for you at school,' Rory said. 'I wanted to catch you before you went into your disco, but then I saw you walking and it was the perfect opportunity.'

'For what?' I wrapped my arms around myself, jamming my hands into my armpits.

'I need you to do something for me,' Rory said.

What did he mean? He came closer to me and I shrank away from him, not wanting him to touch me. Rory looked shocked.

'Not like that,' he said. 'Not like your perv dad.'

I felt a tear run down my face and I wiped it away.

'What then?'

'I need you to read this out, and I'll film it,' he said, waving a piece of paper at me. 'I'm going to stream it on the local news sites and send it to the TV channels. Because everyone needs to know the truth.'

'What truth?'

'That your mother is a scheming, lying, rape apologist bitch and she needs to be punished.'

I winced at his angry words, more tears falling down my cheeks.

'That's not true,' I said.

'Ah, but it is.' He nodded. 'And I need everyone to know so that Billie can come home.'

306

'I don't understand.' I was bewildered. 'What does my mum have to do with Billie?' None of this made sense to me.

He put his hands on my shoulders and pushed me so I was sitting down on the sofa. Then he started to arrange his phone on the coffee table in front of me. He had a little tripod waiting there, like the YouTubers I followed used, and he started to screw the phone into it, checking it was at the right angle. As he worked, he talked. Chatty and informal, ignoring my sobs and sniffs.

'My daughter Billie wanted to be a TV presenter,' he said. 'She did media at uni, she did work experience at the local channels. All that. And then she got an internship on *Good Morning Scotland*.'

Suddenly I knew where this was going. Billie was one of the women my dad had . . . I shuddered. Rory saw.

'I know,' he said. 'Your filthy father got his hands on her. And he made her . . .' He looked sickened.

'That was my dad's fault,' I said. 'Not my mum's.'

Rory didn't answer. He just kept talking like I'd not spoken. 'I knew she was finding her job tough. I knew she wasn't happy. But I didn't ask her why. And then I was reading the Sunday paper about your dad being arrested, and how your mum was standing by him. Billie asked if I believed him and I said that his wife was on his side. And she was a lawyer and she'd said that the rumours were made up.'

He glared at me. 'And I said that I believed her. That she had to be telling the truth and that the women who were accusing Robertson obviously had a grudge against him.' He looked stricken. 'I said they were sluts who'd slept with him and then got annoyed when he wouldn't leave his wife. I said he was a lucky bastard to have young women throwing themselves at him.'

I thought about Rory's daughter, hearing those words from her own dad, and felt horribly sorry for her.

'What did she say?'

Rory's voice cracked. 'She didn't say anything. She just walked out of the house and she never came back. Wouldn't take my calls.

A week or so later, her mother called me and told me she was one of the women who'd accused Robertson. I wanted to support her, but she wouldn't let me go to court. I sold my house to pay her legal fees and she wouldn't take the money.'

'And now?'

Rory shook his head. 'I don't even know where she is,' he said.

I closed my eyes, thinking about how I'd loved my dad and how he'd let me down so badly. And I thought I'd never hated anyone as much as I hated him at that moment.

'My dad is a shit,' I said. 'I hate him.'

'He is,' Rory said. 'But your mum is worse. Because she made excuses for him. She stood by him. She said the victims were silly girls.'

'She didn't,' I whispered. 'She was talking about something else.'

But Rory wasn't listening. 'It is your mother's fault that I lost my Billie. And when I saw her that day, in the Haven, sitting there without a care in the bloody world, I was so angry. I knew Billie wouldn't come home if your mother was here.'

'So it really was you?' I said. 'You did those things to us? The hanging witch and the skeletons?'

'I wanted to scare you. I wanted her to feel pain like I felt,' Rory said.

'Did you hurt Hermione?' I asked, though I wasn't sure I wanted to know the answer.

He laughed. It was a horrible sound. 'I didn't touch your stupid cat.' Then he shrugged. 'But I did find her collar unfastened and caught on one of the thistles in your front garden. I fastened it back up and left it on your doorstep.'

'That's horrible,' I said. 'Why would you do all these things?'

'I wanted you out of town.' His eyes were wild. 'Billie won't come back if your mother is here.'

'She won't come back anyway,' I said. 'It's you she's avoiding, not Mum.'

Rory lurched at me, his face close to mine. I could see a

bubble of spit on his lip. 'Shut up,' he hissed. 'You don't know what you're talking about.'

I curled my legs up and hugged them to me, trying to make a barrier between me and Rory.

'I want your mother to know how it feels to know that your daughter hates you. I want her – and everyone in town – to know what a terrible person she is. And Billie will see it and know that I looked out for her. And she'll know it's safe to come back.'

'What do you mean she'll see it?' I said, not understanding.

'You're going to tell your mother that you hate her.'

'No,' I said.

'Yes.'

He'd finished fiddling with the camera now and he came to sit next to me on the sofa. I shifted over so there was more of a space between us. 'I'll do an introduction and then you're to read out what's on the paper.'

Rory handed me the sheet of paper and I took it. He'd not threatened me or been violent or anything like that, but there was a look in his eye that scared me and I was focusing on just doing whatever he told me to do.

I looked down, scanning the typewritten page. It was horrible, nasty stuff about Mum and Dad and the things they'd done – or not done, in Mum's case, but that didn't seem to matter to Rory.

'And if I don't read it?' I said.

'I will hurt you,' Rory told me. His eyes were dark with hate. 'I will hurt you and I will hurt your mother. All those other things I did were just games. I just wanted to scare you. Imagine what I can do if I really want to upset you.'

I was shaking. I took a deep breath to steady myself. 'Fine,' I said. 'I'll read it.'

'You need to sound like you mean it,' he warned. 'I need everyone to know what you think of her.'

I pinched my lips together and nodded.

Rory leaned forward and pressed record on the phone.

'My name is Rory Baxter,' he said. 'My daughter was one of the women assaulted by disgraced paedo Alistair Robertson. I recently discovered that Robertson's wife Tess had moved to my hometown and I was disgusted that she could go on with her life like nothing had happened.'

I thought that going on as if nothing had happened was the very opposite of what Mum and I had done, but I was too frightened to speak out. Rory went on: 'I am here with Jemima Robertson, daughter of sicko Robertson and his whore wife. And she has something to say.' He smiled at the camera. It looked odd on a face that had been twisted with hatred just seconds before. 'Billie, darling, this is for you. You can come home now.'

He reached out and moved the phone and now I could see myself on the screen. My sticky-out skirt looked stupid now. Getting dressed for the Halloween disco seemed like days ago.

Rory pointed to my paper. 'Jemima has a statement to read out,' he said. 'Whenever you're ready, Jemima.'

Very carefully, I positioned my hands on the paper, with my thumbs in front and my fingers behind, hidden from Rory's view. And then, I crossed my fingers, hoping Rory wouldn't notice the gesture on camera but that Mum would see and know I didn't mean anything I was saying.

'My name is Jemima Robertson,' I read. I made my voice sound mechanical and monotonous, so it was obvious I was reading and not speaking naturally. 'I wish to state my intent to sever all ties from my mother Tess Robertson.' I took a shuddering breath inwards and carried on. 'I will no longer consider Tess Robertson to be my mother and I will no longer be her daughter.'

I was fairly sure none of this was legal or binding, but it sounded so plausible I felt sick just saying the words.

'The reason for me disowning my former mother is because she is unfit to be a parent due to her support for my father who is a rapist and a paedophile.'

I stumbled over the words and Rory prodded me in annoyance

making me jump. I swallowed again. My throat was so dry I wasn't sure I could speak.

'My former mother should also be in prison for her actions and I will be filing a police complaint against her immediately. She will no longer be resident in North Berwick and it will once again be a safe place to live.'

That was it. I'd read it all. I slumped against the back of the sofa, wanting to cry. Rory reached out and turned off the recording.

'What now?' I said, dully. 'I'm guessing you won't take me home.'

'Now we wait for everyone to see it,' Rory said with glee. 'People love this sort of shit. Did you see how many people shared that missing appeal I made?'

'That was you?'

'Obviously.' He frowned. 'I thought it would be enough for people to put two and two together and realize who you were. But it turns out the folk round here are too wrapped up in their own worlds. So I had to be more direct. I posted pictures on the Haven's page proving who your mum really is.'

I stared at him. 'Is that why Mum doesn't work there anymore?'

He laughed. 'They sacked her? Brilliant.' He looked at me. 'That's just the beginning.'

'What did you mean about filing a police complaint?'

He shrugged. 'We probably won't need to bother,' he said. 'That was just for the shock value. If you're prepared to go to those lengths, it shows how awful your mother really is. People love gossip and it's so easy to spread rumours, especially when they're rooted in the truth. By tomorrow your mother will be considered a villain by everyone in town. And I reckon she'll be out of here by next week.' He nodded. 'And then Billie can come home.'

'What about me?' I sounded very young to my own ears. 'I've said those terrible things.'

Rory looked like he couldn't care less. 'What about you?'

'It's not true,' I said fiercely. 'None of this is true.'

311

'But it is,' Rory pointed out. 'Everything I've said is true.' He gave me a horrible smile. 'You and your mother are the witches, and I'm the witch-hunter.'

'Fuck you,' I said. I was filled with red-hot rage. This wasn't my fault and it wasn't my mother's fault. I lunged for the phone, thinking perhaps I could call for help. But Rory was quicker. He pulled the tripod away and off balance, I stumbled awkwardly and fell hard against the edge of the coffee table. Immediately my nose began to bleed. Rory ignored me. Scared and sore, I crawled back onto the sofa and curled up in the corner, my cold hand to my throbbing cheek, and blood trickling, as Rory picked up his phone and watched the comments come flooding in.

Chapter 44

Alice

1661

I couldn't look at Ma. I'd gasped when I first saw her on the box. She looked so tiny standing up there. Her dress was grimy, her hair was a tangled mess, and her face was so pale she looked like a spirit. Her eyes were sunk deep in their sockets, with dark shadows underneath. I couldn't believe she'd only been with Malcolm Black for one night. What cruelty must he be capable of? I shuddered to think.

With Davey and Christy behind me, I pushed my way through the silent crowd, as Malcolm Black read out the charges against my mother.

'Who do you think you are, intruding on this trial?' he said to me, turning his cold stare on me. I did not let myself flinch away from him but instead I pulled my shoulders back and looked him in the eye.

'I am Alice Seton,' I said. 'And I have something to say.'

I felt a little hand in mine and glanced down to see Christy Kincaid gripping my fingers.

313

He nudged me and I took the book he'd given me out from under my cloak.

'You may speak,' Malcolm Black said.

'Thank you,' I said. I glanced at Christy and he nodded reassuringly.

'Alice?' Ma's voice was croaky. 'Do not speak, Alice.'

Behind me I felt Davey's hand on my back. It was warm and fatherly and I felt stronger knowing he was there with me. He and Christy. I took a deep breath.

'My mother – Widow Seton – is a good woman. She is no witch.'

I felt everyone in the room take a gasp of air as I spoke. But undeterred, I went on. 'These accusations are false. And they have been made by Gregor Kincaid because he is greedy.'

Gregor's face was red with rage, while Malcolm's was white. His anger was icy cold.

'You are an insolent, ill-mannered girl,' he said. He sounded quite pleased about it. 'May I remind you that speaking out in favour of a witch can be seen as a confession of witchcraft?'

I looked up at Malcolm. 'I understand that,' I said. 'And yet, here I am, speaking out in favour of Widow Seton.'

'You will burn,' Malcolm said.

There was a murmur of fear through the crowd. I raised my voice so I would be heard and brandished Christy's book.

'No,' I said. 'I will not burn. Because I have here a report of a witch-hunt in East Gullane, just last year, where the townspeople all spoke out for the accused. All of them.'

I felt Malcolm's eyes boring into me and tried not to let his hatred make me lose my resolve. 'Actually, in that case, it wasn't the woman who burned, it was someone else. Now where did I read it?' I ran my finger down the page and pretended to look for the name. 'Ah yes,' I said in triumph. 'Here it is.' I looked up at Malcolm and gave him a wide smile. 'It was the witch finder who burned.'

Beside me, Christy punched the air. 'Yes!' he shouted. 'The witch finder.'

'Christy Kincaid, that is enough from you.' Gregor stood up from his chair at the front of the hall. 'You foolish boy.' He turned to Malcolm. 'He has been ill, Mr Black, and Widow Seton treated him.'

I could see Gregor was scared Malcolm would turn his wrath on his nephew. But I didn't care. I knew we were right.

'Widow Seton must have addled his brain with her potions,' Gregor added, quite desperately.

'No.' This time Davey spoke up. 'On the contrary, Widow Seton gave Christy back his health and allowed him to read the – rather dry, in my opinion – court reports he so enjoys.' He ruffled his son's hair. 'I think he will be a man of the law one day, don't you, Gregor?'

Malcolm Black was ignoring the Kincaid brothers hissing and spitting at one another like fighting cats and, instead, focused on me. He gave me a thin-lipped smile. 'I have not heard the details of this case,' he said. 'Which is strange.'

'Perhaps you are not as well connected as you believe?' Davey said. 'I have heard it talked about from several different sources.'

Malcolm nodded, and I crossed my fingers and hoped that his pride would not allow him to admit he had heard nothing whatsoever of this witch-hunt that I had dreamt up when I was hidden beneath the goat shed. It was rooted in truth, of course. There had been cases of townsfolk standing against witch finders; I'd read the reports in Christy's book. But those cases hadn't happened recently and they hadn't happened here. I just hoped Malcolm was as self-aggrandising as I suspected. There was a pause and then he tapped his chin with his finger.

'East Gullane, you say?'

'That's right,' Christy put in eagerly. I rested my hand on his shoulder. This was my fight, not his.

'And every townsperson spoke up for the accused?'

'That's right.' This time it was me who agreed.

'Everyone?'

I nodded. 'Yes, everyone.'

'And that has not happened here.'

I grinned. 'Not yet.'

With a wink at Christy, I stepped to one side and behind me was Mackenzie from the harbour, flanked by the other fishermen.

'I am Mackenzie White and I speak out for Widow Seton,' Mackenzie said. 'I speak against Gregor Kincaid.'

One by one the fishermen all filed to the front of the room, their broad shoulders nudging each other as they said their names and added their support for Ma. With each man that spoke, Ma's back got straighter. I knew most of them, but there were others whose names weren't known to me. A man with orange hair spoke out, saying Ma had delivered his baby safely when his wife was too weak to carry on. And there was Lachlan Murdoch, adding his voice to the group. I flushed as I saw him walk by me, remembering the last time I'd seen him. He tipped his hat to me, looking sheepish.

And then, behind the fishermen, came the women. Ebba White spoke, saying Ma had saved her little girl and called to Ma as she came, saying: 'She's grown so much in just these last few weeks, Honor. Thanks to you.'

Mary, the midwife who called on Ma when she had a difficult delivery, was there, talking of the good Ma had done.

Malcolm stood silently by, listening, but Gregor was getting angry and went to grab Mary's arm to stop her. Immediately, Davey was there, holding him back.

'Let them talk,' he said roughly. Gregor struggled but though he was taller than his brother, Davey was stronger and fitter. 'You are only laird because they allow you to be. It would do you good to remember that.'

There were servants from the big house, farmers and their wives, shopkeepers, the innkeeper. And the minister, hunched over with fear and shaking as he spoke, saying he'd welcomed Ma into the kirk every week since he'd been minister and had seen no evidence of – his voice trembled – devil worship.

Ma was standing straight upright now, stiff-backed. Even her eyes looked more full of life. Less sunken.

It was Christy's turn. He spoke up, clearly and confidently, telling the room how Ma had saved his life when he was sick. 'And my grandmother,' he added. 'She saved her too.'

'And in saving Christy, she saved me,' Davey added. 'This assize is a disgrace and it must be ended.'

Gregor grimaced at his brother, but then his expression lightened and he spoke into Malcolm's ear. Malcolm listened, and then spoke once more.

'It must be every townsperson,' Malcolm said. 'Every person.' He glowered at me. 'Is that what it says in your book?'

'It is,' I said, hugging the book to my chest like a shield.

'This is not everyone,' Gregor said. His voice was strong and tinged with triumph. 'This is not every person.'

With a lurch of horror, I realized he was right.

We had spent most of the early morning, hurrying round town, telling them what was happening, and urging them to do right by Ma. I'd been scared the people would be too frightened but Christy had grinned at me.

'Magnus, my tutor, said people follow the crowd.'

I'd shaken my head. 'But we don't have a crowd.'

He'd tapped the cover of the book. 'So we make one,' he said. 'If we pretend it's happened before, people will be more likely to speak out.'

I'd not been convinced, but we went from house to house, and boat to boat, and sure enough, it had worked.

Except we hadn't thought about the people right under our noses. The people who were missing.

Because old Mrs Kincaid wasn't there. And nor was Kyla.

I felt my optimism desert me. 'Ma,' I said. I went to the box where my mother stood and reached out to take her hands. Gregor tried to stop me but I ducked away from him.

With tears falling down my cheeks, I told Ma I was sorry,

that I'd tried my best. And then I looked up at her and to my astonishment, she was smiling. Because there, walking into the meeting hall was Kyla, with old Mrs Kincaid on her arm.

'Mother, no,' Gregor said. 'You are old and frail and you should not be out in this weather.'

'Oh shush,' she said. 'I heard Widow Seton was in trouble and I wanted to help. She saved my life you know.'

Kyla glared at me, and then glared at Ma. I looked back at her. Would she stand by me now, when I needed her most?

I felt my chest tighten with fear. Everything rested on this one woman. The woman I'd always thought to be my friend. Was she going to betray me?

Slowly, Kyla walked towards me. Her eyes were fixed on mine and she didn't so much as glance towards Malcolm Black.

She came close to me, so we were almost touching. I kept my gaze steady and concentrated on my breathing. And then, to my surprise, Kyla gave a tiny smile and pushed something into my hand. She turned to Malcolm Black.

'Widow Seton has been nothing but good to me,' she said clearly. 'And I treated her badly and I'm sorry.' She looked back at me. 'Sorry,' she said again.

I smiled at her, feeling the round edges of the witch bottle she'd given me in my fingers.

'I believe,' Davey said, 'that's everyone.'

'Not quite,' said Gregor. 'I am a person of this town, am I not?'

'Not anymore,' said Mackenzie White. 'You stood against one of us for your own ends. I think we can all agree that means you no longer belong here.' He turned to the fishermen. 'Isn't that right, lads?'

They all agreed, loudly and vigorously.

Gregor was spluttering and muttering, knowing he was beaten. Davey went to Ma and helped her down from the box and she leaned against him, still holding my hand.

'This is an outrage,' Gregor hissed.

'No, brother. You are the outrage.' Davey looked taller and more confident than I'd ever seen him.

Gregor's face was twisted in anger. 'You owe me, Davey. I helped you when you needed it.'

'You did,' Davey said simply. 'And I am grateful. But one good deed doesn't mean you can do as you please forever more. You were wrong, Gregor. Surely you understand that?'

Gregor glanced over to where the fishermen were standing, shoulder to shoulder like a barricade, and clearly thought better than to argue. I saw the fight drain from him. He knew he was beaten.

Davey gave me the ghost of a smile and then turned to his brother once more. 'You need to apologize to Widow Seton.'

'What?' Gregor's voice was gruff.

'Apologize.'

The fishermen were a little closer now, moving towards Gregor in a way that managed to appear both protective of my mother, and threatening towards him.

Gregor swallowed. 'Widow Seton,' he said, avoiding my mother's eye. 'Would you accept my apology? I think things got a little . . .' He looked round at the fishermen and the other townspeople crowding the hall. 'A little out of hand.'

'Will you dredge the harbour?' Ma said.

'I still think it could be a successful idea . . .' I couldn't believe he had the cheek to continue to argue his case. My mother looked shocked and the men came nearer, like the tide creeping up the beach. Gregor swallowed again. 'I will not dredge the harbour.'

'Then I accept your apology.'

Chapter 45

Honor

I was leaning against Davey and holding Alice's hand, as Gregor apologized to me. I didn't believe he was sorry. Not one bit. But I just wanted this to be over. I wanted to go home to my cottage and wash and change my clothes, and have a good meal and then get into my bed and sleep. But the crowd was restless, moving and jostling like a shoal of fish. I knew it wasn't finished yet.

Gregor and I stared at one another for a moment. Malcolm Black was standing very still, nearby. Obviously planning his next move. I wondered if this had ever happened to him before. I thought not. He was the sort of man who was used to getting his own way.

I watched him as, without a word, he made to leave the hall.

He almost got as far as the door. 'Stop him,' shouted a voice. Mackenzie White skirted the crowd in the room and held on to Malcolm's arm. 'He came into our town and attacked a good woman. Are we just going to let him leave?'

The crowd's murmurs grew louder. The hairs on the back of my neck began to prickle and Alice's grip on my hand tightened.

'Davey?' I said quietly. 'What should we do?'

He looked at me. 'I think we just let him face the consequences of his actions.'

The crowd was surrounding Malcolm now and once more I was reminded of animals – this time of Alice's cats, nudging our legs and climbing over each other in their rush to be fed. The people gathered round Malcolm, pushing him this way and that, and eventually out of the door of the hall.

'We should follow,' I said. Together we – Davey, Christy, Alice and I – walked behind the people as they took Malcolm outside. No one pulled or pushed him. No one shoved or shouted. They simply surrounded him and made it very clear that he had to do as they wanted.

And there, in the town square, were the barrels of tar and the piles of wood, ready for my punishment. I averted my eyes, not wanting to think about what could have been.

The crowd were on the move, taking Malcolm with them to the makeshift pyre.

'Haul him up,' someone shouted. And to my horror, Malcolm was lifted aloft and put on to the wooden pile meant for me.

He wasn't still now. He was struggling and cursing, telling the men who were fighting him that they would burn in hell, that God would have vengeance. But they ignored him.

And then he was tethered and suddenly motionless.

'Do not do this,' he shouted. 'This is the devil making you act in this way.'

'Was it the devil who made you bring this tar and this wood?' shouted Mackenzie and the crowd laughed.

'She is doing this,' Malcolm yelled. 'Widow Seton is responsible. She is an evil, manipulative woman.'

'Rubbish,' said old Mrs Kincaid who was standing close to us, still leaning on Kyla's arm. 'She is just a woman. A clever one at that. That's why you're so scared of her.'

I looked at her in admiration and gratitude and she smiled

at me. Kyla smiled too and I realized that prickle of unease I'd always had when I was near her, had vanished.

The crowd began jeering, taunting Malcolm.

'They won't actually burn him, will they?' I said in alarm. 'I don't want that. We should get him down.'

'Really?' said Christy sounding disappointed. 'I wanted to see him go up in smoke.'

Alice looked at him with a glint in her eye, and then turned her attention back to where Malcolm was beginning to cry as he begged the crowd to untie him.

'Please,' he said. 'Please don't do this. I have a wife.'

A wisp of smoke began to twist up from the bottom of the pyre. Malcolm's nostrils flared and his begging became more urgent. 'Please,' he said.

I looked at Alice, whose eyes were fixed ahead and then I looked at Davey who gave me a resigned shrug.

'Go on,' he said. 'You're a good woman, Honor Seton.'

The smoke was thicker now, catching in my throat as I pushed my way to the front of the crowd. But there were no flames. That was odd. I glanced over my shoulder to where Alice stood, and raised an eyebrow at her. She gazed back at me, eyes wide with innocence.

'Stop this,' I called as I reached the front of the crowd. 'We're better than this.'

There was a disappointed groan from the people watching. 'The best way to get our revenge on Malcolm Black,' I said, spitting out his name in disgust, 'is to run him out of town and tell everyone we know what a silly, scared man he is. Frightened of a woman and a wee girl.'

Laughter surrounded me. I stepped forward and Mackenzie White helped me clamber up on to the pyre. This could all have been so different, I thought. The smoke was drifting away now. Perhaps it hadn't been there at all. I leaned forward and untied the ropes that held Malcolm firm. He was jabbering to himself, crying like a baby and not bothering to wipe away the snot that ran from his nose.

'You are a pathetic excuse for a man,' I hissed into his ear. 'Now get out.'

I shoved him, as hard as I could, and he tumbled from the pyre on to the cobbles of the town square. Scrabbling to his feet, and ignoring his horse, which was patiently waiting where he'd tied it on the other side of the market place, Malcolm Black ran from the town with a group of children chasing him in glee, laughing and jeering as they went.

Mackenzie White put his hand up to me and helped me climb down from the wood, as elegantly as a lady descending from a carriage.

'Where's Gregor?' he said.

'He's over there,' called a small voice – Christy. He had spirit, that lad. 'He's just getting on his horse, look.'

The eyes of the whole crowd swivelled towards Gregor. His horse snorted and stamped its hooves, as keen as its master to be off.

I saw him look at Davey across the top of the people's heads. Davey gave a small, efficient nod and Gregor nodded back. A moment of understanding between the brothers who had spent most of their lives at each other's throats.

Gregor pulled his horse around and kicked, and they were off, thundering down the street in the opposite direction to Malcolm.

'So no one is being burned?' Christy appeared at my side, with his father and Alice close behind.

'No one,' I confirmed.

'Will Uncle Gregor come back?'

'One day,' Davey said. He put his arm round my shoulders and we all watched the dust fly up as Gregor made his escape. 'We'll just have to muddle through as best as we can without him.'

I glanced at Davey. I thought, despite his past troubles, or perhaps because of them, he would make an excellent laird.

Overhead the sky was darkening – another storm was on its way. I turned to Alice and saw she was focusing all her attention on Gregor as he raced away from the town. Thunder rumbled, lightning forked across the sky, and as we watched, the heavens opened. Not where we were, but in the distance – just where Gregor rode.

'Did you do that?' Christy asked, looking at Alice in awe.

She grinned. 'Perhaps,' she said. 'But perhaps not.'

Chapter 46

Tess

Present day

We watched the livestream in silence, all of us staring at the screen of Jem's laptop as my beautiful, loving daughter said those awful things.

She looked so young, sitting there in her funny witch costume. Young and scared. But there was a glint in her eye too and on the piece of paper she was holding, I could see her fingers were crossed. I knew she didn't mean the horrible things she was saying, but it was nice to see I was right. Jem crossing her fingers showed me she wasn't telling the truth. My heart ached for her. She was so bold. So clever.

As Rory turned the recording off, I stood up. 'I need to call the police.'

I fumbled for my phone with shaking hands and dialled 999, and launched into an explanation of why I needed help.

'How old is Jemima?' the operator asked as I paused for breath.

'She's 14.'

'And how long has she been missing?'

'She was meant to meet a friend.' I checked my watch. 'About two hours ago. She didn't turn up. But I know where she is.'

'Where is she?'

'With a man, Rory Baxter.'

'Is he a friend of hers?'

'No, he's a friend of mine,' I said. 'At least, he was.' I could hear the words I was saying and I knew it sounded ridiculous. 'He's kidnapped her to scare me.' My voice wobbled.

'Why would you think that?'

'Because he's filming her and putting it on social media.'

'Are you watching this recording now?'

'We did. I can send you the link.' I looked at Callum and he nodded.

The police officer sounded a bit confused. 'Is Jemima in distress in the video?'

'No but she's saying things she doesn't mean. He's forcing her to do it.'

'And why would he do that?'

I took a deep breath. 'Because I'm Alistair Robertson's wife, and Rory Baxter's daughter was one of my husband's victims. I think he's taken Jem in revenge.'

There was a pause at the other end of the phone and then the operator said: 'I'll have a car there as soon as possible.'

'Please hurry,' I whispered. 'I'm scared.'

Mandy came over and took the phone from me gently. 'They'll find her,' she said.

I nodded, unable to speak. I was worried that I would open my mouth and simply howl. Slightly awkwardly, Mandy gave me a hug. 'She doesn't mean the things she's saying. You know that.'

'I do. But it's horrible to hear it.'

Mandy nodded. 'Shall I get you a drink?' she said. 'A brandy or something? Might calm your nerves?'

I shook my head. I didn't think I'd be able to drink anything. I paced backwards and forwards, hating that I felt so helpless.

Callum and Cassie were both still staring at the laptop screen. 'Is there anything else?' I asked. 'Has he posted anything else?'

'He hasn't,' said Callum. 'But you have to see this.'

Mandy and I went over to where they were sitting and peered at the screen. Beneath the livestream recording, which was now frozen on a still of Jem's frightened face, comments were being added all the time. The number of views was clicking up again and again, 1000, 2000, more. And the comments were appearing too fast to read them properly.

'What are they saying?' I asked, so horrified by the reaction that I began to shake even more violently than before. 'What's happening?'

'Everyone's gone mental,' Cassie said, sounding triumphant. 'They're all posting about you.' She enlarged the feed and started reading: '"Tess helped me with my application for disability benefits for my son. She is not responsible for anything her husband did." There's loads more, here.' She scrolled through. 'You did a school appeal. And raised money for charity. And helped someone get their money back for a dodgy car they bought . . .' She looked up at me. 'Everyone loves you.'

I wiped away a tear. 'No one's saying that Rory's right? That I'm to blame?'

'A few people,' Callum admitted. 'But no one who knows you.'

There was a loud knocking on the front door, and I jumped. 'The police?' I said, rushing to answer. But it was Eva.

'What's happening?' she said. 'What's going on? Why is Jem on the internet?'

I was so pleased to see her, I hugged her tightly as I tried to explain.

'The police said they were on their way, but I've not heard anything.'

'And you don't know where she is?'

'I don't know where Rory lives,' I said in despair. 'He never said.'

Mandy was bent over her phone. 'I messaged Lorna but she doesn't know either.'

'Can you find her on her phone?' said Eva. 'I thought they tracked our every move?'

'We could but she's turned it off,' Cassie said. 'Or probably Rory's turned it off.'

My phone rang and I snatched it up. 'Hello?'

'Ms Blyth? DS Lambert, Police Scotland.'

'Have you found her? Have you got Jem?'

'Not as yet,' the police officer said gently. 'But I wanted to assure you we are working on it.'

'What do you mean working on it? Just go to Rory's house.'

'At present we're unable to locate an address for Rory Baxter.'

I didn't understand this. What was happening?

'He wasn't at his last registered address. But we're confident we'll track him down very soon,' DS Lambert went on. 'I will be in touch.'

He rang off and I let out a screech of frustration and fear. 'He doesn't know where she is,' I wailed. 'He doesn't know anything.'

'I think I know,' Mandy said. She had sat down in front of the laptop and was playing the video again, stopping it and going back and playing the same bit over and over. I looked at her. 'What?' I asked. 'What do you know?'

'I know where this is,' she said. She turned the screen round so I could see. 'This tree outside Rory's window. I know where it is.'

'Ohmygod,' I breathed. 'Where is it?'

'It's near the swimming pool. My sister and I walked past it the other day. Do you see there's a trainer that someone's thrown up into the branches? We were laughing about it and saying why would anyone do that and my sister said it was a gang thing, because she'd seen it online, and I said did she really think there were gangs in North Berwick . . .' She trailed off. 'I can take you there.'

I had already picked up my keys. 'Let's go.'

We all piled into Mandy's car, Eva squashed in the back with Callum and Cassie.

'Put your foot down,' I said.

Chapter 47

Jem

Rory was getting angry. He was reading the comments that were being added to the bottom of the video and snorting and swearing as he scrolled through them.

'That bitch,' he said. 'People don't know what she's like.' He swiped his hand across the coffee table and sent the paper he'd given me to read flying. 'She's got them all bloody fooled.'

I was curled up in the corner of the sofa. My cheek was still throbbing and I was too scared to speak in case I made him angrier. I could feel that my lip was swollen where I'd fallen against the coffee table. I wondered if I would have a bruise. My nose had stopped bleeding but it hurt a lot and I wanted to cry but I didn't. I wouldn't give Rory the satisfaction of knowing I was scared.

I kept looking round the room, trying to work out how to somehow get away but there was literally nothing there. There was the sofa, the coffee table and the bookcase and that was it. Nothing that could cause enough of a distraction for me to make a run for it.

Rory was agitated, walking up and down the room, and that

made me nervous. Every time he came towards me, I shrank back against the cushions.

'Bitch,' he kept muttering. 'Bitch.'

'What's wrong?' I said, wondering if I would regret asking.

'People are on her side.' He waved his phone at me. 'They're all taken in by her act.'

Oh god, if things weren't going his way, he might get angry and hurt me. I was shaking and I put my hands under my bum on the sofa so he wouldn't see. 'What are you going to do now?' An idea struck me. 'Maybe we should go to the police station.' I nodded vigorously. 'That would be the best idea. We should go to the police and tell them everything.'

Rory laughed. It was a horrible sound. 'Not yet,' he said. 'Not yet.'

He looked at his phone again and snorted. Then he scrolled through and dialled a number. I could hear the long beep you got when a number had been disconnected. But Rory spoke anyway. 'Billie, it's your dad. Just wanted to let you know you'll be able to come home very soon. I promise.'

My nose was bleeding again. I put my fingers up to my nostrils and when I took them away they were covered with blood. Like Lady Macbeth, I thought. With blood on her hands.

Another idea struck me and I stared at my fingertips thought-fully. Rory was still pacing and muttering, eyes on his phone. I put my fingers to my nose again, smearing the blood across my hands. I rubbed them together, spreading it more, then I did it again. The blood was sticky and it felt horrible and I hoped this would work.

I took a deep breath and then I shrieked. 'Rory, look!' I wailed. 'I'm bleeding! I need tissues.' I held out my bloodied hands to show him. Rory stopped pacing, looking furious. For a second I thought he'd just ignore me but I put my hand on the sofa cushion, leaving a rusty handprint and he growled.

'Fuck's sake,' he hissed. He spun round and marched off to the

330

kitchen, and seeing my chance, I leapt to my feet. I was at the flat door before I knew it, fumbling with the catch on the door, and then I was throwing myself down the stairs, half sliding, half running, and opening the door at the bottom with shaking, clumsy fingers. And then I was outside, charging down the path hearing Rory's shouts of rage behind me. My heart was pounding and I was crying. I had no idea where I was, but with no time to make a proper decision, I turned towards the leisure centre and ran down the street, my breaths short and panicked.

Then, like a mirage in the desert, I saw Harry Potter coming towards me through the darkness. I rubbed my eyes, thinking I was imagining it. But he was still there, with a witch, and Eva and another woman. And my mum.

'MUM,' I wailed. 'Mum!' And Callum and Cassie. I ran to them, and fell into Mum's arms, just as a police car pulled up beside us.

'It's okay,' Mum said, holding me so tightly I almost couldn't breathe. 'It's okay. You're safe now.'

Epilogue

Jem

Six months later

Rory didn't go to prison. Mum said we'd had enough of courts and questions and stories in the news, and so she made up some story about how it was all a big misunderstanding, and somehow the police bought it, even though I was standing there with blood all over my hands.

And we didn't leave North Berwick. Rory did though. Everyone was commenting on his feed, saying they'd never employ him, and warning others not to give him work. And when the police went to tell him he was off the hook, they found he'd gone and not left a forwarding address. I felt a bit sorry for him in a way, but I was pleased he'd gone and even more pleased we didn't have to move again.

And the best thing was that Hermione came back.

After I'd run out of Rory's flat, Mum's friend Mandy took us back home and we all trooped inside, a bit shellshocked and sort of spaced out by everything that had happened. And there she was, sitting beside her empty bowl in the kitchen, mewing very crossly because she was hungry. She was a bit thin but none the worse for her adventure. And now she follows me round all the time. When I leave for school in the morning she comes with me to the end of the road, and then she jumps up on the wall and watches me walk away. And when I come home again, she's there waiting for me. She sleeps on my pillow every night, and she's honestly the cutest thing. Mum even let me set up an Instagram account for her. She's got more than a thousand followers. Can you imagine?

Mum's amazing. She's got to be really good friends with Cassie's mum and they go running together all the time. And Mandy, the woman who showed up on Halloween, is part of their gang too. Except she doesn't run. She works with Mum at the Haven but she's a singer and she does gigs at pubs and for old people's birthday parties and that, so Mum and Andrea go and watch her quite a lot. I've seen her on YouTube. She's pretty good.

Callum and I are still together. He's awesome. And Cassie's still spending all her time drooling over douchebags.

And we got an A for our history project, so that was cool.

'Stop dawdling,' Cassie said as I wandered along thinking about everything that had happened. We were on our way to the museum, because Heather said she had something to show us. 'Max said he'd be on the beach later and I want to go and see him after.'

'Max is a douchebag,' I said automatically and Cassie grabbed my hand and pulled me along to make me go faster.

Heather was really pleased to see us. She was wearing bright pink today and her nails were painted to match. I liked it.

'I have finally managed to find out what happened to Honor and Alice,' she said, with a bit of a swagger. 'Thought you might want to know?'

'Totally,' I said, grinning at Cassie. Then my face fell. 'Ohmygod, they didn't die, did they?'

'Well, yes, eventually,' Heather said. 'But not in the witch-hunts.'

I was really pleased. 'What happened?'

Heather had loads of photocopies of old documents. She spread them all out on the table and Cassie and I peered at them. They were totally impossible to read. Heather laughed. 'Honor married Davey Kincaid,' she said. 'There's a parish record of their wedding.'

'The baddie?'

'Perhaps he wasn't a baddie after all,' Cassie pointed out.

'He actually became the laird,' Heather said. 'I don't know why. Perhaps his brother died, though I couldn't find a record of his death. He seems to have been quite popular in the town.'

'So Honor married him?'

'She did. And they had two children together – twins. A boy called Tavish John and a girl called Thora Marion. Both those names mean "twin", which I thought was quite sweet.'

'Aww, that's nice,' I said.

'What happened to Alice?' Cassie wanted to know.

'She lived in the town her whole life. She never married, but she was well into her sixties when she died.' Heather smiled at us. 'Davey Kincaid's son, Christy, married and had several children. And it seems both twins married and had children too. I'm trying to trace their descendants. There would be so many of them, I'm fairly sure we'll find some living today.'

I was thrilled. 'That would be amazing.'

'I'll keep you posted,' said Heather. 'Maybe you could do another project?'

'Maybe,' I said.

Callum was waiting for us outside the museum, sitting on the wall in the spring sunshine. My heart lifted a bit when I saw him.

'Hello,' he said. 'You've been ages. I was worried I'd missed you.'

I gave him a kiss and Cassie made sick noises behind my back. 'Heather had lots to tell us.'

We walked slowly – much to Cassie's disgust – towards the beach to meet our friends, and I filled him in on everything we'd found out.

'Oh, that reminds me,' he said, digging into his pocket and pulling out a flyer. 'Did you see the drama club is putting on another play? I thought you might want to audition.'

He handed it to me, making a face. 'But it might not be your sort of thing . . .'

'*Wicked*?' I said, staring at the picture on the ad, which showed a green-faced witch cackling.

'What do you reckon?'

I crumpled up the flyer and with an exaggerated flourish, I threw it in the nearby bin.

'Nope,' I said. 'I'm completely done with witches.'

Acknowledgements

While I was researching this book I came across a campaign called Witches of Scotland. It's run by Claire Mitchell QC and author Zoe Venditozzi and is calling for a pardon for the people convicted of witchcraft, an apology to those accused and convicted, and a national memorial. You can follow the campaign at www.witchesofscotland.com and sign their petition.

Zoe and Claire also have a podcast, also called *Witches of Scotland*, which is entertaining and fascinating, and was very helpful in my research. If you're interested in witch-hunts, I really recommend checking it out.

Thanks as always to my fabulous agent Felicity, my brilliant editors Abi and Dushi (who didn't even flinch when I sent this book to her without an ending), and my husband Darren. And of course the biggest thank you goes to my wonderful readers. I can't wait to hear what you think of this story.

Keep reading for an excerpt from *The Smuggler's Daughter* . . .

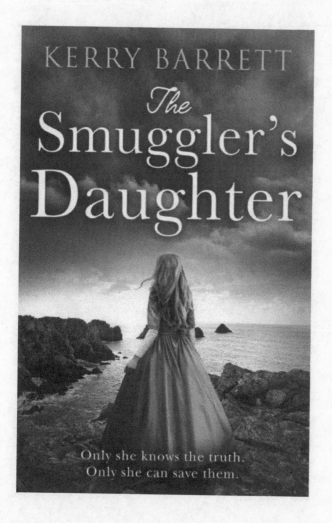

KERRY BARRETT

The
Smuggler's
Daughter

Only she knows the truth.
Only she can save them.

Keep reading for an excerpt from *The Smuggler's Daughter* . . .

Chapter 1

Emily

Cornwall, Spring 1799

I put my hands over my ears and pushed my palms hard into my scalp, trying to block out the sound of the argument. I hated shouting at the best of times, but tonight my parents were louder than ever. They were making no attempt to keep it quiet – normally I heard whispered barbs and hissed insults but tonight it was full-blown screaming. From my mother, at least.

'He will starve us out,' she was shouting. 'He's warned us, and I don't doubt he means it. We'll go hungry, Amos.'

'It won't come to that,' my father said. He was a calm man most of the time but his temper had been short lately, and tonight I heard a tremor in his voice that I'd never heard before. 'He'll get bored and go away.'

'He'll only go away when we give him what he wants,' my mother screeched. 'And if we don't give it to him, he'll take it.'

Something smashed and I cowered under the blanket. I didn't understand what they were arguing about. I only knew they'd been fighting like this for days and days. Weeks, even. I didn't know who they were talking about, nor why my mother sounded so frightened. It wasn't like her at all. She was always smiling, my mam. Or at least she had been until recently. Da always said that most of the drinkers at The Ship came to see Mam, serving drinks and keeping the customers happy, not to drink his ale.

'Your father had this inn, Amos Moon, and his father before him,' my mother said, sounding defeated. 'I don't understand why you want to give it away.'

'I don't,' Da said. 'I want it to be a home for you and Emily.'

'Then let him use it.' Mam was hissing now, her voice sounding urgent and high-pitched. 'It's just once. No one will know.'

'It won't be just once,' Da said. 'If we let him in, he'll keep coming. He'll take more and more liberties, and it'll be me who hangs for it.'

I huddled in my bed. What did Da mean? Why would he hang? I wished I could run to him and ask him what was going on. Da was the only person who took time to explain things to me properly. Mam did her best, but she was always busy, laughing and chatting with the drinkers in the bar. It was Da who spared the time to talk. He knew that I didn't always understand the world. That I couldn't always follow a conversation, that I misunderstood some phrases or took things too literally. I sometimes wondered if he felt the same way – not as strongly as me, but enough that he understood the troubles I had – and that was why he preferred to spend time in the cellar, or with his kegs of ale, while Mam dealt with the drinkers and the entertainers.

'It's not right,' Da was saying. 'How can we be a part of that?'

'God's teeth,' my mother shrieked. 'You and your principles, Amos Moon. Those morals of yours will see us starve to death, you'll see.'

'Janey, calm yourself.'

'Calm myself?'

I heard the clink of a bottle as my mother poured herself a drink. She'd never been bothered by the riches on offer at the inn before. Da said she was as full of fun without the grog inside her, as any man who'd taken a drink. But lately, she'd been helping herself more and more. Her face was more frowns than smiles recently, but when she knocked back a measure of rum or brandy, her lips turned upwards again.

Da said something I didn't hear, and Mam roared. 'Get out!' she screamed. 'I'm sick of the sight of you. Get out.'

'This isn't finished,' Da warned.

'Yes it is,' Mam shrieked.

The whole inn shook as Da slammed out into the yard, whistling softly for his dog, Tully, as he went. I scrambled up onto the window seat, peering out into the darkness to see where he was.

Da was sitting on a barrel, Tully by his side and a flickering lantern at his feet. I wanted to go down to him, but I could hear Mam clattering about in the inn, pouring herself more drinks, and I didn't want to see her. Instead, I reached under my bed, and pulled out my sketchbook and my charcoal.

I loved to draw. I'd done it since I was tiny, and Da – and Mam – had supported me. As I got older, and my difficulties had become clearer, Da had encouraged me to draw people's faces. I found sketching their expressions helped me understand their emotions. Copying the tilt of a lip, or the creases around some-one's eyes taught me what sadness, happiness, or anger looked like.

Now I watched my father, his brow furrowed. My charcoal rasped across the page as I captured his eyes narrowed in thought, and his tight lips. Determined, I said softly to myself. He looked determined.

A quiet knock at the courtyard gate made me and Da both jump. Who was coming to The Ship at this late hour? Surely everyone in Kirrinporth was in bed?

Da turned his head. He could see who was out there, though I couldn't. He sat on his barrel for a moment, then he stood up and opened the gate, standing aside to let the visitor in.

An older man came through into the courtyard, crouching down and rubbing Tully's ears in greeting.

'Some guard dog you are,' I muttered with fondness.

The man was my father's friend, Petroc, I realised now, recognising his wide shoulders and his love of animals. But whatever was he doing here so late? The inn was long closed and Da was only awake because he and Mam had been arguing.

'Take that mutt and tie it up by the stables.' Another man came into sight below my window. I didn't recognise him. He was tall and his face was hidden by the three-cornered hat he wore. He waited for Petroc to take Tully across the courtyard and out of sight. I narrowed my eyes, peering down into the darkness to see better.

'So, do we have an agreement?' the man said. He took his hat off and rubbed his forehead. He had dark hair with one white streak that seemed to glow in the moonlight and a handsome, though rugged, face. On the same page as my sketch of Da, I began drawing the man's expression. He was smiling, but as I drew, I saw that his eyes were angry. That was something I'd not seen before. 'I'll be very disappointed if we don't,' he added.

'No, we do not have a deal,' said Da. He was whispering but it was so quiet that his voice carried clearly across the cobbled courtyard. 'It's too risky.'

'You never used to be frightened of a bit of risk,' the man said. His voice sounded amused, as though Da had made a joke. But I didn't think he had said anything funny. 'Never used to worry when you were younger.'

'Well we all did stupid things when we were young,' Da said. He turned away from the man and lifted the lantern up so it illuminated the courtyard better.

'Stupid?'

My father sighed. 'This is different. The risks are too great; the benefits are too small.' He looked at the man, his chin lifted slightly. 'Except for the benefits to you.'

'Come on, Amos, you're not being fair,' the bigger man said. He reached out and, quick as a flash, pulled my father's arm and twisted him round so they were facing each other again. From my viewing point at the window, I gasped.

'No. You're not being fair, Morgan,' my father said. He sounded angry. 'Things are different now. I've got a wife and a daughter.' He nodded up towards where I sat watching and I shrank back against the wall so I wouldn't be seen, wondering if he knew I was spying on him.

'Reckon your woman will be easier to persuade than you are,' Morgan said. 'Or that pretty daughter of yours.'

My father snorted. 'Janey knows her own mind. You're no match for her.' I smiled to myself; he was right about that. 'Now you need to leave, before I throw you out.' He turned his back and went to walk away, but the other man was getting angry. I flinched, trying to capture the glower on his face on my paper and then watched in helpless horror as the man yanked Da's arm again. There was a flash of metal and my father slumped on to the cobbles.

For a moment, I didn't understand what I'd just seen. What had happened? How did a conversation between two men suddenly end like this? My head was reeling with the horror of it all.

Sobbing, I pressed myself up against the window, watching the blood trickle from my father's stomach. Morgan pulled his knife from the wound, wiped it on his britches and turned to where Petroc had just emerged from the stables without Tully.

'What have you done?' he said, his mouth open in shock. 'What have you done to Amos?'

Morgan shrugged. 'Made things easier for myself.'

Almost without thinking I found a new sheet of paper and started drawing the faces down below. I drew my father's dull eyes, blood pooling around him, Morgan's white streak in his hair and his calm expression, and Petroc's horrified wide eyes. As I drew, tears ran down my cheeks and splattered onto the paper.

'But . . .' Petroc began.

Morgan prodded my father with his foot. 'We'll throw him down one of the mineshafts over Barnmouth way,' he said. 'No one will find him there.'

'No we will not,' said Petroc. 'We need to get help for Amos.'

He went to crouch down to my father, just as he'd crouched next to Tully, but Morgan grabbed him by his collar and threw him against the wall. There was another flash of metal and I saw the knife at Petroc's throat.

'We will throw him down one of the mineshafts,' said Morgan. 'Or you'll be joining him.'

I was frozen with shock and fear. I wanted to scream and bang on the window, but I was scared of what the big man would do to me if he knew I was watching.

Shoulders slumped, Petroc tramped across the courtyard to where my father lay. As he approached, my father's eyes flickered open and he looked up at me. Still crying, I pushed my hand against the window in a sad goodbye and my father, slowly, painfully, put his finger to his lips. Stay quiet, he was telling me. Stay silent.

Tears ran down my cheeks as the men hoisted my father up onto their shoulders and carried him out of the inn's courtyard. Morgan picked up a rain bucket we left for the horses and emptied it over the cobbles, where the blood was staining the stone. He watched as the water washed away any evidence of what he'd done, then he paused for a minute looking at the inn.

Suddenly, I leapt into action. I had to stop them. Da was still alive; I had to tell my mother. I had to save him.

I jumped off the windowsill and raced into my parents' bedroom. Mam was lying face down on the bed, fully clothed.

I shook her roughly by the shoulders, hoping she would open her eyes. Her lids flickered but I couldn't rouse her. She'd had too much to drink and she was out cold.

Crying so hard I could barely catch my breath, I left her lying there, and ran downstairs through the courtyard and out into the night. But the men were nowhere to be seen. It was quiet and still. All I could hear were the waves breaking on the beach far below. They'd gone. But – I thought, with icy cold fear trickling down my spine – what if they came back? Morgan had mentioned my mother, and me. What if he came for us too?

Trembling with fright, I crept to the stables and untied Tully. He licked my face, drawn to the salty tears on my cheeks, and I rubbed his head. 'Come on, boy,' I whispered. Obediently, he followed me back into the inn. I drew the bolt across the door, checking and double-checking it was firmly closed, and then, with Tully at my heels, I climbed the stairs to my parents' room. Tully jumped up onto the bed, and I lay down too, clinging to my mother's back. I'd stay here all night, I thought, in case they came back, and then in the morning, I'd raise the alarm. Tell everyone what I'd seen.

*

But it didn't happen that way, despite my intentions. Instead, when my mother woke, ill-tempered and sweating from all the drink, she glared at me.

'Why are you here?' she said, heaving herself off the bed. 'Where's your da? He stormed off in a state last night. Is he back?'

I was not much of a talker. Never had been. I couldn't talk to strangers, never passed the time of day with the drinkers in the inn. And even with Mam, I'd only ever said what was needed. I was better with Da, and my friend Arthur. They never rushed me, never tutted when I couldn't find the right word, or finished my sentence for me, too impatient to wait. When I was nervous or upset, or even sometimes if I was excited or happy, it was worse. It was like my throat clenched and my voice just wouldn't work.

Now, I sat up in bed, ready to tell her what had happened, how I'd seen Da's blood spill on the cobbles and watched Morgan drag him away.

'Mam,' I began. 'Mam . . .'

And then. Nothing. The words wouldn't come. Mam stared at me for a moment and then, frustrated, she rolled her eyes. 'He'll be back when he wants food,' she said.

At the mention of food, Tully got to his feet, shaking his fur out and giving a soft bark in my mother's direction. She looked at the dog. 'He left you behind, did he?' she said. 'Then he'll be back even sooner.'

She turned to me. 'Floors need sweeping.' And off she went, downstairs, unaware of what had happened to my da, because I'd not been able to tell her.

Three days went by. Three awful days. The inn was quiet. Mam was silent. Tully sat by the window, his front paws on the sill, watching for Da. And try as I might – and believe me, I tried – I couldn't get the words out to tell Mam what had happened. I tried to mime it, clutching my stomach and falling to the floor. Pointing at the spot in the courtyard where the blood had splattered. I tried to show her the drawings of Petroc and Morgan, but she pushed me away. I wanted to scream in frustration and fear and grief. But I couldn't do that, either.

On the morning of the fourth day, I was awakened by my mother's wails. I was on my feet and downstairs before I'd even properly realised what I was doing, so scared was I that Morgan had returned. But Mam was in the inn, sitting at a table with the parish constable, Mr Trewin. His three-cornered hat was on the table, making me shudder as I remembered Morgan wearing a similar one. I flew to my mother's side and she gathered me into her arms – an unfamiliar state of affairs as usually I shunned physical contact. Her face was blotchy with tears. Had they found Da? I wondered. Was this it?

'Emily,' Mam said softly. 'Your father is gone.'

Mr Trewin nodded. 'Your mother is afraid he has fallen from the cliff.'

I shook my head. That wasn't what had happened. Again, I

opened my mouth to speak, to tell them about the man with the white streak in his hair, and the blood on the cobbles, but again I couldn't make a sound.

'Emily,' Mr Trewin said. He was using the tone people often used when they spoke to me. Many of the people from Kirrinporth believed me to be simple because I didn't talk much and because I was much happier observing from the edge of life than being in it. 'Emily,' he said again. 'Your mother says your father has been gone these last three nights. But the tide has turned so if he had fallen he would have washed up at Barnmouth.'

Desperately, Mam reached across the table and clutched the front of Mr Trewin's coat.

'We argued,' she said. 'We argued and he went off in anger. He wasn't thinking straight. He could have fallen.'

Mr Trewin gave a small shake of his head. 'But there is no sign of him,' he said. 'And if you argued, then perhaps he has just gone for some peace.'

Mam pulled Mr Trewin closer to her. He pulled back but her grip was strong. 'You want to speak to Cal Morgan,' she hissed. I stiffened at the mention of the name. 'Because it was him we argued about.'

Mr Trewin stood up, forcing Mam to release his coat. 'I'd be very careful what you say, Janey Moon,' he said. 'Spreading rumours like that.'

I stood in between Mam and Mr Trewin, looking at the man and trying my hardest to speak. But the only sound that came from my treacherous mouth was a kind of desperate croak.

Mr Trewin looked at me in sympathy. 'Your da is alive,' he said, speaking slowly and carefully as though it was my ears that didn't work, not my mouth. 'He has gone off somewhere.' He gave my mother a sideways glance. 'With another woman, no doubt. Who doesn't argue.'

My mother began to wail again and Mr Trewin patted her kindly on the hand. 'Janey, we men are simple folk,' he said. 'We are often not worthy of the love our women give us. Your Amos has let everyone down.'

There was a scratching at the inn door and with a disgusted glance at Mr Trewin, I went to let Tully in. He bounded inside, his claws clattering on the stone floor, and nosed his way around the inn.

'He's looking for Amos,' my mother said, watching him through swollen eyes. 'Amos would never have left without Tully.'

'I'm sorry,' said Mr Trewin, picking up his hat and putting it on his head. 'But it seems he has.'

As though he'd understood every word, Tully sat back on his haunches, lifted his head up and howled mournfully. My mother followed, her sobs echoing round the empty inn. I tugged desperately at Mr Trewin's sleeve, trying to get him to wait so I could get the pictures I'd drawn and perhaps make him understand what had happened. But he picked my fingers off one by one, as though I was dirty, and then brushed some invisible muck from his coat where I'd been clutching him.

'I have to go,' he said in that tone again. 'Good day.'

Chapter 2

Phoebe

London, February 2019

I yawned and stretched at my desk, glad to be clocking off and not working the night shift. Saturdays were always challenging and I was pleased I wasn't back in the police station until Monday morning now.

'I'm heading off,' I said to no one in particular, just as my colleague and friend Stacey – DC Maxwell – who sat next to me in the CID office, put the phone down and made a face.

'Do you have to go now?'

'What have you got?'

'Missing teenage girl. Probably nothing, but uniform are all tied up with that brawl after the football.'

'Where?'

'Hanson Grove.'

I pulled my coat from the rack and put it on. 'I'll go on my way home,' I said. 'Who called it in?'

'Her mum. But according to PC Malone, she sounded a bit funny.'

'Funny how?'

Stacey shrugged and I groaned. 'Give me all the details, and I'll check it out.'

'Will you be all right on your own?'

'I'll be fine.'

As I walked to my car, I read the paperwork Stacey had given me. The missing girl was called Ciara James, and she was sixteen years old. I frowned. She'd probably just gone off with her boyfriend somewhere. This was a job for the neighbourhood PCSO, not CID. Still, it was on my way and it would only take five minutes.

My car was iced up when I got to it. I had no scraper, obviously, so I had to improvise with my Tesco Clubcard and when I finally got inside, I had to peel off my wet gloves, and use them to demist the windscreen so all in all it took me ages to get to Ciara James's house. It was gone 10 p.m. when I finally pulled up outside. There was a light on in the front room, though, so I knocked on the door.

A man looked out of the window, frowning. He was wearing a thick jumper and he had reading glasses on his nose.

'Mr James?' I said through the glass, showing him my warrant card. 'DS Bellingham.'

He looked worried as he dropped the curtain and a few seconds later, the front door opened.

'Is everything okay?' he said. 'What's wrong?'

That was strange. 'We had a call from your wife? She said your daughter Ciara is missing.'

A shadow crossed his face, but then his expression changed to look more confused than annoyed. 'Ciara's not missing,' he said.

'Where is she?'

'Cinema, I believe.' He looked at his watch. 'Her friend's dad is dropping her home. I don't like her getting the bus this late. I worry about her being out on her own. There are some dodgy people around. I'd have picked her up myself but I don't like staying up late on Saturday because I have to be at church early in the morning.'

'But your wife said . . .'

'She gets muddled,' he said quietly. 'She takes pills to help her sleep and sometimes they make her misunderstand things.'

I looked at him. He seemed totally genuine. And yet, there was something niggling at me. 'Have you seen Ciara this evening yourself?'

'No, I'm afraid not. I've been at my choir practice.'

'At church? Which one?'

'St John's.'

I nodded. 'And your wife was here?'

'I assume so. When I got home she was in bed. Perhaps she took a pill and couldn't remember where Ciara had gone.'

'Can I speak to her?'

He made a face. 'If she's taken a sleeping tablet, I won't be able to wake her.'

'Could you try?' I smiled at him. 'I really should speak to her, or my boss will give me grief.'

I was still standing on the doorstep, and the evening was bitterly cold. I didn't wait to be asked, but just stepped inside. He looked like he was going to say something and then changed his mind.

'Wait here.'

I had a good nose round the hall while I waited. It was very ordinary. Dull, in fact. Neat and tidy. Ciara's school photo on the wall, showing her to be a pretty but unremarkable teenager. Boots stacked neatly in a rack and three coats hanging from pegs. Three coats. I frowned.

'Does Ciara have another coat,' I asked as Mr James came downstairs again.

'Pardon?'

'Does Ciara have another coat?' I gestured to the coat rail. 'I presume that's hers? But it's very cold outside.'

He screwed his nose up. 'No idea, sorry. I don't pay much attention to what she wears.'

'Right. Is your wife awake?'

A noise upstairs made me look up. A middle-aged woman was coming downstairs, wearing pyjamas and looking pale and sleepy.

'So sorry to disturb you, Mrs James,' I said. 'We had a call that Ciara was missing.'

She rubbed her eyes like a toddler. 'Ciara is at the cinema.'

'That's right,' her husband said. He looked at me and I saw a flash of something in his eyes – triumph? 'You get back to bed.'

Obediently, Mrs James turned and went back upstairs before I could stop her.

'Terribly sorry to waste your time,' Mr James said with a smile. 'I trust my wife isn't in trouble.'

'Not at all.'

We stood in the hall for a second. I looked at him and he looked back at me. All my instincts were telling me that something was off, but I had nothing. I wished Stacey had come with me. Another pair of eyes on this outwardly normal family would be useful.

'If Ciara doesn't come home, please call the station,' I said.

'Of course, thank you so much, Constable.'

I forced myself to smile instead of correcting him about my rank. 'Call us if you need to,' I said again, more sternly this time.

My car was already icing up again, so I blasted the heater and drove a little way down the road, before I parked up and called the station.

As I waited for someone to answer, I thought about calling uniform out. Being a bit forceful with Mr James. Pressing him. Checking Ciara did come home later. But then I shook my head.

'Have a word with yourself, Phoebe,' I said out loud. He was a boring bloke wearing slippers and corduroy trousers, who went to bed early on a Saturday night so he wasn't tired at church. Uniform would probably laugh at me if I asked them to come round.

And so when my call was answered, I asked to speak to Stacey. 'She's not missing,' I said when she answered. 'She's at the cinema.'

'Okaaaay.'

'The mum got confused, apparently.'

'Fine,' Stacey said. 'Good.'

'Can you flag the name?' I asked. 'And ring me if anything else comes in.'

'I thought she was at the cinema.'

'Just in case.'

'All right,' said Stacey amiably. 'See you Monday.'

*

It was Monday morning when I got the call to say that Ciara James was gone. I felt my stomach plummet into my shoes, leaving me with a sick feeling that stayed with me for days and days as we searched fruitlessly for the missing teenager.

'There's definitely nothing on the parents?' my boss, DI Blair, said on the Friday evening, fixing me with his steely glare across the room.

I shook my head. 'I've been over it and over it,' I said. 'They're just . . . normal.'

I twisted my hair into a ponytail in my hand and pulled it over my shoulder, the way I always did when I was thinking. 'But it was all just misunderstandings. The mother – Molly – she can't even remember phoning us last weekend. She's in a state. Blaming herself. And the father – Steve – he's the same. They were up early for church and it wasn't until the evening that they realised Ciara was gone.'

DI Blair nodded.

'I should have searched her bedroom,' I said. 'I should have pushed the mother more.'

'You had no cause to search the house, and the mother sounds like she didn't know whether she was coming or going,' DI Blair pointed out.

I said nothing. I knew he was right, but I felt completely awful.

'Do you think it's the parents?' DI Blair asked, looking at me intently. 'What's your instinct telling you?'

I shifted in my chair, feeling uncomfortable under his glare.

'I just don't know,' I admitted. 'My heart said they were to blame, but my head says no. They're so . . .'

'So?'

'Nice.'

He sighed. 'You know as well as I do that bad things happen in nice families, too.'

I bit my lip. He was right. Of course he was.

'We should speak to them again,' I said, firmly.

'Sure?'

I shrugged. I really was at a loss. I'd spoken to everyone in Ciara's life. She was a happy sixteen-year-old girl growing up in the suburbs of south London. Her teachers had no concerns. Her parents were normal. Her friends were sweet. There was nothing suspicious about the family whatsoever. Her mother didn't sleep well but apart from that she was ordinary and her father – well, stepfather actually though he'd brought her up since she'd been tiny – was an all-round nice chap. But her parents being to blame was the only thing that made sense. Wasn't it? I had no idea anymore.

'Focus,' DI Blair said. 'And let me know when you're ready to decide on a next step. I might even come with you.'

He marched off towards his office and I sighed. He'd never been this bolshie or unpleasant to work with before, but I understood the strain he was under. Ciara's picture had been on the front of every newspaper today. She smiled out at me on every news website, her drab school uniform unable to dull her youthful prettiness.

The rest of the team were looking at me, waiting for a decision, so I forced myself to focus.

'Right,' I said to two uniformed PCs who were helping with

the door-to-door inquiries. 'Benny and Joe, can you go through the information from the neighbours and friends?' They nodded and I turned to another colleague. 'Stacey, you double-check the reports from her school, and I'll reread the parents' statements. We must be missing something.'

There was a bustle of activity. Stacey – DC Maxwell – squeezed my arm as she walked past me to her desk, letting me know she had my back. I gave her a grateful smile. Eventually everyone settled down and silence fell as we all read through every bit of information we had about the girl's disappearance.

Ciara's mother, Molly, was a nursery school teacher, and the stepdad, Steve, had his own business doing accounts. He rented a desk in an office near the station and everyone there said he was always pleasant. As I already knew, they were both fairly religious – regular churchgoers. Upright. Moral, even. Steve, I'd heard, had turned down the contract to do the accounts for a local betting shop because he didn't approve of gambling. Molly was sweet-natured and kind. No criminal records. Not so much as a speeding ticket. Nothing.

Ciara had been messaging a boy online – someone from a nearby school – and we'd originally thought she might have gone to meet him. But he'd been playing football the evening she disappeared, and he admitted – slightly sheepishly – that he'd never met her.

I put aside the statements from Ciara's parents. This was getting me nowhere.

'Phoebe, I spoke to the dad's mates at his golf club,' Benny said, appearing at the side of my desk. 'I just uploaded the statements.'

'Anything worthwhile?'

He shrugged. 'Just what a nice bloke he is.'

'I'll have a look,' I said half-heartedly.

I scanned the statements. This was so hard. There was just nothing to go on at all. Gut instinct went a long way in police investigations, even though lots of my fellow officers would deny it and claim it was all legwork and asking the right questions. But just now, my gut instinct was switched right off. I had unfounded doubts about the dad and that was it. All I could see was that Ciara was a nice, normal sixteen-year-old. In fact, I thought, she was even nicer than her parents made her sound – but that wasn't unusual. I had friends who claimed their babies were absolute nightmares while smothering them with kisses. Maybe parents of teens did the same?

I sighed, looking at the statement from Steve's friend. 'Steve's one of the nicest blokes I know,' he'd said. 'We all thought he was really good to take on Ciara as his own.' Yawn. I rested my head on my hand, and scrolled on. 'Considering,' the friend had added. I sat up straighter. 'Considering,' I murmured to myself. What did that mean?

I pulled my phone to me and dialled the number on the bottom of the statement. The friend answered straightaway.

'Sorry to bother you,' I said. 'This is DS Bellingham from Lewisham police station. I just wanted to double-check something in your statement.'

'Right,' the man said, sounding nervous.

'When you said Steve was good to take Ciara on as his own child, considering . . . What did you mean? Considering what?'

The man laughed. 'Well,' he said. 'You probably know more than me. But she sounds like a right handful. Always in trouble. Last I heard, she was messaging some lad. Steve was worried about it. Sounded like she was sending him all sorts, if you know what I mean?'

I had no idea. We'd found Ciara's phone in her very tidy room – another odd thing about her disappearance. What teenager went anywhere without their phone? There had been the messages to the football-playing boy, and to her friends, and that was it. Nothing dodgy. No sexting, or inappropriate photos. Just a few sweet words saying how much she wanted to see the lad she'd been getting to know.

'Is Steve a strict father?' I asked.

'He has to be, by the sound of it,' the friend said. 'That girl would be on the streets if it wasn't for him.'

I thanked him for his time, and hung up the phone, shouting for Stacey as I pulled on my coat. We had to go and see the parents again.

From there on, it all unravelled. It turned out, Steve was more than just strict. He regularly punished poor Ciara for any perceived misdemeanour, from not stacking the dishwasher properly, to a poor mark on a test. And the messages from her new friend had tipped him over into disgust.

'She was messaging some filthy little turd,' he hissed at Stacey and me, his lip curled. 'I check her phone, of course, and she didn't even try to hide it.'

I thought about how innocent the messages were, and how I'd been mildly surprised by their chaste tone, and winced. 'What did you do then?'

He lifted his chin up, looking pleased with himself. 'I said to Molly that she needed to be punished and Molly agreed.'

Molly, sitting next to him, looked alarmed. 'We hadn't agreed on that,' she said. 'I felt a bit of a hypocrite. I had boyfriends at her age.'

'And look where you ended up,' Steve spat at her. 'Pregnant.'

Molly stayed quiet after that, as Steve explained how he wanted to teach Ciara a lesson, so he'd taken her to his allotment on Saturday afternoon and left her in the shed.

'It's freezing,' Stacey said. 'And her coat is still here. She must have been so cold.'

The thought of poor Ciara in the icy shed made me shiver. I shook my head. 'But we searched the shed,' I said. 'And the allotments. She's not there.'

'I just wanted to give her a scare,' Steve said. 'But when I got back to the allotment after church, she wasn't there.' He shrugged, not looking remotely worried. 'She'll be with that lad,' he said. 'Getting up to all sorts.'

'She's not with him.' My voice was cold. 'They never met up.'

Molly gave a little gasp and he patted her hand. 'She'll be fine,' he said. 'They'll find her.'

We did find her. In the woods, behind the patch of allotments, that skirted the railway line. She'd obviously found her way out of the shed, but in confusion from the cold, she'd curled herself into the roots of a tree, gone to sleep and never woken up. The freezing February weather, and the vest top and thin leggings she'd been wearing made sure of that.

'She wouldn't have suffered,' the pathologist reassured me.

But I kept thinking about how scared she must have been, and how cold, and how if I'd followed my instincts right at the start, we might have found her sooner.

'It's not your fault,' DI Blair said over and over, as we watched Steve being put into a police car and Ciara's mother wailing from inside the house. 'The only person to blame, is that bugger. This is not your fault.'

But somehow I felt that it was.

Dear Reader,

We hope you enjoyed reading this book. If you did, we'd be so appreciative if you left a review. It really helps us and the author to bring more books like this to you.

Here at HQ Digital we are dedicated to publishing fiction that will keep you turning the pages into the early hours. Don't want to miss a thing? To find out more about our books, promotions, discover exclusive content and enter competitions you can keep in touch in the following ways:

JOIN OUR COMMUNITY:
Sign up to our new email newsletter:
http://smarturl.it/SignUpHQ
Read our new blog www.hqstories.co.uk
🐦 : https://twitter.com/HQStories
f : www.facebook.com/HQStories

BUDDING WRITER?
We're also looking for authors to join the HQ Digital family!
Find out more here:
https://www.hqstories.co.uk/want-to-write-for-us/
Thanks for reading, from the HQ Digital team

If you enjoyed *The Secrets of Thistle Cottage*, then why not try another sweeping historical fiction novel from HQ Digital?

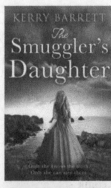

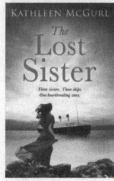